OOYAY

By Stanley Rumm

http://www.ooyay.com

Cover image by John McSweeney
Design by Kevin Forde

First published by Dog Ear Publishing
4010 W. 86th Street, Ste H
Indianapolis, IN 46268
www.dogearpublishing.net

ISBN: 978-159858-280-2
Library of Congress Control Number: 2007920125

This book is printed on acid-free paper.
This book is a work of Fiction. Places, events, and situations in this book are purely Fictional and any resemblance to actual persons, living or dead, is coincidental.

CHILDHOOD

Childhood is a time when anything is possible. Anything can -and often does- happen. We don't examine it to wonder if it is possible. We're no more surprised by the extraordinary than we are by those facets of life we continue to encounter for the first time day by day. Life itself is an adventure.

ADOLESCENCE

Adolescence brings doubt, insecurity, confusion, upheaval, mystery, excitement. We can see our future, but we resist the commitment to a dreary, mundane existence where nothing is fun and everything is planned. We search for meaning in a seemingly-meaningless world. As part of that search, we feel the need to ditch our childish past, yet continue to carry it on our backs like a great sack that stunts our progression.

ADULTHOOD

Adulthood is where we quit moaning about the broccoli and go find our own dinners. We put aside our childish ways and take control of our own selves and our own destiny. We pay the price and are prepared to suffer the consequences. It is a time where things are put in perspective and hopefully some clarity is found.

MATURITY

Maturity allows us to embrace the child within.

CHILDHOOD

THE CALM BEFORE THE STORM

"Welcome!" beamed the Professor as he extended an arm toward young Lucy Lucey.

She had been last to set foot in the greenhouse where the Demonstration was to take place. Even now she remained in the open doorway, full of uncertainty. She wasn't sure why she had even been invited to this exclusive unveiling. All the other guests were very important adults. Lucy was only nine years old. Was it possible that this great and famous man could have made some kind of mistake with the invitation?

One representative from each of five national newspapers was in attendance. The Sun, The Moon, The Star, The World and The Daily Rag all had people there to see what the old man had come up with this time. The town's mayor was present, along with four government ministers, and even the Prime Minister himself.

As instructed, all the guests had changed into soft white boiler suits before they quietly crammed into the little glass room. The Professor had given strict instructions that no cameras or pens or notebooks or tape-recorders or laptop computers or handbags or shoes be allowed in.

The Prof had also insisted that nobody say a word once inside until after he first spoke to the assembly. He had been insistent on this, stating it seven times in his invitation letter and restating it several more times before he had waved everyone in.

"You must be from Smisslewig?" enquired the old man, as he noted Lucy's reticence.

Only then did she relax somewhat. The invitation had been addressed to "A Representative of The Smisslewig News", but until that point, she thought that he might have been expecting a teacher.

St. Mary's School for Little Women and Young Gentlemen was known locally as SMSLWYG (-or 'Smisslewig') and was situated next door to the Professor's estate. Lucy and her friend, Milo Mooney, worked hard putting out the monthly school journal, although they had no idea that it had been read by Professor Crastinator himself.

Now the ancient man himself stood before her and was awaiting her reply. He wasn't wearing the white uniform of his guests. Instead he wore pink fluffy bunny slippers with black socks up to his knees. The knees themselves were quite knobbly looking and bulged out over his long skinny legs. A pair of cream bermuda shorts were tied by a dark string above his stomach, which made him appear even more comical than the slippers did. He also wore an unbuttoned red Hawaiian shirt over a string vest.

The front of his head was bald and bulging. It looked like his brain had grown so large that there was too much space for his hair to cover it all. Still though, around the side of his head and at the back, his long grey hair curled slightly as it brushed his shoulders. He had large, happy-looking eyes and he smiled broadly at the young girl.

Remembering instructions, Lucy replied to his question with a silent nod and polite smile. She then reached out to shake the Professor's hand, but before she could do so, the old man gently prised the pen and notebook from her grasp and quickly tossed them to the ground outside. He closed the door and, as he walked to the glass podium, his fluffy bunny slippers let out a squeak with each step. Some reporters began to snigger but he held his index finger to his lips, which reminded everyone they must not talk until after he introduced the mysterious invention.

Strangely, every seat was really comfortable. The Prime Minister sat up front in a white luxurious armchair that he almost disappeared into it was so soft. Just his large nose and pointy knees could be seen protruding from the fold of cushions. The mayor sat next to him in a similar but non-matching red armchair. His nose was not so large so it wasn't sticking out, but he had an enormous tummy that made it look for all the world like the chair was empty apart from the extra-large white cushion that bulged out of it.

Behind these two chairs, the four other politicians all sat on one long sofa that was also soft and luxurious but did present them with a bit of a squeeze. The five people from the press were assigned the smaller single couch behind the sofa so two reporters needed to sit on the lap of the other three who were lucky enough to have a seat.

Lucy Lucey looked around for someplace to sit but didn't fancy squeezing onto a spare lap amongst the reporters. Just then she noticed a small blue beanbag at the back of the greenhouse. It was only after sitting down that she found a little blue dog had been curled up in one corner of it. As Lucy flopped into the middle of the beanbag, the edges bulged, sending the small dog straight up into the air, immediately landing on Lucy's legs.

As he struggled to move away Lucy gave him one single gentle stroke from the top of his head down to the end of his little blue tail.

"There, there little boy," she whispered. "I'm sorry for disturbing you."

The little blue dog had almost walked out of her reach when he suddenly, but slowly, began to walk backwards, allowing the school reporter to rub him from his tail up to his head. Only then did Lucy notice how the blue dog's coat wasn't furry or hairy like other dogs, but was only slightly furry like a peach or like suede shoes. Up close he looked like a sheep that had just been sheared ...a blue sheep ...with slightly shorter legs. Lucy thought it strange that the dog was blue, but only strange in so far as she had never seen a blue dog before.

"Why have I never seen a blue dog?" she briefly wondered, then had to laugh as she noticed the little fellow continuing to walk forwards and backwards so that he could rub himself off her outstretched hand.

Meanwhile Professor Crastinator was about to speak from the top of the room so Lucy snapped to attention, forcing the dog to curl up in her lap.

I SAY TOMATO

It was at the grand old age of sixty-one that Professor Crastinator made his first million by inventing the lamppost with in-built loo for dogs and other animals. Instead of screaming at their animals not to do it and instead of running behind their pets with little brown-paper bags, owners could now encourage little Rover or Trixie or Pogo to go pooh-pooh or wee-wee on a lamppost, safe in the knowledge that the lamppost would flush and clean itself afterwards.

For years after that, the man had introduced many inventions that literally changed the way people viewed the world itself. He was the one that invented the Silent Motor (used in everything from automobiles to ultra-quiet vacuum cleaners) and Plug-in Knowledge-Enablers (PKEs). Professor Crastinator also invented the Exershoe that does the walking for people who want to exercise but are too lazy to put one foot in front of the other. It had been this same man who came up with the idea of high-rise fields where farmers can grow much more crops on a single acre of land that rise like a tall car park into the sky. He also invented the Bridge-On-Demand, Thammer, Squeeze-Freeze Process and many, many other items and ideas.

Now, after so many world-changing inventions, he was rich beyond belief. People said he had so much money that he had videogame consoles, games and whole movies made just for himself to watch and play and enjoy. They also said that he never drove the same car twice. One rumour spread far and wide that he used paper money for toilet roll. Soon crowds gathered every day at the town's sewage plant to try to find cash that was flushed from the professor's lavatory, but all anybody ever found there was number ones and number twos.

"Ladies and gentlemen I would like to thank you all for coming here today," the Professor began.

He had no microphone but because the greenhouse was small enough and because his voice bounced off the glass walls, Lucy Lucey had no problem hearing him from the back of the room.

"I won't keep you too long. I would simply like to show you my new invention that has occupied *all* of my time for the last *sixteen weeks!*"

He emphasised the words "sixteen weeks" as if he couldn't believe it had taken him so long to come up with the goods.

"Without further ado, I give you... THIS!" he said, awkwardly pulling a metal stick out of his short sleeve.
"And THIS!" he added, slowly taking what looked like a small tomato from his trouser pocket and holding it aloft.

Next he screwed the metal bar onto the tomato and held the whole thing in the air for all to see. A stony-silence echoed around the room. Then the mayor's tummy sunk deep into his chair and bloated out again as he gasped.

"INCREDIBLE!" he cried.

The Prime Minister's nose twitched. The other four politicians gazed blankly at each other, wondering what they had missed and what they should say. One of the ministers opened his mouth in a wide-O as though he had something to state, but closed it again when he realised that for once he couldn't think of anything. Suddenly, all of the reporters jumped up and began screaming questions, although nobody could understand a word because they all did so at the same time.

The little blue dog sat up and started shaking like crazy. He seemed to be whining or barking quietly, but Lucy couldn't hear him over the din.

"Don't be frightened little doggie," she softly whispered in his ear as she wrapped him tightly in her arms. "I'll look after you".

The Professor waved his stick in the air and motioned for everyone to be quiet.

"PLEASE!" he shouted. "It is of the *utmost* importance that you all keep ab-sol-utely quiet for the remainder of this demonstration!"

The noise immediately ceased and everybody sat down. The Prime Minister's hand arose from the fold of cushions on his chair, scratched the tip of his nose, and then lowered once more. Calmness returned to the assembly.

The Professor now twisted part of the stick, making the whole device into a T-shape. The top of the T now appeared as though it was made of rubber, the main bar still looked like a normal metal rod, and at the bottom was the small tomato. Nobody moved and nobody spoke for what seemed like forever.

The white cushion on the mayor's chair once again sunk-down then bulged out in preparation for a declaration.

"AMAZING!" bellowed the Mayor.

The Prime Minister's nose twitched twice. The politicians had no idea what to do. Once again they all looked to each other for inspiration -and found none. Once more the room shook as all the reporters shouted out statements and questions and queries and points of order and remarks. Lucy couldn't understand a word they said as everyone jumped up and down and waved their hands and screamed. The reporter from The Daily Rag quickly lost interest and seemed like he was simply bouncing on the cushions of the chair for the fun of it. The little blue dog again seemed to shake uncontrollably in her arms.

"STOP IT!" Lucy shouted at the people, but nobody took any notice. "SSSSTTTOOPPPPPPP IIIITTTT!!!" she screamed now in obvious distress.

A hush filled the air. Everybody froze and turned to look at the young girl at the back of the room. They hadn't noticed her before now.

"Everybody please be quiet!" Lucy instructed as she began to calm down, gently massaging the blue dog's neck. "...You're giving lit-tle doggie here the shivers!"

The politicians and reporters all broke into laughter as they returned to their seats without further ado. Just then, how-ever, they noticed that the Professor had begun using his invention to scrape the condensation from the glass walls in the greenhouse. Everybody sat quietly as they watched him quickly scrape the fog from each pane of glass. Only after he had finished did Lucy notice that the roof was not glass, but was made from a soft blue fabric that merely looked like it was a window to the sky.

Having scraped the foggy dew from his glass podium, the Professor now stood at the top of the room once more, unscrewed the tomato from the T-bar and held it in the air. It had grown visi-bly bigger since it was first attached to the window wiper and it was now too large and too heavy to comfortably fit in one hand.

The white cushion up front sucked in, then immediately blew out again.

"WHAT A LOAD OF RUBBISH!" shouted the mayor. This time nobody else moved or spoke.

The lady from The World newspaper quietly raised her arm to ask a question and the Professor nodded for her to speak.

"So it's to make juicier tomatoes then?" she queried.

Ignoring her question, the Professor pulled what looked like a small food blender from out of his pocket. He placed the tomato inside, and then pressed a button. Quiet laughter was immediately heard from the blender, followed shortly by a voice that said

"There, there little boy, I'm sorry for disturbing you."

The Professor pressed STOP, and slowly turned to look at Lucy Lucey.

"I told you all not to speak before I spoke, didn't I? You *had* to speak little girl didn't you?"

Then he sighed and pressed play once again.

"I wonder what the old quack has come up with this time?" came another voice from the blender.

"I bet it's an odourless fart" said somebody else, then both of them tittered.

The professor gazed at each person in turn, trying to figure out who had said that. Two of the politicians seemed particularly red with embarrassment, but there was no way of being certain it was them so the matter was ignored. Next came his own speech:

"Ladies and gentlemen I would like to thank you all for coming here today. I won't keep you too long. I would simply like to show you my new invention that has occupied all of my time for the last sixteen weeks. Without further ado, I give you... This. And this."

Now the Professor pressed STOP again and spoke to the room.

"As you can see," he began, "I have come up with a way to play back everything that is spoken in a room. Just as a disc or a tape stores words and songs and music, so too are all our own words from our own lips stored in the air all around us. I have simply been able to gather that air and play it back in the correct way once I have it."

"Incredible!" came the mayor's voice from the blender as PLAY was again pressed. Everyone laughed and leapt in the air and clapped.

"But there's more!" insisted the Professor as he urged the crowd to sit down. "...Because this device plays back each voice individually, we can hear what each person says in a noisy, crowded room."

A hush descended on the greenhouse as everybody stretched to hear what the blender would say next.

"Professor, Professor, what is it?" said the voice of the man from The Sun.

"Does it predict the future?" came the voice of the man from The Moon through the blender.

"It's a laser that will slice our enemies in two!" pronounced the man from The Star via the blender.

"Is it a juicer?" enquired the lady from The World newspaper.

"Do you sleep in the nude Professor?" asked the man from The Daily Rag.

"Oh no, don't mess it up this time please!" cried some other voice that the guests assumed to be from one of the politicians.

"Don't be frightened little doggie. I'll look after you" came Lucy's own voice next from the blender.

Professor Crastinator seemed flustered now. He pressed STOP and spoke once more, hiding his own embarrassment.

"Uhrm... Well, uhrm... As you can hear, nobody's voice is shouting or whispering in this playback. This device can play what was spoken, but the volume of the speech is not recorded on our breath. I'll now play the rest of what was said before I cleared the windows."

"Please! It is of the utmost importance that you all keep absolutely quiet for the remainder of this demonstration!" The Professor smiled as he heard his voice coming from the blender.

"Amazing!" came the voice of the mayor next.

"Is it to help with mountain climbing?" the man from The Sun asked.

"It's a laser that can shoot in two directions at once! Isn't it Professor?" said the man from The Star.

"So it's for drying tomatoes on your washing line then?" asked the lady from The World newspaper. Everyone laughed when they heard this.

"Does it predict the future by any chance?" asked the man from The Moon.

"What colour underpants are you wearing Professor?" asked the reporter with The Daily Rag.

"Stop with the dramatics and get on with it you old fool!" came the same strange voice as before.

"Stop it! Sssstopppp it!" said Lucy's voice, much calmer now from the blender than when it had originally been screamed. *"Everybody please be quiet. You're giving little doggie here the shivers."*

The laughter from the blender was now joined with the fresh laughter from everyone in the room, including Lucy herself this time.

While this playback was occurring, the Professor took another tomato from his pocket and attached it to the window-wiper. The room once again hushed as he bent into the chair with the white cushion and wiped the foggy-build-up from the mayor's spectacles. The Professor placed the new tomato into the blender and pressed PLAY.

"What a load of rubbish!" said the mayor's voice, and everybody in the room broke into laughter once again.

STICKY BUNS

As the laughter died down, Lucy raised her hand to ask a question.

"What if this room was not made of glass?" she enquired. "Doesn't glass trap people's breath better than normal walls do? ...Or anyway, what *use* is this invention?" she enquired.

Not for the first time in the short meeting there was a hush in the room. Everybody studied the young girl's questions before turning quietly to the Professor for some answers.

"...If we all had to have reasons for everything prior to doing anything then we'd all do nothing all of the time," he said. "We'd only ever see the world as it is now -never as it could be if we tried something *different*. We would never know how our world could change."

"But why must everything change all the time?" pressed Lucy, stroking the blue dog in her lap all the while.

"If it doesn't change it'll all become boring," the Professor immediately replied. "We can't laugh at the same jokes forever. New jokes are a type of change. If we get fed up with an old joke then that too is a type of change.

"What you thought and did at three years of age is different to what you will like doing when you are twelve or twenty or sixty. Why? -Because of *change*. What you do at *your* age is different to what *I* did when *I* was that age. When I was your age I wore short trousers and was thrilled if I received a potato on Christmas morning. *You* wouldn't be happy with that and that's because things have *changed*. If everything stayed the same there would be no progress. None of us would get anything done, ever, because there would be no point in doing anything if everything was going to stay the same anyway!"

All the adults in the room nodded in agreement to these wise words.

"I like your questions," added the Professor with a smile, "but sometimes we just have to do things and work it all out afterward. If something is totally new, people won't even know they need it until it is there. We have no hope of making any real change until after we introduce things that are totally new. *Plus ça change, plus c'est la même chose!*"

Lucy didn't know what this last phrase meant but she wasn't afraid to find out.

"What does that mean?" she asked quickly.

"It's something my good friend Dr. Flocky Nocky always says. It means, the more things change, the more they stay the same. The world is forever turning and moving. We need to move and change to be able to keep up."

Lucy found it strange that Professor Crastinator mentioned his rival, Dr. Flocky Nocky, in this way. She had always assumed that the two inventors were mortal enemies or something. After all, they seemed to be trying to outdo each other all of the time.

For many years, Professor Crastinator was in a league of his own when it came to releasing world-shaping inventions. Nobody could match him for consistency or quality. But then came Dr. Flocky Nocky.

It was Flocky Nocky who invented the non-stick magnet (AKA The NS-Mag). This revolutionised travel because it led to him later inventing the uncrashable car.

[Experiment:
Take two magnets and place them together.
If they stick, turn one of them around.
Now they push each other away and it is not possible to keep them attached.
A magnet has two charges: Positive and Negative.
A magnet's Positive side will stick to another magnet's Negative side, but two positives or two negatives will push each other away.]

Dr. Flocky Nocky's NS-Mag meant that metal objects did not stick to these magnets, but by making all automobiles out of this same substance he could ensure that, for instance, two cars that were about to crash would suddenly swerve away from each other (since the outside of every car was now made out of "negatively-charged NS-Mag"). Soon, all road barriers also used NS-Mags. Since people preferred not to be knocked down by speeding automobiles they also took to wearing clothing made from finely woven NS-Mag.

Children were taught from an early age the importance of not putting a sweater on backwards. To do so would mean almost certain death because you would likely be dragged out in front of the first passing car.

Lucy had never seen Dr. Flocky Nocky either in person or on television or in a photograph. In fact Lucy had never heard of anyone who *had* seen Dr. Flocky Nocky. The Doctor was a recluse and reportedly lived on a small island in the middle of nowhere on the opposite side of the planet. Thankfully nowadays it was quite easy to get to any small island anywhere on the planet, again because of another travel invention by the Doctor himself.

CAT Bouncing was now the most-used method of travelling long distance. It quickly all but replaced the aeroplane as the most popular form of travel for long-distance journeys. CAT stands for Catapult Air Travel and works like this:

1. People climb aboard an ATV (Air Travel Vehicle) just as they have always done with aeroplanes.

2. Since no pilot is necessary, somebody (traditionally the youngest person on board) presses the LAUNCH button.

3. Using NS-MAGs (again), the ATV is pulled down through a large hole in the ground. When it is down far enough, the charge on the NS-MAG is reversed, which immediately sends the ATV shooting up into the air like a bullet from a gun barrel.
For this reason, ATVs are referred to as "Bullets" by most people.

4. The Bullet proceeds up, up, up and up, past the birds and over the clouds and through the earth's thin-air crust and out into space. There it hovers for a while as the world turns below.

5. In time, the Bullet begins to fall back down to earth, guided now by a pull from the appropriate NS-MAG landing area.

Because CAT Bouncing uses the direction and speed of the earth's turn, aeroplanes are still used for most shorter westward journeys. Even so, many people prefer to CAT Bounce "once around the planet" simply because it is *more fun* than sitting in an aeroplane. Also, to date it is safer, with no major Bullet accidents reported since its commercial launch ten years previous.

Lucy suddenly realised she had been daydreaming. She had never been on a CAT Bounce, but all that was all about to change in a couple of days' time. The annual school trip was going to be bringing her and twenty other girls and boys from

Smisslewig on a weeklong tour around the planet. The mention of the name of the inventor of CAT bouncing had caused her to re-imagine for the umpteenth time what the school trip was going to be like. Her eyes had glazed over for a while, but now she shook her head so as to clear irrelevant thoughts from her mind.

As she came round, she found herself gazing straight into the eyes of the little blue dog. Those eyes seemed like dark holes of infinite depth, but still they sparkled brightly as though all the stars in the night sky were winking at her through a pair of small black specks. The dog appeared to be silently studying her. He tilted his head slightly to his left and continued to gaze directly into her eyes. Lucy found herself blushing under the intense glare. Then she giggled to herself as she realised that she was embarrassed because a dog was looking at her.

The meeting had more or less come to an end by the time Lucy returned her attention to it. All the other reporters had left to file their copy, leaving only the Professor and the politicians standing around, informally chatting amongst themselves. The little doggie scrambled from Lucy's arms and waddled straight over to Professor Crastinator, who was talking to both the leader of the country and leader of the city.

"Oops!" the Professor stifled a laugh as he took a step backward and almost tripped over his pet pooch. "Sorry about this Prime Minister, I believe it's time for din-dins and little Ooyay here isn't one to let me forget that."

"Quite all right Professor," said the Prime Minister.

"...Even cricket breaks for tea, wot wot?" added the mayor with a guffaw, eager to say something. Anything. Noticing how everyone had turned to look at him, the mayor continued.

"I'm rather stumped by events myself I don't mind telling you," he laughed aloud once more.

His pockmarked face was red from heat and excitement. As he chuckled, his whole frame shook wildly in every direction. His hair seemed to be a step behind the rest of his head as it moved. When he saw that nobody else spoke or was making any gestures, he suddenly felt ill at ease by their quiet stares.

"...Erm, a sticky wicket an' all that!" he stuttered, now visibly shaken, but trying desperately to show a brave face.

Since he realised he had no idea what he was talking about or what he was trying to say, he wanted very much to steer peoples' attention away from himself.

"...Or a sticky bun perhaps!" he laughed once more. "Sticky buns Prime Minister, wot wot? Sticky buns?"

The Prime Minister also clearly had no idea what the mayor was talking about.

"Yes Mayor," he smiled politely, "I'm sure you have."

HERE TODAY, GONE TOMORROW

Outside in the garden, the Professor nodded and waved goodbye to everyone before squeaking off toward his big house. The blue dog was nestled comfortably in his arms. Lucy stood and watched as the Prime Minister climbed aboard his helicopter and sat up front with the pilot. The four ministers followed behind, taking each of the four seats in the back. The mayor had driven to the venue by himself, but now he clearly expected to leave on the helicopter. He tapped the glass door next to the Prime Minister, who opened it as the overhead blades began to rotate. The noise was quickly growing but was not yet too loud for Lucy to hear the PM shout.

"We're going to government buildings in the Capitol," he yelled.

The mayor held his hair firmly in place as he shouted back.

"You couldn't drop me home on the way could you?"

Lucy was unable to hear what was said next but it ended in the Prime Minister extending his hand for the mayor to shake.

"NO!" cried Lucy, but she couldn't be heard now over the deafening hum from the helicopter.

"THE BLADES!" she screamed in warning to no avail once she saw the mayor absentmindedly take his hand from off his head.

Lucy had seen this happen once before and it was too horrible for her to witness again. She shut her eyes tightly and turned away.

As soon as he had moved his hand, the mayor realised the mistake. The toupee on his head immediately blew away under the rotating blades and he shot his arm after it. The PM shut his door as the helicopter rose into the air. The arm that had been reaching for the lost hairpiece now stretched for the country-leader's handshake. But it was too late. The helicopter had departed and the mayor had neither a handshake that he could boast about nor a hair to stretch across his gleaming head.

Lucy had been present at the attempted-christening of her cousin, Baby John, the previous year. Everything had been going smoothly up to the point of the actual ceremony itself. As Father

George bent to fetch some holy water from the font, Baby John innocently grabbed the wig from the priest's head and threw it in the water. Everybody apart from Lucy and the priest sniggered. Some laughed out loud. Father George was rigid with shock and embarrassment. Lucy immediately launched into action. She ran behind the altar and dragged a heavy chair over to where the priest was standing. Grabbing the wig from the holy water font, she stood on the chair and quickly slapped it on his head. Since it was still soaking wet, however, water proceeded to run down the priest's face, making it look like he was now crying. This caused everybody to fall around and laugh out loud more than ever as they pointed at the wet wig and the mock-tears.

Months passed before Father George finally agreed to have another go at christening Baby John. This time it was done quietly at home, with only the parents and godparents allowed witness the event. So Lucy wasn't there, but apparently it all went ok without her. Somehow.

Back in the garden, Lucy now turned around and opened her eyes to see the once-proud shoulders of the mayor sink under the weight of his bald head. After what seemed like ages, the mayor finally stirred, turning now toward Lucy to look straight at her. Both of them knew there was nobody left on the ground who had witnessed the events. The mayor's head slumped down once more and his arms flapped limply in the wind. Minutes passed in silent reflection. Lucy was too scared to say a word. Finally the mayor took a step, then another. Without looking up, he was now walking slowly and calmly in Lucy's direction.

She was frozen to the spot. The mayor had reached half way when Lucy quickly began looking left, then right, possibly for somewhere to escape to or maybe to call out for help. She wasn't sure which herself. Still he approached, little by little. Lucy had no doubt that he was coming for her. Up until that moment she had always assumed the mayor was a bit of an idiot, but never reckoned he was capable of harming anyone in any physical way. Now his large frame cast her body into shadow as he loomed directly overhead. He stopped within striking distance, then paused. Too afraid to look into his eyes, Lucy winced as the mayor's hand suddenly reached out toward her. She felt something being untangled from her hair, then looked up as the mayor removed the toupee from the top of her head to place it back on his own. She hadn't noticed that the wind from the helicopter had blown it directly onto her head.

The mayor looked briefly into the young girl's sad eyes before turning to face his parked car near the side of the Professor's mansion. Now he cast his chin in the air and gave a quiet "wot wot!" as he set off with a nod.

Lucy watched his heavy feet leave a straight line of prints in the damp grass as he walked away. Just before reaching the large black mayoral automobile he must have clicked a button on the car keys in his pocket because the indicator lights all flashed and a loud PTWEOOO PTWEOOO echoed across the otherwise-silent grounds. Lucy also heard the buttons snap up and as soon as the mayor opened the door, the quiet hum of air-conditioning and soft music seemed to leap out with open arms to welcome the mayor inside. He fell into his vehicle like an old wet carpet being piled on top of a rubbish tip, then drove off without another look back.

She felt sorry for him. A few minutes earlier she was convinced he was about to murder her, chop her body up into little pieces and bury her some place nobody would ever think to look. Now she was sad and realised she had been cruel to him to even believe he was capable of doing such a thing. And that nasty old Prime Minister wouldn't even give the poor mayor a spin in his helicopter!

THE CRASTINATORS AT HOME

Only Lucy was left now, alone in the Professor's large garden. He had obviously forgotten all about her. Since the mayor had just driven away, however, she was sure the front gate at least would be open.

Everything was deathly silent. In fact, that wasn't quite true, because as she stood still and listened, Lucy began to hear more and more noises. First she heard some bird whistling a high-pitched tune. She looked around but couldn't see it anywhere. Then she noticed some crows were fighting and cawing on the gravel pathway that surrounded the house. Overhead she saw and heard yet more birds fluttering-by in a V-shaped group. As she tilted her head to look at them, she noticed the familiar sound of school children shouting and screaming in the yard around the far side of the big building. From this distance and with the house in between, this noise wasn't too loud, but still Lucy found it curious that she hadn't noticed it until she deliberately listened for it. Then an old-fashioned motorcycle engine noise drew her attention to other sounds outside the high walls: some cars, a reversing lorry, a barking dog or two. It seemed to Lucy that everything had been totally silent until she listened. Then everything was deafeningly loud.

With a shrug and a smile to herself she turned to look for her pen and notebook. The Professor had tossed them through the greenhouse door, but she had forgotten to pick them up when she first came out. Now they didn't appear to be there at all. Had someone stolen the school reporter's pen and notebook? This mystery could lead all the way to the *top* and bring down the government of the country! Perhaps she should first go and interview the mayor to find out if he...

Before Lucy could continue imagining the *Tale of the Missing Notebook & Pen*, she spotted the pen in question a few feet from the greenhouse entrance. It had obviously been blown away (in the direction of the house) by the helicopter.

In one fluid motion, Lucy took a few steps, stooped, scooped up the pen in her right hand, tumbled heels over head, then as she leapt forward she deliberately stabbed her right shoulder with the butt of her pen so that by the time she was standing once more, the nib of the pen was extended and ready for writing. She held it in the air like a trophy or a javelin and cried out "YEAH! BRING IT ON!"

This was a favourite joke of hers whenever she dropped her pen (which seemed to happen quite a lot). She didn't really have a reason to do it, but she enjoyed it nonetheless. Why not? It was fun. Nobody else saw a point to it, but Lucy found it hilarious. Her teacher had once told her that the pen was mightier than the sword. Ever since then, Lucy had an image in her mind of armies of men and women waving pens at each other in a great battle.

If the pen was mightier than the sword, she should be allowed wield it like a sword if she wanted to. After all, who was going to stop her? Someone with a sword wouldn't be able to stop her because, obviously, she had a pen. YEAH!

But what use was a pen without something to write on? Looking around now, Lucy couldn't spot the writing pad. It must have been blown further up the grassy knoll upon which the house itself was built.

As she climbed the small rise, she spotted the notebook splatted against the wall of the house, just under a large open window. Voices could be heard coming from inside. It sounded like an argument was taking place. Lucy decided to grab her pad and leave without intruding further, but something caught her attention as soon as she picked up the notebook.

The Professor was standing by a door inside the room, to Lucy's right. He hadn't seen Lucy and had just quietly shouted.

"Look! I've told you before," he cried, "the whole *idea* of the One Key itself was flawed."

Nobody else appeared to be in the room.

"Don't be a fool all your life," came another voice from the computer monitor that stood on the desk. The blue dog was sitting up on the seat in front of the screen and his head was in Lucy's way so she couldn't see who was speaking.

"The One Key was as perfect as everything else I've done for you," the voice continued. "The problem was that *you* had to get involved that time. You wouldn't keep quiet like we had agreed. *You* wanted to spend millions on that stupid advertising campaign and to go on all those TV chat shows. As soon as there was any small problem after that we were mocked by the silly jingle *you* wrote."

Lucy recalled Professor Crastinator's most-recent invention before today. A few months back, he had released *The One Key*. It was hailed as a revolutionary way for people to protect their valuables.

The *One Key* was a tablet-sized electronic key that was to be used to open or operate all devices. It could work even from *inside* the human body (to be swallowed up to five times a week). The television adverts sang:

> One Key with the car.
> One Key for the house.
> Keep room for your money
> With a One Key in your mouth.

The idea was that each person had just one key. Any lock could be opened by any one person, as long as the lock's owner gave permission for a specific key-code in advance.

[So, say if your friend "Johnny" was calling for a visit, you could give Johnny's key-code to the front-door (using your mobile phone). When Johnny arrives he can simply let himself in without waiting for you to open the door. This door would open to Johnny's touch (no need for him to put the key in the door). Nobody else could open the door without that code. Since the key would be <u>inside</u> Johnny, nobody would be able to steal it.]

Shortly after launch though, it became apparent that if an electric shock was given to a lock in a certain way, this caused it to "lose its memory". As a result, the lock would have no valid key code so it would automatically ask for a new code. This meant that everyone could easily bypass the One Key by using any series of numbers. Soon anyone could open or use *anything* locked by the One Key system and it quickly became known as "The Wonky System."

The manufacturers overcame this problem without delay, but before long another one developed: People kept losing their keys by accidentally flushing them down the toilet. The One Key could be used simply by carrying it in your pocket, but that defeated at least part of the initial problem (i.e. it could now be lost or stolen and it took up valuable space).

Professor Crastinator (or so everyone thought) came up with a solution that involved having the One Key stitched onto people's skin, but that proved a little awkward and by then schoolyard songs had all but scuppered the whole One Key idea:

> Wonky with the car.
> Wonky for the house.
> Say goodbye to your money
> With a Wonky in your mouth.

Everywhere he went, Professor Crastinator would hear this song from even the youngest of children. Of course, because he lived next door to a schoolyard, he didn't have far to travel in order to hear it. In fact, now that she thought of it, Lucy and Milo had printed that very jingle in The Smisslewig News at the time. So that was why she had been invited! -Clearly the old man had read that piece and decided to show them a thing or two with this new invention.

"Look, if that invention had worked properly there wouldn't have been a problem!" said the Professor, obviously trying hard not to explode with rage.

"The deal was," continued the much-calmer voice from the monitor, "that you go to bed, *I* invent something, then you get up, make my dinner, then launch the invention. The whole world was waiting to see what you were coming out with next. There was no need for you to sing and dance about it. People were queuing to see anyway."

Lucy was amazed at what she was hearing. Could this possibly be true? Was the Professor just a front-man for whoever was speaking through the computer? Who was this mystery inventor anyway? Lucy could only think of one other living person who might fit the bill -but *why* would Dr. Flocky Nocky invent things for Professor Crastinator to pretend to have made himself? It just didn't make sense. The Professor now sighed.

"I'm going to bed" he moaned.

Lucy stretched to view the screen as the dog's head turned to the right, giving her some room to see past.

"You can't go until you make a hot dinner for me!" shouted the voice, clearly angry now for the first time.

Lucy was puzzled. On the monitor was a card game. So where was the voice coming from?

"Besides -your work in launching this Tomatocator has only just begun! You need to initiate further tests and sign up a company for manufacturing. If you go to bed now I won't have hot food for weeks! ...Again!"

Lucy was certain her eyes were playing tricks on her now, because it looked to her that the blue dog's lips were moving as the voice shouted. She clearly knew how ridiculous it was that the voice would come from a dog.

"Well, as that young girl immediately noticed," answered the Professor, "this one is also obviously flawed. What good is this Tomatocator in most cases? You need a sealed, glass-walled room to be able to gather enough condensation for it to work. In most normal rooms there is too much ventilation for it to work. It'll never work. Face it. I'm going back to bed. Call me when you come up with something new."

As much as Lucy was flattered that she was mentioned and as much as she was amazed at what was said, she quickly narrowed her eyes squarely on the dog's lips as the professor left the room.

"NOOOOOOOoooooooo!" howled Ooyay, closing his eyes and shaking his head high in the air.

There was no mistake. This dog could speak! And invent! And Professor Crastinator was a fake! And this new invention was as wonky as the last one! And the mayor was bald!

SLEEPING IN THE DINING ROOM

Whistling was the way William communicated. He had no need for words, since he expressed every thought and feeling that he had entirely through the mood, speed, volume and intensity of his tunes. From the moment he woke in the morning, to when he would go to sleep later that night, William would stop whistling only for a brief bite to eat every few hours. Whether someone was nearby or not, whether replying to a question or posing his own, William whistled and was understood immediately by everyone who heard him (no matter if they could speak whistle or not). William whistled while he worked. William whistled while he walked and whistled while he whittled on a piece of wood. In fine weather, William whooped warm-hearted tunes and would be heard whistling wistful, watery wibble-wobbles when it was wet. During funerals or at the end of a long hard day, William would be heard whistling a weepy, weary, woe-begotten, weightless warble.

He had wooed his wife with witty witterings and when he was being wed the priest asked if William took Whilomena to be his lawful wedded wife. To which William whinnied with a positive whirligig of uplifting emotion that could only be taken by everyone waiting to mean one thing: Oui.

What else would William work at if he wasn't a postman? He certainly needed to be outdoors whenever possible. Whilomena loved her husband as much as ever, but his constant whistling could be too much in the enclosed confines of their two-room house. It was best for everyone if she unlocked the front door and set him free each morning to do his whistling in the open for all to enjoy.

As he wandered the streets and the housing estates with his letters, people would stop and wave and ask William how he was doing or if he had seen the match the night before, just so they could listen to his unique way of replying. The children called him Wee Willy Whistle (which was strange because he was over six feet tall) and laughed and danced and played imaginary flutes as they circled around him on the road. Of course William enjoyed this attention and would whistle all the more beautifully for it. The children weren't mocking him, after all, they were simply joining in the reverie of his music. Indeed it was impossible to meet William and to leave without a smile on your face. Everybody who met him would immediately forget to even ask if he could speak normal words. His whistling was above words. His tunes and songs and general whistling-conversation seemed to work on a deeper level of communication than normal spoken language. William's whistling spoke directly to the heart and didn't need to go through the brain first to be understood.

In time-honoured tradition, Ooyay climbed into the newspaper rack in the hallway once he heard the familiar whistling coming up the driveway. Then, putting his feet through the bottom of the rack, and arching his back, the small blue dog was able to comfortably wear the newspaper rack as someone would wear a coat. Of course this was a strange coat, with two open saddlebags on each side for newspapers, magazines, letters and junk mail.

He hadn't been outside yet that morning, but from William's whistle, Ooyay could tell that it had been raining once again all night long. However, the sun was already shining brightly and Mrs. Silverpottotea down the road had at last found the lawnmower she mislaid the week before.

The blue dog in the newspaper rack now stood quietly underneath the letterbox in the front door as the mountain of mail flowed into the saddlebags on either side. William whistled from his big heart as usual while he pushed the mail through from the other side of the door. As the weight grew in the newspaper rack, Ooyay grew in strength and confidence and happiness from the joyous melody he was hearing from the postman.

The little dog felt that it was like having a one-off beautiful concert performed solely for him every morning. Each day it was different, as he knew that it was different for each person William met. The postman didn't do it deliberately to boost others. He did it for the fun he had and the excitement he got from whistling.

After the post had all come through William was still in mid-whistle, singing of colours and shapes and blocks and leaves. Ooyay didn't want it to end. He could happily sit and listen to William all day long. A sudden flash of emotion (or something) sent a shiver down his spine and out through his tail. This usually meant he had had an idea of some sort. However he now heard the postman leaving the front door and walking down the path from the house. This immediately shook the little dog from his trance.

"Wait!" Ooyay cried in agitation.

William paused as he heard the command from behind the big door. He wasn't aware anyone had ever been listening from inside Professor Crastinator's home.

"Where did Mrs. Silverpottotea find the lawnmower?" Ooyay enquired out of the silence.

The postman smiled as he turned down the path once more. His whistling continued where it had stopped, but now the answer to this question seemed to fit exactly into the part of the tune he was just coming to. Her lawn mower was in the fridge all along, apparently.

The main bedroom had been fitted with one of those automatic doors so as to allow Ooyay easy access while the Professor rested. Inside, Professor Crastinator would lie in his open-top four-poster bed for weeks on-end. Each post of the bed was an arm that moved to do the Prof's bidding: The two head posts might fluff his large pillows, while the bottom two were busy tucking him in for a good night's sleep. During mealtimes, they would prop him up, turn on the radio and hand him a menu with pictures of the food he might like to eat.

Once he had made his selection, a tray would be placed before him, full of cereals, fruit, ice cream, jelly, cold meat, vegetables or whatever he had selected. It was part of Ooyay's job to ensure these food items were available for the bed-posts to present to the Prof. Unfortunately, since Ooyay was such a small dog he was not allowed use the cooker, so neither the dog nor his master could eat a warm meal as long as the Professor stayed in bed.

As he now entered the room, Ooyay didn't have to look around to know exactly where everything was: The wall on the far-side beyond the bed contained two large windows that looked out on the gardens (beyond the gardens on this side of the house was Smisslewig School.) To his left was the Professor in his bed. Behind the Professor's head was a wall full of books from ceiling to floor. However there was one slot in the middle of this wall, through which dinner trays were passed back and forth. A dark red curtain completely covered the wall to Ooyay's right (at the foot of the bed). Usually, this curtain remained closed.

The bedroom itself was large enough to hold everything the old man needed without being cluttered, but small enough to be warm and cosy. Apart from the moving bedposts, everything else looked just like they might in a normal bedroom -except for one thing: it was completely upside down.

On the plain white floor was nothing, apart from the professor's bed and a foot-long light fitting that stuck up from a hole in the centre. An upside-down shade guided brightness all around the "real" floor, which was on the ceiling. This ceiling was carpeted. Next to one of the windows, on the upside-down ceiling/floor, stood (hung) a rocking chair. Beside the rocking chair was a small table with a jug and wash-hand basin, which looked to be full of water. Windowsills were at the *top* of the windows and each one was covered in cushions, as if an upside-down person might sit and rest in this cosy enclave whilst gazing at the world outside.

In front of the wall with the large curtain, hung an upside-down roll-top desk behind an upside-down stool. In the centre of the room, on the ceiling, was a dining table, six chairs and place settings for six people. Above the Professor's bed was another small table, on which stood a table-lamp. Since the main light in the room was in the middle of the floor and since the light-fitting itself was *below* the height of the bed, if the professor wanted more light he needed only to switch on this table-lamp on the table on the "floor" above his head.

In most rooms there is a gap between the top of the doors and the ceiling. Because this room was upside-down, there had been a two-foot drop inside the bedroom at the *bottom* of the door. *(Another reason to have an automatic door was because the door-handle was too high to reach from the floor.)* A ramp had been installed that lead from the door down to the floor/ceiling. Ooyay made sure that it was painted white -the same colour as the ceiling, so that it looked like this ramp was the underneath part of a stairs (if you were sitting upside-down in the room).

It was of the utmost-importance to Ooyay that every detail in the upside down room be exactly as it should if the room was right-way up. He was forever insisting on things being moved around overhead and adding miniscule details that nobody would ever know about. The bedposts could take care of most rearrangements, although every now and then the blue dog would have to telephone a local handyman to come and sort out any bigger tasks.

One of the main reasons for this project was to ensure that Professor Crastinator had some source of mental stimulation. The Professor had a habit of lying there, doing nothing, for long periods. So for him to wake up after a long sleep to find himself stuck to the ceiling, upside-down in a dining room was a dizzying experience that would exercise even the most tired of old brains -no matter how many times it happened.

But! It only worked if *everything* was exactly as it should be overhead. So there was a lace mat under/above the table-lamp over the professor's head that drooped *upwards* as though gravity pulled it in that direction. Inside the opened roll-top desk Ooyay made sure there was paper and pens stuck in place where they should be. Each night, while the Professor slept, the upside-down objects in the room were gently sprayed (by the bed-poles) with a slightly sticky substance, then tiny powder molecules were added with a puffer. This made it appear as though dust was settling on these upside-down objects. Every few days, as he examined the dining room above his head, picturing himself sitting at the table for a meal, the Professor would suddenly cry out the same thing, as though he had never screamed it before. "LOOK AT THE STATE OF THIS PLACE!" he would cry. "BY GOD IT'S FULL OF DUST!" Then the bedposts would have to take out the polish and the vacuum cleaner and spend some time removing the sprayed-on dust.

Just as Ooyay was descending the ramp in this bedroom he could tell such a moment was in fact about to occur. The Professor had been in bed sitting back on his pillows, gazing calmly at the ceiling. Now he seemed to concentrate on one particular location on the overhead table. Next he looked around the rest of the overhead floor as he sat up, stretching to see more clearly. He slowly looked at the carpet, on the windowsills and on the roll-top desk.

"LOOK AT THE STATE OF THIS PLACE!" he cried out at last. "BY GOD IT'S FULL OF DUST!"

He looked genuinely surprised every time. Each time it happened, Ooyay had to bow and shake his head in laughter.

He had imagined the upside down room would help the Professor think about and look at things in new and different ways. Being the man he was, however, the Professor had his own views and still looked on the world from the practical, *functional* viewpoint as he had always done.

Ooyay was a dreamer and each of Ooyay's dreams had to first pass the inspection of this cranky old man.

WHAT IT SAYS IN THE PAPERS

Once he came to a halt and was standing in the correct spot next to the bed, an otherwise-unnoticeable panel rose from the ceiling under Ooyay's feet and lifted him to bed-height.

"HAVE YOU SEEN THIS!?" cried the Professor, waving at the overhead floor as Ooyay stepped onto the bed. "I'll get pneumonia and die from all this dust," he coughed, lowering his voice.

"Do you get pneumonia from dust then?" asked Ooyay with a curious grin.

"Shut up and hand me the papers!" demanded the Professor gruffly as he made a grab for the saddlebag.

To an outsider, it might appear as though the Professor was unnecessarily harsh with his dog by telling him to shut up, but this was simply how things were. Ooyay enjoyed poking gentle fun at his master. The old man enjoyed moaning.

"Ah ah!" said Ooyay, leaping out of reach.

"C'mon, let me have one newspaper," pleaded the man.

"You know the rules Crasty!" the little blue dog taunted. "No paper until you do your exercises!"

"Go on then, fire away," sighed the crusty old Crasty.

The Professor had a tendency to lie in his room, doing nothing, until Ooyay prodded him in some way that would exercise his brain.

"Say the alphabet!" commanded Ooyay.

"That's easy," laughed the old man. "A-B-C-D-E..." -but Ooyay stopped him short.

"Backwards!" he grinned an evil dog grin.

Eight minutes later the Prof had completed his task and was allowed pull the first paper...

THE SUN

For The Hottest News Around

THE WALLS HAVE EARS!

By Smiffy Sheehan

The next time you tell somebody a secret, the next time you confess all your sins to a priest, the next time you are singing badly in the bath —*BEWARE!*

For Professor Marcus Crastinator, Inventor-supremo of many things, including the world's largest foot-stool, the man who brought us the pocket automobile and the deep fried hat (for when it must be eaten) has yesterday unveiled his most devious invention yet! —details on page 7

Are you over-weight?
Perhaps you're a little too skinny?
Do you <u>look</u> different to everybody else?

Well obviously you just don't fit in with the rest of us. -Take our compatibility survey on page 2 to figure out if you should run away from home today!

YETI SPOTTED IN LOCAL FIELD

By Stuart Pumpkinspit

Police have today confirmed that rumours of the abominable snowman holidaying in this country are **true**.

Pictured here by ace photographer, Snappy Feelgood, the Yeti (or "Shadwell" as he likes to be called) says he just wanted a break from his cold mountain. "Even the birds get to fly south sometimes" he added.

Shadwell tells us he is a hard-working Yeti who hasn't had a holiday in 39 years. "It's not like I won't return to the snowy, stormy nights-in with the wife, but for now I just need to get away."

Shadwell asks that he be left in peace for the duration of his visit. More photos on page 11 – 17

"I like that" smiled the Professor. "The Walls Have Ears! -I like that one, I do. It's nice to get the front page, isn't it Ooo?"

"Of course we got the front page," Ooyay sneered, "but that silly Yeti story has more coverage. What's the world coming to? He even looks nothing like a Yeti, does he?"

"What we really need here is some tea," the Professor beamed.

He liked nothing better than to read the morning newspapers whilst sipping from a glass of iced lemon tea.

"Would you like some, Ooo? Tea? Hmm?"

Ooyay looked into his friend Crasty's eyes and not for the first time wondered if he had any sense at all. The Professor was a good master and companion, but would rarely do anything that didn't suit himself. This selfishness annoyed the little dog at times and made him wonder if the Professor would even notice if he wasn't around anymore. Ooyay knew he wouldn't be where he now was if it wasn't for the Professor, but he sometimes wished Crasty would *want* something more from life than to be so happy with just a glass of iced lemon tea while he read the newspapers every morning.

Why didn't Crasty bring Ooyay for walkies some mornings instead? Or take him to the parlour for a manicure and some pampering? Or how come Ooyay had never caught a Frisbee in his mouth that was thrown from his master's hand in slow motion? Ooyay could think of millions of things he'd rather be doing.

"Go on then," he finally sighed. "I'll have some tea."

THE MOON

Mooning The World Every Day!

GOOD HEAVENS WHAT HAS HE COME UP WITH THIS TIME?

BY Frank "Stinky" Polyester

The day began when I first fell from my bed following an early morning telephone call at 11:30am.

My editor informed me that either I carry my posterior down to the Professor's greenhouse or I would not be allowed access to the office Christmas party this year. **See P2**

PEAS ARE GOOD FOR YOU! –new study proves it

Following extensive studies in the offices of reputable newspaper *THE MOON*, we are pleased to announce that we have *positive proof* that people can live on nothing but peas for a <u>at least</u> four weeks.

A group of three fearless reporters quickly volunteered for the experiment. Due to an unfortunate pong from each of them by the end of day two, however, we had to send them home for the rest of the month.

Join us as we examine the fallout on page 3 – 19.

"Typical coverage from The Moon I see," huffed the Professor. "They're more interested in talking about how everything affects *them* than they are in actually reporting the news itself. I'm thinking of cancelling my subscription to The Moon. Hear me Ooyay? I think I want to cancel The Moon."

"Yes Crasty," replied the dog.

This too was a common phrase from the Professor. One time Ooyay *did* cancel the paper following his master's request but the next morning there was hell to pay from Crasty's temper when he didn't get his traditional five newspapers.

The tea arrived in a large jug on a tray, along with two empty glasses.

"Shall I pour?" enquired Ooyay with a mischievous grin.

This was yet another line used by Crasty every morning as soon as the tea arrived. Ooyay was happy this morning to have the chance to say it first.

"Certainly not!" cried Professor Crastinator incredulously. "What with your paws, we'd have spilt tea all over the bed. We can't have that now can we?"

He paused as though waiting for an answer. Then with a deep breath, he spoke again.

"Shall I pour?" he asked, as if Ooyay had not already used these very words just now.

The Professor never knew when Ooyay was mocking him. After filling both glasses he reached for the next newspaper.

"Ah, this is more like it!" gushed the old man, reading the headline.

THE STAR

Why buy another paper when they're the same as us anyway?

PRO PROF PRODUCES PROOF OF PROSE!

By S. Hawn Lane

Have you ever listened to someone speaking and suddenly found yourself wanting to rewind what was said to hear it again? Well now you can.

Thanks to that marvellously madcap man we all love to hear from, Professor Marcus Crastinator.

Not content with almost eradicating world-hunger by introducing the concept of high-rise fields, or making it easy to cross rivers and to walk from the top of one tall building to another using the Bridge-on-Demand, as well as many more **-See Page 2**

20-CARROT BAG OF TURNIPS GOES MISSING FROM CITY CENTRE STORE! –Page 6

"THE EASTER BUNNY STOLE MY HEART" –SOAP-STAR TELLS <u>ALL</u>!
–**Page 3**

ELVIS TURNS LANDLORD, LETS THE BUILDING
–Page 7

2 + 2 = ?
REPORT SAYS CHILDREN ARE DUMBER THAN EVER –**Page <u>4</u>**
(if you can find it)

"PRO PROF PRODUCES PROOF OF PROSE!" Professor Crastinator read aloud. "It doesn't get much better than this, does it Ooo?"

"I guess not" sighed Ooyay, not for the first time wishing that it *did* get better than this.

For Ooyay, the whole thrill came from the *idea* itself (whatever it was), and in seeing that idea develop into a useable item. He enjoyed sitting at his computer most days inventing and designing whatever came to mind. Just a while ago, he had had one of those sudden flashes that usually meant the birth of an idea for a new invention. These flashes would come to him, then go again before he even knew what they were. He would often be in the middle of something when suddenly he would pause as a flash came through his mind. He might then finish whatever it was that he was doing before realising what the flash was. Only by thinking about it later would he come to know that he had had... *an idea*.

Just now he realised what the earlier flash was an idea for: He would like to try making some device that would help him (and everyone else) speak whistle. How much better off the world would be if we all whistled like pretty songbirds all day long instead of being held back by language and its forms and rules. What if he invented something that you could speak into and out would come beautiful whistles and streams of music that was an interpretation of what you had said?

The final two newspapers were now an obstacle for Ooyay to get past before he could run off to begin inventing this new device.

GOLDEN FISH CAUGHT!

Fishermen have made the biggest catch ever known to man (or woman.)

They said he didn't exist, but the fabled golden fish is now <u>dead</u>! -P2

I SAY, YOU SAY, IT SAY!

So imagine this, right? You're in a room, talking to someone. You are asked to repeat what you just said, but instead of simply saying it again, you can now have the <u>walls</u> say it for you. Bizarre? You betcha! But that zany guy we all know and love thinks he has cracked it.

Personally, this reporter thinks the old boy has finally cracked himself, but if you want further info, turn to page 13 now.

8 out of 10 people believe everything they read. FACT! –A new report on the reason why so many reports are carried out today revealed startling information. Page 3

"Nice fish," mumbled Professor Crastinator.

He didn't appear to have anything to say on the coverage that The World newspaper gave to the new invention.

Ooyay considered again how his whistling machine might work. Sadly, he quickly realised it would never do the job: For one thing, the beauty in the postman's whistling was that the whistles spoke *more* than words. If this new whistling machine was going to whistle only what was said and not *felt*, then it was pointless. Not for the first time did the small dog find that he had to cast aside a seemingly great idea after a little thought.

Most ideas of his died at this stage. For instance, he once thought he might develop a way for people to plug themselves into an electrical socket so they could recharge for half an hour instead of having to sleep, but that idea fizzled away in no time. He usually had ten to twenty such notions per day in fact, but only a very small number of them went on to design stage. Then only a small number of those were actually developed. Very few developed inventions became useable items, and fewer still were ever successful in terms of return-on-investment. It wasn't easy being an inventor and it seemed like only one in a million ideas made it possible to pay for the other mad notions.

The fact that Ooyay had come up with so many big, useable, beneficial, world-changing inventions and ideas was really the result of tens of thousands of other, madder notions being discarded before anyone even heard of them.

THE DAILY RAG

Summut t' blow yer nose wiv

CAT GIVES BIRTH TO TWIN BUDGIES

Ok, it might not have been a cat -it was a hamster. And it might not have been twin budgies -it was one. And he was a hamster also. But nonetheless this hamster looked very much like a cat and its offspring looked exactly like two budgies stuck together. See for yourself on Page 6.

This Christmas don't give yourself a Life-Sentence

Celebrity couple split!

World-famous screen actors and off-screen couple, Sam Sheen and Leah McSween decided to leave a restaurant yesterday before they even finished their desserts!!

No sooner did our ace reporter, Joel Aines, enter the room, than the quick-paced pair quickly leapt up and left Billy's Bistro on Brewery Lane.

No reason was given for their sudden scarper, but a good friend of the duo has informed us that all is not well between the two.

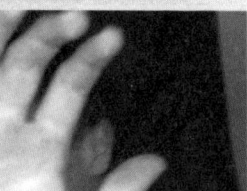

Sam Sheen's ear!

Check it out! The mad doc is at it again!!

INSIDE!!!!

Ooyay tried running off as soon as the Professor seemed to have finished reading, but was called back instantly.

"Look at that! Typical of those scoundrels at The Rag! 'The mad doc is at it again!! ...*INSIDE!*' I'll give them *Inside!*"

The Professor didn't mind being referred to as "The mad doc" but the fact that the story wasn't covered on the front page particularly grated.

"Typical," agreed Ooyay, once more attempting to slip away quietly.

"Don't forget to leave the news rack," reminded Crasty. "There might be some interesting post -and besides, that cute little journal from Smisslewig School is out today too. I hope she spelt my name correctly."

LUCY GOES FORTH

David Swoon was the cutest boy in the school. He had large, bulging blue eyes that seemed to promise the world when they stared straight at you. His long, blonde hair looked like it was folded into place each morning. One large, beautiful curl usually bobbed up and down across his forehead as if it was a finger calling you toward him. Other boys might take pride in such a curl, but David always looked like it bothered him no end. The agitation on his face as he quickly flung the curl out of his eyes was the main thing that attracted Lucy to him. She had always pictured herself walking up to David Swoon and calmly moving that curl out of his way so it would never bother him again. David would then smile one of his glorious smiles just for her.

From that point on the two of them would be friends forever. He'd call to her house and they'd regularly do their homework and school projects and go on newspaper assignments together. When they got older they would open a shop together and Lucy would work mornings and David would take the late-shift. On weekends they would be free to have walks in the park, but not to swing on the swings because they'd be very grown up by then. They'd probably sit near the bandstand and read books like proper grown-ups do.

But David was eleven years old and almost grown up already and, as far as Lucy knew, was unaware that she even existed -Until now.

As she entered through the front-gates of the school she could see that virtually everybody in the yard had a copy of the paper. Her editor, friend and news-dogsbody, Milo "Moo" Mooney, had obviously printed extra copies to cover the demand. Now it seemed that the latest edition of the Smisslewig News had finally grabbed *everyone's* attention. It would almost certainly be impossible for David not to notice her now.

Because of the special invitation to Professor Crastinator's demo, she had thankfully been excused from classes for the whole of the previous day and had spent the remainder of the time writing-up what she had witnessed. Only Milo knew of her discovery and both agreed that neither should mention it to anyone until after the report had been published the following morning.

Lucy had found it particularly difficult to keep it to herself when her parents had quizzed her over dinner for news on the invention, but she simply insisted they would have to wait until the Smisslewig News came out.

Nobody said a word to Lucy as she entered the building. Each person in turn looked up and immediately stopped talking as she approached. The main corridor in Smisslewig School looked much the same distance end to end as any other in any school Lucy had ever seen on television, but when you have to walk its full length through throngs of dumbstruck children and teachers who are all staring straight at you, it makes the journey seem as long as a slow-bicycle marathon ...over broken glass ...in the rain ...wearing no clothes ...carrying an anvil ...while the world watched ...silently.

Standing around three-quarter-ways down the corridor, in the centre of a circle of friends, was David Swoon. He too looked directly at Lucy as she drew near.

Just as she passed, she noticed a movement from David out of the corner of her eye. Quickly she spun around, but immediately saw that he was merely wiping the curl from his face. She had thought he was going to say something to her and now she was embarrassed because both of them were looking directly at each other.

"Ehhh..." said David Swoon, trying to gather words.

"Yes?" encouraged Lucy, eager to hear any reaction to what she had uncovered.

David shyly handed his mobile phone to Lucy. She took it and looked back to him, wondering what this could mean.

"A friend of mine wants a word with you," said David sheepishly.

"Oh?" asked Lucy as she looked at the phone and put it to her ear. "Who?"

"It's my dog" laughed David. "He says he has a fresh scoop for you!"

With that, the whole school burst into laughter. People clapped David on the back as they doubled up from laughing so hard. Children waved the Smisslewig News in the air, taunting Lucy with it, crying out that they had never read such a load of rubbish in all of their lives. Teachers behaved much as the children did. It took all of Lucy's strength to wade past, back through the corridor and out the main door, eyes filled with tears the whole way.

As she made it to the gate, Milo caught up with her and swung her back by the arm. He was quite strong for his age and always wore a T-shirt that appeared two-sizes too small for his large, chubby arms.

"I thought you believed me!" bawled Lucy as she lashed at his chest.

Milo stood there and took it as he continued to pin her to the gate by her shoulders. His red frizzled hair blew wildly in the wind.

"I did believe you. I *do*. I never even thought of it as being funny until I saw everyone else laugh just now. You have to admit -it is funny Lucy."

Lucy stared at her friend Milo's wide, watery eyes and snotty nose and knew instinctively that he was telling the truth about believing her. For the past year he had been her editor and best friend. Milo had been beside her all the way when they waged that campaign to keep books in the school library.

The head teacher's plan had been to replace all the books with twenty computers that each contained more books than the library already held, but Lucy was outraged at the proposal.

"We might as well not bother coming to school, but work from our home computers instead if that's the case," she argued.

"Why do we need teachers if computers have more information?" she asked.

"Why do we need schools if we don't need teachers?" she reasoned.

"Why do we need head teachers if we then have no other teachers?" she demanded to know.

After a lengthy campaign that had seen the school newspaper temporarily shutdown, Lucy's parents being called-in several times and Milo accidentally falling from the upstairs library-window (long-story for some other time), the headmaster finally backtracked on his plan.

Virtually all of the children and some of the teachers were against Lucy and Milo on that one too. They had been looking forward to surfing the internet and playing games and sending emails instead of having to read boring old books all the time, but in the end, the school got five new computers anyway and they all fitted into the library without having to remove any books.

She hadn't been certain that they were right all that time even though she fought so hard. What had kept her going, possibly above all else, was that every time she caught a glimpse of David Swoon he never seemed to even notice the battle she was waging. That had made her fight on all the more.

With so many people against them it had been hard to believe in the goal, but still something in Lucy's stomach churned at the thought of replacing all those beautiful books with a few plastic computers that would fade away and lose their memory in time. That simply could never be right no matter what everyone else was willing to go along with.

Now however, Lucy knew she was on her own on this one. She was aware that Milo would believe anything she told him and would always back her to the hilt, but she also knew that it was up to her to prove what she had said and to show *Mister* Swoon who was right.

"Let me go Milo" said Lucy calmly, wiping the tears from her eyes and gently taking his hands from off her shoulders. "I have a tail to wag."

A WAGGY TALE

"Ooyay! Ooyay! Where are ya fella?"

Instinctively the little dog's tail began to wag when he heard the excited screams from his master. Could it be that at last Crasty wanted to go for a walk? Were they going to play fetch and roll around on the grass together in the park? This was surely a joyous day.

"I'm in the Den, Crast!" shouted Ooyay in response as he ran to get his leash.

He no sooner grabbed it and began running to the door than Professor Crastinator burst in with a look of deep worry on his face.

"There you are boy!" he gasped as he caught his breath.

Ooyay knew at once he wasn't being called for walkies. He dropped his leash in the middle of the floor, then turned back to the computer.

"What's wrong now?" he sighed. "Did you miss the sale at the mattress factory again?" he added sarcastically.

"No, worse than that!" answered the master, who never understood sarcasm. "Have a look at this..." he said as he held out the front page of the Smisslewig News.

"Crastinator a Fake! by Lucy Lucey" read Ooyay aloud, then quietly read the rest to himself, moving his head from left to right as he took in each line.

SMISSLEWIG NEWS

NEWS FOR PEOPLE WITH CLASS!

CRASTINATOR A FAKE!

By Lucy Lucey.

Professor Marcus Crastinator never invented anything. In fact, all he does is sleep all day long until the true inventor gives him something worth getting up for!

Yes, the inventor of all those things was none other than Professor Crastinator's dog, "Ohyeah". Have you ever seen a blue dog? Well this reporter certainly hasn't, but that's not all. He is blue, but also he can talk. He talks very well in fact.

This reporter was present when this little blue doggie pleaded with his owner to make him a hot dinner before he went to bed.

The Professor just sneered and said that Ohyeah's new invention was obviously faulty and deserved to fail like the "One Key System" and that he would get no dinner until it was fixed or until there was something else worth his time getting out of bed to see.

(More all the way through...)

Artist's impression by Milo Mooney, Aged 9.

"You are stupid!" laughed Ooyay finally. "Look! It has me telling you that you're stupid. That's the best piece of reporting I've seen all day. I don't think I said that, but they can quote me on it anytime. Ha ha!"

"You're missing the point *dear* Ooyay," sighed the Professor in a condescending manner. "Have you not noticed that it more or less spills the beans on our little arrangement!? I mean, how did she know about our argument yesterday?"

The Prof walked to one of the windows in Ooyay's den and looked outside.

"She must have been spying on us the whole time! What are we going to do?"

Quickly he glanced around outside each of the three windows in the room, but noticed nothing strange there now.

"Calm down Crasty. Keep your hair on," said Ooyay without looking up from his monitor. "Who's going to believe this write-up from a schoolgirl? This will all quieten down in no time -even *if* anybody takes any notice. Anyway, whoever heard of a talking dog?" asked the talking dog.

"But, but, but... There are more people than just children involved here you know!" Professor Crastinator now began waving his arms as though he was desperately trying to smash his way out of a fire in a glass bubble. "Some people will begin to suspect something -after all you *are* a *blue* dog. That in itself is unusual. Even if they don't believe it they will now look at you and wonder where you came from. No matter what they believe, it will draw too much attention to you."

"...And away from you!" finished the dog with a nod and a crafty smile.

"That's not the problem and you know it!" cried the master, not knowing where to look now or what to do, before swinging back around to gaze out the window.

"Besides, someone like Flocky Nocky would *kill* for even a sniff at this half-rumour. He would never overlook such a tale no matter how outlandish-sounding."

The blue dog looked up now, for the first time curious about what was being said.

"What do you mean?" he asked. "Flocky's your friend. You've always said so. The two of you often talk for hours on your secure satellite line."

The Professor hesitated, then sat down on the seat by the window.

"Well I wouldn't say *friends* exactly... We're more like... *colleagues*."

Ooyay was genuinely puzzled. Dr. Flocky Nocky had never physically visited their house and the little dog himself had never been admitted to the room while the Professor was speaking with him, but still he was under the impression that the two men got along well together.

"Look!" gasped the Professor finally, "I've never told you this before because I didn't want you to... be bothered by it... but... well, The Doctor usually spends most of his time trying to convince me to join up with him. He says that great minds such as ours should work together for the greater good. Most of the time I'm just trying to get him off the line because I don't know what he is talking about, but he can be quite insistent. ...Now I'm afraid he'll begin questioning me about you and I don't know how I can stand up to that from *him*."

Ooyay was surprised. He had no idea Dr. Flocky Nocky wanted to work with Crasty.

"...And you would prefer to have *me* do it all instead!" he howled.

"No. That's not it at all fella!" The Professor now ran to his best friend and rubbed him gently behind the ears as only he knew how.

"Don't you see what I'm saying? How could *I* work with Flocky Nocky when it is *you* he is really looking for?" He took a deep breath, then added, "Besides, I've seen how restless you're getting. You want to leave me. You've outgrown your old pal Crasty. I was afraid - I *am* afraid - that if I told you about Flocky Nocky you'd jump into his arms... I don't want you to leave me, boy. You're my best friend!"

The professor looked down now and as he rubbed at an ear, his best friend turned his head to look into his eyes. Both sets of eyes were filled with tears as man and dog looked sadly at each other.

"I'll never leave you Crasty!" burst Ooyay. "You're my master and my friend. You know I'd do anything for you!"

"And I'll never leave you Ooyay! You know I'd never let you come to any harm. You are a *part* of me. I'd rather cut off my right arm than part with you." The Professor now hugged his pet and kissed him on the nose and between the eyes several times.

"C'mon" he said finally. "Forget about your inventions for now. Forget about that newspaper article and forget about that silly girl. Let's go see what's in the freezer. I'll cook you a nice big juicy steak if it's there!"

The dog's tail slammed off everything in the room as it wagged away while man and pet immediately left for the kitchen.

Lucy reached the same spot from where she had seen and heard the dog talk the day before. Following a brief inspection, she discovered that one of the windows was unlocked. Opening it just enough to squeeze through, she climbed inside and immediately slammed it shut behind her.

Having made a louder noise than she had anticipated, she quickly dived behind the sofa and lay there quietly for some minutes until she was certain nobody was coming to investigate.

Finally she stood up and surveyed the room, looking for just one thing. Amazingly she spotted it almost straight away, lying on the dog's computer desk in front of the monitor. Walking over, she picked up the metal rod and twisted the rubber shaft so that it formed a T-shaped bar -just as the Professor had demonstrated the day before. On either side of the keyboard two large red balls rested in trays, but Lucy knew at once that they were not the tomato-type objects Professor Crastinator had used in the demonstration. For one thing they were too big, but also these balls each had a number of buttons and seemed to be moulded to fit a dog's paw.

Looking around the room for the first time she quickly spotted a bowl of real tomatoes on the coffee table in front of the television. Had he *really* used real tomatoes to gather that condensation? There was only one way to find out! Choosing a small one, Lucy screwed the tomato into the bottom of the T-bar. Amazingly it seemed to fit and stayed in place at once.

Each window in the room was made from several glass panels. There wasn't much condensation on any of them, but she scraped the T-bar across each one anyway in the hope that *some* record of the dog's speech had been stored there. The computer monitor looked like it hadn't been cleaned in a while, but there was certainly a little moisture on there someplace because as she scraped the screen the tomato seemed to noticeably expand. At least she thought it did.

Looking at it again, the tomato now appeared to be much the same size as when she had attached it. There seemed little point in continuing, but she pressed on, scraping the desk, each of its legs, drawers, television, coffee-table, flower-pot, petals, mantelpiece, door, doorknob, walls and for good measure she rubbed the T-bar along the carpet and curtains, before detaching the tomato. It now had definitely grown somewhat since she began, but what had she gathered? There was only one way to find out.

Without looking for it, Lucy had already spotted the blender in an open drawer in Ooyay's desk. Pulling it out, she took a few steps back, sat on the couch, inserted the tomato and pressed the button marked with a triangle. Voices instantly sprang from the device and a wide smile spread across Lucy's face.

"At last I have proof!" she thought to herself, but immediately the smile froze on her face as she realised the importance of what she believed she was hearing...

"She must have been spying on us the whole time! What are we going to do?"

"Keep ... schoolgirl ... quiet ..."

"Some ... suspect something"

"... where you came from... draw too much attention... someone ... kill ... sniff ... rumour"

"...and you would prefer to have me do it"

"I am afraid"

"You're my master ... You know I'd do anything for you!"

"come to ... harm ... that silly girl ... I'll cook you a nice big juicy steak"

The voices stopped. The little humming noise that came from the blender itself stopped. Lucy remained hunched over the machine with the same stiff smile still plastered across her cheesy face as she gazed blankly at the carpet. The shock from what she believed she had just heard left her frozen with fear. It was clear to her now that Professor Crastinator had taken out a contract with his wonder dog to bump her off. After several seconds, the eyes rolled upward in her head and she fainted quietly onto the chair.

OOYAY LEADS THE WAY

Waking up on a couch can sometimes be a nice experience. One time, when she was much younger, Lucy fell asleep whilst watching cartoons on the telly. All through the snooze she could hear the cartoons, but now they were kind of mixed in with her dreams. On the television, a rabbit would ask "*What's up?*" and in her dream, Lucy would answer that the sky was up. Later in the same snooze, Lucy was part of another cartoon where the kids were riding on a sleigh down a snowy mountain, avoiding trees and fences and leaping over houses where people ate their dinner. After that there was another dream where she was inside the belly of a big fat purple dinosaur that was pretending to be nice to the children, but was really going to eat them all like he had already eaten Lucy. Lucy shouted to warn the other kids, but they only laughed and sang along with the purple dinosaur as he danced all the way to the child-sized oven. When she woke up from that nap, Lucy stretched hard and laughed out loud as she recalled the different dreams. Her dad was sitting on another seat nearby, engrossed in an animated feature about a duck and a balloon. He asked Lucy why she was laughing, but she answered "nothing". It was too silly to tell anybody about such dreams.

For an instant when she opened her eyes now, Lucy believed she was on that same couch at home in front of the television. Almost immediately however she recalled which couch she *was* lying on-and why. Quickly she snapped up her head and spotted the blue dog sitting at his computer, no more than a few feet from where she lay. It would have been impossible for him not to have seen her. Too afraid to budge, she held her breath without moving a muscle.

Ooyay was on a seat that was almost the same height as the desk itself. His front paws were leaning on the two red balls Lucy had earlier noticed by the computer. On the monitor was a three-dimensional model of the Tomatocator device that had been demonstrated by the Professor and used by Lucy herself just before fainting (she had no way of knowing how long she had been out). As Ooyay rotated one ball under his paw, the onscreen Tomatocator rotated in the same direction. The dog's far shoulder moved and Lucy observed how the onscreen model zoomed in and out. Obviously the two red balls were a type of computer mouse used by Ooyay to control whatever was on the screen.

"I call them boobies," said Ooyay suddenly, without looking around.

Too afraid to speak, Lucy couldn't bring herself to say a word. The dog continued as though he was talking to someone else, but stealing a glance, Lucy didn't see the Professor anywhere in the room.

"...With the right one I control the X/Y axis," he continued, still looking at the monitor. "The left one can be user-defined to any purpose, but obviously controlling the Z axis is the most obvious application, as I'm doing here in this program."

Still Lucy couldn't bring herself to say anything to the dog that she believed was contracted to kill her for the price of a juicy steak. She knew how it worked. She had seen all the movies. She knew that the bad guy would be nice to the hero or heroine, talk about pleasant things -maybe invite her to dinner. In the end however, he would hang her over a shark-infested swimming pool and try to kill her slowly and painfully by lowering her into the water. Still Ooyay continued talking.

"These are my boobies," he smiled. "Each one has three buttons for each of my main paw-fingers, and a fourth button on the base of the paw."

Now Lucy saw an opportunity to show this blue dog that he wasn't as clever as he might like to think.

"Boobies don't have four buttons on each one!" she sneered.

Ooyay turned around and looked straight at her.

"You're forgetting that I'm a dog!"

Lucy felt herself going bright red, both because of what he had said and because he was holding her gaze. She was unable to look away.

"You're sick!" she finally declared.

"...I know what you've done and what you think you know," said Ooyay slowly, changing the subject. "...And let me tell you that you are incorrect."

"So you're not a talking dog?" asked Lucy with a straight face and without a hint of irony, which made Ooyay smile.

Crasty was the only other person he had ever spoken to, but Crasty never appreciated or understood irony or sarcasm or any other type of sly wit the dog enjoyed.

"I like you Lucy," smiled Ooyay once more. "So I've decided not to kill you."

With that, Lucy burst into tears, despite trying hard not to. Just hearing him say the words "kill you" made the whole plan all the more real and was further proof (if it was needed) that he was indeed going to kill her.

This panicked the little dog. He thought they both knew that they were only joking with each other.

"I -I was *joking!*" he stammered, then ran over to sit next to her on the couch. She was too upset to even notice him.

"Look!" he commanded sternly. She looked. "I've listened to the evidence you have gathered in the Tomatocator. Let me tell you, what you've heard was *nothing* like what we were talking about. What am I going to do? *Nuzzle* you to death?"

Lucy noticed once more that he was only a small dog (small enough to curl up comfortably in her lap) and that he didn't seem that fierce.

"But I heard the tomato," she reminded him.

"Tomatoes were a bad idea," confessed Ooyay. "They lie all the time. ...But seriously, remember when you asked what would happen if the air was not trapped properly in the room? Well now you know! You can't have gathered much juice to power that little bit of conversation. *Think* about it. You just heard little snippets and put two and two together to make nine. Or twenty nine!"

Lucy looked once again into Ooyay's eyes. When she had done so the day before, she was unaware that he could speak. Still at that time she saw a depth of understanding and quiet *wisdom* that had overwhelmed her. Now, in his jet black eyes she saw *truth*. As he looked straight at her, she felt like she was falling into the dark eyes, but it wasn't a frightening fall. It was like a nice warm *uplifting* fall. It was like Ooyay knew everything and he was there to help Lucy understand everything too.

Her lower lip stopped trembling. More than anything he had said, those eyes had convinced Lucy that she had somehow gotten it wrong. It was silly to believe this little doggie would want to kill her. She knew that now. He was simply too cute for her to believe he could be a killer.

"Wha..." she began, when suddenly Professor Crastinator glided into the room.

"Ah you're up I see!" he smiled, giving a distant wave in the air. "Allow me to take you home."

"No, allow me Crasty!" cried Ooyay excitedly. "I'll take her! No one will see us. We can go in the HB!"

The Professor looked amazed. He had thought they agreed that they would try to confuse the girl and to pretend she was only dreaming it all.

"What are you doing?" he asked in confusion. "I thought we agreed you wouldn't speak? Why are you talking? Stop talking you *mutt*!"

"She *knows* I can talk Crasty," sighed Ooyay. "Put a sock in it. Besides, nobody believes you, do they Lucy? Otherwise you wouldn't be here."

"They laughed at me," mumbled Lucy, jamming her hand under her chin. "All of them."

Not for the first time, Professor Crastinator was amused and pleasantly surprised at Ooyay's reasoning. That dog was always more on top of things than he himself found possible.

"So I just deny everything about having a talking dog then?" he asked his talking dog.

"No need to deny it," laughed Ooyay. "Just laugh at any questions about it. After all, it *is* a very silly thing to imagine. Remember that."

The dog knew that his master was still thinking through the consequences of what should be done and picturing different scenarios that might occur and how he would deal with them. Crasty tended to over-think and over-plan every single thing he did long in advance of actually *doing* anything.

"Why don't you go back to bed Crasty?" suggested the dog. "You have a lot to work on there. Let me take care of things here for now."

"Yes," agreed the Professor, distantly. "This is a new tactic. A new approach. Change! Everything must change. Always change." Slowly Crasty turned and waddled from the room like a penguin at a funeral.

"It's ok, he gets like that," smiled Ooyay to Lucy. "He can easily spend hours choosing between apricot and strawberry yoghurt, but once he does, he is full of confidence in his decision. If you offer him some new flavour after that it is liable to send him ducking under the blankets for a week while he considers all the new parameters."

Now it was Lucy's turn to be confused.

"But he said yesterday that he *welcomes* change. How come he can't cope with such small changes?"

"He's old," replied Ooyay sadly. "He finds it hard to deal with change, but I think change is what holds him together. If things stopped changing for him now he would probably fade away and die. These little changes are just enough to keep him ticking over."

Ooyay appeared thoughtful as he stared at the door that his master had left through.

"Besides!" he laughed suddenly aloud, "it gives him an excuse to go to bed and have a think about it. He loves his bed, does Crasty! You'll see! When he gets up he'll be a new man. Come along now -follow me!" he said, nudging Lucy's arm with his bottom as he leapt off the couch and walked over to the television.

Ooyay pressed the power button, then sat on the ground below the TV, craning his neck as he looked up at the silent black screen. To Lucy's eyes it was a normal-enough looking television. It had a large, flat screen. It was pretty big, but nothing out of the ordinary. Lucy's uncle Kevin had one just like it. She could see no reason for the dog to examine it as intently as he was doing -especially since nothing seemed to be coming on.

"Maybe the plug is out?" Lucy began to wonder.

Then Ooyay suddenly jumped up and disappeared into the television.

"This waaayy!" he yelled to Lucy, sounding like he was falling.

Lucy was stunned. She ran to the TV, threw a hand at the screen she had earlier scraped with the Tomatocator, then immediately noticed that there *was no screen*! Ooyay had been waiting for the glass to move after he pressed the button, she now realised. Studying it more carefully, she spotted a hole inside the television that Ooyay had obviously jumped into. How bizarre!

Still, Lucy was long-since past being surprised at anything she found in Ooyay's house -oops! ...Professor Crastinator's house. She climbed into the television and dived into the black hole within.

WHAT'S IN TELEVISION?

Down she fell, too shocked to scream. She had expected to slide on something slippery, but instead there was just nothing. Nothing above her, nothing below her, nothing to the side. She could see nothing. She was falling but she couldn't see or feel a thing, apart from the air rushing past her as she fell. After what seemed like a very long time she finally composed herself enough to find her voice.

"AAAAAAAAAAAAAAAAAHHHHHHHHHHHHHHHHHHHH-HHHhhhhhhhhhhhhhhhHhhhHHHHhaaaahhhhhhhhhhAAAAA AAAhhhhhhhHAAAAAAAAHhhhAaAAAAAAAAA"
she screamed.

After a few screaming minutes, Lucy became confused once more. How could she possibly be falling for so long? Even if she fell from the tallest mountain in the world she would have hit the ground and splatted into tiny pieces by now. Still she was falling. Gravity was pulling her downward and air was wrapping around her as she quickly fell. But it was taking much too long. She should be dead long since. Or was she dead already? Suddenly she remembered what she had heard on the Tomatocator. Was this *really* it? Did the dog kill her after all?

"Hello?" she called out into the falling darkness.

There was a click and a light came on. Around three feet below her was what looked like a large metal bowl with holes in the bottom. Out of the holes, air was quietly, but forcefully being blown up at her, holding her in place. A few feet above her head, she noticed the hole she had come through. At most she had fallen five feet.

Looking around, it seemed to Lucy that she was dangling in mid-air in some kind of garage. Shelves full of old tools, tins of paint, oil and junk decorated three walls. The fourth wall was made of wood and looked to be a door. In the centre of the garage Lucy saw what looked like a giant ball of black rubber decorated with little stars all around.

Peeping out from behind the ball, Ooyay couldn't help but laugh. He stretched his nose over to the nearest wall, hit a switch and the air beneath Lucy slowed, then stopped, allowing her to land softly in the bowl with the holes.

"That wasn't funny," she scolded him. "Not funny at all."

Climbing out of the bowl, she now stood next to the rubber ball and examined it up close. Lucy was pretty tall for her age, but this ball was at least twice her height. As she pushed at it gently, her fingers sunk ever so slightly into the rubber, but the ball itself didn't budge.

"You're right of course," admitted Ooyay. "It was cruel of me to trick you that way. I didn't mean it. Not really."

"Not really?" asked Lucy. "What does that mean?"

"Well, you jumped in before I had time to switch on the light. Usually I just leap in in the dark and the air compressor cushions my landing. However, instead of switching on the light I accidentally pressed the button to keep the air on full (normally it slows and stops itself once someone jumps through). That's what kept you up all that time."

"And what does '*not really*' mean?" asked Lucy again.

"Well," said Ooyay with a sly, sheepish grin. "I *could* have helped you down quicker I guess, but I couldn't resist checking your reaction."

He laughed again and this time Lucy found herself joining in. It *was* funny she had to admit to herself. This laughter added to her relief upon finding that she was not dead after all. So far, twice on this day she had believed she was about to die. She didn't get a chance to laugh after the first time, but now the relief was so great she spent many minutes doubled up with laughter until suddenly she paused, spread open her arms and stared silently wide-eyed into the distance.

"What is it?" whispered Ooyay, suspecting she heard something.

With that, a backward-swallow rumbled slowly from Lucy's tummy all the way up her throat. When it reached the back of her mouth she swallowed it down again. Part of it fell back to her tummy, the rest of it exploded out from her lips in the form of a loud belch (just like her mother made all the time).

Ooyay laughed. Then Lucy laughed. Then she hiccupped.

"Oh *hic*... no!" she moaned. She hated hiccups.

"Have a look!" suggested Ooyay, changing the subject and nodding at the big rubber ball. "What do you think of this?"

Lucy studied the large rubber ball once again. It had grooves much like a tyre would have. *"Hic"* Up close, the shiny objects that she had thought looked like stars, now looked more like... *"Hic"*... they looked like... jellyfish. *"Hic."* She reached out to carefully feel one, then quickly pulled her hand back once she had done so. It felt *squidgy* but firm, like what she thought an eyeball might feel like -Or maybe a bit harder than that. *"Hic."* These jellyfish were dotted around the rubber ball, each one no more than a foot away from any other.

"They're like jellyfish. *Hic"* whispered Lucy.

Ooyay considered this and had to smile as he found himself agreeing.

"Have you ever seen our rubber glass?" he asked.

At once Lucy recalled the problem the local supermarket used to have with people accidentally running through the large glass doors. *"Hic."* The manager asked Professor Crastinator if there was something could be done. Soon after, the Professor installed some rubber glass that merely bounced a person back onto the pavement whenever he or she hit it.

"...Well that's what they're made of," continued Ooyay.

"Jazzy!" said Lucy. She thought it somehow strange but brilliant that the same invention was now used in *"Hic"*...in this ball. However, she still had no idea what it was all for.

"Open up," commanded Ooyay at once.

Lucy briefly feared he wanted to examine her teeth, but with that, a door opened in the rubber ball. Lucy breathed a sigh of relief once more, then looked in. It was dark but the red light inside showed what looked like another, smaller, white ball in the centre of its flooring. Apart from this beach-ball-sized ball, the only other thing Lucy spotted in there was a comfortable-looking seat, much like would be found in any car.

"Climb in," Ooyay invited.

So she did, sitting in the chair. Ooyay stood on his hind legs as he rested his front paws on the base of the door of the vehicle.

"We call this The Hamsterball!" he said, smiling as he examined his design.

Immediately Lucy imagined herself running around inside this large ball as it banged and bumped its way through traffic and around pedestrians.

"No way!" cried Lucy, as she stood up. "I'm not running around anywhere in this thing!"

"Relax!" smiled Ooyay as he extended his nose toward her, then nuzzled her back into the seat. "You don't have to move. Just sit there. I'll do the driving. There's no running required. Look..." he said, pointing with his nose to the opening where his paws rested.

Lucy noticed how there appeared to be two layers on the wall of the Hamsterball -One layer was coated in rubber. This was the visible part from *outside* when the door was shut. However, since the door was now open, Lucy could see a second ball wall *inside* this outer wall.

"This rubber wall moves," explained Ooyay, indicating the outer shell, "but the main ball that *we* sit in, doesn't move."

Lucy looked around once again and noticed there was only one seat.

"But where do *you* go?" she asked the hound.

Ooyay leapt in and planted himself on the white beach ball directly in front of her. His hind legs now stood on the ground of the vehicle. His body draped over the beach ball, and his front paws stretched around the far side from where Lucy sat.

"Ready?" asked Ooyay.

Lucy had no idea what she was supposed to be ready for, but she answered yes nonetheless.

Much like with the "boobies" that Ooyay demonstrated to Lucy earlier, he had a number of buttons on this "beach ball booby" under each of his paws. Pressing one of them now, the outer door closed by itself, then the inner metal door also slid shut. He pressed another button and the red light went out, then the circular wall inside the Hamsterball all but disappeared.

Lucy gasped as she looked around the garage from her seat inside the vehicle. It wasn't that the wall of the Hamsterball was now invisible, but that the inside of the Hamsterball itself (in every direction) now seemed like the screen of a curved television.

"Ahhh!" exclaimed Lucy. "So that's what the jellyfish are for! - They're cameras!"

"Yes," said Ooyay. "But there's more! As the Hamsterball moves, the cameras will also be moving around and around, but the Onboard Hamsterball Computer (OHC) will ensure that *we* will only see things the right way up all the time. Watch!"

With that, Ooyay pressed another button and the garage door opened, revealing an uphill slope with just blue sky visible at the top of the ramp.

Pushing up with his hind-legs now and rolling forwards over the ball, Ooyay was overjoyed to finally get the chance to drive the Hamsterball on his own. He fell back down again as he wiggled to improve his position on the beach ball. He hadn't bothered telling the girl that this was his first time driving without Crasty barking orders and setting the directions and pushing Ooyay out of the way when he didn't like the driving style. Crasty could be such a bore at times. Obviously the Hamsterball had been fitted with the same NS Mags as all other vehicles, so it wasn't as if it was possible to even *crash* into most things.

Lucy was amazed that they had moved ever so slightly when Ooyay had rolled forward on the beach ball. As he repositioned himself, the whole vehicle rocked from side to side. They went into reverse once he allowed the beach-ball roll backward, giving himself more leverage on his hind-legs.

She wasn't prepared, however, for the sudden jerk forward as soon as Ooyay stretched up, still balancing on the beach ball. His hind legs were now in the air above the floor, between Lucy's legs. The Hamsterball launched itself out the door, up the ramp and leapt into the air as Ooyay's tail slapped Lucy's face left/right/left/right since her nose was now stuck almost in the dog's bottom.

They circled the mansion a few times while Ooyay grew used to the controls and Lucy found some alternative location for her head (she opted to shift slightly to the dog's right, away from his wagging tail and protruding posterior. Then Ooyay steered the Hamsterball out the main gate and into the quiet early afternoon traffic.

"My hiccups have gone!" declared Lucy since she could think of nothing else that would possibly do justice to the situation.

"Well if this didn't do it for you," laughed Ooyay, "nothing would!" Then, wagging his tail, feverishly added "Man I'm having *fun!*"

SUCKER!

They rolled along streets and roadways, over bridges and through tunnels, out of the city, over the hills, into fields, across rivers and up and down mountains.

Lucy clearly shared Ooyay's excitement as neither noticed time passing or thought of much to say, other than the occasional "oh look at that!" when they passed a cow or nicely shaped mountain or a funny-looking tree.

Finally Lucy noted that the sky had darkened as grey clouds huddled-in overhead.

"Where are we?" she asked.

Ooyay threw his head around as if looking at the surrounding countryside for the first time.

"I have no idea" he had to admit, but sensing Lucy might be upset at that, added "don't worry though, I have a homing-button here to guide us back. I just need to stretch my legs before we head home."

With that, the Hamsterball slowed to a stop, the screens shut off, the red light came on, the inner and outer doors opened and Ooyay jumped out. Lucy climbed out after him and admired the view.

They had stopped in the corner of a field, close to a hedge and some trees. Since they were quite high up, they could see for miles down the hill, across a valley and all the way up the mountain on the far side. A river ran through this valley and out into the sea. Lucy was amazed that from where she stood there appeared to be such order to how things were arranged in the countryside: Grey rocky walls separated large green and yellow fields, like the seam on a patchwork quilt. Cutting through this quilt was the tree-lined blue river. Where the blue/green sea met the land, Lucy noticed patches of yellowy-white that could only be far off sandy beaches. She felt grateful there were no high-rise fields around here. Although they were a wonderful innovation by the Professor -oops! -by Ooyay, it was nice to have such an open view, where you could see so far and so much all at once.

The sun still shone brightly on the hill on the opposite side of the valley. The shadow of the clouds over Lucy's head moved slowly across that far off hill. While these clouds were cold and dark where Lucy stood, over on that hill they looked like the kind of funny shadow-shapes that her dad would sometimes make on a wall at home with his hands.

"It's funny..." began Lucy, smiling as she pointed to the moving shadows, then looked around to find Ooyay. She was surprised to note he had already set off on a walk along the hedgerow, away from the Hamsterball.

"Where are you off to?" she shouted after him.

"Just for a walk," he called back. "Not far. ...Stretch the ole' legs!"

Recognising that there wasn't much for her to do while she waited, Lucy decided to join him.

"What type of dog are you anyway?" she panted as she caught up with the small blue dog.

"I don't know," he answered, clearly not taking much interest in what she was asking.

"What do you mean you don't know? How can you not know what type of dog you are?"

"Nobody ever asked or told me before. What type of person are you?" he asked.

Lucy thought about that as she half-ran to keep up with the dog.

"I don't know," she said instinctively, then realised that was what he had expected her to say, so she added "I guess I'm a *good* person. Yes. I'm a *good* person. Do you think I'm a good person?"

"I do," he admitted, "but it's not for me to say if I'm a good dog, or what type of dog I am. Somebody else needs to tell us who we are."

"But why?" asked Lucy Lucey, now scrambling to take notes, after quickly pulling her pad and pen from her pocket.

"Ok! I'll tell you why!" said Ooyay, suddenly coming to a halt and jumping on a nearby rock so as to be a little closer to the girl's height.

"...A long, long time ago when the world was in black and white, people could never lie. They still always said things that weren't true all the time, but even as they said them suddenly what they said became truth. So one person would say *'I'm taller than you'* and suddenly -*he was*!

"Then someone else would say she had arms longer than the street. Suddenly her arms would be longer than the street!

"...Her arms wouldn't have grown just because she said it, but it was like as if they had always been that length. People *remembered* they were always that way because the girl had said it and there were no such things as lies in those days.

"*'Who spilt milk in the kitchen'* a mother would ask her children. *'My brother,'* the little girl would answer. Suddenly it *was* true that her brother had done it.
'Did you spill the milk?' the mother would then ask her son.
'It wasn't me it was the man on the moon' the son would declare. Suddenly the man on the moon had done it. And that was *the truth*.

"...Now clearly such things couldn't go on, because everybody said things that contradicted everyone else all of the time, so things kept changing and people kept changing and *the truth* kept changing.

"One day, a long-forgotten boy who had been asleep for a long, long time suddenly woke up and looked around and noticed how nothing was the same as it used to be. *This is not how things work* he said to himself. And suddenly that was true. *That* was not how things worked any longer. Since then, it's always been up to others to tell us who we are because now it's rarely true when someone says something about themselves" declared Ooyay with a triumphant nod.

Lucy wiggled her nose as she thought about this story.

"That's rubbish," she said. "They were lying. The man on the moon couldn't have spilt the milk. He doesn't even exist. He couldn't even *breathe* on the moon if he did exist anyway."

"But in those days he *did* exist," explained Ooyay. "The moon was also made of cheese back then. Only later did the cheese go off and suffocated him to death. That's why you can't breathe on the moon nowadays."

"Oh," said Lucy, but shot Ooyay a quick sharp stare that showed him she didn't believe a word she had heard.

"If I was talking to you yesterday on the phone before we met," began Ooyay, "and I told you that I was a dog -would you have believed that?"

"No," she admitted without a thought.

"So what's so outrageous about the man on the moon?"

Lucy studied this for a long time.

"I guess," she said at last.

"You guess!?" exclaimed Ooyay aloud. "There is absolutely not *one* adult on this planet who would disbelieve *anything* he or she was told by a talking dog. Dogs do not tell lies. Has a dog ever lied to you before?"

"No," Lucy had to admit.

"There you go. *Always* believe a dog," said the small talking blue dog, then quickly turned his back on her, sticking his nose in the air with a huff.

Lucy didn't know what to say. There were a million things running through her head all at once, but she knew Ooyay wasn't happy that she didn't believe everything he said.

"Did the world really used to be in black and white?" she asked, recalling those old movies she had seen where everybody wore hats and walked kind of funny like.

"Did I tell you it was?" huffed Ooyay, clearly still upset.

"Yes."

"Then don't... ASK -AGAIN!" he snapped, seeming angry at her now for some reason. She suddenly feared he was going to bark. Somehow the thought of Ooyay barking made her laugh out loud.

"Oh do act your shoe-size," he sighed, then leapt off the rock and walked over to relieve himself on the bushes.

Lucy felt embarrassed. It wasn't the first time she had seen a dog cock a leg in the air, but now since this was a talking dog she hadn't expected such... such... candour! *"Is candour a word?"* she wondered to herself. *"Is it the right word?"* she further wondered, then scribbled it on her pad, determined to check it later on.

Looking over the rocky wall before her, Lucy spotted a small lake at the end of the next field. It looked so pretty, reflecting the bright blue of the far-off overhead sky that she decided to take a closer look. Ooyay showed no signs of stopping any time soon and she didn't want to speak with him "mid-stream", so she decided to go on ahead and to let him catch up when he was ready.

Green grass soon turned to brown grass the further she walked. Brown grass turned to brown reeds. Before she knew it, she was walking in a bog and her shoes were squelching and sucking the ground beneath her feet. She had no idea of time, but a lot of it had passed when she began to wonder how much longer it would take. The lake looked no closer than when she had begun. What Lucy didn't know before then, but what she was in the process of discovering, was that distances can be deceiving in the open countryside.

"Where is that dog gone dog?" she said quietly to herself as she looked behind, putting her foot down without checking.

SQUADGE-KHHURROOAAWWWWKKK-GURGLE!

Lucy's foot had landed in the middle of a mud-filled puddle. Try as she might, she couldn't now pull it free.

"OOYAY!" she called out as she tried raising her leg. It wouldn't budge. She wrapped her hands around the back of her knee and tugged hard. No good.

"OOYAY! Where are you boy?" she yelled, clearly upset now as bog water and mud and dirt and who-knew-what started seeping into her shoe.

"IF THIS IS ANOTHER TRICK I'LL KILL YOU MYSELF!" she cried out, clearly upset.

But there was no sign of the small, cute, talking blue dog that had brought her to this place.

In fact there was no sign of life anywhere as she looked around. Everything was quiet. Dead quiet. She tried keeping calm in order to hear things like she had done in the Professor's garden the day before, but the silence here was somehow not like most other silences. This silence sounded like the air sounds underneath a heavy blanket. Even as she called out for the dog again she knew that the silence was eating up her words and that nobody more than a few feet away would be able to hear.

She gave a series of small, sharp tugs on her leg but it wouldn't come loose. As she examined the water and mud around her ankle, she was horrified to see a small, quick ripple in the middle of the puddle. She looked around and saw another ripple, then another in other puddles.

"Oh no!" she mumbled softly to herself.

Suddenly an avalanche of rain washed over her like a horde of mad schoolchildren at the beginning of mid-term break. Within seconds she was soaked from head to toe. Now that her fear of getting wet was gone, she easily slipped her foot from the trapped footwear, pulled out said shoe, then proceeded to climb back along the path she had just trekked, shoe in hand.

"OOYAY!" she yelled again, more as a distraction this time.

She was no longer expecting to see the dog come leaping to her aid for some reason. Her main motivation for yelling his name now was so she would be able to keep from crying.

Standing still, she took a deep breath. She no longer had the energy to walk and shout at the same time.

"   ," she said, then exhaled as tears streamed from her eyes.

Where was he? Why had he brought her here? Why had he lead her away from the Hamsterball? She thought she was getting to know him. She thought she *knew* him. He seemed like such a nice dog. One minute he's curled up in her lap, enjoying a rubdown, next minute he's going to kill her, next he's not, now she's dying again, then they're laughing, going for a ride, he's telling her silly stories... Now he has dumped her in a bog in the middle of nowhere. It hurt her so much to think how much this dog seemed to mean to her so quickly, but all this death and abandonment simply had to stop!

Finally she reached the wall and paused once more, without looking over, as she gathered her thoughts. She really didn't want to know if the Hamsterball was gone. The thought of being left out here alone in the middle of nowhere was not what upset her. What *really* bothered her was the notion that Ooyay may have in fact planned this all along. Taking a deep breath, she placed her shoe on top of the wall, then gripped it tightly as she peeked over. The Hamsterball was gone! Definitely. It was gone. Up and down the neighbouring field she peered, but the strange vehicle was no longer where it had been.

Lucy quietly squeezed her shoe even more tightly and

buried her head in the back of her hands as she began to sob her eyes out. It was all a trick! He was a cruel dog and she didn't realise it until now. How could she have been so stupid? Of *course* they weren't happy with what Lucy had done. They must have laughed themselves silly when they thought of how they'd gain her trust, then dump her in the country. *"Stretch the ole' legs"* he had said to her as if it was the most natural thing in the world.

She rocked her head left and right on the back of her hands on the wall as she bawled and wailed now. It didn't matter if she was lost. The only thing that mattered was that she had lost someone -some *thing*- she had thought was a friend. How *could* she have been so stupid!?

The rain had stopped, she noticed as she turned around to rest her back against the wall. Suddenly she thought she saw something move out of the corner of her eye. She snapped to her right and, through tear-stained eyes, was amazed to see the Hamsterball leap into view as it bounced over the far-off ridge. More tears burst from the nine year old (now they were tears of joy) as she leapt up and threw her shoe in the air.

"YYYYYOOWWWWWHOOO!" she yelled, overjoyed at the sight of the large rubber sphere plunging in, then bouncing out of small bog holes as it changed course and headed directly toward Lucy at top speed.

For a moment, she wondered if Ooyay had decided to come back to finish the job and make sure she would not be returning, but once it drew within a few feet of her, the Hamsterball suddenly stopped, its doors opened and her pal Ooyay beamed out at her.

"Hey pretty lady, need a lift?" he smiled, looking particularly silly, stretched over the white beach ball as he was.

Lucy had to laugh. Then she picked up her shoe and flung it at him, hitting the inside of the vehicle, but not the dog.

"STRETCH THE OLE' LEGS!" she cried, running at him now. "STRETCH THE OLE' LEGS!" She stopped a couple of feet from the Hamsterball, but couldn't think of anything else to say.

"Wh..." he began, but Lucy wouldn't let him speak. She had thought of something to say.

"YOU LEFT ME THERE! Where did you go? Why didn't you follow me? I thought you were gonna follow me! *"Stretch the ole' legs"* you said, then ran off back to leave me here! My foot got trapped! I couldn't get out! I screamed for you but you didn't come! What kind of dog *are* you? You didn't come!"

She cried again as she slumped at the door of the vehicle, arms and head leaning inside.

LUCY THE HERO

Children screamed through the corridor and burst out the main door of the school like a horde of mad women at the January sales. It was Friday and the beginning of mid-term break. The idea of a full week and a half without Mr. Klept and Mr. Fulsome and Ms. Canditooth and Mrs. Gangtua and Sister Crysalot and Brother Murphy and all the others was simply too overwhelming to allow pass without a cheer and a cheery stampede from the building.

Just one boy wasn't happy. Nothing had been heard from Lucy all day long and Milo Mooney had insisted Ms. Canditooth ring her parents to make sure she was ok. She wasn't ok. At least that is, nobody had seen her to know if she was ok or not. Then Milo had insisted some teacher should call to Professor Crastinator's house, but nobody was willing to "disturb the great man at his work."

A number of children still lingered in clumps around the yard when young Master Mooney moped out the main doors of the school, just in time to witness a large rubber ball roll silently through the gates and come to a stop next to the parked teachers' cars.

After a brief pause, everyone ran to the ball for a closer look, but didn't get too close since they had no idea what it was - and anyway, the car park area was out of bounds to pupils. Milo could only think of one person who could possibly be driving such a vehicle, and if indeed it was Professor Crastinator, there could only be one reason why he had come to Smisslewig: Obviously he was bringing Lucy back.

He pushed his way past the other students just in time to see the rubber ball roll away once more. Everybody breathed an "Ooh" as they watched it tumble off. Then, once they turned back to where the ball had parked, they clapped as they saw a lopsided Lucy Lucey standing there, looking wet and miserable, holding one of her shoes. Milo ran to help, propping himself under her left shoulder since she looked like she was about to fall.

"Cheeses Lucy! What did he do to you!? Are you all right?" he screamed.

"Thanks Milo" she smiled wearily. "I'm ok. Nobody did anything to me. I was stuck in a bog and... *he* rescued me."

As the two of them began to leave the yard together, others circled closer to hear what had happened.

"What was that?" someone asked.

"It was the Professor wasn't it Lucy?" answered someone else tentatively.

"Does he really have a talking dog?" enquired another pupil.

Nobody was laughing now.

"The dog doesn't talk!" said Lucy suddenly as she stopped and hung her head in shame. "I'm sorry to everyone for the confusion. Professor Crastinator is a bit of a trickster and also an excellent ventriloquist. I fell for it hook, line and sinker," she admitted. "But at least I was tricked by the world's best!" she laughed with a shrug.

Everyone around nodded in agreement, then joined in another round of applause while they laughed and patted her back and gave a hearty cheer. Some commiserated with her for being fooled by the old rogue, but all were well impressed that the man himself had taken the time to drive her back to school -and in a large rubber ball no less!

"So tell me..." said Milo with a sly glance to Lucy, who was resting an arm on his shoulder as they walked home.

"Tell you what?" she asked coolly, as though she had no idea what he was talking about.

Few things got past Milo. Top of his class since ever, he was constantly feared and ignored by everyone his own age (and older). He seemed to be wise beyond his years, but never needed to study anything. Frequently a teacher would defer to Milo if some puzzle proved particularly difficult. He would always have the solution.

Other pupils would probably have beaten up Milo regularly, except he was so big and strong and well able to take care of himself. But he had never had a friend. Other kids were too weary of him, even if he just wanted to play. It had always been that way. It seemed like the *natural plan* for how things would always be for him in the future. He had grown somewhat used to it in fact. In nursery school, if Milo was sat in the centre of the room, all other children would be found huddled together in one corner or another. It wasn't that they despised him. They just didn't want to play with him. Nobody did. Ever.

Then one day Lucy joined with him in reviving the old school journal and Milo's life and whole future seemed to change overnight. No longer was he seen as the dusty old encyclopaedia in the corner, now he was *the editor* and *the work colleague* and *the friend* of someone. And not just "someone" -he was the friend of Lucy Lucey -the most beautiful and intelligent girl in the school (in Milo's opinion at least).

Lucy had always been popular and didn't need to work on the school journal to garner attention from anyone. Milo was mesmerised by her. She could easily suck all the attention from a room without even trying. If someone had a camera it would inevitably be pointed at Lucy before too long. If a teacher was looking for a volunteer to perform some task, he or she would almost certainly choose Lucy. If she missed a class or two or indeed a whole day from school, it didn't matter -it was Lucy.

She could easily use that popularity to fulfil any selfish urge she might have, but Lucy was above such material gains. She wanted nothing and so wanted *for* nothing. She wanted to set up the school journal and she wanted Milo's help in doing so. To Milo, that was like having a princess beg him to eat chocolate cake with her and drink fizzy drinks and play video games all of the time. Milo would do anything for her, but she only ever asked him to do the things that *he* liked. This girl was his idol.

But he knew she was hiding something now. It wasn't that he thought the Professor had a talking dog -in truth he didn't know what to think about on *that* score. But he only knew that when Lucy ran to him the day before and told him about that dog and gave so much detail about what had happened and who said what and where and how and why, she was not even *thinking* about what was being said -she was just *remembering*. Now he knew she wasn't saying too much because she didn't want to give away some secret.

"What secret?" he wondered. *"She cried this morning when she thought I didn't believe her talking-dog story. Now she says it was the Professor playing some trick? -But she is soaking wet and is carrying her shoe. Why is she carrying her shoe? Is there some secret in the shoe? Yes!*

That's it! The answer is in the shoe!"

"Will I carry your shoe for you?" Milo asked with a large grin and extended arm, confident that Lucy would refuse and so give the game away.

"If you like," she answered, before tossing the shoe to him.

He checked it inside and out, but discovered nothing new, other than proof that leather stinks when wet.

"Strange" he thought. *"She seems to be on to me!"* He decided to change the subject.

"How come I've never seen one of those rubber balls before?" he asked. "That definitely looks like an interesting invention. Why hasn't it been released for everyone?"

"I asked him that -the Professor I mean" she replied. "On the way back he told me that it was the only one ever made. They had planned to launch it last year, but that tyre manufacturers complained it would be too tough to change the rubber if needed. Their factories aren't geared up to cater for that type of structure. He told me they hope to be ready in five to six years time. That will be some fun to look forward to, huh?" she laughed. "I'm gonna drive a Hamsterball when I'm older!"

Suddenly something unrelated occurred to Milo... Lucy must have been holding that shoe in order to divert attention away from the *other* shoe that she kept on her foot... for safekeeping!

"Don't you feel silly walking with one shoe?" he changed the subject, again with a sly, confident grin. "Why don't you give me that one too so you can be more balanced as you walk?"

"Forget the shoes Milo," said Lucy suddenly. "You're on the wrong foot. -Look, you only needed to ask! -I'll tell you exactly what happened if you promise to keep it to yourself. Do you promise?" Milo nodded eagerly.

"Yes, yes I promise" he said.

Lucy drew a deep breath and proceeded to tell him everything, up to the point where Ooyay found her.

"And where was he after going to?" asked Milo after she had finished, "...while you were stuck in the bog I mean..."

"He said he was looking all over for me and that he climbed back into the Hamsterball to find me. He didn't know I had gone over the wall. He said he thought I was angry at him -or that he thought that I was afraid that *he* was angry at me."

"Hmmm, makes sense I guess" he shrugged.

Lucy agreed.

"But he never thought to look over the wall?" Milo continued after thinking about it.

Now it was Lucy's turn to shrug.

"Surely he would have thought to look over the wall? You were in plain sight all the time from that wall weren't you?" he asked.

"That's what I was thinking. But how do *I* know how a dog's mind works?" she explained.

"A dog can find things and people easier than we can!" stated Milo.

Lucy knew this was true.

"And he is a more intelligent dog than most -almost certainly *the* most intelligent dog ever! ...And he didn't think to look over the wall?" Milo was puzzled.

"So why did he come back?" questioned Lucy, certain now Milo was not making sense. "You're too grown up Milo! I *know* him. He apologised and I *know* he was sorry. You didn't meet him. You don't know him. I know him. He is my friend and he came back for me and he saved me."

Milo didn't say anything for a few minutes but Lucy knew he was analysing the situation.

"Y'know," he began, "it would've looked real bad for the Professor and his dog if you had gone missing the day your news-article came out. I knew you were gonna go to the Professor's to prove your case. Other people would have known that too. If you suddenly went missing, *everyone* would have known it was something to do with him."

Milo paused to let this thought sink in, before continuing.

"...What if Ooyay thought of this while he was on his way back home in the Hamsterball?"

Then he had another thought -"Or what if Ooyay was never going to leave you there, but that his plan was to make you *think* he had left you there so that he could return and rescue you and make you grateful to him and to promise to keep quiet about his little secret! -Who's idea was it to say Professor Crastinator was a ventriloquist?" he asked, shooting his index finger at his friend.

Lucy didn't quite grasp all that Milo was saying. He was thinking and talking and confusing her too quickly. Still, she didn't like the gist of his argument. Whether he was right or not, she didn't *want* him to be right this one time. She considered her answer carefully before replying.

"Well... it was his idea to say that -but..."

"I knew it!" cried Milo, cutting her short and waving his finger in the air. "He had it planned all along! He *knew* what he was doing alright! We're up against a devious brain here, Lucy, and we need to be extra-careful. He's two steps ahead already! What we need now is..."

"No!" Lucy cried. "We don't need anything. Ooyay is my friend! I *know* him. It's not like that! I don't care! Even if what you say is true I don't care -it's not true and I don't care anyway!"

She knew she wasn't making much sense, but felt that Milo wasn't considering everything either. *Milo* hadn't seen Ooyay's water-filled, sorrowful eyes after she threw her shoe at him. *Milo* wasn't there when Ooyay licked her face with joy after he found her. Milo wasn't there as they talked all the way home about what had happened and what they should do next.

"It's not like that" she again insisted. "We're *friends*. And we're going sailing tomorrow!"

Milo suddenly leapt in front of his friend, blocking her path.

"You're going sailing tomorrow?" he gasped, disbelievingly. "The school trip is tomorrow!"

Lucy silently closed her eyes as she rolled them up into her head.

"The school trip!" she echoed. "I forgot all about that!"

That Lucy would have been able to forget about the school trip before it happened would have been impossible to even *think* a couple of days earlier. In fact she had spoken to her parents and relatives about little else for the past year.

Initially they had said she was too young to go, but after she pestered them and had Milo pester them and had some teachers pester them, they gave in.

Then they changed their minds a few months later, during the time of that "library trouble" at school. They said she was incapable of doing what she was told while she was at home and it would only lead to disaster if she was out of their reach.

By the end of that trouble, though, they changed their minds again. Since she had been proved right all along (or at least since things had gone her way) they reluctantly again agreed to allow her to go on the tour.

Yet again they changed their minds a couple of months back, simply because they could.

"We're your parents and we think you're too young to go foreign places without us," explained her mother. "...Tell her, father!" she ordered Lucy's dad.

"Hmph!" said her father as he waved Lucy and her mother out of his way (they were standing in his view of the television at the time).

"See!" added Lucy's mother. "Let that be an end to it. Your father has spoken!"

It was only after Lucy was picked to be one of the few people to witness the launch of Professor Crastinator's latest invention did her parents again relent and agree to allow her go on the week-long tour to *foreign places*. Lucy's mother had said that if she was big enough to sit in a glasshouse with the Prime Minister and Professor Crastinator then she was big enough to go CAT Bouncing around the planet with some teachers. Lucy's father had said "Harrumph!" because he was busy trying to listen to the radio at the time.

Now, just as her lifelong ambition to go bouncing around the planet was about to be realised, she found she had made alternative arrangements to go sailing with a talking dog on the very same day. Life could be so cruel sometimes.

"So what are you going to do?" asked Milo excitedly.

He had missed the turn off to his house and they now stood outside Lucy's front door.

"...It'll do you good to get away from that dog for a few days anyway," Milo's eyes narrowed. "I don't trust him. He's too conniving. He may have been planning on throwing you overboard. No doubt he'll abandon all thoughts of killing you once you leave him cool off for a while."

"He's not trying to kill me Milo!" Lucy assured her friend.

Milo tilted his head in her direction as he raised his eyebrows and looked straight at her, without saying a word. That said it all really, that did.

"All right" said Lucy in exasperation, "I'm going!"

It wasn't that he had convinced her to fear the Professor and his dog, but she had made an enormous effort to go on the school trip. If she didn't go now it would mean she had lost that battle and set the idea of her Children's Rights Movement back by years.

Her friend cheered up immediately.

"On the tour you mean?" he smiled as he handed back her shoe.

"Yes. I'm going on the tour!" Lucy sighed and twisted the key in the door.

"I'll see you at the airport then!" he shouted as she let herself in, quietly closing the front door behind her.

PARENTAL CONSENT

Things can only be said to be truly beautiful if there is some added *flaw* that contrasts against this beauty that shows us how striking the beautiful thing itself really is.

Take a clear blue sky for instance. If you look up to see nothing but blue overhead you think nothing of it. *"That's the sky,"* you think. Now add a little cloud far off to your right. This cloud is nothing special in itself. In fact it is a kind of flaw in the blueness of the sky. It has no place there since there is no cloud anywhere to be seen, except for that one small little cloud defacing the beautiful blue sky.

However, *because* you see such a little cloud all on its own splodged onto such a large, open, clear blue sky, you think "oh that sky looks beautiful." (If you don't think that, there is something wrong with you. Seek advice or start looking at skies before it's too late.)

So it was with Lucy's mother. Her eyes, ears and cheeks mirrored each other perfectly. She had perfectly-aligned teeth across a perfect mouth. Her nose was long (but not too long) and straight (but not too straight). Her hair was soft and always smooth and shiny. Her face was so perfect in fact it would have been easy to overlook just how perfect it was (in the same way you would overlook a blue sky), if it wasn't for the large wart in the centre of her right cheek.

Everything else on her face matched left-to-right so well, that the wart stuck out all the more and made you almost wish there was another one on her left cheek so it too would have a match. But this wart also enhanced Beauty Lucey's face in the same way that the small cloud defines the size and scope and blueness of the clear blue sky. This wart caused everyone who looked on her to notice and appreciate how well the rest of her face fitted together. The most common phrase people would use upon first meeting Lucy's mother was "Oh my, you have a beautiful wart."

Lucy had tried closing the front door without making a sound. She had cringed when Milo spoke so loudly just now, but it seemed she had gotten away with it. Quickly and quietly she began to make her way upstairs, but forgot to skip the third step.

"Corrrrreeeeeeeeeeeowaaaaeeeek!" creaked the third step.

"IN HERE NOW MADAM!" shrieked her mother instantly through the crack in the door to the kitchen.

There was nothing for it, but to follow such an order. Slowly widening the door, Lucy noticed her mother sitting at the table, having difficulty drawing oxygen into her lungs as she looked on her only daughter.

"Wha...?" she began as she stared at the dirty, wet, shoe-holding nine-year-old before her.

Lucy's dad looked up from the newspaper that was stretched across the table.

"Hmmm" he said, as he widened his eyes, then slowly lowered them (without moving his head) to the open pages before him. Meanwhile, his wife rubbed at her face and counted to ten before continuing.

"Take a seat," she said finally to Lucy, offering a chair across the table from where they sat.

"It's ok I'll stand" answered Lucy, who didn't fancy sitting in her wet garments any longer than she had to.

"So, what happened you now?" asked Beauty Lucey.

"I... My foot was stuck in a hole in a bog and it started raining and..." but before she could continue her mother cut her short.

"Where *were* you today?" she enquired.

Lucy Lucey looked to her dad, who pursed his lips and widened his eyes again as he waited for the answer. When it didn't quickly come, he began to look down at the newspaper. Examining it more closely now, Lucy saw that it was *her* newspaper that he was so interested in.

"I..." she began. "They all laughed at me and I had to..." but again Lucy's mother interrupted.

"We've been worried sick here all day, haven't we father?" Beauty tapped the table to get her husband's attention.

"Uh-huh!" said the father.

"See!" said the mother. "Worried sick! That nice Ms. Canditooth rang this morning wondering if you were ok and we had no idea where you were. Then we received a copy of... *this!*" she added pointing at the Smisslewig News, "and we wondered if you were maybe losing your marbles altogether or something. Talking dog! I hope you didn't say that to the Prime Minister! ...Talking dog indeed."

"It's..." Lucy began again, but was once more cut-short by her mother.

"Your father wants a word with you. Go on father," she cried, waving a hanky in the direction of Lucy's dad, then holding it over her nose.

Lucy turned to her dad, more curious than anything else to hear what he was going to say. He didn't talk much, but always made sure that what he said was just enough to convey the idea of what he was thinking.

"Hmm. A-hmmm" he said, trying to find the words.

It had been a while since he asked a question. Questions tend to lead to answers that require further questions and discussion, he found. So generally he preferred not to ask anything of anyone.

"Lucy," he said at last, quickly eyeing his wife in a way that told Lucy this question was *really* coming from her, "...are you on drugs?" he asked softly and they both stared directly at her, checking the reaction.

Lucy couldn't believe what she was hearing. She shot her dad the same forward-tilting-head-with-open-eyes that Milo had just given to her. Then she blinked once slowly for added effect.

"Dad" she said. "I'm *nine!*"

After her shower, Lucy sat at the computer, gazing blankly at the screen. The "conversation" that her parents had had with her ended as Lucy guessed it would: She was no longer allowed go on the school tour. In fact, Lucy's mum wrote a letter there and then, excusing her from the trip. Lucy was to give that note to Milo in the morning so their teacher would know she wasn't going.

Under normal circumstances, this would have launched

the nine-year-old non-drug-user into a frenzy of scheming plans. She would have worked around the clock to ensure she was on that Bullet at all costs.

After they told her their decision, however, Lucy's parents had seemed surprised when she merely shrugged and answered "Ok."

As she left the kitchen, she overheard her mother tell her father "I have no idea what is going on in that girl's mind," before adding "she's too *young* to be a teenager!" Lucy wasn't certain what that meant, but she liked the sound of it.

It was a tough-blow not to be allowed go on a foreign tour with her friends, but it wasn't every day she met a talking dog. And even if he *was* trying to harm her, he was still at least *as interesting* as a foreign tour. In truth, Lucy was relieved that the problem of choosing to go or not had been taken out of her hands. Now that she knew she wasn't allowed go, she could sit back and look forward to a relaxing cruise in a sailboat instead.

Even as she thought of this, her heart skipped a beat when she considered how Ooyay might have had something else in mind. She quickly typed CRASTINATOR SAILBOAT into her computer to check what might be in store and soon found this website...

One of Professor Crastinator's lesser-known inventions (among landlubbers at least) is *The Farting Sailboat*.

Shunned by the popular press because its name was deemed too rude, this boat has nonetheless marked the most controversial introduction to maritime travel since Jesus walked on water.

HERES HOW IT WORKS

As the boat travels, tiny grooves in the mast take in air. This air is stored in the specially-modified keel underneath the boat. Once this keel is full, a red button flashes for the captain to know the boat is ready to break wind. The button is pressed and air is quickly expelled from the backside of the boat (underwater), giving a *turbo-boost* type effect, which shoots the sailboat along faster, which causes air to gather in the keel faster, which allows the captain to break wind even faster.

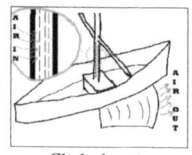

Click the pic

FREQUENTLY ASKED QUESTIONS

Q. Doesn't this trapped wind cause the boat to go slower?
A. Yes. Initially speed is slower than normal, however,   NEXT PAGE

She clicked the picture to get a better look...

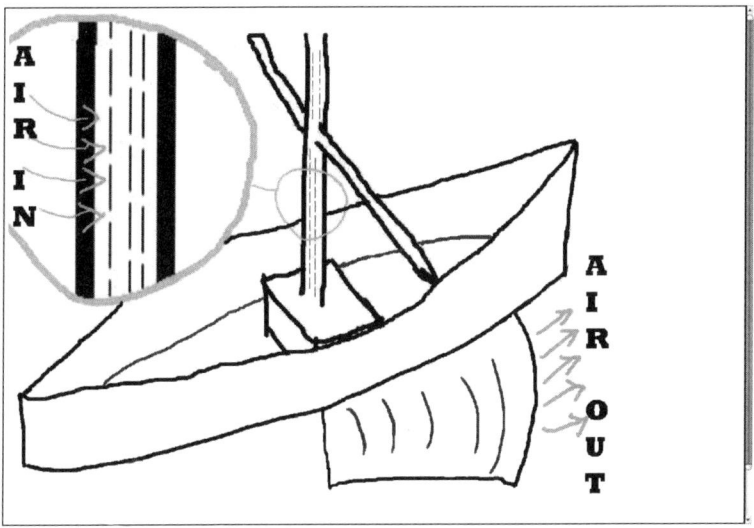

"Jazzy!" smiled Lucy as she pictured herself holding onto the railings while Ooyay pressed the fart button. This was going to be good.

PARTING ON BAD TERMS

"Shall I pour?" asked Professor Crastinator as he held the jug of iced-tea.

Ooyay's mind was elsewhere so he didn't hear even though he was already on the bed, standing not two feet from where his master sat.

He was dreaming of his ears flapping in the wind like it was when Crasty used to take him for spins in the car. Nowadays, the Professor rarely drove anywhere and when he did, Ooyay was no longer allowed stick his head out the window. "That's too dangerous" he'd be told. Time was, both of them would have their heads stuck out the window together, while Crasty steered the speeding automobile with his feet. Slowly things changed (as they always do). Crasty no longer wanted to drive with his head out the window. Then he didn't want to go too fast. Then he didn't want Ooyay putting his head out the window. Now he had almost given up driving entirely.

Ooyay knew why this change had occurred in the Professor. One small part of it was because he was getting too old. It's hard to drive faster than your age when you're almost ninety years old.

There was another, more important reason though: Jealousy. Since Dr. Flocky Nocky had invented the uncrashable car, Crasty was jealous that himself and Ooyay (or more particularly - just Ooyay) hadn't invented it first. Now whenever they went out in the car -any car- Crasty was reminded of Dr. Flocky Nocky's great inventiveness. This made Crasty seem more like a fake, because he now knew there was someone who might be more deserving of having a dog like Ooyay. Dr. Flocky Nocky actually *invented* things. Professor Crastinator didn't really do anything.

With old-fashioned *crashable* cars, Crasty was not beholden to anyone. Now though, the sight of every car -any car- reminded him of "The Doctor". It was not possible for Crasty to think of The Doctor and to be happy.

The sense of freedom that Crasty used to have when he stuck his head out the window at high speed was now taken away when he realised this freedom was being provided by that other inventor. Crasty was jealous of him.

For that reason, Ooyay invented the Farting Sailboat so

Crasty could "own the water" like Flocky Nocky now "owned the roads." But Crasty got seasick whenever they went out on the water.

Ooyay's main hope for the Hamsterball was that it would help Crasty put some fun back into driving. He might not be able to stick his head out the window, but at least he could now think of something other than Dr. Flocky Nocky whenever he drove.

But now Ooyay thought of his own wish for speed and for his ears to flap in the wind. He often spent hours floating in mid-air in the hole in the television for that very reason, but it wasn't the same. Today he was going to experience that *outside*, without the Professor for the first time ever.

He and his new friend, Lucy Lucey, would merrily break wind all around the open waters as the air flapped through their ears. *That* was the type of fun that everyone should have every day (if possible) or at least once a week.

What the Professor failed to grasp was that the little blue doggie *needed* this type of fun. Fun was possibly the most essential part of being an inventor. Ooyay suspected this was why so many of his most recent inventions were not as successful as older ones: There simply was not as much fun to be had as there used to be. Fun is food for the imagination.

"Ooyay?" came a distant, disembodied voice echoing through the little dog's thoughts.

"Yes?" he replied before thinking where the voice was coming from.

Only after that did he at last notice what was directly in front of him:

"Shall... I... pour...?" asked The Professor slowly.

"Yes. Yes. Do. Pour. Yes," answered the dog as he rejoined the land of the living, then added "No!"

Crasty put the jug down and stared at his dog.

"Yes, yes, no? Which is it fella? Do you want some iced tea or not? Make up your mind. You're beginning to sound like *me!*"

Ooyay smiled and cringed at the thought of it. Sometimes, if he found that he couldn't make a decision on something, or if he wandered the whole house looking for something he had mis-placed, or if he noticed that he just wanted to stay curled up in bed some mornings, he would suddenly realise that *that* was exactly how his master behaved. Other times he would catch a quick glimpse of himself as he passed a mirror in the hall and swear that his own face looked just like Crasty's, but once he stopped to examine it more closely, he would find that he looked less like Crasty and more like... *Ooyay*.

The small dog seemed to share lots of characteristics with his master -whether he wanted to or not. More often than not, he would spend his time trying hard to *not* be like Crasty. Maybe that was one of the main reasons why he invented so many things? -To be unlike his master? Still, he found there was no escaping it. He was his master's dog. And he was happy to be so, really.

"I must go" he informed the Professor. "I have work to do."

"What work? Where are you going? With whom?" enquired Crasty suspiciously. "You're not going out with that girl again! I told you already you are never to take that Hamsterball out without me!"

Many reports of sightings of "a big, strange rubber ball rolling through the hi-ways and byways" had made it onto several news desks in the city. Soon Professor Crastinator received several phone calls asking if he knew what it was. Of course the Professor had known at once what it was and who was driving, but admitted nothing to any reporters. However, as soon as Ooyay had returned, he received a stern talking-to from his master. The Professor had always been careful to only take the Hamsterball out late at night when few people were around. Ooyay was too impatient to wait though. He would insist on playing with his balls whenever he felt like it.

"You'll get us into trouble!" cried Crasty, wagging an index finger. "That vehicle isn't registered and you don't have a driving license."

He spent the rest of that evening chastising the dog for taking too many unnecessary risks. But Ooyay was having none of it.

"The girl found out about me," he had reminded his master just before bedtime. "She was going to continue telling the world you had a talking dog. There was only one way out of it... befriend her. Now she is my friend and I am a loyal friend and I will be seeing more of her from now on. We will be *having fun* together since you no longer ever want to have fun."

That had hurt the Professor and they ended up going to sleep without another word between them. Ooyay was sorry he had said it, but neither had spoken to the other until he quietly entered his master's bedroom just a while ago. Trying to make up for it, Ooyay brought the papers as normal and made like nothing had happened. Likewise, the Professor was also trying to be nice to his dog on that morning by offering him some lemon tea. However, Ooyay was still being too evasive for his liking.

"Do you hear me?" Crasty demanded to know. Now that each of them had failed in being nice to the other, all bets were off. "I *forbid* you from taking out that Hamsterball again!"

"Fine!" declared Ooyay finally, running now to the door. After making it to the top of the ramp, the small dog stopped, then turned to the Professor and shouted "I won't take it! See if I care!" before running out of the bedroom.

"Where are you going?" cried Professor Crastinator. "Bad doggie! Where are you going? Bad doggie!"

They didn't know it at the time, but those were the last words to be shared between Ooyay and his master. If either had any idea of what was going to happen next, they would certainly have never parted on such terms.

ADOLESCENCE

SETTING OFF

"Where are you off to young lady?" Beauty Lucey demanded to know at 8:30 Saturday morning.

"I'm meeting a talking dog and we're going sailing on a farting boat," answered Lucy truthfully.

Her mother looked troubled.

"Lucy," she said in the kind of hushed voice that people usually use when they have no strength left, "*What* are we to do with you? We've talked about this haven't we?"

Lucy nodded sorrowfully, even though she wasn't sure which talk her mother was talking about.

The older Lucey approached her daughter, then knelt down and carefully held the young girl's head to make sure she was looking straight into her eyes.

"...There are certain things that little girls just do not do," she informed her only child, "and one of those is mentioning certain words... such as..." she couldn't bring herself to mention the word so instead said "...break wind. ...Ok?"

Lucy tightened her mouth and again gave a sorrowful nod. In truth she hadn't heard a word her mother had just said (apart from "break wind ok?") since Beauty Lucey was rubbing Lucy's ears as she spoke. However, the mother was happy with the daughter's mature response and allowed her to leave without another word.

Now, another story must be introduced that will in time be of utmost importance to the tale at hand. That is the story of Matthew Cratchett and his family...

There was nothing extraordinary about Matthew's early years. His father worked as a piano teacher and tuner. This didn't pay extremely well, but thankfully he was also able to earn some extra money from farming the acre of land surrounding the small semi-rural Cratchett cottage where Mr. and Mrs. Cratchett reared their six Cratchett children, including Matthew's sisters Joan, Jenny and Penny and his brothers Mike and Martin (who was the youngest). Matthew's mother worked hard in the home, in the garden and in the grocery shop down the road where she spent most weekdays.

Joan was the eldest of Matthew's siblings. She worked as a waitress on the railway and as an assistant in a large newsagents. Jenny was next. She became a seamstress and cook to a wealthy family in the city from the age of thirteen. For as long as anybody could recall, Mike serviced automobiles as well as later becoming joint-owner of an unusual cinema with a man named Pierce Kratinsky (more on this later).

The whole Cratchett family was constantly busy from one end of the day to the next -apart that is from Matthew, his older sister Penny and younger brother, Martin.

While the others cooked and toiled and tuned and tinkered and travelled and sewed and served and sweated, the three youngest family members spent their days in idle appreciation of their surroundings. That was *their* job.

Penny was a year older than Matthew. From the age of five, she would always ensure that he and Martin arose by noon (most days), after she had fed them cold soup and toast in bed. Throughout the rest of the day the three of them would normally take long strolls with no destination, where nothing would ever happen.

Martin was three years younger than Matthew and usually had a cough or runny nose or a fever of some kind. It was because of the ailing baby-of-the-house that the three of them always went on these walks and also because of this that they mostly walked in oxygen-giving woodlands. And it was also because of Martin's sickly frame that no excitement was allowed during these excursions in case they proved too much for him.

They would roam the local fields and meadows and woodlands almost every day, picking daffodils and counting the spots on ladybirds and chasing butterflies and scooping frogspawn into jars and collecting tory-tops and chestnuts and anything unusual they could find. Back at home, they stashed this bountiful collection in a large chest at the foot of Penny's bed, where they would spend their time playing on wet afternoons.

Martin was known as Mucus by everyone in the family. Nobody could recall how the name first came about, but it probably derived from Matthew's or Penny's resentment at being held back by their brother all the time. It takes a lot of effort from small, capable children to deliberately *not* overexcite their younger siblings. Mucus's presence forced them to slow down and take things easy.

Over time though, the three youngest came to appreciate their surroundings all the more because of this slowness and carefulness. Soon the youngest child's nickname became a term of endearment.

"Where's my Little Mucus?" Mother Cratchett would call out after coming home from the shop.

"There's some soup on my Mucus," Father Cratchett would regularly point-out after dinner. (Despite the many jobs held by its members, there was never much money in the house and each meal was rarely anything more than soup).

Matthew's sister Jenny lived in the home where she worked for as long as Mathew could remember. One weekend, a little before Christmas, when Matthew was around seven or eight years old, she came home carrying the largest, creamiest cake any of them had ever seen in their lives.

Not that they had seen many cakes at all by then, but this one was certainly fit for a king: Its base was made of sponge and had little chocolate sticks poking out in mismatched directions. Another sponge sat on top, squashing out a layer of jam-filled cream all the way around. This cream remained on the chocolate sticks, making it look like winter snow was resting lightly on a bird's nest. To decorate this cream exterior, peach and strawberry pieces were balanced in an upright position on this snowy nest, somehow silently reminding everybody of little winter birds out in the cold. The top of the cake itself was glazed with a milk chocolate icing and sprinkled with icing powder. A single sprig of holly completed the festive theme.

Joan was working around the clock that whole weekend so she never got to see the full cake, but all of the other family members could only gasp as they looked upon Jenny's confectionary masterpiece.

After tea that Saturday night, each of them was given a slice, much to everyone's delight. It was only after Martin slowly bit into a strawberry did Jenny remember that he was allergic to the fruit.

"No!" she cried, leaping across the room to smack the cake and fruit from Martin's hands.

Everyone looked up through frozen creamy stares and immediately realised what had happened. The first (and last) time before this that Martin had eaten a strawberry he was just two years old. Within an hour he had bloated out and turned redder than the strawberry he had swallowed. For days he had remained in that state and the doctor said it was touch and go whether he would survive. He did survive at that time and nobody in the house (including Martin himself) was ever in any doubt thereafter that eating strawberries was not a wise thing for him to do.

Now the cake (and its design) had been so distracting that Jenny hadn't even considered Martin's allergy while she pieced all the ingredients together, until she had seen it sink between her youngest brother's teeth.

"Why did you do that?" they all asked Martin, who slowly gazed around the room, examining the face of each concerned family member.

"...I didn't want to spoil the moment" was his only reply.

Afterwards, he spent the rest of that night wrapped around the toilet bowl, sleeping between bouts of vomiting.

TROUBLE AT THE PIER

Anyone who has ever seen a soppy, romantic movie would have expected to hear a soft orchestral soundtrack as Lucy stood by the pier, waiting for her date to show (the fact that the date was with a dog in this case shouldn't affect the score). The music at this stage would sound kind of like plink-plink.... plink... plink-plink... ....plink, as she wanders slowly around in circles, gazing anxiously into the distance every now and then, seagulls soaring overhead. They had arranged to meet at 9a.m. and it was already 10 to 10.

Now the music stops as Lucy's eyes fix on something far off. Could it be? Is it he? Yes! At last Ooyay has arrived! He hasn't stood her up and their friendship is confirmed! The orchestra BLASTS a swelling score that echoes the crashing waves from the ocean as the blue dog begins to run down the hill toward the young girl. The tempo drifts into a type of ballet music as Lucy dances around the pier with joy. All the while Ooyay approaches. He was never the fastest of dogs, but it doesn't help that he is now running in slow motion to better accompany the dreamy soundtrack.

Suddenly there is a loud bang as trumpets roar and the music changes to indicate danger. At the same time a large net descends on the helpless blue dog, scoops him up, then drags him behind a building. Lucy freezes and screams. She hears an engine start up, then a white van screeches out from behind the building, tearing up the main road away from the pier.

Soon the only thing left with the crying young girl is the original plink-plink music. Scene fades like the slowly closing eyes of a tearful nine-year old girl.

CRASTINATOR CONSIDERS ACTION!

The doorbell had rung and the knocker had knocked for at least half an hour before the noise finally ceased. Calm returned to the bedroom and Professor Crastinator was once more able to pull his head from under the pillows with a gasp for air.

"Honestly I don't know what is getting into that dog," he grumbled aloud to himself, rubbing both sides of his head to flatten his tossed hair. "He won't even come to tell me who's at the door these days." As he sat up and fluffed his own pillow, he continued to mumble.

"...Have to suffer through all sorts of racket 'til they go away... Never any peace... Can't rest..."

He was busy playing a computer game when the din had commenced. The game involved hitting a ball in such a way as to ensure that it avoided or bounced-off various objects in its path in order for it to reach the target wall. However, to hit this wall, you only have one shot. Once you fail to hit the wall with this one shot, you lose a life. If you *do* hit the wall with your one shot, another player must hit the same wall with the same ball from where it lands.

The Professor always played alone, since

a) he was the only person who had ever seen or played the game,

and

b) he was terrible at it, losing a life with almost every shot he made.

and

c) Ooyay was too good to play against.

Just as he happily returned to the game, he heard small, quick-paced footsteps in the hall.

"Who was that at the door?" he called out.

But it wasn't his dog that peeped in through the bedroom door after it automatically swished open. It was a young girl. The Professor quickly pulled the blankets up to his neck, hiding his favourite white pyjamas with the red and yellow teddy bears.

"Who are you?" he cried. "How did you get in here? I have a dog! Ooyay!? Sic Ooyay! Ooyay hurry boy! Sic! Sic!"

The young girl was clearly out of breath and took a moment before she could find her voice.

"Pro -Professor," she panted, "Ooyay -Ooyay's been taken. Kidnapped! He... He... Men! There was a big net! ...pulled into... back of a van... Gone! He's gone!"

The Professor clearly had no idea what she was saying.

"What? Who are you?" he repeated. "What do you want in here? You'll have to leave now! Ooyay? Where are you fella?"

"He's not here!" cried Lucy once more, slowly finding her breath.

"That's what I'm trying to tell you! He's been kidnapped! Dognapped!" She took a few careful steps onto the ramp inside the door.

"Professor!" she almost whispered as a single tear flopped down her cheek. "It's me -Lucy Lucey. We met yesterday. Remember?"

"Lucy Lucey?" he echoed, slowly dropping his arms as he studied the name. Lucy was buoyed up somewhat to hear him say her name and she ran now to the bed.

"Where is he?" shouted the Prof angrily. "Where's my dog? What have you done with him?"

He began crawling now toward the end of the big bed where Lucy stood.

"That's what I've been trying to tell you!" she cried, slowly again stepping backward. "I was meeting him at the pier. He was running toward me when some men snatched him and pulled him into the back of their van -a white van. They screeched off before I could even get close. He's gone! I don't know who it was!"

The Professor heard it this time. He froze there on the bed on all fours for what seemed like ages. A river of tears welled in his eyes, but somehow none of it fell.

"Goh..ne?" his voice wobbled as he stared upward.

Lucy followed his gaze and was surprised to see a large table and chairs hanging from the ceiling. As much as she would have liked, she didn't have the heart to change the subject by asking why they were there. She suddenly felt dizzy and had to look away.

Some time passed. There were only two people in the room and neither was capable of thinking of time during that period. It could have been minutes. It could have been hours. In fact it was two minutes, forty-seven seconds, but neither Lucy nor the Professor ever knew that -or cared.

"Flocky Nocky," whispered the Prof finally, returning now slowly to his pillows. Lucy moved around to the side of the bed.

"You ...ooOOOOOoo!" she cried as the pad beneath her feet suddenly rose and carried her to bed height.

Quickly she stepped from this pad (which immediately descended), onto the extra large bed.

"You think Dr. Flocky Nocky took Ooyay?" she asked, standing now next to where the Professor sat.

"I know it!" he stated with certainty.

"But *why*? -Why would he want your dog?" she asked, even as she knew the answer.

"I thought you two were friends?" she continued, "How would he have even known about... Oh!" she stopped, suddenly realising the part she may have played in the kidnapping.

He had obviously read her news article. Another long silence ensued, after which, the Professor slowly turned to face the young girl, although he remained silent.

"Maybe it wasn't Dr. Flocky Nocky?" suggested Lucy. "Someone else might have read that stupid report I did and decided to capture him?"

The Professor looked like he just wanted to fade away into the bed. He seemed to barely have the strength to speak.

"No" he said at last, "it was Flocky Nocky. I know it. He knew I had a secret. Nobody else suspected a thing. He was waiting for a hint. Obviously he was waiting..."

The Professor's voice faded away. His lips now moved but nothing was coming out. Quietly, he began to cry.

"You don't know what that dog means to me," he told Lucy. "He can't be gone... Why did I shout at him? I should've let him take the Hamsterball!"

He turned away now, sinking his head into the pillow. Lucy looked on, feeling helpless. It was all her fault, she knew. How could she put things right?

"Where does he live?" she asked. When she saw he wasn't listening, she pulled on the Professor's shoulders and asked again. "Where can we find Dr. Flocky Nocky? Professor?"

Eventually he wiped his eyes and responded.

"I don't know" he said. "I have no idea."

Lucy thought long and hard.

"Well we can work it out!" she declared. "Come on! We can find him! We'll find Flocky Nocky and we'll get Ooyay back!"

She shook the old man until he turned to face her.

"How?" he asked, clearly not believing it could be done, but straightening himself where he sat, in anticipation of some good news.

Again Lucy thought hard. Looking up, she noticed the red curtain that normally covered the wall beyond the base of the bed. It was open now, revealing a large projector screen that currently showed a computer game of some sort. She quickly spun around to the Professor, eyeing two of Ooyay's booby balls, each one on either side of where he sat.

"Can you bring up a map of all Bullet-Hole Airports on the planet?" she asked, pointing at the screen.

The Professor looked confused.

"Yes" he answered, shaking his hands and head, "I probably could. But that would be nonsense. There are thousands of them everywhere."

Lucy rubbed her chin. This helps people think.

"Dr. Flocky Nocky lives on a small island somewhere -we know that! Everybody knows that."

"Yes!" said Professor Crastinator, almost showing happiness. "...It's his own private island on the other side of the planet!"

"Good!" answered Lucy, continuing the thought. "Bring up all small islands with Bullet-Hole Airports on the other side of the planet that are not part of some bigger country..."

The image on the screen changed and soon showed a map of the world. Lucy looked back to see how the Professor was working. Deep in concentration, with his tongue poking from the side of his lips, he looked up to the screen, both hands spread out on the boobies.

"Out of interest..." asked Lucy softly, "...how many buttons do *you* have on *your* boobies?"

The Professor stared at Lucy in shock. He quickly crossed his hands over his chest.

"What are they teaching you children these days?" he asked, horrified at such a question. Then he considered the overall situation more clearly.

"You'd better leave," he said. "You can't be in here. This is my bedroom!"

Lucy looked at the melon-sized balls the Professor had been using and was surprised to find that they didn't have buttons like Ooyay's had, but each one had a number of keys, like a keyboard. Obviously, the Professor was able to type using these boobies (or whatever they were *really* called) as well as using them to move things on the screen. The one thing Lucy hated about computers was having to think about where to put her hands all the time. At once she resolved that when she grew up she wanted to have boobies just like this old man had.

The Professor's eyes were watering up again now. This time he looked straight at Lucy as he continued to hold his chest. She was surprised to see he appeared frightened of her all of a sudden.

"What's wrong?" she began to ask.

Just then, the screen bleeped and she spun around to see what was happening. Red dots had appeared all over the world map as it rotated on the screen. The result, *2256 ISLANDS FOUND*, was shown in the upper right-hand corner. She hadn't expected that many.

"That's a lot of islands," she said.

With Lucy facing the other way, the Professor now felt free to return to his work.

"I'll narrow the search to places furthest away," he said.

At once the result changed to *952 ISLANDS FOUND*. Without saying anything, they both knew it was still too many.

"Hang on!" cried Lucy all of a sudden, "Dr. Flocky Nocky *invented* CAT Travel, so he probably had the first Bullet Hole Airport ever! Can you find the oldest one?"

After a few seconds the Professor shook his head.

"No" he said, "the records only seem to go back ten years."

"Great!" yelled Lucy, "bring up all of the ones older than that!"

The Professor didn't move. Soon dots began disappearing from the screen and the result changed to... *25 ISLANDS FOUND*.

SHOVEL HEAD

It was risky, but it was a risk she would have to take. The window of opportunity was small. Professor Crastinator hadn't wanted to leave immediately. He said that he needed time to think about it some more, but Lucy pushed and prodded and cajoled and finally convinced him it had to be done straight away.

"But *you* can't come!" he suddenly realised as they left the upside-down room, "you're a little girl!"

"It'll be all right," Lucy assured him, "we'll stop by my house on the way to the airport. Let me talk to my parents first and once they know I'm going with *you* there won't be a problem."

"Well, let's see what your parents say I guess..." said the Professor, not at all sure about it.

Normally a decision would take a long time for him to arrive at. Just this morning he had spent fifteen minutes wondering if he should scratch his big toe or let it itch until it stopped by itself. In the end, he had the bed-pole scratch it for him. Also, he had spent *years* wondering if CAT-Travel was a good idea or not. Since Flocky Nocky had invented it rather than Ooyay, he was not at all happy with the idea and had long-since come up with many theories and explanations as to why it was so bad.

Now though, Ooyay was gone and the Professor was at a loss. He felt like how a cartoon character might behave after being banged over the head with a shovel. It now took only the clear, decisive direction of a nine year old girl to lead him on a journey around the planet in search of his missing dog.

Lucy had explained the situation in full to her parents: *...Professor Crastinator had heard Lucy was not allowed go on the school tour so he had agreed to accompany her personally to ensure she came to no harm.*

She wasn't happy about having to lie to her parents, but there was no way she could explain the real situation to them and still be allowed go. This was all her fault after all and the Professor was clearly in no state to take care of things by himself.

Her father was speechless. There was nothing new in that. Her mother was overcome with emotion.

"Professor Crastinator is insisting that my girl go on the school tour!" she cried in joyous disbelief.

For a long time, Beauty had wondered if Lucy was perhaps a kind of child prodigy, but she had never dared to assume that a true genius and world-shaper of Professor Crastinator's calibre would see how bright she was. That he would take a whole week out of his busy schedule just to make sure her daughter was all right was unbelievable to Beauty.

"What are you waiting for?" she asked Lucy through floods of tears, "show him in!"

As soon as Lucy ran outside, however, her mother called after her once more.

"Oh wait! Wait!" she cried, quickly spinning around to find the ribbons for her hair.

Thankfully, she already had both pink ribbons to hand in a nearby drawer. Hurriedly, she affixed one to her head, while the smaller one she tied to the long hairs growing from the wart on her cheek, just as Lucy returned, leading the great inventor into their kitchen by the hand.

Beauty Lucey was impressed right off the bat. The man was every bit the eccentric genius she had expected. It wasn't everyone that would walk into another person's house wearing nothing but white pyjamas with yellow and red teddy bears. It was only when Lucy saw him standing next to her parents did she realise he had forgotten to dress before leaving. She now wished she had given him at least enough time to think of getting changed.

"Exceptional!" declared Beauty for no apparent reason.

The word did not sound like anything Lucy had ever heard her mother say before.

"Dear Professor!" she then added, bowing her head and spreading her arms wide. "Welcome to our humble abode."

The Professor raised a hand toward the woman before him.

"Oh my," he said absentmindedly, clearly eyeing the small pink ribbon dangling from her cheek. "...What a beautiful wart you have!"

Any doubts Lucy had as to the successfulness of her plan were immediately banished from her mind. The Professor had said the magic words and it would be hard now for anything to go wrong.

"I'm very sorry about that business with your dog," Beauty apologised for her daughter's newspaper report and once more Lucy feared the worst.

"Yes" said the Professor, thinking of the kidnapping, "it's -it's a terrible blow..."

"I have no idea what Lucy thought she was doing," continued the mother, wondering how her daughter could have come up with such a tall tale as that of a talking dog.

"...She must have been too distracted by events," agreed the old man, regretting the fact Lucy had not been able to rescue his doggie or take note of a license plate number.

"Exceptional!" announced Mrs. Lucey once more, taken aback by the forgiving nature of this unequalled genius.

The young girl decided it was time to nip this conversation before it went any further.

"Mother says it's ok if I go on that trip as long as you take care of me," she informed the Professor.

"She did?" he enquired, surprised the parents had agreed so readily.

He really was out of touch with how people reared children these days. He didn't understand it at all. Neither children *nor* the parents made any sense to him. The whole world had gone mad as far as he could see.

Before leaving, Lucy searched and found a pair of slippers and a bathrobe belonging to her father. She asked if she could give them to the Professor. Her father said "Hnnn" through his nostrils and shrugged -a clear YES if ever there was one.

As they climbed into the Hamsterball, Beauty handed her mobile phone to Lucy.

"I know we said you couldn't have one until you were twelve," she sobbed, "but best bring this along with you so we can keep in touch."

"Thanks," said Lucy, delighted she at last had a mobile phone of her own, but deeply saddened it had been given under such circumstances.

Now more than ever she regretted lying to her mother and father. As the outer door began to shutout the sight of her parents waving anxiously to their daughter, Lucy had pangs of sorrow and doubt for what she had done.

"Goodbye," she cried and tears tumbled from her eyes.

Once the cameras came on inside, Lucy began waving feverishly, as did her parents continue to wave even though they could no longer see her through the outer shell of the Hamsterball.

As soon as the vehicle rolled out of sight, Beauty turned and collapsed into her husband's chest.

"Our baby has grown up" she sobbed.

"Yes" he whimpered with a heavy sigh.

They were walking to the main desk at the nearest airport when Lucy quickly dived behind the Professor as she spotted Milo and the rest of the school tour gathering near a large glass statue.

"What's wrong?" asked the Prof, nearly tripping over the schoolgirl.

"Nothing" she answered, trying to be nonchalant (also secretly storing the word *nonchalant* in her mind so she could look it up later on). Then added, "There is someone I have to talk to."

"Ok" said the Prof, "I'll be at that desk over there. I'll have to see about hiring one of those... Bullets."

Lucy suddenly realised they had made no plans for how they were going to travel.

"But you don't have any money!" she declared. "No cash or credit cards! Do you?"

The Professor patted her head softly.

"Don't worry," he told her, "when you're me, *this* is the only plastic you need," pointing at his big cheesy, plastic smile.

Then he pointed above the heads of the school tour.

"See!" he beamed and Lucy looked.

The statue was a glass sculpture of the Professor himself, wearing the exact same cheesy, plastic smile.

"PSSST!"

Milo looked behind, then quickly turned back to face the door. He had been waiting for Lucy, but so far there was no sign of her.

"PSSST!" he heard again.

This time he half-spun around with an agitated frown on his face, before spinning back to check the front door again. It was getting late now and he didn't want to be distracted. Where had that girl gotten to!?

"MOO!" bellowed Lucy, then ducked behind the pillar as fast as she could.

Others looked around before returning to their business, but only Milo "Moo" Mooney realised who had called his name. He walked to where he believed the call had come from and was quickly pulled out of sight by a pair of nine-year-old hands.

"Lucy!" he cried, "you made it! I was beginning to worr..."

"Milo!" she interrupted, "I'm not going! Here, give this letter to Ms. Canditooth and don't tell her that I'm at the airport."

She handed over the letter her mother had given her the night before, excusing her from going on the school tour. Thankfully she had held onto it or Ms. Canditooth would have contacted her parents, wondering where she was.

"But but but..." stammered Milo.

"It's ok," Lucy told him. "Ooyay has been kidnapped. I need to go with Professor Crastinator to get him back from Flocky Nocky. We know he has him and we're going to get him back. It's all my fault and I need to put this thing right."

"It's a trap!" shrieked Milo. "Don't you see! This is all part of their plan!"

"No Milo, it's for real," she assured him, although his reaction did offer a viewpoint she hadn't considered before now. "He was kidnapped. I saw it with my own eyes," she informed him

"They're going to bump you off Lucy! Don't you see?" he pleaded with her to listen.

"Don't be silly, Moo" she once more practiced her nonchalance (still vowing to look it up to check its meaning later on).

She brushed his shoulder with her hand -not that there was anything there to brush away, but she needed to reach out to her friend in some manner. Milo was at a loss for what to do or say.

"Even if it's not about getting rid of you, Lucy, it's a trap somehow." He was certain of it. "This man -or his dog- or both of them together are responsible for making many things on our planet. He is *not* the fool you take him for. He is *not* going to take your interference lightly!" Milo could see he was getting through in some small way. "He won't let you get away with it Lucy. He plans to teach you a lesson one way or another. I *know* it! Don't you see?"

Lucy considered her friend's words carefully.

"No," she said finally, "I have to go with him. He *needs* me. We need to find Ooyay. We *are* going to find him and bring him back... Give the letter to Ms. Canditooth," she instructed with a quick hug to her best friend, before running off, at once vanishing into the crowd.

A tear-stained Milo sighed deeply and looked at the envelope in his hand. Even if Lucy hadn't realised, she was placing him in a terrible position. He could be involved in a conspiracy to her own murder if he passed on that note to their teacher. Slowly he ambled back to the rest of the group, not at all certain of what he was going do. Without even thinking, he automatically tapped Ms. Canditooth on her arm and handed over the envelope.

"Oh what's this?" she asked, although neither she nor Milo bothered with the answer.

She was already tearing it open as he walked away, shoulders drooping below his chest.

Dear Miss Canditooth

Lucy will not be joining your group on the world tour, as her father and I have decided she is too young to go.

Yours Sincerely
Beauty Ludey

oOOOo

The inside of an ATV is the size of a large, enclosed, circular Jacuzzi or hot tub, capable of seating twelve. NS-Mag seats, along with the compulsory extra-strength NS-Mag clothing (now a part of most people's daily attire) eliminated the need for seatbelts. This also allows people slide around on the seat, but not to fall out of it. Larger ATVs have multiple floors, each capable of holding twelve passengers, but this private bullet had just one level. In the centre of the circular seat was a large metal table.

Professor Crastinator sat in front of the main control console that included a keyboard and two large buttons (one green and one red). An electric buzzing noise filled the air in the ATV as soon as he pressed the green POWER ON switch. A large three-dimensional globe suddenly appeared above the table in front of them.

Taking a piece of paper from his pocket, the Professor unfolded and examined it carefully. There was no order to the list of islands he had printed and most of the coordinates did not even have names. His head shook and his shoulders shrugged and his hands waved in the air.

"How am I to know where to start from?" he cried. "I don't even know what I'm doing here! ...Where are we supposed to go next? ...This was all a mistake."

Lucy calmly took the list from his hand, then immediately chose one of the islands.

"Here!" she said, pointing at a name on the printout, "this one definitely looks the most interesting."

The Professor read the name and coordinates of where she had chosen, shrugged again, and turned back to the rotating sphere. His tongue poked from between his lips as he searched the globe. Eventually he spotted the relevant bullet-hole and touched it with his finger once it moved within reach. Instantly, the globe disappeared and was replaced by a rotating three-dimensional map of an island. A single word rotated in the opposite direction in mid-air above the map. It read:

"UTOPIA"

RIDE THE BULLET

The big red button marked LAUNCH now flashed.

"Ready?" asked Lucy with a smile, at once assuming her responsibility as the youngest person onboard.

"Ready as I'll ever be," sighed the Professor, sliding out of the way to give her room.

She knew most smaller kids normally slammed their foot down on the red button (she had seen it done that way plenty of times in movies and on television), but Lucy made a point of reaching over and calmly pressing it with her hand.

At once the ATV slowly began its descent to the bottom of the gun-barrel tube while the female computer voice began its standard announcement.

"Please remain seated and ensure your safety goggles are securely fitted."

Oops! They had forgotten to put their goggles on! Quickly they reached under the table in front of them, grabbed their eye-protection sunglasses and pulled them over their heads.

"...We are currently descending into the earth in preparation for lift-off," continued the computer. "Once we reach the bottom you will hear three beeps. On the third beep, this Air Travel Vehicle will launch and begin its journey to..." (the voice now changed to a low-pitched male tone), "...Utopia."

The nine-year-old girl and the (almost) ninety-year-old man looked silently at each other. It was something new for both of them, but of the two, Professor Crastinator looked the more worried. Lucy took his hand and gave it a slight squeeze.

"For Ooyay" she said. The Professor tightened his mouth and looked straight ahead.

"For Ooyay" he whispered with a nod.

Now the descent ceased as the island-map disappeared. A beep sounded and a large 1 appeared where the map was. Another beep rang out as the number changed to a 2. The passengers squeezed each other's hand again as the two changed to a 3 and the bullet shot upward.

It took a few seconds, but once they heard the loud "THOOOOOP" sound they both began to breathe, realising they had cleared the tube.

Lucy was surprised to find it wasn't at all as bad as she thought it was going to be. She had expected a loud deafening noise and violent shaking and a feeling that her head was going to be pulled through the floor of the bullet, but instead there was no noise and no great shakes. She *was* clung to her seat though, due to their speed and the gravitational pull.

It took a while, but eventually she managed to tilt her head slightly to be able to see the window. Through the dark blue glasses she could tell it was blue outside. Then white. It remained white for some time. Then the rattling started and the white outside the window turned blue again. Now the rattling grew worse -a lot worse as the blue turned darker. Lucy tried hard to keep her eyes open but they were being pulled shut by the pressure inside the vehicle. The window now looked like it was shaking three-feet in every direction with each split-second. A roaring noise grew to a deafening pitch before she even realised that the volume had been increasing all the time.

Just as her eyes finally closed, she saw the dark windows begin to glow ever-brighter orange. Soon, even with closed eyes and thick sunglasses she could see a brightness all over as if she was entering a pure-white ultra-bright tunnel.

"Is this... what death... feels like?" she could hardly hear herself think above the rattling roar and wild shaking. She didn't believe it could actually be so hard to go CAT-bouncing. People did it all the time -too often for it always to be like this. No way would everybody put up with this much discomfort time after time. Something *had* to have gone wrong with their jump. They were dead. She knew it.

...But if they were dead, how come the shaking and loud noise didn't stop? If anything, it was still growing louder and the shaking was growing stronger. It had gone beyond bearable some time ago, but now it was continuing to grow. Louder. More shaking. Louder. Louder. L-OU-D—E——R...

Then, it stopped.

Quiet.

Silence.

Nothing.

A feeling of relaxing warmth filled her face like warm
water being poured into a hot-water bottle.

This warmth was filling from the top-down.

Starting at the crown of her head it poured through her forehead and washed over her eyes and past her nose and mouth and chin. It went down into her heart and filled her with warmth and eased her body and made it tingle all the way down to her toes.

She opened her eyes. Nothing. She hadn't managed to open them. She tried again. Slowly they opened and at once she saw her two arms floating in front of her. She hadn't realised they were no longer by her side.

She turned to look at the Professor. He had pulled his glasses off and they floated now next to his face. His eyes were open wide in disbelief and his head floated slowly this way and that as he too took in his surroundings. Looking directly at Lucy now, he asked if she was ok. At least that is what she believed he had said, since it sounded so quiet, like he was speaking to her from the next room.

"Yes" she answered, then laughed as her ears popped and the air seemed to clear. "Ask me again!" she instructed, hearing at once that her own voice was now much louder and clearer than she had heard from him.

"Are you ok? Is everything all right?" he enquired.

She was surprised to hear him speak so quickly since their heads and arms were both floating around so slowly.

"Yes" she laughed aloud. "I'm brilliant! This is... this is *too* jazzy for words!" she cried.

She wasn't lying. There are no words to describe the thrill and excitement of floating in space. The Professor's eyes looked like they were going to pop out from excitement. Lucy realised hers were the same. She pulled off her glasses and tossed them away in order to see them float around inside the vehicle.

"NS-Mag disengaged," said the female computer and at once the two passengers floated up.

Lucy held onto the wall and her feet continued to float upward. At least she *felt* like they were going upward until she realised it wasn't really up at all. It was down. As she looked down to her feet she suddenly felt very dizzy, realising she didn't know which way was up and which was down. The Professor seemed to be ahead of her once again.

"WHICH WAY IS UP AND WHICH IS DOWN?!!" he screamed.

Somehow his terror relaxed Lucy and she found herself laughing aloud once again from giddy, excited dizziness, pure joy and pure fear. It was like watching the scariest movie ever, whilst being tied to the moving arm of a windmill. Only worse -A lot worse. And a lot better too.

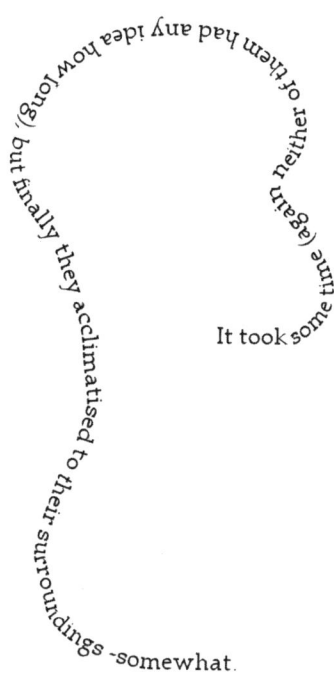

It took some time (they neither of them had any idea how long, but finally they acclimatised to their surroundings -somewhat.

Eventually they plucked up the courage to look out the window.

"Come on, let's look outside" said the old man with a youthful, nervous giggle, taking Lucy's elbow and doing his best to guide both of them up or down or left or right or whichever way it was, over to the nearest view-port.

Surprise and a nervous, giddy tingle followed through waves of dizzy joy as they gazed outside. *There* was planet earth below them -or above. Whichever. It was there. The *Earth.* ...*Planet* Earth!

It was too large to take in as a whole in one view. Whichever way they looked in every direction through the window, *there* was Planet Earth.

It was a mass of blue water (they both knew it was water but found it hard to believe what their brains were only just beginning to comprehend). Both the young and the old had tears of wonderment now from keeping their eyes open so wide for so long as they tried so hard to absorb everything that was happening all around.

There was the water. *There* were clouds.

"Look at that storm!" Professor Crastinator pointed to a swirling tornado far off in one direction.

"There's another one there!" cried Lucy pointing in another direction.

They spent some time indicating cloud anomalies and discolorations in the land and what looked like shimmering sparkles in the water before they quietly retreated into their own heads to gather their own thoughts on this most-private feeling of insignificance and greatness. For a long time they floated there. Lucy considered how tiny everybody was. The whole planetful of people down there were too small to be seen. Each and every one of them was a whole person like Lucy herself was, but was so tiny she couldn't even see *one* of them from the height she was now at.

Then she began to consider how tiny she herself was. For a while she had forgotten she was just nine years old. It was like space had made the old man younger as well as making her older, so that now they were both the same age.

But now she began to feel like a nine-year-old again. She wanted her mammy. She needed her dad to hold her in his big arms and not let go until she stepped on the solid ground once more. She began to consider how she might not see her parents ever again -or that she might not see *anyone* ever again since they were all so tiny now.

They would never find Ooyay and they would never return home and she'd be up here in space for ever more until her bones and the Professor's bones withered away to dust here inside this Air Travel Vehicle. They would never see another single living soul.

Their own ATV had just one flooring level to it. However, any bullet that had seven floors or more was usually called *a worm*. The largest bullets had twelve floors, each capable of holding twelve passengers. These were commonly referred to as Bakers' Worms (or Baker Bullets) for some reason.

Now as she gazed tearfully out the window, silently contemplating the futility of life and her own nothingness, one of these giant Bakers' Worms soared seemingly within a few feet of their own bullet.

As their vehicle spun around to the nearest window of the other vehicle, her over-popped eyeballs widened even further to see Milo Mooney staring right back at her through the other window! Clearly he couldn't believe what he was seeing either. His mouth looked like it was screaming as his eyes grew wider than wide. Then Lucy spotted Ms. Canditooth next to Milo. She had slowly begun to turn her head in the direction he was looking. It wasn't easy under the circumstances but Lucy ducked or spun or twisted or wiggled out of sight as fast as she could, praying she had done so fast enough.

TERRA FIRMA

Penny was ten. Matthew was nine and Martin was six. It was a warm, bright, sunny afternoon and they walked through fields as they normally did. This day was not unlike any other.

Martin puffed as they neared the top of a ridge, but Penny pulled him up by walking in front of him, with both arms stretched backward, holding his outstretched hands. Matthew was a few feet in front and had come to a halt. He was sitting on the dirt path and his neck craned as he stared now at something small and interesting on the ground.

"What is it Matt?" called Penny.

Martin looked out from behind her back and coughed a deep phlegm-filled, throat-full cough as he tried to speak.

"Take it easy Mucus," Penny said as she turned around, "we're almost there."

"Ants!" whispered Matthew, holding his open hand in the air to stop his brother and sister from approaching further. "...Hundreds of 'em -Probably *thousands!*"

Penny and Martin continued to draw closer.

"No! Stay back!" shouted Matthew in an urgent whisper, waving his palm at them.

"Why?" asked Penny in her normal voice as she dropped Martin's hands, taking the last few steps alone.

Matthew was always over-dramatising his discoveries.

"It could be dangerous for Mucus," he tried to convince his older sister but she was having none of it.

"Rubbish," she said, "ants don't carry diseases. They're not going to eat him up or carry him away y'know!"

Martin made it now to where his older brother and sister sat examining the ant highway that crossed the three-foot wide path the kids were on.

"There are two ant paths!" gasped Penny as she looked more closely.

"I know," said Matthew, quieter than Penny, annoyed she was disturbing the moment with her loud voice. "...One going that way," he pointed to his right, "the other that way," pointing left.

Once the ants left the path they all but disappeared in the grass to either side.

"Let's follow and see where they live!" said Martin as he bent down to look.

"Don't be silly," Matthew replied, "it'd take forever to follow one of them. And anyway, we don't even know which direction their house is in."

"Look!" said Martin, pointing a finger to the ant-trail that went left, "that lane are carrying nothing, but the ants going *this* way all have leaves and things on their backs," he stated, pointing to his right. "I bet they're taking food back to their house."

Mathew laughed. He had been looking all this time and didn't notice, but little Mucus had just arrived and spotted the obvious with a single glance.

"There's no flies on our Mucus," he said and they all laughed together.

Penny had no concern for ant trails so she sat playing loves-me-loves-me-not with daisies while the boys went following insects.

The older brother lost track of ants within a couple of feet of the path, then quickly lost interest, running off to examine the stream he spotted a few yards further on. Martin continued to walk slowly with both hands on his knees as he stooped to find where the ants lived. He soon came to a large oak tree, at the base of which the ants seemed to be gathered in much bigger numbers. They ran and crawled and climbed over each other in what looked like chaos. It was like a big ant party at the bottom of the great oak tree. When he looked closer, he noticed that each individual ant appeared to have a particular goal or destination to be reached or possibly a particular job to be undertaken. They all moved like they had somewhere in particular they wanted or needed to get to. Still Martin couldn't figure out where they all lived, since they approached and departed this party from every direction. The food on their backs seemed to be passed from ant to ant for no obvious reason.

Just then Matthew called out.

"Mucus!" he cried, with one foot in the ankle-high water, "c'mere!" but Martin was too busy checking the ants to answer.

"It's a frog!" shouted Matthew, but Martin paid it no heed.

Soon Matthew came running to his younger, sickly brother, holding something in his hands. As Martin stood straight he noticed a small green frog looking directly at him from within the older boy's grasp.

"I caught a frog," boasted Matthew. "Here! Spit on him!"

"Huh?" asked Martin, unsure what his brother was talking about.

"Spit on him," he repeated. "It'll bring ya luck. Go on, I already spat on him. You need the luck anyway."

"But I can't spit," complained the youngest child, "I don't know how. I never get it right."

"It's ok if you get my hands too," insisted Matthew. "I don't mind. Just stand over it and drop a glugger down on his head. Go on!"

Martin craned over his brother's outstretched hands and was just about to aim a spit on the frog when Penny spoke up. She had been approaching quietly but said nothing until now.

"Don't be stupid the two of you!" she interrupted with all the sense young girls demonstrate when confronted with silly males.

"...You don't get luck from spitting at frogs," she explained, "...you have to spit in their mouths and ask it to take away your toothache!"

"But he doesn't *have* a toothache" said Matthew, "...so just spit on his head Mucus, go on!"

Penny looked around and picked up an acorn from the ground.

"Here," she said, handing it to Martin, "have this instead. *An acorn should be carried to bring luck and ensure a long life,*" she informed the six year old.

"And spit on the frog too!" insisted Matthew. "You need all the luck you can get!"

Penny shot Matthew a dagger stare as Martin quietly took the acorn and walked away.

"Here, I'll spit on him for ya!" said Matthew, then dropped a glugger on the frog's head before throwing him back in the direction of the stream.

"MATTHEW!" cried Penny, disgusted at her brother.

"WHAT?" shouted Matthew, pretending he didn't know what upset her.

Penny huffed, then turned to follow her younger brother without another word.

Ooyay felt like someone had hit him over the head with a shovel. One of his hind legs throbbed as though it had suffered a heavy blow and his eyelids were too hot and too heavy to open. He was fading in and out of consciousness. One minute he could hear someone talking or shouting over a loud engine noise, the next he was asleep. Now he was stirred by rattling and banging and another far-off thunderous engine.

What had happened? He was running toward the girl. He was ensnared in a net, then tossed into the back of a van. He had struggled to escape but the doors slammed and he was trapped. After a few minutes' drive, he managed to open the back door and leap from the moving van. The vehicle screeched to a halt as Ooyay tumbled and spun out onto the road. He had barely found his feet when two or more arms reached out and quickly grabbed him. Then his leg stung hard and soon he was in this half-awake/half-asleep state for some unknown length of time.

But his eyes would not open and his mind was unable to concentrate on what was happening. For now he just ...needed... sleep.... Sleep.... Sleeeeeep.

TOUCHING DOWN

The journey into space wasn't so bad for Professor Crasti-nator. In fact he kind of enjoyed it because he was feeling so awful in himself for what he had done to Ooyay. They had fought and he called him a bad doggie and hadn't allowed him take out the Hamsterball and now Ooyay had been snatched away from him and he (the Professor) was nothing without his beautiful blue dog. The only thing he could think of through all the discomfort and fear while they burst through the earth's atmosphere was "I deserve it, I deserve it, I deserve it."

Space itself was too beautiful. He didn't deserve that and he knew it. Space made him sad. For years his dog had pleaded with him to bring him on a CAT Bounce. Ooyay said it would help expand his horizons, but Professor Crastinator would have none of it. There were always too many reasons to do nothing.

But space had made him feel young again. He now didn't feel a day over seventy-two. His body was telling him "I want to live!", but his mind and broken heart were shouting "lie down, old man, your time has come." The only reason he had for going on was to do it for Ooyay. He *needed* his Ooyay.

The only reason he *had* gone on was because this little girl had forced him into it. He had no idea who she was really or why she had taken it upon herself to help him like this. But there she was once again holding his hand as the ATV began its descent to planet Earth, telling him it would all be ok.

"Don't cry," she smiled sympathetically, "it won't be so bad going back down."

He cried. He cried harder and louder now because this child had gotten it so wrong. He wasn't crying because he feared the journey down. He was crying because space was too beautiful and too *fun*. He didn't deserve fun and didn't want it (though while it was there it was impossible not to enjoy). He only wanted his dog. He was crying for his lost doggie.

But the journey down proved *worse* than the outward leg. For one thing, the shaking and loud roar didn't build gradually as it had done earlier. On this trip, the ATV drifted quietly toward the planet, then suddenly there was a loud BANG as they smashed into the Earth's atmosphere. The worst of the shaking and the rattling and the roaring all happened right in that moment. It was like an explosion, but this explosion lasted *minutes*. For every second during that period he was certain everything was just going to burn away, crumble to dust and rain down on the world below in a light sprinkle of ash.

Eventually however, he noticed he could once more open his eyes (a little). Then the noise lowered to almost nothing, but the violent vibrations continued through the silence. In time, the shaking eased to a level that allowed him look around, just as the girl began to scream.

"AAAAaaaahhhooooooo!" she screamed for joy, throwing her hands in the air, obviously relieved they seemed to be over the worst of it.

Despite himself, Professor Crastinator couldn't stifle a loud laugh. He found himself grabbing the girl's closest arm and waving it around clumsily as they both whooped and yodelled with delight.

After some minutes there was a FUUUMP sound as the Bullet fell into the Bullet-hole, fitting perfectly inside the walls of the tube.

"You have reached..." began the female voice from the computer console.

"...Utopia" completed the male voice before the original tone took over once again.

"Please remain seated until this Air Traffic Vehicle comes to a complete stop." (Despite the NS-Mag seating, it *was* possible to slide forward and shimmy out of your seat, or to even remove your clothing in order to escape that way, if required.)

The Bullet eventually slowed to a halt and both passengers felt like they were being pulled down into the ground. "Cheeses" said Lucy under her breath. The old man shot her a frowning stare.

"I said *cheeses*" she clarified. "Y'know -like *cheese* -only ...more cheese ...Cheeses."

She would have smiled only it felt like something was dragging her mouth and her whole body downward as the ATV began to climb back up the tube to ground level. She suddenly felt heavier than an elephant in a vacuum cleaner.

It took a while before either of them could speak again due to the forces at work. Finally the Professor opened his mouth.

"I have no idea what you kids are saying these days," he complained.

"Whose fault is that?" asked Lucy with a directness and wisdom that surprised the old man.

In his day, no child ever spoke to an elder in such a tone. He was about to chastise her when he found himself agreeing with her sentiment. He was out of touch. Ooyay would know how to speak her language. The Professor didn't.

Still the ATV was climbing slowly in the ground. Too slowly for Lucy as she looked around now, wondering what to do or say next.

"I thought we were going to die," she mumbled to the Professor.

"Me too," he confessed at once, surprising Lucy.

If she had thought about it, she would have expected him to either pretend he didn't hear or to pat her head and say it would all be all right. The man really didn't know how to speak to children. This made her smile.

"What's so funny now?" he asked, genuinely puzzled as the two of them looked to each other.

"Is it really true you are ninety years old?" she asked, ignoring his question.

"No," he stated. "I'm eighty nine."

"Aren't people usually dead by the time they reach that age?"

"No" answered the old man with certainty. "No dead people ever reach eighty nine."

Sunlight warmed the inside of the Bullet now as they slowly reached ground level and came to a halt. Then the ATV seemed to shift a little in a horizontal direction, before sliding downward briefly, ending in a splash.

"NS-Mag disengaged," said the computer -not that it made any difference to the passengers. They were stuck to their seating anyway.

"I can't move," said Lucy, beginning to panic now as she realised that she didn't have the strength to raise her arm.

The Professor eased back in his headrest, grateful to finally have the chance to rest. If he couldn't move, that suited him fine.

"Professor!" cried Lucy in horror as he began to snore.

It was no use. He was asleep and no amount of shouting could wake him.

A half hour or more passed before she heard a noise coming from outside. First there was a clink, then a clunk, followed by a knock. Then the hatch in the roof opened and two figures appeared overhead. Because it was so bright outside, for a few seconds Lucy couldn't make out their faces. Then one of them moved slightly into the light's path and she saw two bare-chested men gazing silently into the ATV.

"Welcome to Utopia," they both smiled finally in a pleasant, youthful manner.

UTOPIA

Toothpaste-blue, bath-warm seawater quietly lapped the sandy white beach. The island's Bullet-Hole was positioned on the rocks at one end of the beach, but the ATV they had arrived in was now sitting in the shallow water a little below the mouth of the Landing-Tube.

Lucy stood in the ankle-high water, next to (and slightly behind) the Professor. On either side of them, the two men who had greeted and helped them from the Bullet now assisted in keeping them steady on their feet. A smiling round man with a long grey beard was standing on the sand before them. Next to him stood a beautiful young woman. On either side of them stood two more young men, much like the two who helped Lucy and the Professor. All of the inhabitants were wearing nothing apart from loincloths, coral jewellery and pearly-white smiles.

The round man raised his arms in a light-hearted, uplifting manner.

"Welcome to Utopia!" he laughed as if bursting with excitement. "You'll have to forgive us. We're not used to visitors and we weren't expecting anyone on this day. We are usually OTM here..."

"What's OTM?" enquired Lucy immediately.

The round grey-bearded man smiled at her directness.

"Off-The-Map" he explained, resting his hands on his knees as he bent to speak to the young girl. "Utopia doesn't show on any map or geological representation of the planet... at least it shouldn't do... I'm not certain what happened in your case..."

Suddenly he stopped talking as he examined the features of the thin, sad-faced old man before him.

"Professor?" he asked, unsure he had the right man. The Professor glanced back with the briefest of smiles.

"It is you! Professor Marcus Crastinator! It is! It's you! Everybody! This is Professor Crastinator -The Man Who Fixed the World!"

The man in question gave a slightly broader smile now as he remembered how the newspapers used to describe him, back when he was regarded as the only inventor of his kind.

"...It's a long time since anyone called me that," he blushed.

"Well that explains everything!" laughed the bearded man to the others around him. "The Professor here has the freedom of the planet, of course. He can come and go anywhere he pleases! ...And can I say what a great honour it is for us to have you here in our land. I am Bink, official Greeter of Utopia."

Turning now to the young woman beside him he said "This is my daughter, Wakanista." Wakanista bowed silently as did the Professor and the girl.

"And over here," added Bink, pointing to each of the handsome young men in turn, "are Shadow, Derry, Sandy and Philip." The men smiled, mumbled their greetings, then bowed.

"Let us walk to our home," said Bink, pointing in the direction of some stonework that was just about visible at the other end of the long beach. "That way you can stretch your legs and I can tell you a little about this land."

To their left was the sea. To their right, a green margin of tropical, leafy palm, coconut, banana and other fruit trees. The beach was a straight, golden, deserted roadway to the village.

Overhead, the sky was clearest blue in every direction, save for one small white cloud far above the sea. Even as they slowly ambled through this picture postcard world, Lucy suddenly found herself again missing her parents -her mother most of all now, for some reason.

"I'm Lucy Lucey!" Lucy piped up, since she was feeling so left out and it looked like nobody was going to introduce her.

"Yes!" continued Professor Crastinator. "And we're looking for Dr. Flocky Nocky! He's not here by any chance is he?"

"Flavius Flocky Nocky?" smiled Bink. "Now that really would be something special -to have the two of you here on Utopia with us! Alas no, he isn't here, but anything we do have -is yours."

Shadow and Sandy suddenly broke from the group to grab a giant sea turtle. They lifted it by either side of its shell as it kicked the air with its flipper-like legs, then rejoined the group, carrying their catch in one arm each.

"Turtle soup!" smiled Bink. "We try to pick some up whenever we're by this way. Delicious!"

As soon as the Professor saw Lucy raise an arm as if to ask a question, he jumped in with one of his own.

"So tell me Mr. Bink, how did Utopia come about? Is this the *real* Utopia?"

"Bink," he corrected. "Just Bink. Yes. It's the real Utopia. Yes it exists! ...We were part of a government-program that was setup many years ago..." Bink began as they walked.

"Which government?" Lucy interrupted immediately.

The Professor turned to face her, whispering quietly, but firmly.

"How about we let Mr. Bink do the talking my dear, hmm?" he suggested with a smile. "We can leave the questions 'til later. ...Let's hear what he has to say and see what he has to show us before blurting out the first thing that comes into our minds, eh?" Turning back to the round man now he continued "I'm sorry Mr. Bink, do carry on."

Bink nodded with a toothy smile, before beginning again from the top.

"Bink," he stated simply. "Just Bink. Ah! Yes! ...We were part of a government-program that was set up many years ago to check out the possibility of creating the *perfect* society," he explained.

"Not too perfect for turtles," mumbled Lucy under her breath, but if they noticed, nobody reacted.

"...We were carefully selected as a representative cross-section of people who had a wish to live in quiet, peaceful seclusion in trouble-free splendour..."

"Do you have loud music?" Lucy enquired.

"Lucy!" said the Professor, which made her smile because it was the first time, that she could recall, he had spoken her name.

Bink laughed.

"Yes we have loud music," he answered.

"...So if this place is perfect and one person wants peace and quiet," said Lucy anxiously, "and someone else wants to dance... what happens?"

This was the question that was burning in her mind since she had chosen Utopia as their destination. She had half-heard something about this place being a kind of heaven on earth, but had no idea how everybody would be able to agree on what was good and what was bad. Lucy herself hated the taste of fish, but her parents loved it. Would she be forced to eat fish in Utopia? How perfect was that?

"I think you're looking at this all wrong Lucy," the Professor chimed in. "It's not about music - loud or otherwise. It's about *choice* and the ability to escape the harsh realities of daily existence in the world today. It's about starting anew in a beautiful island, free from trouble and hardship and pain. Isn't it Mr. Bink?"

"Bink. Er, yes" Bink replied, unsure, "but everyone here wants the same things. We live for peace and tranquillity and pleasantness. There *are* no problems in Utopia."

"So what happens if there *is* a problem?" asked Lucy, still unsure how it all worked. "I mean, what if someone does something wrong or doesn't want to do the same as everyone else? What then?"

"Lucy I don't think you get the gist of it," the Professor smiled briefly to Bink as he explained once more. "This place is about forgiveness and understanding and tolerance of other people's faults and about the ability to get along one and all with each other. Isn't it Mr. Bink?"

Bink rubbed his chin. This helps people think of an answer to a question they don't know how to answer.

"Bink. Er, no" he said, "not really. We all do get along here, but we don't tolerate trouble-makers."

"So what happens if..." Lucy began again, but the Greeter of Utopia cut her short.

"We banish them," he stated matter-of-factly. "If someone no longer wishes to live in peace and happiness and understanding, then they can go and live elsewhere ...can't they Wakanista?"

The smile on Bink's daughter's face faded somewhat now for the first time. Immediately, both visitors knew there was a story behind Wakanista's faded smile, but neither had the courage to ask. Instead, the Professor chose to ask a different question, curious now about the island's justice system.

"So is there a punishment scale to fit different crimes then Mr. Bink?" he wondered.

"Bink," laughed Bink, not in the least upset at the question or the fact that this man continued to get his name wrong. "There is only one punishment in Utopia," he said.

"So if..." began Lucy.

"Yes!" Bink interrupted. "If someone commits murder, he or she is exiled -never again to set foot in Utopia. If someone steals, they are exiled -never to return. If a person ever played loud music continuously and wouldn't stop when asked nicely by peaceful, caring, well-intentioned neighbours... then that person is banished from this land," he said. "Forever!"

"We are one here," added Bink, "...or we are *nothing.*"

"Sheesh!" whistled the Professor, "That's tough."

Bink opened his eyes wide and threw his index finger in the air as he smiled a mad, toothy grin.

"*BINK!*" he exclaimed for no apparent reason.

As they approached the village, the Professor noticed the large walls that seemed to be growing out of the jungle.

"How come you have such large walls?" he enquired. "I mean, nobody knows you are here. Why do you need such protection?"

"Utopia is the most beautiful place on Earth" smiled Bink with a pat to the older visitor's shoulder. "It is worth protecting at any cost. Inside, we are happy and want for nothing. You will see. Utopia is the fulfilment of all your dreams. Such beauty needs a border."

"Why?" asked Lucy, unconvinced. "...If all that beauty is inside then isn't there *less* beauty outside for everyone else?"

Bink's smile faded a little.

"Everyone else is free to have their own beauty," he answered, then laughed again. "We like ours just the way it is. You'll see! Utopia is everything you imagined and more!"

"My mother's name is Beauty," Lucy grinned boastfully.

"That's nice my dear," said Bink, smiling to the others.

An awed silence now descended on the group as the gates of Utopia drew near. Lucy felt dizzy as she walked, looking up to the large double doors. There was no comparison between these and any other entranceway she had ever seen in real life, but she couldn't help thinking that if her house had doors this size, she would easily be able to climb through the keyhole in order to get in -"*Keep room for your money with a person in your keyhole*," she laughed as she thought of a possible jingle that would sell the idea to people.

But there were no keyholes here. She had seen such doors in many movies, but they were usually used to keep large monsters and dinosaurs either in or out. It is one thing to see those doors in a movie, but it's another when you are slowly approaching them on foot and they are growing bigger and bigger before you, as you proceed. Lucy felt like she was floating again now -not moving her legs at all. Her eyes remained on the top of the gates as she glided onward. By the time they came to a halt, some yards in front of the gate, Lucy's head was nearly bent backward from looking up so high.

Professor Crastinator, on the other hand, wasn't as impressed with the gates as the young girl was. He looked around now, taking in his surroundings some more. On either side of the doors, a large stonework wall rose as high as the wood and metal frame. Each slab of rock was over six feet tall and twice as wide. He began counting the number of rocks there were in one straight upward line, but lost count at ten. It became too dizzying for him to look up any higher. Ten rocks high was still less than half the full height he reckoned however. Utopia must really be something special if their joy and happiness needed to be encased within barriers of this scale.

Lucy stood to his left, Wakanista to his right. On the other side of Wakanista was Bink. The four men were spread out haphazardly nearby. A loud, metal scraping noise could be heard now as a large bolt was slowly being moved out of the way on the other side of the gates. Then came a clank and clunk and a clonk. Next, a rattling, screeching chain noise rang out, followed by more heavy metal jangling. The Professor began to grow fidgety and turned toward Wakanista now. He wondered what it was that had made

Bink's daughter so sad a little while ago. Just as he drew breath to ask, he broke off, uncertain it was a good idea to mention it.

However, Wakanista had now noticed he was about to speak to her so she turned to look at the Professor, expectantly. He had no idea what to say. She was a beautiful young woman, perhaps eighteen or nineteen years old. She was wearing a loincloth bikini and a white coral necklace. It had been years since Professor Crastinator had even looked at such a female, let alone stood next to one. What could he say? What did they have in common? He had no idea what interested people of that age or how they even conversed with each other. Not for the first time, he realised he was out of touch with the youth of today.

The door finally juddered and slowly began to open. A thin crack of bright, golden light gradually spread across Lucy's face as her mouth formed a large O and her eyes widened to take in the beauty of Utopia. Just then the Professor thought of a youthful phrase he had recently heard. Turning to the young woman on his right once more he smiled tenderly and asked

"How many buttons are on those boobies of yours?"

Within minutes they were back on the Bullet. Lucy now frowned as she folded her arms tightly across her chest, looking anywhere but at the old idiot sitting next to her. The most beautiful, secretive, protected land in all the world was about to be revealed to them and he had picked that precise moment to say something senseless and stupid. What in the world was he talking about when he asked such a question!?

"I thought that's how you young people speak!" he pleaded with her in answer to the question that her anger prevented her from asking.

She huffed, stuck her head in the air and deliberately made a show of looking as far away from him as she could manage.

The Professor was about to say more but the manner in which Lucy had turned away suddenly reminded him of his dog. Ooyay always turned away and stuck his nose in the air like that whenever he was in a huff. He knew there was nothing he could say and he didn't have the energy or the heart to attempt it anyway.

THE DEATH OF MUCUS

Even since before he was born, Martin's demise had been an imminent certainty. After a six-month pregnancy, Mrs. Cratchett was told by her doctor that it was all over. The baby in her womb was all but dead. There was nothing could be done for the little blighter. She just had to go home and wait.

A few days later, having given birth to a baby boy, she cried for hours before anyone could make it clear to her that he was not dead. He was very sick, but not dead yet. He was smaller than an average adult hand on the day that he was born. He needed care and affection, warmth and protection from the outside elements. His first bed was made from one of his father's comfortable old shoes, padded with soft lamb's wool.

For three and a half years, the rest of the family more or less held their breath in anticipation of Martin's passing away. The curtains were forever drawn in case the light hurt the poor baby's eyes. Everybody was made whisper for fear any loud noise disturbed him. Nobody with so much as a cough was allowed inside the front door lest they passed on their infection to little baby Martin.

One time, the eldest son, Mike, came home with a sniffle and his mother wouldn't let him into the house. So the sick teenager had to go stay with his aunt Clara for a while. He ended up living in that house for over a year, since the pressure had become so unbearable at home.

Matthew had had enough by the time the baby was almost four. For all those years they expected him to die *tomorrow*. But tomorrow never came. Coming home from school one afternoon, Matthew slammed the front door and shouted.

"IS HE DEAD YET?" he cried out in an off-hand selfish way, as children often do.

This outburst lead to an eruption in the Cratchett home that had been building for many years. Father, mother, sisters and brothers all quarrelled for hours. In the end, it was decided that Matthew had to be punished. Following further arguments, it was decided that Matthew was to be sent away for his bad behaviour.

The next morning calmness settled on the house for the first time in years. Mother Cratchett smiled and made toast for everyone before informing them that she had slept on it and there was going to be a new plan of action: Martin was to be allowed outside. Matthew was to take him on daily walks in the country-side to help clear his lungs. Penny was to accompany them to make sure no harm came to the two boys.

Thus the country walks began whether the children wanted them or not. Martin didn't die. In fact his strength grew somewhat from all the fresh air and exercise. He was still a sickly boy, but at least he was now able to *live* a little instead of being locked up in that dark and dreary house all day, every day.

The rest of the family also finally learnt how to live with a sick child. No longer did everyone tiptoe around the house, but instead they began to treat Martin as a full and proper *human being* for the first time. Martin had to wash the ware sometimes and he was often made set the table for dinner. He wasn't allowed sweep the floor for fear of dust contamination, but he was allowed (and forced to) make his own bed.

Soon his illness was something to be laughed at. It remained and there was nothing could be done about it, so the family made jokes of it. Humour helped them cope. They took to calling him Mucus, not to laugh at the child, but to laugh in the face of his illness.

The day came, however, after Martin had just turned eight years of age that he became too sick and too weak to go outside any longer. For the last six months of his short life he was too weak to climb out of bed. There was nothing could be done for him in the hospital so he was allowed home to die with his loving family.

At first, Mother and Father sat by his bedside every minute of every day. Mike, Joan, Jenny, Penny and Matthew all remained nearby also. But as the days turned to weeks and the weeks turned to months it had become harder to expect Martin was going to die in the next five minutes. There were cars that Mike needed to fix. Joan was offered a job abroad, working on posh trains for rich and famous people. Jenny had to return to her work in the big house in the city. Mother and Father Cratchett began taking turns minding Martin while the other went to work. Each day Matthew and his sister Penny quietly went to school, came home, ate their dinner and went to bed. There was nothing else could be done.

One Saturday morning there came a loud banging at the front door. Father Bishop burst into the house in a sopping wet overcoat as soon as Matthew raised the latch to see who it was.

"You must come at once!" cried Father Bishop to Matthew's dad, "the church organ is playing B-flats instead of As and we have a VIP wedding this afternoon!"

Mr. Cratchett looked up from Martin's bedside, unsure how to respond. His wife had left for work and it was his turn to mind the boy. Martin was weak but conscious.

"Go," he instructed his father with a weightless wave, "Matt and Penny are here," he reminded him.

Emmett Cratchett gently pecked his youngest son's sweating forehead and promised he'd be back within the hour. The priest had already anointed and prayed over the sick child many times in the past. He didn't feel this was the time to do so again. Not with an organ-tuning emergency on their hands.

As soon as they left, Martin began coughing. He whooped and schewed and phlegmed and cooeckled. Penny ran to the door to go call their father, but Martin stopped her.

"No!" he wheezed. "It's ok... It's time."

Penny and Matthew slowly approached the bed as little Mucus eased back down on the pillow, resting both hands on his chest. The coughing had stopped. He looked up to his brother and sister (as he had always done), then closed his eyes for the last time. The wheezing eased, then stopped. Matthew and Penny froze to the spot. Both knew exactly what had happened, but neither knew what to do or say.

Then one of Martin's arms slipped from his side and something fell out of his hand. It rolled off the bed and hopped on the floor twice before Penny grabbed it.

Matthew couldn't believe it when he saw what little Mucus had been carrying with him the whole time. As Penny opened her hand, a waterfall of silent tears fell from both siblings' eyes when they saw the acorn that Penny had given to Mucus on that day, more than a year earlier.

Matthew took and rolled it slowly between his fingers. The words Penny had spoken that day suddenly ran through his mind as though they were being said right now:

"An acorn should be carried to bring luck and ensure a long life."

It was all too much. He flung that liar of an acorn as far away from him as he could manage. Then he fainted on the floor.

CAGES OF FEAR

Ooyay was in a boat race with the wind whistling through his ears. Crasty smiled at him and pointed out that he too could whistle just like Wee Willy Whistle. Ooyay was overjoyed to hear this. That postman had always been his idol. Ooyay had never even thought to attempt to whistle with his ears instead of his lips. He quickly flapped his ears up and down, one at a time and Crasty sang along as the boat sailed on through the high seas.

Suddenly there was a loud crash. Crasty fell forward and Ooyay quickly shut his eyes to brace himself against the weight of his master.

When he once more looked around, Ooyay saw that he was lying in a metal cage. But unlike the boat and the whistling, this cage was no dream.

A man in a long white coat, who had his back turned to the cage, was picking himself up off the floor, having fallen over a metal wheelie-cabinet. He was too busy cursing and tidying away a range of scary-looking surgical instruments that he had knocked from the top shelf of the cabinet to notice that Ooyay had woken up.

In one quick glance, the blue dog surveyed his surroundings: His cage was one of many in the cold, hall-like, echoey chamber. At either end of the room, large cabinets housed an array of multi-coloured liquids and tubes and glass beakers and Bunsen burners and safety goggles.

The middle of the room was filled with tall-standing bright lamps all trained on a metal table. Attached to this table were different kinds of straps -some metal, some leather, some wooden. On each of these straps he at once spotted the remnants of a struggle: There were animal hairs of various colours and consistency. On one or two of the straps he could see and smell dried blood that had not been washed away after previous uses. That was when he took a deeper breath and smelled the dying animals in the room all around. Mostly the place smelled of sawdust and disinfectant, but beneath those odours was the unmistakeable whiff of sickness, disease, pain and suffering.

In the cage to his right, a dirty-looking brown and white bull hound terrier sat huddled in one corner. As Ooyay's head had turned, it caught the attention of this animal. He quickly scanned

Ooyay for any sign of danger, then stood straight as if ready to fight. He didn't bark or growl. He just stood and stared. His most distinguished feature was that he had only one eye. Into his empty eye socket, someone appeared to have inserted a green golf ball. The ear above this missing eyeball was also missing, but nothing was used to replace it. Below the eye-that-wasn't-there, a long, badly stitched black trail ran from the corner of his mouth, all the way down his neck.

To Ooyay's right, there lay a beautiful collie with soft gold and white hair. Her head was facing the blue dog and she appeared to be asleep. Looking beyond her face, Ooyay noticed that the hair on a large part of her side was missing. More than that, it looked as though it had been deliberately plucked-out. It was like a big, burnt clearing in a forest after an explosion or a plane crash. A long red, ugly scar streaked through this bareness like a line of lipstick on a bald man's head. This line of red on the dog wasn't a cut though. It *was* actually a line of lipstick (or simi-lar). The realisation that it wasn't a cut was more upsetting to Ooyay than if it had been a cut. This line could only mean one thing: It was *going* to be a cut.

Beyond the cages to his left and his right, Ooyay could see more sad and angry dogs. Over on the other side of the room were cages, piled four-high and twenty-long. As every school child knows, and as Ooyay could tell in a fraction of a second, this meant there were eighty cages over there. Almost every one of them contained a scrawny-looking, mangy cat. Toward the far-right end of the room he could see several cages with rabbits. He couldn't spot any other animals at this stage, but he was certain that the person running this laboratory was also using rats and guinea pigs and possibly monkeys for whatever despicable exper-iments were going on here.

"Ah!" said the man in the white coat, now almost sticking his head through the door of Ooyay's cage. He had thick milk-bottle glasses and long, straight, slightly wet hair, combed carefully. He appeared to be no more than twenty years old. "...And here at last is the star of the show!" he added with a mad wide-mouth gasp that (along with his enlarged eyes) lent him the look of some kind of toad or giant bug that had spotted a tasty-looking meal.

"They must have roughed you up well, my boy" he gloated. "You were out for quite a bit."

Noticing how Ooyay was still silently surveying the surroundings, he allowed the dog get his bearings.

"Allow me to introduce myself!" he said, after a pause. "My name is Seamus Shafford and I will likely be... looking after you... for a few days." Seamus smiled briefly before continuing.

"You like what you see here?" he asked, tossing his head backward, which jerked the hair from his bulging eyes at the same time. "...A little primitive I agree, but it serves its purpose."

Ooyay looked at Seamus to check what he could possibly mean by that, but failed to find any explanation in the overjoyed comic-book expression on the man's face.

"Ha ha!" laughed Seamus Shafford. "You don't trust me! That's understandable, but you mark my words..."

The young man now raised his right arm as he spoke and Ooyay noticed a syringe sticking into the top of his index finger. The man also clearly hadn't noticed this syringe before now.

"AAARHHHH!" he yelled, flapping his hand up and down, sending the syringe flying into the air over his shoulder.

Without even looking to see where it had landed, he spun around and ran from the room without another word.

The syringe, Ooyay noted, had stuck in the paw of a hitherto quietly dozing kitten in a cage at the far side of the room. This kitten leapt in the air in pain and fright, but couldn't move because the syringe had nailed its paw to the floor of his cage. The cats around him started screaming. Then dogs barked from every angle. Soon the whole place sounded like a festival on Noah's Ark.

Ooyay sunk his head into his legs and quietly huddled in a corner of his small cage. *What* diabolical activities had he gotten mixed up in? *How* had he come to this place? Where was Crasty? Why was he here? Did this 'Seamus Shafford' know he could speak? -It appeared he did. *How* did he know? -The school journal?

There were a hundred questions running through his head all at once, but most of all, the one that screamed louder than any other was:

"Why can't I just go home?"

LIFESTYLES OF THE RICH AND FAMOUS

"So how come Ooyay can speak?" asked Lucy Lucey. "I mean, where does he come from?"

It had been early afternoon when they first departed. The Bullet had launched in a slight easterly direction, which would have gained them some time. The world turned below as they had floated outside the Earth's atmosphere, although the Bullet itself remained in much the same position (relative to the sun) as when it had emerged into space. Because of this, the "local-time" when they had first reached Utopia was about the same as when they took off, even though some hours had elapsed. Now they were lying on deckchairs, next to a swimming pool, beside a beach on the exclusive island of Linsi, overlooking the picturesque Linsi Sea. They had decided that another blast into space so soon after the first one would have been too much for them both.

Thankfully, Catapult Air Travel facilitates an NSLA (Non Space Lob Angle) for shorter journeys. It works like this: The upper section of the Bullet-Hole can be targeted in different directions. If the angle is too severe, the Bullet will not be able to penetrate the outer-crust of the Earth's atmosphere. Such angles are used to simply 'lob' the Bullet to a specific nearby Bullet-Hole, without the need to go into space. Because of possible weather interference it would not be safe to lob a Bullet further than one hundred miles.

Luckily, Linsi (which was not an island on the Professor's list) was only eighty miles from Utopia, so Lucy had instructed the Professor to head for there. Since he was already in her bad books and since he had no fresh ideas of his own, he was unable to think of a reason why not.

From early twentieth century, Linsi was seen as *the* place to be if you were ultra-rich or fabulously famous (or both). A bottle of water on this island cost more than most people spent in a week -although champagne flowed freely in the island's only river. If you had to ask the price of anything here, you couldn't afford the time it would take the person you asked to answer you.

Although they accepted plastic on Linsi, none of the gold-plated hotels (which were the only hotels here) would go so far as to accept Professor Crastinator's plastic smile as part-payment on a couple of their rooms. The manager at the Marcsi Sea Hotel recognised the inventor, however, and invited them to rest on some poolside loungers for as long as they wished.

"Professor?" Lucy spoke up again, but he appeared to be asleep. "Do you hear me?" she continued. "Professor? ...How come Ooyay can speak? Do all dogs talk *really?*"

She left the echo of her voice fade to nothing before starting again. "Hmmm? ...Professor? ...Huh? ...Huh? ...Pro..."

Just as Lucy was losing hope of inducing a response, he spoke -louder and clearer than she would have imagined.

"No," he answered clearly. "They don't." His eyes remained closed.

Excited now that she had gotten some reaction, Lucy decided to launch as many questions as she could, in the hope that he might answer at least one or two. There was no telling when or if such an opportunity would arise again.

"So how come Ooyay can talk? Where did you find him? Was he part of some experiment? What..."

"I don't know," the Professor interrupted calmly, then at last opened his eyes to look at the young girl. "...I don't remember. We've always been together. I *need* to find him. I need to bring him home -back where he belongs. It's none of your business anyway. He *belongs* with me! Do you hear me? He is *my* dog. Not yours. You can't just come along and think you can take him away from me you know!"

As he spoke, he sat forward and gradually raised his voice until he was almost shouting by the end.

Lucy was shocked. So far, she had run the show and dictated where they go and when and why. Especially after Utopia, she had thought that *she* was the boss in this operation. Yet somehow it now appeared that something had changed. Somehow, the Professor now had the right to chastise *her.*

When did that happen? She had no idea.

"I ...I never..." she stuttered, unsure what to say.

The Professor said nothing further. Both of them lay back in their recliners without another word. Their conversation quickly faded and was washed away by the ever-present swish of the waves.

Have you ever been lying by the sea, facing the sky, saying nothing, looking at the dark purple colour of the inside of your eye-lids as you half-listen to the eternally lazy tumbles of dissolving foam on the sponge-like beach before you? No? Well you should try it some time. Don't rush it. In fact, it can't be experienced *at all* if it is rushed. It might happen within seconds of closing your eyes, but usually it takes a few minutes. Let's practice now -but keep your eyes open or you won't be able to read the following...

Your eyes are closed. You are not tapping a finger or a foot. You are not thinking of the fun you had that time when you splashed your sister. Don't bring to mind what your parents always told you about crossing the road. Put all thoughts of games and sport and food and drink and fun and pain and sadness from your head. Free your mind to the sound of the waves -just like your shoulders would free themselves to the soft kneading of massaging fingers. Swish... Swish... ... ...Swish... (Every now and then a wave sounds like it's not going to fall, but it does -just a little later than the one before it did)... Swish... Soon you find yourself wrapped snugly in the sound of the waves as if you were tucked up in bed, enjoying the most relaxing lie-in ever.

Nothing should ever deliberately disturb such a moment. Nothing. But something always does. Normally, let's face it, it's your mother, calling you to wake up for one pointless reason or another. In this case it was...

"Professor! Hello! Allow me to introduce myself. My name is Johannsen. Blurt Johannsen. I've been studying your work and I must say... I *do* like the cut of your jib."

It was as if someone had suddenly switched on a radio, tuned to an over-enthusiastic advert. The voice jolted both Lucy and the Professor from their relaxation and both sat bolt-upright mid-way through this introduction, trying to open their eyes despite the suddenly-unbearable glare of the sun.

Once they could finally see again, both were surprised to find a tartan cowboy (of sorts) standing before them. He wore a tartan ten-gallon hat, a plain white T-shirt and his thumbs rested in the front pockets of his tartan trousers. He also wore dark glasses and a big smile. Beyond that, there wasn't much to say that would describe the man. He wasn't tall. He wasn't short. He wasn't fat or thin or dark or light. His age wasn't immediately apparent.

Once Mr. Johannsen noted that he had the Professor's attention, he continued.

"...And this here with me, is the lovely Susan," he added, waving an arm at the palm tree immediately to his right.

Professor Crastinator examined the tree, briefly wondering if it might be a person in fancy dress. But the tree *was* a tree and it had almost certainly been standing there long-before *he* had set foot on the island. He turned to Lucy, who shrugged. She had no idea what was going on either.

Since Blurt was obviously waiting for a reaction, the Professor paused, then turned and saluted the palm tree.

"How do you do, Susan?" he asked.

Blurt smiled.

"She doesn't talk much" he laughed aloud at some private joke. "So tell me Professor -What brings you to Linsi? I don't believe we've seen you here before? I've been here many, many times myself. I'm a regular here I guess you could say. Yes indeed. I don't think anyone stays at Linsi any more frequently than I do. Never go anywhere else, me. But it *is* great to finally get the chance to meet you. Say! -Are you hungry? We should do lunch. Ok by you? Fine! We'll do that!"

Blurt bent down and briskly shook Lucy's hand, then turned to walk away.

"I'll go get the waiter," he added before directly stepping off the ledge and disappearing under the water in the pool with a large splash.

Lucy and the Professor stared at each other in stunned silence. What had just happened? Suddenly there was a sound from somewhere far away, out of sight.

"Yap yap yap yap yap," it went, as it came closer.

"Yap yap yap yap yap."

A small, hairy Shih-Tzu dog came bounding into view.

"YAP YAP YAP YAP YAP."

Without stopping, it too jumped straight in to the pool in the middle of the rippled circles that formed above Blurt after he sunk.

INTRODUCTION TO MR. BLURT JOHANNSEN

Linsi was first developed as a party and/or getaway island for celebrities and business tycoon types back in the 1920s. It was at that time that the infamous and slightly unusual Linsi Laws were first drafted -each one developed by bored socialites with nothing better to do.

CONSTITUTION OF THE ISLAND OF LINSI

1. Nobody is allowed go to bed before 10:37pm. If you are sick you can sleep outdoors (by the pool or wherever), otherwise you must party.

2. If your name is David or Kevin or John or Jack or Gillian or Mary or anything like Mary (e.g. Marie, Maria, Maura, etc.) then you must sing for each meal in front of at least seven people.

3. Only those who can successfully complete two full cartwheels together are allowed eat meat on weekdays. Everyone else must have vegetables or fish or wait until weekends. Turnips are illegal at all times, except before noon on the first Sunday of every month.

4. Murder is <u>legal</u> if you give twenty-six-and-a-half hours notice, in writing, to your proposed victim. Having given that notice, you must not impede or restrict (or have someone or something else impede or restrict) the movements of your victim.

5. If you must steal, leave an uncooked sausage in the place of whatever you are taking.

6. Nobody allergic to red onion or pickles or yellow peppers is allowed show their nose on Linsi. They can remain on the island, but their nose must be covered at all times.

7. If more than three people find you boring, you must leave the island at once -unless you can keep a hoola-hoop in the air, using just your hips, for longer than sixty seconds.

8. No animals can be tied-up or encaged on Linsi Island. They must be free to roam, on pain of death.
(This law was later amended to exclude Bengal Tigers after the famous poet, Derek Rust, brought one with him, with disastrous consequences, whilst visiting in the seventies.)

9. No appointments or dates can be made on Linsi for a time that is divisible by five
e.g. Instead of meeting at 8pm or 2:45 or 11:20, you can arrange to meet at 8:01 or at 2:47 or 11:18.

10. No lists are to be made with an even number of points. Anyone found making a "Top Ten" list on anything must be shot at the first dawn following twenty-six-and-a-half hours notice. Make lists of nine or eleven if you must make a list.

11. Inventing a nonsensical eleventh point, just to avoid being caught making a list of ten is <u>not permissible</u>.

Blurt Johannsen had made hundreds of millions from selling his toenail-clippings internet site before the Dotcom-Bubble had burst. Since then, he wandered the planet in search of something to give meaning to his life. He already had everything money could buy, but there seemed to be nothing left for him to actually *do*.

Besides *meaning*, there was only one other thing Blurt craved but couldn't have: His eyesight.

He used to be one of those children that sat too close to the television. This in itself was bad enough for his eyes, but it wasn't the reason he went blind. He also watched television during every spare moment of the day. That too was bad for him, but in itself, didn't explain his blindness... One day, whilst watching a movie, a man and a woman started kissing on-screen. Being the sensible young boy that he was, young Blurt had no time for that kind of carry-on. So, as he had always done before, he quickly raised his hands to block his eyes from the offending kiss. Unfortunately, he had forgotten he was eating his dinner at the time, and so he failed to put his knife and fork down first!

But that was years earlier. Now Blurt had a more pressing problem. Namely that he couldn't swim. Being the resourceful chap that he was however, he at once recalled the months of sur-vival training he had gone through at management school. This taught him to never panic in an emergency, but to sit back and do nothing until someone else fixes the problem.

"*After all*" (the management course instructor had told him), "*the sun will rise again tomorrow whether you fix the problem or not.*"

Thankfully, his little dog, Susan, had not attended the same course. She was attending a guide-dog training course at that time. The instructors had informed Blurt that she was too small, but Blurt was someone who never let go of an idea once he came up with it. Susan was going to be his guide-dog, he had decided. It simply wasn't good enough to explain to him how something wasn't possible.

"*IMPOSSIBLE*" (his management training course had taught him) "*is just another way to say I AM A FAILURE!*"

Susan wasn't the best seeing-eye dog ever. For one thing, her six-inch height off the ground meant that she simply didn't *see* many dangers and obstacles until they were right on top of her. A sprightly young Shih-Tzu can easily zigzag around the feet of oncoming pedestrians or even leap from the path of an oncoming automobile, but a blind man on the other end of her leash tends not to come out of it as unscathed. Blurt had suffered many bumps, bruises, broken limbs and pairs of dirty shoes, but he would not admit that Susan was a bad choice as a guide dog.

Because of his blindness and keenness to try out new things, he always said he was braver than anyone he had ever known: Everyone else did things with the help of their eyesight - but *he* did it all with no eyes! If he got rid of the dog simply because she was the cause of a broken bone or two, that would be seen (by Blurt himself) as cowardice. And Blurt was no coward. He would not surrender. Never!

What Susan lacked in stature and ability (and often in common-sense), she made up for in loyalty and feistiness. She may have been taking advantage of the eighth Linsi Law when she failed to stick by her master, but nevertheless she didn't think twice about rushing to his aid once the danger appeared.

She leapt into that swimming pool without a thought to her own safety: Her master had gone, so she must follow. But how does a tiny Shih-Tzu rescue a drowning man? -*With her teeth*, of course. Under the water, she bit the man's nose. At once, Blurt flapped his arms and wiggled his body and threw his legs down-ward. Finding the bottom of the pool, he sprung back, leapt up, then coughed and spluttered and waved in every direction as his head broke the water. He was still waving and yelling when he finally realised that his head and shoulders were totally out of the pool and that he was standing in no more than four feet of water.

A few seconds passed in relative silence as Blurt waited to hear who or what was nearby. Feeling the wall behind him, he turned around to face where the Professor and the girl were sitting. They still didn't know what to make of this show and neither had yet realised that the man in the pool, wearing sunglasses, couldn't see.

"So how's your belly for spuds?" he asked with a broad grin, whilst rubbing his nose.

FOUR FOR THE ROAD

"If you're blind, how come you knew the Professor was right here?" Lucy Lucey brazenly enquired as they finished the meal that Mr. Johannsen was kind enough to pay for.

Despite him being a bit of a loudmouth show-off, she found herself actually *liking* the brash blind man. This made her angry, though she didn't know why. Blurt smiled.

"Kid," he said.

Some people can say "kid" and make it sound like a slap in the face, as in "kid, go away and don't annoy me." Other people say it as a term of affection and it really does mean something nice -as in "kid, I like your style." The problem for Lucy was that Blurt said nothing *except* "kid", despite his non-stop talking throughout their meal. He had spoken constantly about himself and his "management training" and his toenail clipping internet site and his miniature guide-dog, Susan. Now he just said "kid" and smiled when she most-wanted to hear what he'd say next. What made Lucy even angrier though was that she still liked him. Immediately, she liked him even *more* now for the way he had simply said "kid."

Susan was the only one still eating. She was standing on the table with her face stuck in the remains of Blurt's dinner. Lucy and the Professor stared at the small, hairy dog packing away so much food. She seemed to be eating more than her total bodyweight.

"Oh for God's sake!" declared Lucy, as she noticed the quiet tear that was trickling down the Prof's cheek.

Clearly he was thinking of his own dog. She rolled her eyes just as her mother would do if Lucy had walked into the kitchen with blood dripping from her elbow. She was too angry just at that moment to feel sorry for him. If he was going to cry like that every time he clapped eyes on a dog, this was going to be one long weepy journey.

Blurt was confused. He had been eager to please the Professor's young friend. He *envied* her, travelling the world with the great inventor. He had thought that as an elder, he should smile and say nice things to her like "kid." But apparently this upset her. Why had she said "oh for God's sake" like that? Had he offended her in some way? He really didn't know how to talk to young children.

"Excuse me Lucy," he said. "You did say you were nine years old didn't you?"

"Yes," answered Lucy, unable to stop herself adding a further question. "Why?"

"It's just you seem... older," he shrugged.

Lucy smiled, blushed and said no more. After a few seconds silence, Blurt continued.

"I really envy you kid" he said, and meant it. "You get to travel with this man of great vision. I might be blind, but even *I* can see what a gift that is. You should be grateful. I hope you are."

Looking briefly to the frail-looking, hunched Professor, she turned back to Blurt.

"He's a bigger idiot than you are!" she informed the blind man with a laugh. "He can't decide if he should make one knot in his shoes or two. He hasn't a clue!"

Blurt was stunned. Even Susan took her snout from out of the grub to see if the girl had lost her marbles entirely.

"That's no way to talk about Professor Crastinator!" insisted Blurt. "This man helped change the world! You don't know how lucky you are! Without him there'd be no high-rise fields or Bridges-On-Demand or silent hair-dryers or Melon Controllers or so many other things! This man has been an inspiration to me and to millions of others! You can't talk about *him* like that!" he declared.

Now it was Lucy's turn to be confused (not to mention embarrassed). She had spoken in a half-joking manner. She didn't think it'd be taken so seriously. She hadn't meant to call either of them an idiot really, but after finding herself blushing like that, the most natural reaction was to laugh and to call everybody an idiot. It *had* seemed like a good way to escape the giddiness she was feeling at the time. She also felt embarrassed now because what she had said (albeit in jest) had been quite correct and that what this man was chastising her for was incorrect, although she couldn't tell *him* that.

"...But it's true I'm afraid," confirmed the Professor, at once reliev-
ing the pressure. "I'm in a spot of bother at the moment and I *have*
been in a bit of a tizz. ...Not myself at all -I haven't been for some
time now... We need to find Flavius Flocky Nocky. I've lost my dog
you see and we think Flocky Nocky might know where he is."

Blurt seemed quite concerned with their plight, now no
longer upset at the young girl.

"I'd be lost without my dog too," he said, rubbing the large potato
on his plate.

"*Doctor* Flocky Nocky?" he asked, after giving the problem some
further thought. "Doesn't he live on the other side of the planet?"

"Yes," answered the Professor with a nod, "but this *is* the other
side of the planet."

Blurt shook his head.

"Not from here it's not," he declared.

The statement was a revelation to the old man and to Lucy.
Everybody knew that Dr. Flocky Nocky lived "on the other side of
the planet," but nobody seemed to have considered which side it
was they should start from in order to get there.

They both buried their heads in their hands at the same
time.

"We'll have to widen our search" said the Professor.

"This could take forever!" sighed Lucy.

One trip into space had been enough for one day. If they
were to do justice to searching for Ooyay and Flocky Nocky, it
could take months just to go to each possible island now. The
school tour was only going to take a week. Her parents would be
worried if she didn't come home by then.

"I'll take you home first thing" said the Professor, as though reading her mind.

"No!" Lucy protested, but only half-heartedly.

At that point she felt helpless. This adventure was proving
too much for a nine year old and it now looked more impossible
than ever. Being in space was possibly the greatest experience of
her life to date, but she wasn't certain she could do it every day for

weeks or possibly months on end. She was out of her depth and now she knew it.

"There is an island..." said Blurt now, remembering something he had heard. "It's a place I've been meaning to check out for some time. I've heard talk of a strange man there with many strange objects and inventions. The more I think about it, *he* could well be Dr. Flocky Nocky. I hadn't thought of it before."

An excited look passed between the Professor and the girl. It was the first positive piece of news they had heard since setting out. Neither one needed to ask the other if they should go for it. Both called out at the same time.

"Where is it!?" they cried.

FROM THE FRYING PAN INTO THE FIRE

When Matthew finally woke up, days had passed. He had missed his brother's funeral. Unfortunately there was even more bad news awaiting the young eleven year old: His father was also now dead. Nobody would tell him exactly what had happened, but as time passed, he pieced some things together... His dad had blamed himself for not being there when Mucus died. At some stage, his mother had also blamed his father aloud, in front of others. They said it was a heart attack. Matthew heard half-whispers of suicide. He didn't know what to believe in the end, but found it hard to think that his hard-working, life-loving father could possibly have taken his own life. It must have been a heart attack, he concluded.

Strangely, Matthew found the loss of two family members easier to handle than the loss of one. It was painful to think of either of them for a long while, but any time he felt sad for one of them, he would automatically chastise himself for not feeling as sorry for the other. This drew the sad thoughts further from his mind.

Also, he took comfort in the knowledge that, wherever they now were, they at least were with each other.

Joan came home for a brief period, before setting off again to work on her foreign trains. Mike immersed himself in his mechanical work, opening a garage in the city. Jenny too returned eventually to her job in the big house. She was never to bring home another strawberry cake like she had done all those years before.

This left Penny and Matthew to take care of their mother, who had taken to bed after the death of her husband and youngest-born. It was all too much. Her heart was broken in too many pieces. No amount of help or coaxing or pleas from her two near-teenage children could pull her from her stupor. For months, she just lay there and ate soup when they spooned it into her mouth.

Penny insisted that Matthew continue with his schooling while she stayed home to mind their mum. For his part, Matthew didn't need too much convincing. He was relieved to be able to escape each day and usually dragged his heels when the time came to come home. The teachers marvelled at his enthusiasm in signing up for any and all extra study-sessions or voluntary extracurricular activities. He was the star pupil.

At home however, if Martin's illness had held the family back, his death seemed to have ripped it apart. The older children rarely called home now and seemed not to want to hear when Penny continued to claim that their mother needed psychiatric care. Increasingly, mother cried out for her husband and baby boy.

"Martin. My lovely boy," she would suddenly scream out into the silent, dark night.

"Emmett, I'm sorry!" she'd yell as she pulled tufts of hair from her head.

Eventually she stopped screaming and stopped crying and more or less stopped eating altogether. Penny might get two spoonfuls of soup into her per day if she was lucky. Being so young, she wasn't to know that this was not enough to sustain their mother. Penny was someone who simply dropped her head and got on with whatever needed doing. As far as she was aware, her mother was now in no pain, so there was no reason to call a doctor.

At around the same time as their mother's death, Mike was having some difficulty at work. The garage was attached to the back of a large, old cinema called *"The Flock-In Occulorum,"* which showed strange (and often twisted) movies from all over the world. However, the market for strange movies was drying up. Fewer people came than ever before and the cinema was quickly going out of business. The place was becoming run-down and needed extensive renovation. Its owner (and Mike's landlord), Pierce Kratinsky, no longer had any option. The whole building (including the garage) would have to be sold.

For Mike, business was booming. He had taken on six new mechanics and had three vans constantly on the road, towing and mending broken-down vehicles. He didn't want to move. Neither did Mr. Kratinsky.

As the oldest son, Mike found himself inheriting the old family home. Neither Penny nor Matthew wanted to live there any longer. For the first time in years, it seemed things were beginning to fall into place for the Cratchetts. The house was sold. Mike bought a part-share in the Flock-in Occulorum (which paid for renovations) and Matthew and Penny went to live with Mike above the garage, at the back of the cinema.

FROM THE FIRE INTO THE FRYING PAN

Nobody ever accused Ooyay of being stupid. That's because he was never stupid. But shortly after Seamus Shafford returned, Ooyay realised something that did make him feel slightly foolish.

Seamus ran to the syringe that was still stuck in the kitten's paw and quickly yanked it out. He then opened the cage and burst into tears as he hugged the upset little tabby.

"Oh my word what have I done!" he cried. "I'm *so* sorry little kitty. I didn't mean it. Please forgive me. How *could* I have been so callous?"

Just then a big man in a chunky red jacket burst in, carrying a large wooden box.

"Only one for now Seamus," said the man, dumping the box on the floor with a heavy thud.

"How dare you do that!" Seamus Shafford at once complained, tenderly putting the kitten back into its cage. "I've told you before not to drop it like that. You have no right to be so cruel!"

"Whatever..." shrugged the man in the chunky red jacket, as he turned and walked from the room without another word.

Seamus now ran to the box and lifted the lid. From his vantage point, Ooyay could clearly see the black mongrel that was sitting quietly inside, gazing up at the man with the milk bottle glasses and white lab coat.

"Ah!" said Seamus, bending to pick up the dog. "And here at last is the star of the show!" He held him in the air to take a good look and to check him for signs of mistreatment. "You seem to be in good enough health my boy."

He now walked to the cage below Ooyay's. Placing him inside, he continued to speak.

"Allow me to introduce myself -My name is Seamus Shafford and I will likely be... looking after you... for a few days."

Closing the latch on the cage door, he quickly looked around, then turned again to the new arrival.

"You like what you see here?" he asked the dog. "...A little primitive I agree, but it serves its purpose. I can see you are a trusting little fellow. That's nice. I hope I can prove myself worthy of that trust. We'll do all that we can to find your owner and to have you back home as quickly as possible!"

Throughout this one-way conversation, Ooyay had slowly begun to feel a little silly. But only now did he truly wish he could slap his forehead the way humans do when they realise that they had been wrong about something. This was not a place for diabolical experiments, but simply a refuge for stray animals! His mind had run rampant at the possibilities of where he had landed and who might have been responsible (Flocky Nocky being top of the list), when all along he had been captured by the dog warden! He suddenly wanted to sing and shout for joy. Of course he didn't give away his little secret quite so easily. This Seamus character now seemed like quite a nice fellow, but who could predict how anyone might react when confronted with a talking dog? Ooyay knew human nature. Most human beings would suddenly think only of bags of money if they met a talking dog. Such thoughts would not see him returned to his rightful owner any time soon.

"My, what deep, thoughtful eyes you've got!" Seamus was now looking directly at Ooyay, head pressed against the cage. "Quite beautiful," he added, opening the door and reaching for the blue dog.

"I'll have to give you a scrub down I think... remove some of that paint. Did those baddies rough you up? Yes they did, didn't they?"

Seamus now rubbed noses with the blue dog. Ooyay knew such activity couldn't possibly be allowed by the rules for fear of infection, but it seemed that Seamus Shafford was too caring and *involved* with animals to bother with the rules.

Ooyay was carried out of the large room, into a reception area where another man stood behind a desk. A teenage boy had just walked in the front door, with a small black and white terrier following behind.

"I found him there on the street," said the boy. "I think he's sick."

Seamus stopped and looked-on as the other man beckoned the dog onward, past the counter.

"Go on!" said the boy with a nod of his head. The dog immediately followed after the man.

"There's a small fee for admitting a dog," explained the man. "You don't know who owns him do you?"

"No," answered the boy. "I just found him."

Ooyay could see that the slow-moving, clearly-unwell dog had stopped to look back at the boy one last time. The teenager and the dog quietly looked in each other's eyes, before the dog slowly turned and followed the man into the room that Ooyay had just left. As the boy reached for the handle on the front door, he quickly brushed his cheek, then walked out. Ooyay distinctly heard a sniffle before the door closed behind him.

Seamus too had stood and watched the same scene, but now the spring on the front door caused a loud slam to echo through the reception area. Both Ooyay and Seamus seemed to react with a jolt. On Ooyay's part, this jolt coincided with the real-isation that he had missed his chance to escape. The front door had been wide open all the time! He could have leapt to freedom at any second! Instead he had been distracted and become too engrossed in the sight of that dog and young boy. Now Ooyay tried jumping from Seamus's arms, but Seamus himself also seemed to have woken up with the slamming door. Casually readjusting his grip, he carried on through another door and down some steps to a sweet-scented basement. In one corner of this basement, bubbles decorated a small metal bath of water. Above this bath hung shelves full of cleaning and washing products in glass jars and bot-tles and cardboard packaging. A scissors, brush and hand-mirror were within easy reach on the bottom shelf.

Again Ooyay struggled to break free, but Seamus was obviously a seasoned dog handler. He seemed to know all the right moves. With a simple tuck of a rear leg, he easily folded Ooyay into the water and immediately started brushing the dog's head with the brush from the shelf. At first, Ooyay found it to be quite hard and unpleasant, but as he relaxed himself, it soon felt ...not exactly discomforting ...almost *enjoyable* even really.

"There now," said Seamus softly, "it's coming off already."

Ooyay had to smile at the thought of this man thinking he was covered in blue paint. He had been a dark blue colour since always and it was not about to wash off with any amount of hard scrubbing. Still, it did feel kind of nice now in the water and it wasn't too cold. He'd just have to grin and bear it.

Seamus Shafford paused as he looked again into the blue

dog's jet-black pupils. Once more he was struck by how deep those eyes looked, as though he might tumble into them and fall forever. He could easily lose himself in those big black sparkling jewels.

"Oh my," whispered Seamus, quite taken by the unexpected beauty in the blue dog with the crown of suds on his head. "I shouldn't really, but I'll have to give you a name. Tell me, what do they call you little fellow? Hmm?"

Feeling somewhat mischievous, Ooyay pretended to yawn. He opened his mouth wide, closed his eyes, shook his head and said "Oooo-yay!"

"Oh my!" Seamus gasped. "You are the tired little fellow, aren't you? I'll have to get you out of there before you fall asleep on me! That's what I'll call you ...Sleepy!"

He pulled the blue dog from the bath and stood back as he allowed him to stand on the table in order to shake himself down. Ooyay played his part. He shook hard and enjoyed the quick wet flapping of his ears and tail. Since he didn't really have a furry or hairy coat like other dogs, he had never made a big splash while shaking himself in this way. Still though, most of the simple pleasures in life are free. Ringing the wetness from his body with a quick, sharp shake was about as much pleasure as he could hope to have under the circumstances.

Just then, a loud rumble started up at the other end of the basement. It was quite dark in that area, but Ooyay could guess that the orange glow coming from behind a slightly-open large metal door was the fire from the building's boiler. Immediately he realised the use to which these large flames were most likely put - Dead animals needed to be disposed of somehow.

This realisation sent a shiver down his spine. How long did he have before they would toss him into this fiery furnace? Didn't animal homes have a policy of 'terminating' unwanted and unclaimed pets after a certain period? How much time did he have? A couple of days? A week? He stared now at Seamus, trying to figure out if maybe he should speak up.

If Seamus had only taken a *little* more time at that point to once again look into Ooyay's eyes, the dog would probably have said something and most-likely saved himself. But instead Seamus saw the shivering dog before him and ran to get a towel.

Just as he was about to wrap up the dog, Ooyay suddenly

leapt from his spot on the table and knocked over almost all the contents of the overhead shelves, most of which tumbled into the bathwater. The small mirror fell and smashed on the cold, hard basement floor. Ooyay dropped clumsily to the ground and was busy scrabbling to find his feet when the large towel landed on his head, blocking his view and pathway to freedom.

Once Seamus scooped up the blue dog, now wrapped in the towel, he noticed the broken mirror on the ground. Standing quietly for a few seconds, he examined the pieces before turning again to face the dog, whose head was now sticking through the wrinkled cloth in his arms.

"Oh," muttered Seamus softly. "That's seven years bad luck you know!"

He was visibly upset at the development and said nothing further the whole way back to the cage.

"Seven more than is planned for me now" thought Ooyay sarcastically to himself.

"There you go, Sleepy," whispered Seamus as he unwrapped the blue dog and placed him into his enclosure.

No sooner had the animal-handler gone than Ooyay opened his mouth wide. In the folds of his long tongue (which he now carefully unfurled) he had stored a piece of broken mirror.

It wasn't easy, but he managed to slot this mirror between two toes on one of his paws, then placed this paw up to the thin metal bars in his cage. Using the mirror now as he had seen them used in countless prison movies (to see left or right of a cell) he at once spotted Seamus in the outer reception area, talking on the phone. Seamus had removed his glasses, which caused his eyes to look very small, and was making large gestures with his hands as he talked animatedly to someone on the other end of the line. Now Seamus Shafford pointed back into the room with the cages and wiggled his finger as he spoke. Then he wiggled at the door to the basement and made what looked like brushing motions. His free hand waved in the air, palm-upward, before snapping back in the direction of the room with the cages once more. Ooyay quickly pulled his paw back to hide the mirror as Seamus turned to look into the room.

Although he hadn't heard what Seamus had been saying, it was obvious to Ooyay that he was talking about him. What did *that* mean? What *could* that mean? For now, he had no idea, but resolved then and there to escape this place at the earliest opportunity.

HARRUMPH!

Imagine opening your eyes to the sight of a six-inch-high dog floating silently past, upside down, not a foot from your nose. This was the first sight that greeted Professor Crastinator as he pulled the safety goggles from his face. The Shih-Tzu, Susan, was staring into space (literally) as she glided around the Bullet. Her long, tossed hair stood out at strange angles, although somehow her eyes appeared to bulge even further. She was mesmerised by the experience, even though it was obviously one of many CAT bounces she had been on with her owner, Blurt Johannsen.

Susan wasn't the only one with transfixed, bulging eyes in this ATV. Everyone else wore the same eye-popping expression - even Blurt (who still had on his own sunglasses and couldn't even open his eyelids) appeared as though his eyebrows were now stapled to the uppermost part of his forehead.

In fact few people ever get used to being in space to the point where simple, everyday objects and details become boring. Everything you've ever witnessed and taken for granted suddenly magnifies and seems breathtaking for the first time ever. The inability of your brain to know which way is up (or to even realise that there is no longer any "up" or "down" as we know it) takes a lot of getting used to. For the Professor, it reminded him of the experience of waking in his upside down bedroom -except for the fact that *that* disorientating experience usually lasted only a few seconds. Here in space, dizziness, giddiness and an inability to look on anything in only one way was the norm. Ooyay would love this, he knew.

The sight of people or (sometimes) animals suspended upside down or at a sharp angle to your own position is hard to fathom, but there is a seemingly-infinite number of other, more basic, fantastic experiences to be discovered at every moment of your stay outside the Earth's gravitational pull:

Your toes float around in your shoes -no longer pulled flat onto the inside sole. It might seem like a small thing, but it's the small things you have always taken for granted that you now notice the most, because it's all *different* when in space. You need to re-learn almost everything you've ever learnt about almost anything. Your *skin* seems like it pulls in every direction and no direction all at the same time -it feels as though the skin is no longer holding in all your blood and guts and bones, but that everything is just floating around in pieces all over the place. At times you would swear that your stomach was in your head or that your heart was in your feet or that your knees were moving around from head to toe. There is no constant "tug" from Mother Earth, letting you know where all your bits and pieces are located at any one time.

Many people to this day still don't like such out-of-this-world experiences. Thankfully there is an option for these individuals: Most two-or-more-level Bullets have at least one level where the NS-Mag remains activated throughout, thus keeping everybody firmly in place in their seats. However, it cannot escape the attention of even these people that the blood inside their bodies feels like it is now flowing in every direction at once. It's like your blood vessels have disappeared and there is room for this somehow-soothing red liquid to seep through everywhere and to rejuvenate the parts of your body that you never even knew *needed* rejuvenation. You can feel the blood rushing here, there and everywhere -and it feels *good*.

Even a nine year old like Lucy Lucey could feel stronger and quicker and lighter and more able to deal with any occurrences up here in space than she would ever think possible on Earth. If she hadn't been so busy examining the feeling it gave her to hold one shoulder in her hand as she rode an imaginary bicycle in circles, she would certainly have laughed at her earlier belief that space travel was too much for her. In fact, space travel, she now felt with every inch of her body, was the *absolutely* best experience it would ever be possible to have.

The first CAT Bounce had been pretty traumatic from start to finish. The second proved not much easier in terms of having a bumpy ride out (even though they were now travelling in Blurt's padded, leather-interior Bullet), but the reward in terms of the freedom you feel once you reach space itself, was as big and bold and as bursting-with-joy as ever -If not even *more* so the second time.

"Well done *again* Blurt," said an excited female computer voice after they reached their destination and once more returned to Earth.

"Your bravery knows no bounds. We have now landed in... Har-rumph!"

Lucy looked to the Professor to see if he was going to say something. He wasn't, but he did look like he was amused at the voice message commenting on Blurt's bravery. Sensing a quietness, Blurt spoke up.

"You're probably laughing at my message," he smiled. "Well, it's true! Look at me! You know that in space it feels like your body is in bits and that you've burst into pieces. For you, it's easy to just *look* and see where your elbows are, or to make sure your legs are still attached to your body. No matter where I go, I need to feel my way with my hands, but at least on land, I know my feet are on the ground so that gives me *some* bearing. Up in space, though, it's like I'm blinder than ever -not in a *totally* bad way -it can be quite pleasant in fact. But still, I tell you it's scary up there with your eyes closed. Try it sometime!"

He did go on at times, did Blurt.

"You have a point," agreed the Professor after a brief pause. Lucy too nodded in agreement. Again, she could think of nothing to add. Blurt was good at covering every angle, she noted appreciatively.

Outside, they found that the island's Bullet-Hole was situated on a path, halfway up a mountain. They could go up, or they could go down (not being in space now, they could easily tell which was which.) The upward path appeared to lead to a snowy peak. The path down the mountain seemed to be lined with grass and flowers. There was another downward option, but that entailed walking off the unguarded edge of the cliff, down to the jagged rocks and crashing waves below. Since the path itself would have been wide enough for an elephant to comfortably walk along, there wasn't much danger of falling off by accident.

"Let's go downward" said the Professor, pointing down the hill.

Lucy looked at him in amazement. Was *this* the same Professor she had been journeying with all this time? Here was the first *decision* he had made since they met. And he made it seemingly without a thought. And from the way he announced that decision it was clear that nobody would disagree with it or with him. It was like when Lucy's mother burnt the Christmas turkey one time. She cried for half an hour, not knowing what to do. But then her dad came home, having collected some relatives for dinner. At once he saw the situation and announced *"Right -let's go to the hotel!"* Nobody disagreed or was upset at the decision. Everybody knew it made sense. Even Beauty Lucey was relieved that Aunty Madge would now not have the opportunity to sniff at her Brussels sprouts-on-toast side dish.

"Blurt! Come back you're gonna fall!" cried Lucy when she saw that Susan had led him dangerously close to the precipice.

The little dog hadn't done it deliberately of course, but her natural curiosity had brought her to check out the drop. Blurt had cooperated by following along on the other end of the leash. He now turned around and walked back to the others, pulling his guide dog behind.

"Keep in by the wall Blurt!" suggested Lucy, pressing him toward the mountain wall.

"Here Blurt," she added, taking his hand and pushing it out to touch the rock-face that marked the safe edge of the downward path.

They followed Professor Crastinator all the way down. Lucy assisted the blind man's walk with probably a few more *This-way-Blurt*s than were strictly necessary, but Blurt didn't mind. He quite enjoyed the attention, even if it was from a solitary nine year old.

He was rarely awarded the proper attention he believed was due for his courage, endurance, perseverance, outgoing affable nature, cheery disposition, keen dress-sense (as he was told), fun, interesting and exciting personality, good looks, or even for his wads of cash. People tended to not approach him (possibly admiring him from afar, he guessed) *because* he was blind -this infuriated him no end. He *lived* for attention, but was always disappointed with what little was given him.

Blurt had always been an outsider for as long as he could remember. He loved life and loved living and he loved people, but still he knew he didn't quite *fit-in* anywhere. Since selling his business, now more than ever he felt that he had to find something *more*. He didn't know what or where that might be, but he was determined to keep going until he found the place where he truly belonged.

DANCING IN THE STREET

"Halt! Who goes there?"

A large man with a spear suddenly leapt in front of the group as they reached the bottom of the mountain. Lucy couldn't remember *ever* seeing a spear being used outside a museum, but now it appeared to be the weapon of choice -amongst island people at least.

Bulging chests also seemed to be the norm for islanders. This particular islander had a chest the size of a mountain and he clearly now pushed it out as far as it could go as he posed with his pointed spear in one hand, the other showing a wall-like flat-palm that is the universal signal to "halt." His legs were spread and slightly bent at the knees. His face betrayed no humour under a sheet of icy seriousness.

The man's clearly-practised Olympian stance would have been a hilarious sight to the visitors if it wasn't for the fact that he was the only one carrying a weapon.

Blurt, who (obviously) hadn't seen the man with the big chest or his spear, stepped forward, waving his hand in greeting.

"'Tis me," said Blurt, "big chief Wibble Wobble! Take me to your leader!"

He spoke in a deadpan tone that mocked the other man's seriousness. Not knowing how to react to such a bold reply, the man silently eyed Blurt and the rest of the party, as he considered what to do. Most other people would have read Blurt's outburst as a sarcastic, joke response, but not this man.

"Follow me," he announced at last, before turning on his heels and strutting purposefully away along the path, without waiting to make sure the visitors were in tow.

The Professor shrugged at Lucy, once more unsure what to do. This time however, Blurt took the lead.

"Well, what are we waiting for? You heard the man! Follow him! Let's go!" said Blurt, arms out, waiting for direction.

"This way Blurt" said Lucy, as she led him away by the hand, Susan in tow. Again Professor Crastinator shrugged before following on.

They soon reached the edge of a mud-hut village. For some time they had been hearing jungle drums and singing and whooping, but hadn't seen another person until now.

Now the group came upon some kind of festival or celebration amongst the villagers. A large group of people sat on the ground in the village square, while one person danced in circles around a great bonfire. Nobody took any notice of the new arrivals.

One person played drums, though it sounded like a whole group of drummers were playing, he moved so quickly and played them so well. In fact, it sounded as though each drummer in this non-existent drumming band *each* played a separate tune, all of which (somehow) managed to come together to form one song.

The dancer kept everyone enthralled with her movements and perfect rhythm. If it sounded like five or six people were drumming, it looked as though this dancer had a movement for each beat of every drum. She appeared to be stepping to an Irish jig with her feet, while her shoulders and arms waved and performed breakdancing, as her hips gyrated like they were swaggering to rock n' roll. All the while, the dancer's fingers spread and waved and wiggled in every direction. Her eyes and ears and nose and mouth and tongue danced all over her head. Her belly cascaded like the waves of the sea and her knees knocked together in a chicken-dance effect. There wasn't an inch of the woman's body that wasn't dancing to its own song in its own unique manner.

Only one villager was sitting off the ground on a kind of bamboo-pedestal. She was a large woman in her fifties. Her body was covered in flowers and feathers -red, yellow, blue and white. A headdress, made of black and white feathers stuck into a straw crown, flowed over her head and down her back like a lion's mane.

The music beat to a crashing finale and the dancer kicked somersaults over, through and out the other side of the fire as she continued to shake and roll in every direction. At last the breath-taking song and dance ended -abruptly, like the bursting of a balloon. Everybody remained in their places and began yelling.

"HARRUMPH HARRUMPH!" they called, clearly pleased with the performance.

Lucy couldn't contain herself any longer. She applauded as hard and as quickly as she could manage. She shrieked with joy and admiration at what she had witnessed. The crowd stopped their harrumphing and turned as one to look at this odd child hitting her hands together, making strange high-pitched noises. Some of the villagers looked concerned, as though they feared Lucy was ill. Others seemed amused. Still more appeared impatient or even slightly angry at her antics. Lucy slowed her clap and quietened down as she noticed everybody staring. Silence descended on the crowded village square for the first time since their arrival.

Blurt whispered to the professor.

"Point me at the leader if you see him," he instructed.

Professor Crastinator turned Blurt to face the woman on the pedestal, but before he could open his mouth, Susan walked ahead, pulling Blurt behind. Making the most of the situation, he brazenly stepped forward with a cheery wave.

"Hello there! Johannsen's the name," he began.

Management Training had taught Blurt to attack rather than to wait to be spoken-to. "*Silence is the first sign of weakness,*" he had been informed by his training master, Elder Bell. "*If you fill a silence with the first thing that comes into your head, you disarm the other party, placing you in command of the situation.*"

However, as Blurt walked toward the pedestal, Susan had drifted slightly toward a plate of food at the feet of a small, bald man who was sitting on the ground with others, to the right of the platform.

The man was clearly surprised to find the shaded, tartan cowboy address him directly.

"This is some swanky shindig you put on for us," continued the blind man. "I must congratulate your ingenuity -and I use that word frankly because it's the first one that comes to mind, I don't mind telling you. ...And I can tell you don't mind me telling you either. In fact, you're my kind of chief, chief. Put it *there!*"

Blurt extended his arm for the bald man, who now looked around, unsure what to make of this attention. He glanced at the decorated woman on the pedestal before reaching to take the cowboy's hand. As they clasped and shook, the crowd harrumphed once more.

"Harrumph Harrumph" they harrumphed.

"You see further than the wind over many tall trees," said the bald man, pulling himself to his feet with Blurt's grasp.

"I am like wind," agreed Blurt. "I travel everywhere in search of nostrils, that I may be inhaled like breath and like truth itself."

"And you find truth no matter where you travel, no doubt," nodded the villager, who somehow seemed to know what Blurt was talking about (even if Blurt himself didn't).

"Tell me Johannsen," he continued, "How come you approached me and not our most-favoured person here before you?" indicating the woman on the pedestal.

Blurt at once removed his glasses for all to look upon his sewn-together eyelids.

"I need no eyes to see truth!" he declared. Everyone gasped in awe and harrumphed all the more.

"Harrumph Harrumph Harrumph," they harrumphed.

Once the harrumphing subsided, the bald man looked to Blurt's companions.

"And who do you bring along with you, Johannsen?" he enquired.

"I bring my trusted guide and Shih-Tzu, Susan," answered Blurt, giving a single, quick tug on the leash.

Susan leapt in the air and into Blurt's waiting arms.

"Harrumph Harrumph," harrumphed the crowd.

"And here I give you, the man himself, Professor Marcus Crastinator!" announced Blurt, spinning around and waving in the air toward the Professor.

"HARRUMPH HARRUMPH HARRUMPH!" The villagers had obviously heard of the great inventor.

"And last, but by no means least," intoned Blurt, getting into the spirit of the occasion, "...is the young and beautiful, Lucy Lucey!"

One, possibly two of the villagers harrumphed. Others sniggered and laughed aloud. Lucy was confused. When confused, Lucy asks questions.

"How come they're laughing?" she asked the bald man as she walked forward.

The bald man dropped his silly grin and forced an overly-serious expression on his face as he answered.

"I'm sorry," he said. "We don't normally hear such names... but yours... is just *too* funny."

He now broke out in a roar of laughter, as did most of the crowd. Again, Lucy was confused. She needed a *little* more information in order to know if she should join in the laughter or be angry at the people of Harrumph!.

"What's so funny about Lucy Lucey?" asked Lucy Lucey, and the laughter grew louder than ever.

The bald man held his waist as he tried to stand straight. Giddiness had made him feel dizzy.

"What's *your* name?" enquired Lucy, now beginning to feel embarrassed and somewhat annoyed at these people.

The bald man stood straight and pushed his cheeks together in an effort to stop himself laughing any further. He knew it was rude to behave in this manner, but he couldn't help himself. He had never heard such a silly name before.

"My name is Granny's Cat," he replied, "and I am the leader of this community."

OOYAY MAKES A MOVE

He waited hours for things to quieten down after the staff had gone home. During this time, Ooyay sat motionless as he considered each of the possible obstacles, problems and outcomes to the action he was about to take.

Was it possible that this "Animal Shelter" was merely a ploy in order to draw him out? If so, it was very well done -the building and its workers all appeared genuine. There was no doubt that Seamus Shafford in particular was an experienced handler who cared for the animals in his charge. Such attention, knowledge and concern could not be faked for very long.

Then again, if someone such as Dr. Flocky Nocky had the forethought to set all this up, he would know that a simple pretender would not fool Ooyay. He would be extra-careful not to arouse the blue dog's suspicions in any way by ensuring that the building and its workers were all as real as could be. In fact, this person would probably pay a *real* Animal Shelter just to look after this particular dog for a few days while *he* monitored proceedings from afar.

Was he even now monitoring Ooyay's behaviour -waiting for him to make some unconventional move? The blue dog counted four cats on the other side of the room that definitely hadn't moved for hours. Might they actually be video cameras wrapped in fur? He stared motionless at these "kitty-cameras" for over half an hour each. Finally he determined that two of them were definitely cats, but the other two were either sleeping or dead if they were not cameras.

There were no proper windows in the room, except for some small slit openings near the ceiling that would not have been big enough even for a little dog like Ooyay to fit through. All but one of these openings now showed nothing but darkness. On the border of the opening furthest to the right, however, Ooyay spotted the faint reflection of a blinking red light. Could this be the light from a camera installed to monitor his progress?

After another hour spent staring at this reflection of a red flashing light, he determined there was no way he could tell why it was there.

A ventilation grille on the wall to his right masked another shadowy location in which it would have been possible to hide a camera or motion-sensor of some kind. Another hour should have been sufficient to sit staring at this, but after doing so, each time he made to turn away, he swore he saw something move from behind the grille. Were his eyes deceiving him in the darkness? Was there a movement that time? ...How about now? When he tilted his head slightly to the left and squinted so much his eyes were nearly shut, it looked like... *maybe*... hmmm... again he couldn't be certain.

Finally, he decided the time had come to make a move. It simply wasn't possible to determine if his actions were being recorded. It was a risk he would have to take -whilst being careful not to do anything *too* spectacular (if at all possible.)

The latch on his cage proved quite difficult to open from the inside. The bars were too close together to allow his teeth or paws or nose through in order to slide it open. So again, the mirror that he had sequestered from the basement came into use. He carefully slotted this mirror between two bars, catching the latch, then pulled it slightly out of its lock. He then had to take the mirror back into the cage and out again through the adjacent bars in order to pull the latch further from the lock. It took a couple of minutes fiddling before the door itself swung silently open.

Ooyay looked now into the dark room without the metal bars interrupting his field of vision. Again, he examined the kitty-cameras. Again, he checked the red flashing light. Again, he squinted at the ventilation grille. Now he noticed more possible surveillance devices: Many of the cages on the far side of the room had little labels or badges on the doors. Could *these* perhaps be cameras?

Wracked with doubt, he was about to leap from his cage when something grabbed his attention out of the corner of his eye: The brown and white bull hound terrier with the golf-ball eye-ball was standing stock-still in his pen, staring at the blue dog. Again, he didn't appear angry and didn't make a sound. He simply stood and stared.

"Could he be a camera?" Ooyay found himself briefly wondering, before shaking the thought from his mind.

"Of course not" he immediately responded to his own thought.

He realised he was just being paranoid. After all, it *was* still likely that this building was a simple animal shelter and that no untoward monitoring was taking place. Even if there *were* some surveillance devices in operation, why would anyone go to the trouble of making such a life-like canine camera? It was too silly to even consider.

Onto the tiled floor he landed and was about to step toward the door when he turned once more to the golf-eye-ball hound.

He was still watching. Silently.

Now Ooyay felt a little pang of doubt. He didn't want to admit to himself that he still thought that this dog might be a cam-era -he had already decided that was a foolish notion. However, this one-eyed dog looked like he could do with a good turn in his fortune. If Ooyay released him, he might turn out to be a helpful companion.

If anyone had asked Ooyay why he chose to release the golf-eye-ball hound, he would have answered *"out of pity"*. In fact, one of the main reasons *was* pity, but also he found that he couldn't escape his *own* curiosity. ...What *if* this dog *was* a camera? He sim-ply had to know.

Jumping up wouldn't do it. If he was to open the latch on the other cage he would have to find something to stand on.

'Golfeyeball' and quite a few other animals silently looked on as Ooyay pushed into place the wheelie tray that Seamus Shaf-ford had earlier fallen over. Still, he found the latch was just out-side his reach as he stood on his hind legs on top of the tray.

With this tray being on wheels and full of dangerous sur-gical instruments, it was never going to be easy to land safely once he jumped. Nevertheless, the little blue dog launched himself into the air with a single leap, which sent the tray scattering under-neath in a loud crash.

If someone had walked into the room at that point, they would have at once spotted a small blue dog suspended in the air, attached to the latch of a cage by his teeth.

But the latch was pointing downward. Ooyay needed to use his legs to gain a grip on the cage-door so he might have some support. Next he had to raise his head upward and crossways, all whilst balancing above a floor that was now covered in sharp sur-gical implements.

Amazingly, he managed it. The door swung open and Ooyay flew back with it. He fell. The last thing he would later recall was the sight of Golfeyeball leaping from his cell door on top of him. Then all went quiet and all was dark.

GRANNY'S CAT

It had always been the tradition on Harrumph! for its inhabitants to name *themselves*. Every baby under the age of two was referred to only as "baby" or "the baby". On their second birthday (or as soon as possible thereafter if the child is slower to talk) he or she was placed in the circle of everyone in the village. The first word or words from the child's mouth became its name forevermore. For the purpose of this exercise, certain words -such as Mama or Dada, were normally ignored (for obvious reasons).

Lucy would have laughed at the leader's name, but she found herself too confused to know how to react to such a moniker.

"Granny's Cat," she repeated, trying to figure out how a person might come to be called such a thing. "What kind of name is that?" she asked with all the unguarded curiosity of a nine year old.

Granny's Cat wasn't pleased in the least with such a disrespectful question.

"Hmph!" he said and stuck his nose in the air in the same way Lucy had done when she was angry with the Professor, and in the same way Ooyay had always done in the past.

Seeing his dog's reaction reflected in this island chief, the Professor was once again reminded of the reason for them being there.

"Excuse me, Granny's Cat, we're looking for..." he began but the leader now interrupted him.

"Ah Professor Crastinator!" he gushed, at once remembering the presence of their eminent guest. "...How rude of me to ignore you like that. Allow me to welcome you on behalf of the people of Harrumph!" Granny's Cat bowed slightly to the Professor.
"You join us on a very special day of celebration. We are today celebrating the presence of our *best cook*, Iwanna Peepee," he continued, with a slow wave to the decorated woman on the pedestal. Now Granny's Cat paused, craned his head into the air, then let out another, single "HARRUMPH!"

Most of the people ran into nearby homes and returned at once with tables, chairs and large trays of food. The tables were arranged around the square and Granny's Cat invited the guests to join in the feast.

Only after they sat did they inspect the selection of grub available: wild salmon boiled in vinegar and mushy pea soup; roast, badly-plucked chicken with the heads on; wild boar (again with heads) in cherry curry and onions. Side dishes included every kind of vegetable, dipped in extra-hot wolf-droppings sauce or stir-fried with eels and frogspawn.

"Ewww, I'm not eating that stuff!" declared Lucy. She was sitting between Granny's Cat and the Professor as she spoke.

"Lucy! Don't be so rude!" scolded Professor Crastinator, smiling apologetically at the village leader.

"Mmmm! This looks *delicious!*" he then lied, spooning a piece of wild salmon, dripping with mushy peas, into his mouth.

The old man's eyes widened in shock as the overpowering taste of stale peas, vinegar and rotted fish invaded his senses. He managed to hold it all in for over five seconds before raising his head and spitting it in an arc over the table, onto the ground near the fire in the middle of the square.

"Eurgh!" he cried, wiping hairy peas from his mouth and trying to scrape the taste of the dish from off his tongue.

He had never known that it was possible for such a disgusting taste to exist on this Earth (or beyond). Mid-way through the tongue scraping, he finally realised that everyone had gone quiet and were now looking directly at him. Blurt picked that precise moment to nudge him in the ribs to ask a quiet question.

"Crast, what's happening?" he whispered aloud.

The best cook in the village, Iwanna Peepee, wore a stern frown as she stood up from her seat next to Granny's Cat. She hadn't moved her head from its forward-facing path. Slowly now her eyes began to move to the left, toward Professor Crastinator, as her eyelids dropped. Just as they closed altogether she turned in the opposite direction and walked away, leaving nothing but the faint rustling sound of her floral robe.

Professor Crastinator was speechless. He wanted to melt into the ground from embarrassment. Lucy wanted to run for her life. Blurt wanted to know what was going on. Susan wanted more to eat. She had already finished a full bowl of broccoli and parsnips in wolf-droppings sauce.

Granny's Cat slowly shook his head as he stared at the old man before him.

"Unbelievable!" he muttered. "Simply unbelievable."

"I'm so sorry..." the Professor began, but again he was cut-short.

"You truly are an amazing man!" said Granny's Cat. "I bow to your superior intellect."

"But aren't you upset that the Professor spat out your cook's food?" asked Lucy.

"It's not her food!" Granny's Cat declared with a laugh.
"This is *her* festival so all of *us* cooked the food to give her a break," he explained with a large wave toward the other villagers.

"Of course we can't cook as well as Iwanna Peepee can, but on Cook's Day we pretend to be worse than we really are so that she can be happy about how much better than us she is at cooking (- also it's nice to make sure she won't want *us* to cook more often)."

"How bizarre!" stated the Professor, "but why did she leave in such a huff?"

"Well, *we* can't tell her we know our own food is terrible. Normally on Cook's Day we keep picking-at and hiding food for a few hours, pretending to enjoy it. We tease Iwanna Peepee by telling her she will have to work harder to make sure she can beat *this* lovely grub!"

"That's cruel" said Lucy, no longer afraid of losing her life. "The poor lady is stuck in the kitchen all the time!"

"No no," Granny's Cat was quick to correct. "Iwanna Peepee *likes* to cook. She is a great cook. Today is *her* day. Everything we do on this day has to be done to make *her* feel better. Today she re-learns the fact that she is certainly the best cook in the village. We always end our Cook's Day festival by pleading with her to remain our cook. Then we confess that we hated our own food even though we have tried so hard to reach her standard."

When he noticed that the guests were still unsure how it all worked he continued to explain.

"...She left just now because she felt that the Professor hurt *our* feelings by spitting out our food. Iwanna Peepee has always been too polite to voice her distaste of our meals. The Professor's spitting has saved her from actually *eating* a plateful of it this time around. She will be most-grateful," he smiled.

Looking around, Lucy noticed how the other villagers also now all smiled and laughed quietly into their hands so as not to give the game away to the absent cook.

Lucy was still confused.

"But why do you have a Cook's Day?" she asked. "Why not a Butcher's Day or a Singer's Day or a Beekeeper's Day? ...Why Cook?"

Now it was Granny's Cat's turn to be confused.

"I don't understand," he admitted. "Today is Cook's Day. Tomorrow is Best Hunter's Day. The day after that is Bravest Person's Day. After that is Most Intelligent Person's Day... We each have our days."

Granny's Cat obviously had never thought of any other way to name the days of the week or month or year.

"So who's the best hunter?" enquired Lucy.

"That would be Blanky over there" answered Granny's Cat, pointing at a bronze-skinned woman, dressed in the fur-hide of many animals.

"And who's the bravest?" asked Blurt, attentively.

Granny's Cat smiled again, enjoying the guests' curiosity.

"Why, you've already met Oo-Sing-a-Car!" he declared. "He's the one who greeted you at the mountain and brought you here. I must say, it's rare for people to come this way. Most visitors *climb* the mountain path to visit the giant -for some reason. Nobody ever comes to see us."

"*Giant?*" the three visitors asked as one, but before Granny's Cat could answer, another villager piped up with a suggestion of his own.

"Since we now have the Professor here," he ventured, "I say there is a new most-intelligent person and we no longer need *you* Granny's Cat."

The village leader guffawed at the suggestion. Ignoring the upstart and turning to his guests he said "This is Baby Poochie Doggie -he is the Most Argumentative here."

"No I'm not," Baby Poochie Doggie complained at once.

Again ignoring him, Granny's Cat continued.

"We try not to award positions for such negative traits," he explained, "but Baby Poochie Doggie does nothing else but argue, so..."

"...So why do we need you?" asked Baby Poochie Doggie, refusing to be ignored.

The leader now had no alternative but to answer.

"You need me because what happens as soon as Professor Crastinator is gone?" he asked, intelligently. "The Professor isn't about to stay in this mud-hut village for very long with the likes of *you* around, now is he?" continued Granny's Cat.

Before Baby Poochie Doggie had a chance to reply, Blurt jumped in again.

"So is everyone here best at one thing? I mean -everyone has their own one thing to do?" he asked.

"That is so," answered Granny's Cat. "We each know our place and each other's role."

"And what happens if someone is *not* the best at anything?" continued Blurt, clearly interested in this type of village life structure.

"People can choose their own thing. If they are not the best at fishing, they can work hard to be the best at sewing or basket weaving. I-Have-Poops over there is best at throwing Frisbees," he explained. "Each single achievement is treated equally. We celebrate everyone on their own days. Only one person is the celebrated best at any one thing -of course."

Blurt seemed agitated, like something was itching him all over. He kept shifting in his seat and moving his lips as if he was about to say something. He put his finger in the air several times, seemingly to raise a point or to ask a question, but always held back, unsure how to voice his query. Management Training had taught him to be weary of showing too much interest too soon. *"Don't ask anything important until someone else first asks for your input,"* he had been instructed. *"Create an interest in your interest before you declare an interest."*

Granny's Cat looked concerned. He wanted to ease the discomfort Blurt seemed to be having.

"Is there something I can help you with, Johannsen?" he asked.

"Well..." began Blurt. "Let me see if I got it... Anyone can be anything in your village -and anyone can join the community once they're best at that one thing?" he asked.

"That is correct" Granny's Cat confirmed.

"So the only thing someone needs in order to become a full member of this community," continued the blind man, "and to have a day of celebration in their honour... is to be the best at one thing?"

"Yes," confirmed Granny's Cat once more. "That is correct. We each spend our lives perfecting that which we are best at."

"In that case..." declared Blurt, "I am here and I will stay and I am the *Bravest* Person in this village!"

It was as though a stone had been dropped in the middle of a big puddle. Silence rippled out across the square. Everybody looked at Blurt Johannsen but nobody said a word. In the stillness, a distant *Fuuump* was heard by all as another Bullet landed in the Bullet-Hole halfway up the mountain. Then came a smug snort as Oo-Sing-A-Car stood up from his seat in the middle of the village and slowly swaggered off to check who had arrived.

"My, we *are* popular today," noted Granny's Cat. Now turning back to the brave blind man, he took a breath before attempting to explain things further.

"It's not *quite* as simple as that in some cases," he told Blurt. "For instance, bravery is not something easily assessed. Oo-Sing-A-Car has spent his life demonstrating his bravery. He has leapt from the tallest cliffs into the smallest puddles of water -even though he doesn't swim. He has swamped his head in honey and oyster sauce before placing it in the jaws of lions. He has bravely called our strongest villager names such as "little shrimp" and "cabbage head." And he personally tasted all the food that is before you!"

Granny's Cat nodded as he considered Oo-Sing-A-Car's brave achievements.

"No doubt you are brave, Johannsen," he said. "But it is not for you to say if you are the bravest. Such a title is granted over time. Such a position is *earned*. Such an honour is *awarded* by others. Sometimes only other people can tell us who we are."

Now it was Blurt's turn to nod.

"I understand," he conceded magnanimously. "It is not your fault. ...You do not know the meaning of the word bravery. The word you describe ...is called *stupidity* where I come from. This Singing Car fellow is clearly a nut and should be commended for it. He knows no fear. That is rare indeed."

Blurt could sense people were listening. Recalling that chapter in his Management Training Manual entitled *"Don't Stop Talking If They Don't Stop Listening,"* he continued.

"...But that in itself is not bravery," he declared, standing on his seat now and raising his fist to the air. "Bravery is knowing the danger and the risk and *still* going ahead with it. Bravery is being *afraid* and *still* putting your head down to get it done. Bravery is doing what must be done simply *because* it must be done."

Blurt was clearly enjoying this moment. His hat dipped and swooped on his head as his finger whipped-up a gentle breeze.

"...A person is not brave simply for sticking his head in a fan -that is a fool," he continued. "You could wrestle pythons in the jungle and be nothing but a snake charming idiot. ...I once knew a man who washed himself daily in a river full of crocodiles. Everybody bowed as he passed and he never knew why. It turned out he had simply never heard of showers or baths..."

"Blurt!" called the Professor.

"...People might *see* danger, but not *know* it," continued the blind man, deaf now to all interruptions. "...But brave indeed is the man who *knows* it without seeing and *still* faces the danger!"

"BLURT!" cried the Professor again, pulling now on the belt of the blind man's trousers. "They've gone!" he said. "They're all gone home."

Only Lucy, the Professor and Granny's Cat now remained in their seats. Susan sat on the table in front of Blurt, gazing up at the glorious sight of her master preaching the ways of the world. Everyone else had quietly slipped away.

"Who's gone?" asked Blurt.

"They're all gone," replied the Professor. "Come down."

"Who? -All of them? Where did they go?" Blurt enquired, unable to believe they didn't stay for his summation.

"They're a busy lot," explained Granny's Cat. "I'm sure they would have loved to stay."

"Gone?" cried Blurt, climbing down from his chair. Only now did it begin to sink in that they had deserted him. "You mean they've really walked out? They left? They've all *gone*?"

The Professor and Granny's Cat turned to Lucy as she silently raised a single index finger.

"Bink!" she quietly confirmed, with a malicious grin.

THE FLOCK-IN OCCULORUM

Since before the year 1900, people rushed to movie parlours to see thrilling images from everyday life such as ordinary people waving at the camera, or horses and carriages racing through the streets. One particular movie featured a train rushing toward the camera. This caused many viewers to run in terror from the darkened room, convinced they were about to be runover.

These initial "movies" lasted all of thirty to sixty seconds and featured no characters nor storylines nor sound nor colour. The thrill of seeing a ball bounce across a large screen for a few seconds was enough to have millions of people worldwide flocking to watch.

Nothing like it had ever been seen before. These "moving objects" had somehow been recorded at some time in the past and were now stored inside a box that was able to show this same movement at any stage to throngs who were not present when it had even happened. The public was puzzled. Was there a train inside the projector case? Who were these individuals up on the screen? Were they trapped there? People were afraid they too might be trapped on the screen just for watching it.

Eventually the masses came to understand what it was all about. The excitement of the movement itself began to wear off and soon extra-long shows emerged. Some even had *plots.* Now people began to shout at the screen to warn the hero of an approaching villain -just as they had always done in the past at the theatre.

In time, longer movies with detailed storylines replaced the early thrills from seeing everyday objects. Audiences came to expect a standard tale with a beginning, middle and an ending.

Pierce Kratinsky was an old-school moving-image enthusiast. He believed that cinema should be able to exist simply as a means to view old things in new ways or new things in old ways or as a way to just *look* at things that were not ordinarily looked at. He thought of film as an update to artistic paintings, rather than as an update or replacement to theatre.

"A beautiful painting," he regularly explained to audiences before they watched a show, "...contains the subject of the painting as well as the *form.* It is made from placing paint on canvas. It does not move, but it *can* speak. It talks to each viewer individually, saying something unique to everyone. It is not limited in what it says by having a *script*. A hundred people can view a great painting and have a hundred different ideas on what it is."

Here he would pause to allow his audience digest what he was saying.

"Moving images," he would continue, "are made from running celluloid over a light source, to be displayed on a screen much like a painting's canvas. The greatest of these moving images can touch people and *speak* to them in the same way as can great paintings and sculptures and other works of art."

"A *script*," (at the mention of that word, Mr. Kratinsky would usually spit,) "is a cheapening of the whole medium of film. It is akin to developing a comic-book from Da Vinci's Mona Lisa!"

Once he had made his viewpoint clear, the lights would go down and his *'feast for the eyes and brain'* would begin.

Different shows in the Flock-In Occulorum had different themes. Some were mainly to do with colour or lighting -perhaps featuring nothing but moving shapes on the screen. Others dealt with beauty -showing perfectly constructed moving images that would be most at home on the wall of an art gallery. Instead of walking from one picture to another, however, you could sit still and allow the image on the screen *itself* to move and change into some other 'painting' for your consideration.

The Flock-In Occulorum was mostly known for its 'Chaos Shows' though, where objects on the screen swirled and shifted and people might have several heads and no hands. These shows generally made no sense to speak of, but did indeed seem to say something different to each person who witnessed them. Some folks would denounce them as rubbish and nonsensical. They would laugh and throw tomatoes at the screen. Others might mention how particular scenes affected them deeply -and yet, usually not be able to say why. Some people regularly donated money to Mr. Kratinsky's cinema because they felt his famous (and infamous) shows had inspired them in some way.

Most people thought only of the chaos shows when they thought of the Flock-In Occulorum, but in fact, a whole selection of shows on vastly different themes ran throughout every day, each one introduced by Pierce Kratinsky himself.

Penny worked on the front-desk, selling tickets. During the show, she sold refreshments to the audience. Afterward, she cleaned the cinema room in preparation for the following show, for which she sold the tickets. When business was slow she walked the streets with a sandwich board around her neck, advertising Kratinsky's Flock-In Occulorum -'The Museum of Moving Art!'

At first, Matthew and Penny (and even Mike) laughed together at how awful these shows were.

"There was one on yesterday," Penny informed her brothers one day, "that lasted for an hour and fifteen minutes and showed nothing except a man walking backwards into a room, sitting in a chair, then reading a book... all in slow-motion!"

Other movies were much worse than that one, but most were less boring. This 'slow backward book-read' movie was *the* most boring thing the kids had ever seen. It was so boring it became a running-joke between the younger brother and sister to see which of them could convince Mr. Kratinsky to run it again. They would tell him how *moving* it had been and how *poignant* they found it (the word "poignant" itself being hilarious to the two).

Each time one of them succeeded in having this movie re-run, they would both vow never to attempt to have it shown again. Inevitably though, one or the other would pester the unwitting cinema-owner to put it on "one last time."

Despite his vast intelligence, Mr. Kratinsky never realised that the teenagers were pulling his leg the whole time. Instead, he revelled in having two such enthusiastic youthful followers of his own obsession.

"I'll gladly re-run that show since it seems to give you children such joy," he informed Matthew one morning. "But I must admit I find that particular film somewhat boring -I have thus-far been unable to share your enthusiasm for it."

The biggest downside to this running gag for the two children of course was that, having begged for it to be run, they then had to sit through it all for an hour and twenty minutes (including Mr. K's five minute introduction) -which made it all the funnier when one of them succeeded in having it played again some days or weeks later.

COLD MOUNTAIN

Oo-Sing-A-Car lead the way up the mountain path, followed closely by Blurt Johannsen. Lucy skipped to keep up with the blind man, who was obviously determined to match Harrumph!'s Bravest Person in every way. Guiding himself solely on the footfall sounds from the villager in front, Blurt had removed his hat to make sure he was receiving all the signals he needed in order to safely navigate the passage. Following behind at a more leisurely pace, Susan rambled freely alongside Professor Crastinator.

They had met up with Oo-Sing-A-Car at the bottom of the hill, near the same spot where he had pounced on them before. Apparently, villagers never went any further beyond that point. Whoever had arrived on the latest Bullet must have climbed the mountain rather than journey downward.

Once Blurt sniffed at Oo-Sing-A-Car and declared that *he* was not afraid to meet this giant, the Bravest Villager took this as a challenge and launched ahead.

The new Bullet, next to theirs, was a private "sports" model, much like Blurt's. As suspected, nobody was now on board. This person or persons had clearly come, not to see the lovely village of Harrumph!, but to visit the so-called giant.

"What is so special about this giant that he gets all the traffic?" the Professor asked their guide.

"We do not talk of him," answered Oo-Sing-A-Car flatly, before continuing onward uphill.

Blurt and Lucy were about to carry on when the Professor called after them.

"It looks like you'll need a sweater, Lucy," he told the young girl, pointing at the snow on the top of the mountain.

He had no idea how far up this giant lived, but it wasn't about to get any warmer ahead.

"Blurt, wrap up!" he commanded.

Without another word, both Lucy and Blurt climbed into the Bullet to retrieve some warm clothing from their supplies.

"Should we bring something for Oo-Sing-A-Car?" Lucy asked Blurt, thinking of their bare-chested guide.

"Nah," the blind man laughed. "He's too brave to fear the cold!"

Only after they returned to the Professor did Lucy look to what he had been wearing all this time. He still had nothing on but his slippers, pyjamas and Lucy's father's bathrobe.

"Don't *you* want anything?" she asked the old man, "I'm sure Blurt will have something to fit you."

"Nonsense," he declared, pulling tightly on the cord of the robe and drawing its lapels around his neck.

"I'm snug as a bug in this!" he smiled.

The Professor seemed to have lost much of the uncertainty that he had before. He now spoke with the voice of authority. It seemed as though his strength and conviction had grown immeasurably since they had set out. It was no longer in Lucy's power to lead him in any way (if she had wanted to) or to even question his decisions. Blurt had no idea as to the extent of the Professor's flimsy attire.

As they climbed, the air became cooler and thinner. Lucy noticed how Blurt seemed to be slowing down and tried to help him by distracting the man they had finally caught up with.

"So how come you're called Oo-Sing-A-Car then?" Lucy asked.

Thankfully, the guide did stop to consider the question -if only momentarily. He looked at the young girl out of the corner of his eyes before answering.

"Kid," he sneered, then shook his head and walked on.

Unlike when Blurt had said the same thing, there could be no doubt how it was intended this time. Oo-Sing-A-Car said "kid" as though it was beneath him to even address a person so young. He scoffed as if the word belonged at the end of a sentence like *"I'd answer that question, but I really couldn't be bothered speaking to a kid."* It was the worst kind of way "kid" could be said to a kid -as every kid knows.

Snow began to fall and the wind blew lightly as they zigzagged their way up the mountain path.

"How much further is it, Oozing?" enquired Blurt.

Again Oo-Sing-A-Car stopped and turned and sneered.

"You think I'm frightened of the giant don't you?" he laughed. "No way! Not me. If you think I'm frightened of *anyone* you are wrong! See!"

He turned now, ready to run the rest of the way.

"No," answered Blurt, amused and puzzled at the guide's outburst. "I don't see... but I was only wondering how long it was going to take?"

However, Oo-Sing-A-Car had not run. In fact he had not moved. His line of sight was caught now by something up ahead.

"What is it?" asked Lucy, who was somewhat smaller than Oo-Sing-A-Car and could not see as well through the falling snow.

Although it wasn't falling too heavily where they stood, further-on things blurred somewhat.

"Something's coming!" declared the Professor now as he reached the others.

From out of the white haze a dark shape formed.

"Uh!" Lucy exclaimed in fright as she grabbed the nearest adult's arm.

Realising she had locked onto Oo-Sing-A-Car, immediately she withdrew her hand. Still some yards off, the shadowy figure developed into the shape of a man.

"Uh!" she exclaimed once more, careful to grab Blurt's arm this time.

The man was no giant. He wore a buttoned-up, long, dark coat to his feet, with a wide-brimmed hat that covered most of his face. Still he approached, now no more than a few feet away. His shoes crunched on the snow with each step as he walked slowly and deliberately toward the travellers.

The three men, young girl and dog stood silently, waiting to find out what would transpire next. Oo-Sing-A-Car thrust out his chest in anticipation of an attack or perhaps to instil fear in the on-comer.

"Evenin'," muttered the man, tipping his hat, as he squeezed through the astonished travellers, continuing his journey down the mountain path.

He was some feet away before one of them finally thought to say something.

"Evenin'!" cried Blurt, who could hear the man had passed by.

Management Training dictated that nothing was to be revealed as a surprise if everyone else was also surprised. *"Never admit to not knowing something,"* his personal personnel-trainer had taught him, *"<u>especially</u> if everyone else is confused! A true leader shows <u>confidence</u> when there is nothing else to show. ...When all is lost, the person who shows the way with the greatest confidence is the leader."*

As the others stood and stared at the retreating silhouette, Blurt took Lucy's hand and carried on walking up the hill.

"I'd love to stay and chit-chat," he called back to the others, "but I'm afraid I have a mountain to climb!"

THE GIANT'S GROTTO

"The giant!" exhaled Oo-Sing-A-Car, pointing, as they turned a corner near the summit.

The path had zigzagged up one face of the mountain. This final turn had lead the travellers around to the far side, where a fence had been erected along the top of the cliff. Beyond the fence was a sheer drop hundreds of feet down. At the far end of this snowy road was a log cabin that appeared to have been built into a cave-opening in the mountain. Over the door stood the letters G-R-O-T, three feet tall. Above these letters, a lit-up giant statue of a lumberjack holding an axe stood on the roof.

"That's not a giant!" laughed Lucy. "It's a statue!"

"Afraid of a statue, eh Oozing?" Blurt joined in the laughter.

"I fear nothing!" Oo-Sing-A-Car announced and once more lead the way onward.

"What is GROT?" asked Lucy as they approached the cabin.

"It looks to me like there are a couple of letters missing" suggested Professor Crastinator. "Perhaps it should spell GROTTO -as in a small cave or cavern?"

"But why place the word GROTTO above a grotto?" asked Lucy, not for the first time confused.

After reaching the front door (which was not any bigger than any normal door), Oo-Sing-A-Car announced he would wait outside "to guard in case the giant wakes up," he insisted. Susan leapt into Blurt's arms as the remaining three entered the grotto.

The door creaked open. CREEEeeeeeee... After it was fully opened and had stopped moving, however, it continued to creak. ...eeeeEEEEEeeeAAAaaaaaAAA... the visitors looked around, not knowing what to do. Then, finally, it stopped ...aaaAAAAkkkKKkkkkkkkk.

The first thing they noticed inside was a sign on a small stand. It read:

FOLLOW THE RIGHT WALL TO FIND WHAT YOU SEEK

Behind the sign were three pathways with shelf walls from floor to ceiling, full of what looked like junk.

"There are three corridors here full of junk, Blurt," Lucy informed the blind man. "And a sign that says *Follow the right wall to find what you seek.* -It looks like a maze! But which wall is the right one?" she wondered aloud.

Blurt waved his arm as he walked slowly to his right, finding the nearest wall. Susan was snuggled comfortably in his left arm.

"It's obvious really," he told his friends. "The way to navigate a maze is to keep along the right-hand wall. A blind man could do it!"

Immediately he traced his arm along the right-most wall. Lucy and the Professor stood and watched as he walked down the short corridor in that direction. What they could see, but Blurt couldn't, was that its length was twenty feet at most and there were no further turnings on that path. Suitcases, boxes and other containers of all shapes and sizes were packed onto the shelves in this corridor.

The young girl held her mouth to stop herself giggling aloud as Blurt reached the end and stopped. Then he turned to his left, keeping his arm stretched to the wall on his right, and walked back to the start-point. Now Lucy couldn't help herself. She broke out laughing as he returned.

"Don't laugh!" Professor Crastinator nudged her from behind. "Look!"

Blurt now continued walking by following the "right wall", taking him into the middle corridor and along rows of shelves stuffed with seemingly every kind of electronic gizmo or gadget ever made: Old computers, games consoles, controllers, video game cartridges, tapes and disks fought for space on the shelves beneath a mass of unkempt cables that looked to be growing along the shelves like ivy on the walls of an old house.

Lucy stopped laughing at once as Blurt turned again to the right and disappeared out of sight down another corridor. She and the Professor immediately followed after the blind man and his dog.

Row upon row of clocks dominated a number of corridors as they navigated the maze. Most were running clockwise, some anti-clockwise. Some were not working at all. It looked like every type of clock ever made had a representative here: Grandfather clocks, ball clocks, water clocks, cuckoo clocks, dodo clocks, square clocks; locked clocks that record the time, but don't tell it; clocks that never tell the time, except when you ask them nicely. There were clocks that showed the time in every corner of the planet and clocks that weren't clocks at all (-they were things like wall-safes, pictures of clocks, time-bombs, stop-watches, etc.)

Another corridor had stacks of puzzles and board games - some of which Lucy herself had played, but most of which she had never heard. In fact it didn't seem possible that so many games and puzzles had actually been developed.

"Is this a toy shop?" she wondered.

Next they came across an aisle laden with (of all things) handheld megaphones. Lucy couldn't help herself. A megaphone has got to be tested on-sight. She reached for a small black one with a red handle, but as she did, a loud voice boomed in her ear.

"PUT... THE... MEGAPHONE... DOWN!" roared the deathly-serious voice, causing Lucy to drop the item and leap in the air.

Only after she looked around did her heart begin to beat once more, when she saw Professor Crastinator giggling behind a large white megaphone. Grabbing the nearest handle, she winced in order to hide a smile of her own as she shouted into the loudspeaker device.

"I WILL NOT!" she called out, but what actually came through on the other end was "WILL NOT I!" ...Somehow this megaphone had distorted her words.

"Hey my words are mixed up!" she said into the speaker. "UP WORDS MY HEY MIXED ARE!" is what came through, amplified on the other side.

"Can ...we ...please ...get ...a ...move ...on?" said a robot voice from behind once more.

Blurt was standing there, speaking into another voice-distorting megaphone.

All the world needs champagne buckets. We could live without the drink itself, but every household should have one

champagne bucket. Just *one* mind -any more than that is deca-
dence. Another aisle in this strange supermarket-like maze was
stuffed with nothing but champagne buckets. They all looked
pretty similar, but on closer inspection it appeared that no two
were the same: Gold buckets, silver buckets, brass buckets of every
shape and size. Some with stands, some without.

Other shelves held rows of buttons and switches that
seemingly did nothing special. Above some of the switches were
little lights that lit-up when flicked. More consoles made a beep or
a ping when a button was pressed. Lucy couldn't make any sense
of this aisle, but the two men seemed fascinated, flicking every
switch and pressing every button as they passed.

"That's the problem with technology these days," said the Professor with conviction, "there's not enough physical *switches*. You just
can't beat the flick of a solid switch when you want something
done!"

With that, he launched into a frenzied switch-flicking
spree. TICK TICK TICK TICKTICKTICK... TICK! Lights came on,
beeps and pings rang out, some small monitors lit up, showing sta-
tic or radar-type green screens.

Abruptly, he halted his flicking and stood frozen, looking
at one particular spot on the wall. Lucy walked over, curious to see
what he had found... Among other buttons and dials, a flip-up
glass panel covered a large red button. On this red button were the
words "DO NOT PRESS."

Lucy immediately felt frightened. She looked to Professor
Crastinator to make certain he wasn't thinking what she thought
he might be thinking. With one glance, she knew that he was. His
eyes were wide and his open mouth held a toothy-grin. There
could be no doubt what he was thinking.

"Are you thinking what I'm thinking?" he smiled at Lucy, who
quickly answered.

"No I am not!" she replied and tried to push him past this area.

When she saw he would not be moved she called for assistance.

"Blurt!" she screamed. The blind man stepped closer at once.
"There's a big red button here marked DO NOT PRESS and *he*
wants to press it!"

Blurt's eyebrows appeared from behind his sunglasses and quickly disappeared beneath the hat that was now back on his head. Lucy was relieved to see he was as shocked as she was.

"Press it!" cried Blurt suddenly.

Before she could react, and with a speed she hadn't realised the old man was capable of, the Professor lifted the glass panel and slammed the palm of his hand down onto the red button.

A quick, deep rumble rang out and filled the air. The shelves and floor shook briefly as they might during a small earthquake. Then nothing. The two males smiled approvingly. Professor Crastinator closed the glass lid with a soft double-tap and waved Blurt out in front once more.

"After you, Mr. Johannsen!" he bowed grandly.

Blurt also seemed to be caught up in a silly mood all of a sudden.

"Don't mind if I do, my dear Professor!" he joked.

Lucy almost fainted from fear.

Ugly-looking ornamental statues (most of which were broken) adorned more shelves. Led through the maze by the blind man, at every turn they came across more gizmos, gadgets, trinkets and playthings -mostly useless junk- and apparently all previously-used: Square footballs, bicycles with square wheels, tobacco flavoured chewing gum, potted plastic and fabric plants, hundreds of cameras, sunglasses, CB radios, musical carousels and old-fashioned music boxes, staplers, calculators, hats, playing cards, coloured pens, night-vision goggles, mp3 players, quill feathers, ear-muffs, ... something new was to be found on each aisle -and the visitors were aware they were not seeing half the items as they went.

Finally, they turned a corner and found themselves standing in the middle of a clearing. Here too, the walls in every direction were full of items -mostly fancy-dress costumes hung in this area: Napoleon outfits, pirate-wear, princess ball-gowns, gorilla suits in many styles.

In the centre of this clearing stood a large workbench, a small table and two people. One of these people (the taller one) was... me!

THE WISH TABLE AND THE EMPATHY STONE

Allow me to introduce myself. I have been telling you this story for such a long time now it is bad-manners for me not to have done so sooner, I know. But this is the point where I come in so it made more sense to me to wait until now. I hope you, reader, will understand.

My name is Stanley Rumm. At the time of this tale I was living what I had thought was my dream. Fed up with "the rat race" of life, where I had to sleep, work, eat, sleep, work, eat, day-in/ day-out, I finally escaped one morning to the furthest hole in the furthest mountain I could find. I wanted to be alone. I stuck a statue of an angry giant on my roof to frighten silly people away.

Without dwelling too long on my story, it is sufficient to say that I soon found that I was wrong: I needed to interact with others. A hermit-like existence might sound romantic and adventurous, but it's no fun being a loner if you have no one to talk to about it. I wanted people to come visit -but then to leave.

I was not about to open a hotel or a bar -that would have been too much hassle, looking after the guests, organising ski-trips, etc.. So what could I do to make people visit, then go home?

Inspired by an old TV-show I used to enjoy (when I owned a television), I opened *The Grot Shop.*

It started out in the log cabin at the top of the mountain road, but soon I had to excavate into the hillside itself. A lot of people had an urge to see that their "nice junk" found a good home. Others took great delight in sifting through other peoples' cast-offs. I believe it was the remote, extreme location that somehow attracted only the best kind of "grot". I came to love every item in that store and usually found it hard to part with any of it.

"Good evening!" I greeted the visitors, not knowing at that time who they were or why they were there. Most people knew of the place before they got there. It was very unusual for someone to find that shop by accident.

"Welcome to Grot! My name is Stanley Rumm. If you have any queries I'd be happy to oblige. For more detailed item-requests, please see my assistant, Onoshi Han," I gestured toward the man sitting next to where I stood.

Onoshi Han was my small, hunchbacked assistant. At that time, I was trying to foster a kind of *'madman of the mountains'* image for myself and had searched job agencies across the world for an appropriately peculiar looking individual to act as my gofer. If you've seen any movie that features 'a brilliant madman' you will know exactly why: They always have humble little manservants by their side, eager to do their petty biddings. Of course, I am not brilliant in any way, but nobody coming to the shop for a plastic nose full of fake snot or a pre-chewed multi-coloured pen would be aware of that. After one look at my assistant, however, they would figure I was someone to be reckoned with.

Onoshi was a funny-looking hunchback with bent teeth and eyes that could see in every direction at once. He physically fit the job-vacancy to a tee. However he wasn't very humble and refused to do anything asked of him. These weren't helpful traits for a shop assistant of course, but I kept him on because I kind of liked his ferocious crankiness.

"This is a shop?" asked Blurt, as ever first to speak. He was too off-guard by then to use his Management Training to full effect. A maze is a nice way to confuse people, I've found.

"That is correct," I informed the man. Now it was my turn to be confused. "Might I ask what you have come for if not to shop?"

I had no idea how anybody could possibly have come to this location without knowing in advance what was here -especially *these* people. A blind cowboy, a young girl and a freezing old man wearing a bath-robe seemed to me to be an unlikely group to come across by accident in such an extreme location.

"We are looking for Dr. Flavius Flocky Nocky," said the Professor. "You don't happen to know where he lives do you?" he enquired.

"The inventor?" I asked, making sure I had the right chap. "Sorry I have no idea. This is just a grot shop," I explained. "Feel free to browse!"

They sighed, but decided they had nothing to lose by browsing some more.

"What does that big red button back there do?" Lucy enquired.

"You mean the one that says DO NOT PRESS?" I asked, sternly.

I was preparing to scare her in some way, but when I saw how frightened she looked, nodding slowly back at me, I smiled gently.

"It's funny -Most males coming through here press that button," I informed them, "but no woman has ever pressed it." Both men nodded and smiled to themselves.

"But what does it do?" asked Lucy again, anxiously. "Why is it there? How come it says DO NOT PRESS?"

"Nothing. Why not? Don't know," I told her. I really didn't have better answers.

Still confused, but apparently more at ease, she turned now to the gorilla suit collection.

"How much for that one?" she quietly asked Onoshi Han, pointing at a nice *gorilla-suit-with-chest-implant* that I rather liked myself.

Most of the other gorilla suits were too heavy or too light-weighted, or didn't have the all-important fake chest.

The actual words Onoshi shouted in reply to her perfectly-innocent question I cannot repeat here, but basically the gist of it was *"Go away and stop annoying me you... person."*

Lucy leapt back with a start and both the Professor and Blurt at once took quick steps forward in order to protect the young girl from that raving assistant of mine.

"I'm very sorry!" I pleaded before they had a chance to complain. "He hasn't had his cornflakes yet today," I lied as I pushed Onoshi Han off his stool and pointed him toward the staff-room.

He actually had eaten cornflakes earlier that morning, but the yak out the back that gave us fresh milk had been a touch too cold overnight, and her milk came out in ice-cubes. Onoshi didn't like frozen yak-milk with his cornflakes.

"That gorilla suit is not for sale, miss," I informed her.

"...So, how much for one of those square footballs?" she asked immediately.

"Umm -They're not for sale, miss," I had to admit.

"How much for the megaphone that jumbles your words?" asked the Professor. "I liked that one."

"Yes it is nice, sir, isn't it? But -it's not for sale I'm afraid," I once more declared.

"Is there *anything* for sale in this shop?" asked Blurt.

"No," I stated with glee. "This isn't a sale shop," I explained. "It's a swap shop. We don't take money here. You need to give me something of comparable value in exchange for whatever you would like."

Both the Professor and Lucy seemed to think about it and appreciate the system. Blurt, however, found it harder to comprehend why anyone would do such a thing. He stepped closer to where I was standing as he waved the air with his free hand.

"Why...?" he began, but couldn't think of the words to use.

It was impossible for him to see how anyone would choose to not use money.

"How...?" he started once more but fell silent, as he continued to approach.

He brushed into the small table by my side and, sensing its unsteadiness, his hand quickly dropped to keep it from toppling over.

"What..." he asked, fingering an unusual stone piece on top of the table, "...is this?"

I hesitated because *The Wish Table* itself had been difficult enough to explain to those who didn't already know, but that stone on top now required an even greater explanation...

By that stage in the life of The Grot Shop, this Wish Table had become its greatest attraction. It was a small, wooden, pink platform on one pole that fanned-out at the bottom into four short feet. Basically, it was a gaudy piece of furniture that would not have appealed to any sensible person of taste, if it wasn't for one minor feature: Once you make a wish as you place "the correct item" on this table -and leave it there for its owner ("me") to keep, your wish will be granted.

There was only one rule to The Wish Table: In order for the wish to come true, the item placed there must be something of immense value ...and yet worthless!

The man whom these visitors had met outside on the mountain path had come here to have one wish granted. He brought with him one thing.

I cannot tell you his name, but you *have* heard of this man. You probably even have read -or know someone who has read- one of his books, in fact. He is a very famous author. Unfortunately (he admitted to me), he felt he was getting too old to carry on. He liked to write great books, but he feared death more. He informed me that in his youth he had met 'a tall dark man with no face' (his words) who handed him this stone.

"With the aid of this Empathy Stone, you will be a famous author," said the man with no face, *"but in return, I will have your everlasting soul!"*

Creepy stuff, I know, but this young author was told that The Empathy Stone would need to be buried with him after he died, in order to pay this debt. He was also informed that his books would fade into obscurity once he died, if the stone was not buried with him.

For a proper author (as this man is), the thought that your work would fade away and be forgotten is the worst fate imaginable. This author, however, had spent years wrestling with his conscience and he finally decided he could not risk his everlasting soul.

So he came to me and made a wish as he placed the Empathy Stone on the table: His wish was that his books would not fade into obscurity once he died.

The stone itself was quite ordinary-looking. The whole thing could fit snugly into a large adult hand. If you stood on it on a beach you wouldn't think to look at it twice. Its colour was grey/black and shaped much like a standard slice of cake, although its height made it less like a cake, than a biscuit: A slice of biscuit. For all its ordinariness, it did have one mildly-curious visual feature: throughout its depth, crystals could be seen, like dark, ingrained, everlasting snowflakes.

I had no way of knowing if this author's tale was true or not (after all, he *was* an author and used to making up tales), but either way, it was not in my power to grant his wish. That wish, (as with all others that people have asked of me) is granted only by the table itself. I have no power to decide which ones come true and which don't. If the author had made a false submission, the worst that had happened was that he gave something to me for nothing.

As I explained The Empathy Stone and The Wish Table to the visitors, each of them in turn rubbed the dents and crystals throughout the black slice.

"How does it work?" gasped Lucy, clearly believing the story somewhat more than I did at the time.

All three listened intently as I answered, although I sensed that Professor Crastinator was somewhat more sceptical than the others.

"...Well he told me that after somebody rubs it," I answered, "I must sleep with the stone under my pillow and when I awaken I will know them and empathise with their situation."

Lucy didn't quite grasp the point being made.

"Huh?" she inquired at once.

Still unsure about it myself, I had to think hard before replying.

"...I believe the idea is that when I dream with this stone under my pillow," I told her, "I will see things exactly how other people see them."

Seconds of awed and awkward silence followed, punctured finally by Lucy.

"Jazzy!" she declared with a gasp.

Admittedly, the rest of us were still somewhat puzzled and bemused.

SLIDING DOWN

The Cratchett home at the back of The Flock-In Occulorum cinema, where Mike had his garage, was actually an old fire station. Upstairs was *'the living quarters'* where firemen used to sleep and play cards while they waited to be called to a fire or a kitty-rescue.

Between each other, Matthew, Penny and Mike still called this area *'the living quarters'* even now, as a kind of joke, but also as a nice reminder to the past-use of these rooms, where men would "live" and wait to place their lives in danger at the ring of a bell, after which they might not live any longer.

Linking this area to *'the engine room'* below were some wide stairs, but also the old fire-station slide-pole was still in place in a corner of the room that was now used as the *'front room'* area. Normally, the hole in the ground (upstairs) that surrounds one of these slide-poles has a metal guard around it to stop people falling through by accident. In the Cratchett front room, however, the old railing had been completely removed, making it easier to jump onto the pole itself, without having to skirt around the railing.

Matthew and his older brother, Mike (who was in his early-thirties by now and should have known better), enjoyed hopping from chair to soft chair. Then, after bouncing along the three-seater couch, they would leap with a kick into the air, grabbing onto the pole some distance away. This was how they normally travelled from upstairs to down. They called it "the high kicking kung fu bunny jump."

Penny chastised the pair for their silly, childish behaviour. They would break the furniture, she informed them in no uncertain terms. She complained that the slide-pole was dangerous without the safety barrier and that a cold draft howled through that hole in the floor on chilly winter mornings.

But, as everyone who enjoys such fun is aware, some people simply do not know how or when to loosen up. Penny was incapable of really 'letting go'. For all her pleasantness and her sometimes-playful humour, she only ever slid down the pole once. That was over three years after they had moved in to this place and she didn't do it out of a sense of fun even then...

It was a Friday morning when it happened. She had been calling Matthew to get out of bed for over half an hour before he finally arose. Penny had insisted that her younger brother stay-on at school despite Matthew's wish to go to work for Mike in the garage.

She herself had left school to take care of the house and her brothers and also to work for Mr. Kratinsky. She was insistent that Matthew would finish his education. Lately though, his grades had been slipping and it was becoming harder for her to force him to take his study seriously.

Their older brother was ready for work and had begun his 'bunny jumping' from chair to chair when Matthew entered the kitchen-area of the living quarters. It was only after Mike began bouncing along the runway-launch of the three cushions on the couch, however, that he first noticed his younger brother out of the corner of his eye.

Just as he sprang into the air toward the pole, in his high-kick stance, he turned to Matthew.

"You're up?" he enquired with a mid-air sly grin.

These were to be his last coherent words.

Having been distracted, Mike failed to grab a hold of the slide-pole, but crashed into it with the side of his face instead. By itself, this might not have been so bad, but as he began to fall, he succeeded in catching on to the pole with only one arm. He also forgot to tuck-in the leg he had extended for the 'kung fu kick', so when his falling body reached the hole in the upstairs floor, his foot was caught on the ground of the upper-floor. This happened so quickly that he was unable to grab on tighter, so he lost his grip, which caused his head to stretch away from the centre of the circle.

The back of his head slammed onto the edge of the upstairs floor and his body fell limply to the ground below. Penny, who had been sitting at the kitchen table all this time, ran to the pole and didn't hesitate to slide down after her big brother. Matthew was frozen, unable to move for a long time.

"I WANT TO MAKE A WISH!"

"I have a wish to make!" announced Blurt with a pained, but hopeful look across his face.

"All right" I told him. "Place your item on The Wish Table and tell me your wish. Remember: it must be something of immense value -and worthless."

Although he couldn't open his eyes, the stitches on his eyelids allowed them to open just enough for moisture to seep through. Blurt now removed his sunglasses as tears began to pour down his face. Susan shuffled under his left arm as he wiped at his wet cheeks. Then, taking a deep breath, he lifted up his dog and placed her on The Wish Table.

Lucy couldn't believe what she was seeing, but realised at once what was at stake for Blurt so she kept absolutely still. Susan gazed quietly up at her owner, oblivious to what was happening. Professor Crastinator spun away in the opposite direction, unable to look at this man giving up the dog he loved so much.

Blurt Johannsen took another deep breath in preparation for his wish. Looking at those stitches across his eyelids, there was no doubt in any of us what that wish was going to be.

"I wish..." he began, then faltered. "...I wish I was acknowledged as The Bravest Person on Harrumph!"

The Professor spun back as all three of us shouted at the top of our voices.

"WHAT!?" we all cried.

"Blurt!" continued Lucy. "You could have wished for your *eyesight* back! Why didn't you wish to see again?" she pleaded with him to answer as she slapped him repeatedly across the chest.

Blurt didn't put up much resistance.

"You don't understand, Lucy," he told her. He was still crying now. "...If I could *see* I would still be lost," he sobbed. "This way, at least I know where I belong."

It was the kind of warped logic that I have since learnt to expect from Blurt Johannsen.

"I'm sorry girl!" he apologised to his one-time guide dog, before turning around and staggering quickly in the direction they had entered.

Just then Susan began to bark.

"Yap yap yap yap yap!" she yapped, calling her master.

He didn't come back and Susan continued to yap.

"Can't you give him his dog back?" Lucy begged me as Onoshi Han returned to the clearing.

"I'm sorry," I had to inform her. "He has made the wish. I cannot change that."

Onoshi rubbed Susan's little head with a softness I had never known he was capable of exhibiting. Immediately she stopped barking. He scooped her up and carried her quietly out of the clearing without another word from either man or mutt.

Professor Crastinator was now clearly distraught. He had lost his own dog, for which he was travelling the world. Now he had witnessed the loss of another dearly loved pet. His whole body shivered and shook as he stood there, unable to move. I honestly didn't know what to do or how to react.

"I want to make a wish!" declared Lucy at that point.

Gathering my thoughts and composure, I wiped my nose and reminded her of the rule.

"All right," I said, "but you know the rule -it must be something of immense value -and worthless."

Taking her hand from the pocket of her trousers, she pulled out the mobile phone given to her by her mother as she left home. She had not switched it on once since they departed, because of guilt on her part and also because she didn't know how she would react if her mother pleaded with her to come home right away.

"Here," she announced, placing the phone on the table. "I wish the Professor had his dog back. Right now."

Not knowing at that time which person the Professor was, I turned to check the exit, through which Onoshi had left with Susan.

"Not him," cried Lucy, indicating the direction Blurt had gone, "HIM!" she shouted, pointing at the shivering, frail, old man.

Only now did I notice that his teeth chattered and his nose was redder than a tomato. This man was cold.

"*His* dog was kidnapped and we need to get him back," she explained.

Now I fully understood her request, but I was still powerless to act.

"I'm sorry," I had to announce. "I don't think the table will grant your wish. If it was up to me, I would do everything in my power to see that your dog came back right now, but..."

I meant to try to explain that *I* did not make the rule or grant the wish. I merely accepted the 'payment' in order that the table would make the wish come true. It had seemed to work most-often, though I never understood why.

"Your item is not right," I had to tell her. "This phone is much too valuable. It's just not worthless enough. I'm sorry."

"I don't care," Lucy cried. "Take it! Make his dog appear now!"

Again I explained how it worked.

"I could take your telephone, but it would do no good" I told her. "You can have anything in this place in exchange for the phone," I said, "but I do not have the power to grant you your wish. The Table will not work for you. I know it."

In truth, I didn't want the phone at all. Mobile phones are just not my thing. But I did want to help this young girl and old man through their difficulty.

"I can have anything?" asked Lucy, thinking now, looking to the shivering old man.

Outside, Blurt Johannsen had been trying to explain to Oo-Sing-A-Car what had happened.

"I'm sorry" he told the Former-Bravest Person on Harrumph! "I made a wish. You're out and I'm in. I'll put in a word for you as Most Arrogant, though," he laughed.

Oo-Sing-A-Car laughed too, amused at this blind man's dream and perseverance. He was just about to say something when he saw movement coming from the Grotto. There in the doorway stood a large gorilla, looking straight at him. For the first time in his life, Oo-Sing-A-Car knew fear (for some reason). He screamed and ran, immediately leaping over the fence, falling down the sheer cliff, to his doom.

"OOOOOOooooooooooo!" he cried out as he fell.

Lucy and the gorilla ran to the fence and looked down, but it was too late. Pulling the warm mask from his face, the Professor looked to Lucy, who stared back in shock. Then both turned to the blind man standing behind them, confused.

"What?" asked Blurt.

MATTHEW THANKFUL

Mike Cratchett didn't die immediately after he fell through the hole in the floor in the old fire station. He was unconscious, but still alive. Penny stayed with him, ensuring nobody touched her brother until the ambulance arrived.

Only for a brief few seconds did she stop running her hands through the unconscious man's hair -that was after she looked up to see Matthew had quietly climbed down the stairs and was gazing, open-mouthed at the sight of his crumpled sibling.

"Run!" she told him through tear-stained eyes, "Go get Jenny. Tell her what happened!"

Matthew didn't need to be told twice. Thankful that he didn't have to stay and look at his brother lying there helpless on the garage floor, he ran. Thankful to be able to do something of use, he ran. Thankful for the chance to put his own lazy part in this awful accident out of his mind for a brief period, he ran. He was thankful that there was another older family-member (his sister Jenny) that he could run to, so he ran. He couldn't breathe while he stood there in the garage, so he ran and he was thankful for getting as far away from there as possible.

Had he waited five minutes at the top of the road he probably would have found a bus that would take him to the house where Jenny worked in less than half an hour. But of course there was no way he could have stood around waiting. Even if the bus was already there as he reached the road, he would not have been capable of sitting or standing still as it trundled across the city. He needed to move every bone in his body and move them quickly. There was a thumping, burning, banging *lump* inside his chest that needed to be set free. If he could make it burst out due to his running too fast and too far, he could at last have some release.

Later, he wouldn't be able to recall much about the run or how long it took or what happened afterward, but he would half-remember climbing through a hole in a hedge at the bottom of a garden, to find his sister Jenny standing there at the washing line. He would never know what he said or how she reacted. He would not remember.

At some stage he found himself back home, where he met Mr. Kratinsky, who took him to Penny at the hospital.

"Where's Jenny?" asked Penny as though she was speaking through an echo-chamber.

Matthew could barely hear her or understand what she was saying.

"Did you see her? Did you tell her what happened? Is she coming?"

He was incapable of speaking. He merely nodded his head every time she asked a question.

Mike was in surgery for hours. Afterward, a doctor came and informed them that it was touch and go if he'd live, but he was unlikely to ever be able to walk or even to understand what was happening around him if he did survive.

Jenny didn't come to the hospital that day. Finally Penny stole some time from Mike's bedside the following afternoon to go find her older sister -Alone. Matthew spent that day and most of the following week watching film after film in the Flock-In Occulorum, just to take his mind off what was happening. One film featured the head of a bodiless chicken that spoke constantly for forty-five minutes about the meaning of 'Nothing'. Another film was like a fly on a wall -Literally. The camera moved around and rested in an empty room as though it was a fly. Instead of buzzing however, the sound was like the beating of mighty wings.

When Penny reached the large house, the proprietor's wife, Mrs. Folkard-Nockwell answered the front door herself. She seemed flustered, but polite. She informed Penny that her sister wasn't there and that she didn't know where she was.

"There's been an accident..." Penny began, but Mrs. Folkard-Nockwell already knew about that.

"Your younger brother was here," she reminded Penny, then asked after Mike.

"It looks like he'll live," she said to the lady of the house. "They say he'll never properly wake up though. Will you tell Jenny when she comes back, please?"

Penny was annoyed now at Jenny for not being there and for not taking her family responsibility seriously. Jenny was the older sister -*she* should be the one looking after these matters.

There had been no word at all from their eldest sister, Joan, for a number of months. Before that, Joan would send regular cheques home, along with a letter at Christmas. The previous December had come and gone, however, without any news. Jenny had told Penny she would make enquiries, but to date nothing had come of it. Joan had simply disappeared. Now it looked like Jenny was also disappearing. Was their whole family simply being *erased?* Would there be any record of the Cratchett-family having *existed* in time to come? What was happening here?

"I'll have my husband, the doctor, pass on the message as quickly as possible," answered Mrs. Folkard-Nockwell.

At the time, Penny didn't attach any significance to what was said. On her way back to the hospital, however, those words kept echoing in her mind: *"I'll have my husband, the doctor, pass on the message as quickly as possible."* What did that mean? Was Mrs. Folkard-Nockwell not capable of passing on a message personally? Perhaps she didn't speak directly to 'servants'? The lady had *seemed* to be shy and polite, but who knew what thoughts *actually* lurked behind a polite and smiling person?

"I'VE MADE A TERRIBLE MISTAKE, LUCY"

"There's been an accident," Blurt Johannsen told Granny's Cat. "Oo-Sing-A-Car is dead."

Granny's Cat's eyes filled with tears. He took a deep breath and nodded quickly and repeatedly. All the villagers had stood behind him in the square once the travellers returned without their guide. It was as though they had been expecting some grave news.

Now a low, slow chant began at the back of the crowd and grew louder as each villager from the back to the front started up, one-by-one.

"Ooooooo" they all sang in a continuous open-mouth hum. As soon as the person immediately behind Granny's Cat started ooing, the village leader himself joined in.

"Ooooooo" he sang, then slowly continued...

"...Sing-A-Car! Oooooo-Sing-A-Car!" as the others all carried on with the simple "Oooooo."

Now the tearful Granny's Cat stopped singing as the others began with the "Oooooo-Sing-A-Car, Oooooo-Sing-A-Car!" slowly and repeatedly. Lucy recognised the tune as being the same as that wedding song -'*Here comes the bride, All dressed in white.*' The villagers kept singing Oooooo-Sing-A-Car, Oooooo-Sing-A-Car to the air of those two lines over and over again.

"The giant has claimed another victim," nodded Granny's Cat to Blurt, Lucy and Professor Crastinator.

Blurt shook his head.

"No it's not like that, you see!" he complained. "I made a wish, you see! I wished I was the bravest person in Harrumph! you see!"

But Granny's Cat couldn't see at all.

"...And you shall be granted that wish," he told the blind man. "But for now, let us mourn another brave man, struck down in his prime by the evil giant."

Blurt tried to protest, but the Professor rested a hand on his shoulder, as Granny's Cat began to lead a slow procession around the village, ooing and singing all the way.

"They're not interested," the Professor told Blurt. "Their own truth is simpler and easier to accept. They're not ready for complications. How could it be explained anyway? Oo-Sing-A-Car died of fright? That doesn't make any sense to these people. Perhaps in time they will want to listen," he said, "but not now."

Blurt nodded, then turned and cried on the shoulder of the man dressed in the gorilla suit.

"I've made a terrible mistake, Lucy," confessed Professor Crastinator after dinner. "I'm taking you home first thing in the morning."

Lucy didn't complain. She merely nodded sadly as she left him standing there and went inside the hut Granny's Cat had assigned for her to sleep in.

What she hadn't stayed around long enough to hear, was that his mistake had been in leaving home so quickly. He had come to realise some time ago that he could have contacted Dr. Flocky Nocky via email. He didn't know the address offhand, but he was certain it could be found on his computer somewhere.

He had been in such a tizzy before they left (and for many years before that, he now realised) that the most obvious things - such as getting dressed or sending an email- hadn't occurred to him. Of course Flocky Nocky would have protested his innocence, but at least the Professor would have had *something* to go on. He could have insisted on visiting the doctor and if Flocky Nocky had refused, he would have known some more. Not knowing what had happened to his dog was possibly the worst part of it all. And where was he, himself, now anyway? -Somewhere, lost in a far-corner of the planet, probably thousands of miles away from any-where, dressed in a gorilla suit, frightening innocent villagers to death -and for *what?* What was the point of it all?

He walked to his hut, then went inside as the sundown Oo-Sing-A-Car-Procession passed by.

That night Lucy had a dream. She was standing in water that was up above her knees. Ooyay was standing before her, but because he was so small, he was under the water. Somehow, breathing underwater was not a problem for him. He just stood there, looking up at Lucy.

"C'mere Ooyay!" she called to him, but he didn't come. He just stood there.

"Come on, boy!" she cried, patting her knees now, under the water.

He didn't budge. He looked like he was ready to leap into her arms, but he didn't budge.

She looked around (in her dream) and saw several pyramids rising out of the water.

"Where are we?" she asked the dog.

"Gurgleburglesplurgleurgle," said Ooyay, but she couldn't make out what he was saying.

"You shouldn't talk with your mouth full!" she informed him. "...Now take a deep breath and tell me slowly where we are."

Ooyay took a deep breath of water before replying.

"Gurgle... burgle... splurgle... urgle," he told her more slowly. For some reason this made complete sense to the young girl in her dream. Not only did it answer the question she had asked, but, she found, it also answered everything else she had ever thought to ask. She now knew *everything!*

...And then she woke up, smiling, because she knew all the answers because Ooyay had just told her.

However, once she shook the sleep from her head, she realised it had all been nonsense. "Burgle splurgle!" she laughed at her own stupidity.

Professor Crastinator too had a dream: There were squares and circles floating all around him. As these two shapes blended together, they formed triangles. That was the entire dream.

He woke with a frightened start. The half-asleep Professor

had to think hard before he realised that what had happened was that he had had a dream. It had been *years* since he had a dream of any sort. In fact, he couldn't remember the last time he did dream. He was not the type of person who dreamt.

This was what continued to frighten him. If he now was someone who *dreamt,* then what did this mean?

Change.

Blurt Johannsen dreamt of pirates and space ships and of being king of the world.

The next morning they ate breakfast together in Granny's Cat's hut. Nobody said much throughout. Each of them was lost in his or her own thoughts. Finally, as Granny's Cat's wife, Stringy Dooey, removed the empty plates, Lucy thought to say something.

"I dreamt I saw Ooyay last night," she told the group. When nobody said anything, she continued. "I was standing in water and he was under the water, talking to me."

Still nobody said a word. Since there was nothing better being said, she thought she might as well tell them the rest.

"He was just gurgling, but I could understand him in the dream," she laughed. "There were pyramids all over the place -big ones and small ones..."

"Pyramids?" asked Blurt, cutting her short. "...He was under the water and there were pyramids?" He had never heard anything like that before -in a dream or not.

"...Sounds like Pyrra," said Granny's Cat.

"Pyrra?" repeated the other three at once.

"Yes," Granny's Cat answered, "it is as you describe -pyramids and water. It's an island a few hundred miles south and east of here. You must have heard of it?" But they all answered no.

"I've definitely never seen or heard of that place," continued Lucy. "It sounds like Geography and we don't start doing that in school until *next* year."

The others smiled, although Professor Crastinator was curious to hear more from Lucy. Something in what she had said sparked his interest. Perhaps it was just a feeling. Maybe it was because he had dreamt of triangles. Pyramids were also triangles. ...Could there have been some link to their dreams? Was that why he had dreamt for the first time? Was it possible that Ooyay was somehow linked to this Pyrra place?

Lucy looked into the Professor's sad, confused, curious eyes.

"Do you think we should check out Pyrra?" she asked him with the hint of a smile.

WAKE UP OOYAY!

KUH-LILLOP-IP

Ooyay woke up, but struggled for some time to open his heavy eyelids. It felt like they were stuck tight. Eventually, he succeeded in opening one eye and managed a groggy inspection of his surroundings before finding he had to shut it again due to fatigue.

KUH-LILLOP-IP

He was lying on the metal table in the centre of the room with the cages.

KUH-LILLOP-IP

...

KUH-LILLOP-IP

Using all the muscles in his head, he slowly stretched his mouth to one side, then the other. He twitched his ears. He jiggled his brow-line. Finally he forced both eyes open -just a tiny bit this time. He also managed to raise his head a fraction before falling back onto the table to rest some more and to consider what he had seen.

KUH-LILLOP-IP

He had seen that the door to the reception-area was open. Seamus Shafford was standing in the doorway, talking to someone who was out of sight, near the front desk.

"You shouldn't have done it like that..." Seamus was saying. The other man said something in reply but Ooyay couldn't make it out.

KUH-LILLOP-IP

Opening his eyes and craning his neck once more, Ooyay noticed that Seamus was still distracted by the other person in the reception. Maybe there was a chance to run past them ...if he could ...just... make it off this table.

KUH-LILLOP-IP

He managed to move a little from where he was, by letting

his neck flop closer to the edge of the table. He found that he was able to twitch his front paws, but his hind legs were lifeless. He couldn't feel them at all.

Only then did Ooyay think to wonder what had happened. How did he get there? How come he couldn't move?

KUH-LILLOP-IP

Then he remembered trying to escape. He had opened his cage and set that other dog free. Why had he done that? How could he have been so stupid? One look at that dog should have told him he was nothing but trouble.

KUH-LILLOP-IP

But Ooyay had chosen to ignore the common-sense option and decided to play the hero. He had rescued the savage dog with the golf eye ball and was repaid by being mauled almost to death. The memory of that fierce hound bearing down on top of him was a particularly tough image to remove from his mind just at that moment.

KUH-LILLOP-IP

"...no right... In fact you can stop that right now!" Seamus was demanding of the other man.

Ooyay raised his head again and let it flop closer to the edge of the table once more. Now he pulled a front paw closer to his head. Now the other paw twitched and slid into place next to the first one.

KUH-LILLOP-IP

KUH-LILLOP-IP

'What *is* that strange noise?' wondered Ooyay. It seemed to be coming from the other room and getting quicker now.

KUH-LILLOP-IP

KUH-LILLOP-IP

KUH-LILLOP-IP

A scuffle suddenly broke out in the doorway as the strange noise stopped. Ooyay saw Seamus grab at something.

Then he saw the other man's arm in the air and Seamus was scrabbling for whatever it was that he was holding.

"GIVE... IT..." shouted Seamus.

Ooyay made it to the edge of the table and allowed his
head flop over the side. His front paws followed quickly after. If he
could just make it to the floor he would be a step nearer to home
and to Crasty.

"What the...?" Seamus cried when he caught sight of the dog that
was hanging off the table.

The other man seemed to be distracted for long enough to
allow Seamus casually take the item from his hand. Walking
toward Ooyay now, Seamus marvelled at the dog's strength and
determination.

"Take it easy there fella," said Seamus calmly, "you've had a nasty
fall on some chloroform. There's no way you'll be able to budge for
at least another few hours."

'Chloroform?' thought Ooyay. He had fallen on chloroform? He must have knocked it from the portable shelf when he
leapt to open that other dog's cage. A small dose of chloroform is
used to knock-out people and animals. He must have fallen back
on top of the whole smashed bottle. No wonder he was now so
limp! He hadn't been mauled by that beautiful one-eyed dog after
all! There was hope for him and for all of them yet! There was a
goodness in everyone and nobody deserved to be written-off like
he had done with that badly-treated animal.

Seamus placed the small object from his hand on top of the
table as he picked Ooyay up from where he lay, half-on/ half-off
the bench. As he did so, the dog gave a quick scan to the cage next
to his own, to check on how the brown dog was doing: He wasn't
there at all. In his place was a friendly-looking golden labrador.
Where had his friend gotten to? Had he somehow managed to
escape? Well done that dog! A blow for freedom at last!

But as Seamus swung around to place the dog back in his
cage, Ooyay caught sight of what Mr. Shafford had left on the
table: A green golf ball.

DOCTOR'S LETTER

TO PENNY AND MATTHEW CRATCHETT,

Some months ago, your sister Jenny made enquiries as to the whereabouts of her older sister, Joan. As you know, Joan has not been heard from in some months.

Jenny was unable to locate Joan. Apparently, she failed to turn up for work one day and has not been seen since. Nobody has any further information.

Jenny took the news (or lack of it) badly. I had to sedate her for some time, but she was adamant that she would shelter you from the blow.

Her nerves were beginning to return to more normal levels when news arrived of your brother's accident. Jenny was unable to bear the burden of this news on top of all that has gone before.

Despite her delirious ramblings, she gasped and shrieked in horror as she pleaded with me not to talk to you about this. I had to promise I wouldn't speak with you.

That is why I am writing this letter. Apologies for the delay, but Jenny was not in any state for visitors before now. You will find her at the state mental hospital, north of the city.

I am sorry for all your troubles,

Dr. Miles Folkard-Nockwell GP. MD. BA. BP. WSA. HPQP. RRP. WD40. XYZ.

Coming on the back of all that had gone before, Penny and Matthew took this latest news with little more than a shrug. It was too big to think about for any length of time, so basically they put it out of their minds altogether. More than a month had passed by the time the letter arrived. Mike had already been released from hospital to come home to be nursed by his sister.

"Silver doubloons! Sparkling diamonds... cold... no wushinn, gaasf rubbillumm" Mike would call out from his bed of delirium. He was never again to form an understandable sentence, but would forever tease his listeners with snippets that almost made some sense before fading into a whisper.

"Told you to walk... gannets over water... SEE HIM!!! HIM!!!... fried fish and... wellingtons."

Of course Penny took care of Mike almost entirely by herself. She also took care of the living quarters, her job and Matthew. She insisted that her younger brother work hard at school, and later college, so that he would be in a better position to look after the family once he qualified and had a good job.

Matthew no longer needed much persuasion. He convinced himself that he was taking care of his sister by doing what she asked of him. He stayed out of her way as much as possible and away from his older brother. He buried himself in books and learning and he moved into the back room of the old fire station so as to take up as little space as possible.

Coincidentally, this room was also right behind the screen in the Flock-In Occulorum. One entire wall of the room was taken up by the reverse-image of what people were watching in the unusual cinema. So not only did he see every one of those strange films many times as he did his homework, he got to see them the wrong way around (left to right).

Some time passed before Penny worked up the courage to go visit her sister, Jenny. She found Jenny calm but quite mad. It seemed that Jenny had naturally acquired the same mental illness that their mother suffered from and that Mike now suffered through due to the knock on the head.

As she made her way back home that day, vowing not to say a word to Matthew, she thought about where this madness had come from. It was obvious really: It all went back to their brother, Martin. Poor Mucus lived such a short life. His only comfort came from their walks in the countryside. He was such a nice boy and they all loved him dearly. Penny knew that the family had never recovered from that loss. His death was like the beginning of a rip through an old photograph of the happy family.

Mike lay in bed, talking to himself, crying out and rambling through his own mind for almost ten years. Not once did Penny complain.

Time and again, Matthew made a half-baked protest that he should leave college and get a job to take care of them both, but his sister would not allow it. Matthew was silently thankful. Despite gaining a lot of knowledge, he knew he was pretty useless at anything of a practical nature. Like most boys who never grow up, he barely knew how to make toast for himself. Making money was something at which he wouldn't know where to start.

One day, he came home to find Mike's bed made, but empty. Penny was busy tidying the kitchen. Matthew didn't know what to say or how to ask. Eventually she turned to Matthew and said it for him.

"He faded away," she told him matter-of-factly. "There'll be a short ceremony tomorrow morning at ten."

PYRRA

It's hard to explain in writing how people in Pyrra speak. If you haven't heard them before, you (reader) need to do some work in figuring out how they say things: Just about *all* they say is "Oooo," but they have several hundred ways of saying it, each meaning something different. Don't worry though, you won't be expected to understand the Pyrraoooish in the next few pages - Lucy and the Professor don't speak it either. But to properly get to grips with the sound, try saying the following out loud: "OoooohoOOOOooowwW!"

No! Come on. Say it *out loud*. Really. It won't work if you only say it aloud in your mind. You need to *really* say it. Quickly now! We don't have all day... If you are familiar with Frankie Howard or Kenneth Williams or some other famous raconteurs, you will know how to say it. But don't worry if not...

Imagine someone has just told you a really *dirty* secret -a *juicy* piece of information about somebody else (who you don't really like) that you weren't expecting to hear and you are very surprised that it has been said. Now hold that thought! ...Imagine what your friends and neighbours are going to think when *they* hear it! It will be the talk of the town!

...So scrunch up your eyes and put your lips into a tight O-formation. Turn your head slightly to the left or to the right. Raise your shoulder up to your chin. Breathe in quickly through your mouth. Now say it fast. Say it out loud: "OoooohoOOOOooowwW!"

That's it! Say it again! Come on! Don't be shy!

"OoooohoOOOOooowwW!"

Now you can speak Pyrraoooish. In fact you've just told the person nearest you that his or her shoelace is undone.

Pyrra turned out to be as Granny's Cat had said: pyramids and water. A crowd of Pyrraooni people had formed around the ATV by the time Lucy and the Professor climbed out. They all looked shocked and surprised to see the two visitors, as though they had never seen another living person in their lives.

"Hello!" yelled Professor Crastinator with a cheery wave as he climbed from the Bullet and stood in front of the nearest islander.

"OoooohoOOOOoooww!" cried a number of people as Lucy stepped from the vehicle, but it was too late even if she had understood their howls.

The nine year old tripped and tumbled down the ladder, landing with a splash at the foot of the man standing next to the Professor.

It was only then that she noticed the main difference between this place and her dream: The water here did not reach as high as peoples' knees. Instead it barely covered their feet. ...But *what feet!*

The bare feet in front of her face at that moment were easily twice as long and twice as wide as any adult's Lucy had seen up to then. Strangely they didn't look too ridiculous though because the lower part of the legs were also very wide and fat.

As she picked herself up, dripping wet, Lucy noticed how this man seemed to get skinnier the further up he went. At the top, his head was smaller than Lucy's own head. Looking around now, Lucy noticed that every man amongst them, old and young, appeared to have the same frame: Large, fat feet and small, skinny heads.

"OOOOOoooww!" said a woman as she bent to make sure the young girl was all right after her fall.

Gazing into this woman's kind eyes, Lucy felt embarrassed to find herself staring at the extra-large size of her head. Professor Crastinator himself had quite a big head, but this woman's head was twice as big in every way. Her neck and shoulders were also quite large, but her hips were small and (as Lucy slowly took note), her feet were tiny.

Quickly Lucy looked around for more women and young girls, and yes, she found they all too had the same proportions: Extra-large heads and extra-small feet. Nobody wore shoes here, it seemed. *'I expect they'd have to change their wet socks too often if they did,'* guessed Lucy silently to herself.

"We have come to see Flocky Nocky!" said the Professor slowly and loudly. "Do you know him? Doctor Flocky Nocky? Flavius Flocky Nocky? The inventor? Hmmm?" he asked, examining the puzzled expression on everybody's fat and skinny faces.

"OoooOOOOooowwww yaaooooooh" said one man as his eyes bulged.

The Professor walked quickly to this individual and stopped within inches of his nose.

"Ooyay?" he enquired. "Did you say Ooyay!?"

"OoooOOOOooowwww yaaooooooh" repeated the man, shaking his head up and down, left and right, then around in circles. "...Oooo OOOO ooowwww yaaooooooh" he added.

Lucy wondered if this was all some big joke and desperately wanted to laugh, but the strangeness of the surroundings made her feel ill at ease, even though these people were clearly friendly and meant to cause them no harm.

"Did he say Ooyay?" the Professor asked her, then quickly turned again to the man before him. "Ooooooooooo-Yaaaaaaaaayyyyyyyyyyy?" he asked. "Doggie? Oooooo-yayyyyy? Woof woof?"

The man looked shocked, as if the Professor had said a lot of dirty words.

"OooooOOOOOowwwwwww" he said, looking to his friends and nodding with a hint of a smile, as though thrilled by the newcomer's daring tale.

Then he stood aside to allow the visitors access to the large and clearly-ancient land around them.

Nothing rose out of the flat glass-like ground except for pyramids, near and far. Some were bigger than others. Some had green crops growing on each narrowing platform and fruit bushes up the walls. Some had water running down their sides, making them look like shimmering, triangular, skyscraper waterfalls.

Lucy felt as though nothing would ever surprise her again after this journey was over, but *boy* was she seeing some pretty spectacular places, people and objects since she left home. Could it really be possible that such things *existed* in this world? She felt giddy with excitement, had no idea whatsoever where any of this was going to take her next and hardly cared.

She couldn't think of anything to say as she noticed how the pyramid city before them was mirrored in the water below, causing each building to appear diamond-like in shape, with neither a top nor a bottom.

"Ooooooooh!" she gasped.

"...I know exactly what you mean," nodded the Professor, with a deep breath of his own.

Nobody now came forward to talk to the newcomers. Nobody blocked their path or told them where to go. In fact everybody more or less pretended they were not in the least bit curious about the visitors. Each time Lucy or the Professor looked around, the people close-by quickly looked in the air or kicked at the water on the ground or picked their fingernails or whistled casually.

"They're hiding something!" Lucy quietly declared.

The visitors turned back, away from the ATV, then walked a little to the left. Suddenly, all the nearby Pyrraooni people behind them shifted quietly to the left. They moved right and everyone changed course to follow, barely raising a splash. Nobody spoke. Professor Crastinator quickly looked back and everybody stopped moving and acted overly-casual once again.

For a brief few seconds he wondered if these people were blocking their path back to the Bullet, but as soon as he took a step in that direction, they instantly cleared a path for him.

"I think you're right!" he whispered to Lucy. "They *want* us to leave! They definitely know something!"

Slapping his foot down on the ground beneath the water, he now jumped toward the silent crowd and quickly cried "OOYAY!" as if shouting boo at a child.

Everyone jumped back, then once they had recovered from the shock, looked to each other and nodded appreciatively.

"OooooOOOOOOh!" they all declared, raising their eyebrows, smiling and nodding.

Now Lucy had to laugh.

"They like that," she giggled.

But Professor Crastinator saw nothing funny in it. He turned and looked sternly at the young girl, without speaking. At once, Lucy's laughter faded to a smile.

"Well it *was* funny," she pronounced, before walking off in the direction of the nearest pyramid.

The nearest pyramid appeared to be made of marble. Most others in Pyrra looked much like the more-common desert and jungle pyramids, with block-stepped levels as they rose into the air. This one was smooth from bottom to top. It practically screamed at Lucy to run up it and try to touch its pointed nib, but somehow she resisted the urge. With wet shoes, she was certain it would have ended in a single, embarrassing flop-step anyway.

As she slowly approached the entrance to this marble tower, a group of Pyrraooni cried out and waved their arms in every direction.

"OOOOOooooOOOOooo!" they all cried in one voice as they manoeuvred themselves in front of the young girl, blocking her path.

The Professor was only a few feet away, but before he had a chance to react, they had gathered around Lucy, then opened a path away from him, around the far side of the pyramid. People now waved and oooed and gently brushed against Lucy, encouraging her to go in that direction.

"It's ok Lucy I'm right here," Professor Crastinator spoke up from behind the crowd. "I don't think they mean any harm. They want you to walk around the pyramid I think."

He tried squeezing past some Pyrraooni to join her, but nobody made way for him. They were too interested in guiding the young girl.

Lucy was more curious than frightened. The presence of smiling Pyrraooni children, both older and younger than herself, kept her from even thinking of being frightened. ...But just what *was* at the other side of this building?

Behind the marble pyramid was -another marble pyramid. This one, however, was inverted. The pointed peak of the building was buried in the ground beneath the water. The top of it stretched out in a wide, flat roof. It was as if the pyramid was built, tossed in the air, and that it landed on its head.

The group of Pyrraooni lead Lucy to its doorway, then gestured for her to enter. Just inside the inverted-triangular entrance, a spiral staircase wound its way up into the building. The steps were quite narrow at the bottom, but thankfully they quickly widened, giving more room as Lucy ascended. Having completed one full turn, Lucy found herself at the top of the staircase, opening out into a single large room with a floor that sloped upward toward the centre. A single overhead light in the ceiling beamed brightness on a regal-looking woman who sat proudly on top of a raised throne in the middle of the room. Her hands grasped the arms of the throne and her chin was turned high into the air.

Noticing Lucy now for the first time, she lowered her eyes so as to gaze upon the young girl.

"OOOOooooooouh!" she said in a rather surprised, posh tone.

Lucy shuffled in her spot, unsure what to say or how to address this lady.

"Excuse me your highness," she bowed. "I was sent to talk with you. My name is Lucy Lucey."

"OoOoOOOOOOuh!" said the queen.

"I've come here with Professor Crastinator. He's outside," Lucy explained, then added, "*The* Professor Crastinator," just in case this queen knew of another one.

"OoOoOOOOOOuh!" said the queen again.

"Anyway," Lucy said, unsure if it would do any good to continue, but decided she might as well..."We've come here looking for Dr. Flocky Nocky -the inventor. Do you know him?"

"OoOoOOOOOOuh!" said the queen.

"Ok," Lucy answered. "We think he has the Professor's dog, Ooyay..."

"OOOOOWAY!" cried the queen, distinctly.

Lucy stared in amazement.

"Yes," she laughed. "Ooyay! Do you know him? Ooyay? Have you seen him? Is he here? We've come to bring him home!"

The queen raised her arm, pointing upward.

"OoOOOOOooooouh" she said as she lowered her hand and

pointed down to the ground. "OOOOoooOOOOOooo OOOoooUH" she added, waving her hand left to right, then around in circles.

"OOOoOoOOOOOOuh Oooooooouh OOOOoooo OOOo Oooo ooh ooooo uh... OOOOOWAY!" she announced, looking directly at Lucy as she finished her speech, waiting for the young girl's reaction.

Again Lucy was unsure how to react. The lady seemed to be imparting some very relevant information, but it couldn't be understood. Pulling her notebook and pen from her large trouser-pocket, Lucy took a step forward, holding them out for the queen.

"Could you draw...?" she began, but the queen raised her arm once again, all open fingers upward this time, clearly telling the girl to come no further.

It was probably against the rules to approach the throne, Lucy thought, then paused. The queen pressed a button on the arm of her throne. Suddenly there was a sound of splashing, running water. Then a loud gurgling, belching noise rang out across the throne room. The queen arose and stepped lightly toward Lucy, taking the notebook and pen.

"OoOOOOOoooooouh" she spoke more softly now as she stood next to the young girl, drawing something on the page. "OOOOoooo OOOOOoooOOOoooUH   OOOoOoOOOOOOuh Oooooooouh OOOOoooo OOOo Oooo ooh ooooo uh... OOOOOWAY!" she ended, passing the items back.

Lucy studied the notes and drawing the queen had made, but she still wasn't sure what they meant.

"What does..." she began asking, but noticed that the queen had descended the stairs and had just turned out of sight.

Following a brief but careful examination of the throne room, Lucy was satisfied there was nothing else to see here, so she too left, in the footsteps of royalty.

Outside, the Professor seemed to be making some headway. The locals were treating him to a song, with the women and children all lined up on one side singing "Eeee eee eeeeee" and the men on the other, splashing on the ground, singing "Awwww awww awwww." Each side took turns singing eee, then awww, then eee, then awww. Soon the song changed as the two choirs joined together to sing "Oooooooooooo." Professor Crastinator cheered and clapped, then turned to find Lucy joining him by his side.

"Which way did she go?" Lucy frantically enquired, annoyed that the old man didn't seem to have been guarding the exit.

"Who?" asked the Professor, as she feared he would.

"The *queen*," she answered. "Didn't you see her? She came out just before me!"

"The queen?" he replied. "I was standing here the whole time Lucy and I assure you nobody came out since you went in."

Lucy wasn't waiting for an explanation. She was busy asking the others where the queen had gone, but nobody seemed to know what she was talking about no matter what actions she made or words she used. As before, everybody simply looked around and oooed.

Finally she turned to the Professor.

"Here!" she cried, tearing the page the queen had used from her notebook and handing it to him. "She drew this and said *Ooyay*."

Professor Crastinator grabbed the piece of paper and studied it. Here is what it said:

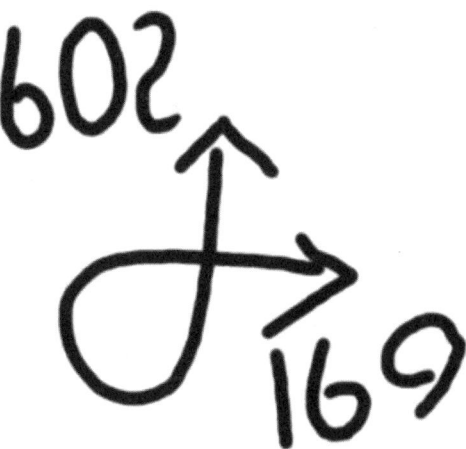

"She said Ooyay?" he repeated, then showed the page to the crowd before him.

"Ooyay?" he asked and to his relief several people nodded. He approached one nearby man who looked particularly knowledgeable.

"Ooyay?" he asked this man once again.

"OoOOOOOooooow" he said as he nodded. Then he pointed up, down, left right and around in circles, before adding "OOOOooooOOOOOoooOOOooow   OOOoOoOOOOOOw Oooooow OOOOoooo OOOo Oooo ooh ooooowww... OOOOO AY!" he said. Others nodded, clearly agreeing with him, some of them pointing at the note.

Now the man himself pointed at the ATV they had landed on, then pointed to the note, up into the air, then back to the ATV.

"Oooay" he nodded and others repeated the same word.

The Professor looked briefly at Lucy before turning back to the crowd.

"You mean we'll find Ooyay at these coordinates?" he asked.

Everyone simply nodded.

Inside the ATV, the Professor was busy studying the computer-generated globe in the centre of the console table. He had calculated 169 miles east and 602 miles north of their current location, but no island showed on the map.

"Oh Blurt," said the female computer voice. "Even you wouldn't be brave enough to try going where there is nothing!"

A large white X indicated a point in the middle of the ocean with no Bullet hole. Lucy sighed deeply and folded her arms.

"What do we do now?" she asked. "He must be there!"

The Professor thought long and hard before finally announcing that he had an idea.

"I could override the safety controls," he stated, looking now to the nine year old sitting next to him. "But first I'll have to take you home."

Lucy was shocked.

"What!" she cried. "After all we've been through! You can't leave me out of it now! I got those coordinates! I'm coming with you!"

The Professor looked to be in pain.

"You don't understand, Lucy," he stated. "If I override the safety and it turns out there *is* no Bullet hole at that location, we'll go crashing into the ocean and we'll *die*. I can't have your blood on my hands."

"But what about *your* blood?" cried the girl. "What about Ooyay? All this is *my* fault. I got us into this mess. I got these coordinates. You *have* to allow me go!"

"No," he whispered, shaking his head softly. "It's time for you to go home."

With that, Lucy stretched in front of the old man, quickly reaching for the launch button. Just before pressing it however, she noticed the notepaper that she had handed to him.

"They're not the coordinates!" she cried out as she read them again.

Professor Crastinator looked on silently as she turned the note upside down, showing:

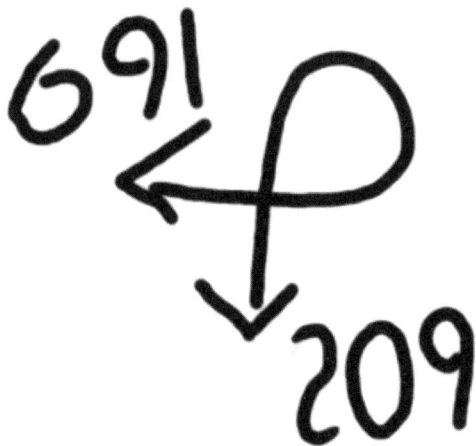

"*They're* the coordinates!"

OOYAY AT IT AGAIN

It was night-time when Ooyay woke again. He still felt somewhat groggy, but immediately launched into action.

'No time like the present,' he thought to himself as he stood up.

He was surprised to find his legs wobble below the weight of his body. After testing his strength for a while, though, he discovered that he could indeed support himself. He searched around the cage for... What? ...He was sure there was something in here that should be able to help him...

Ah! There it was, under some straw: The piece of mirror he had used before. Thankfully it had gone unnoticed by the attendants.

It took him some time to use the mirror on the latch this time and he nearly dropped it through the bars on more than one occasion, but eventually the cage door swung open.

He couldn't see the ground below in the darkness and so misjudged its distance. Thinking, it was slightly further down than it turned out to be, he landed quite heavily on the cold floor, but didn't suffer any cuts or wounds this time. Some other animals stirred and rummaged at the gates of their cages, but Ooyay refused to be distracted this time. This time he was getting out of here. He turned to face the door to the reception area and made straight for it now, without looking left or right.

The door turned out to be closed. However the handle was a straightforward drop-down type and didn't take much effort from Ooyay to leap up and pull it as he fell.

Again, things weren't going easily his way, although he refused to let them bring him down. As soon as he realised that the door was locked from the other side, without missing a beat, Ooyay looked and found some small, empty crates. Pushing these boxes over to the door caused a number of animals to bark and meow and rattle their cages, which in turn woke most of the others. Ooyay was now the focus of a public, daring escape, the likes of which these creatures had never seen before.

He found some paper on top of one of the tables. Taking a single sheet, he placed it under the door before pushing the crates that final few inches.

The handle of a surgical scalpel was held between the little dog's teeth as he pushed the sharp end through the keyhole.

Thankfully the key *was* indeed still in the door and it only took a little effort to turn it slightly, then to push it out the other end.

Once Ooyay pulled the sheet of paper back from under the door, he was relieved to see the key had landed and remained on top of it.

After unlocking the door, he gave only the quickest of gazes over his shoulder at the roomful of howling, screeching cast-off, forgotten and lost animals before leaping with joy from the crates, into the next room.

His happiness was to be short-lived, alas. The heavy front door turned out to be also locked from the other side. This time there wasn't even a keyhole to look through.

"It must be locked with a sliding-bar outside" Ooyay realised. *"What now?"* he wondered as he scanned the room.

There was a large window here, but it too was heavy look-ing, and anyway, he had clearly noted the shadow of bars through the opaque glass when last he was in this reception-area. Breaking through would not do any good even if it was possible.

Besides the phone on the front desk, there was nothing of note in this room. The only other exit from here lead down into the boiler room/ cellar and he really didn't fancy seeing that room again.

With great reluctance, Ooyay quietly stepped back into the room he had come from, trying not to draw any further attention to himself.

"Woof woof woof" barked the big dogs.

"Ruff ruff ruff" went some smaller ones.

"Arf arf arf" shouted a few others. And the smallest dogs cried "Yap yap yap yap yap."

Some cats screeched like a violin in the shower. Some meowed like only the cutest kitties can do. Yet more shivered fear-fully at the back of their cages. Rabbits, hamsters, turtles, guinea pigs, mice and rats all hopped and eeked with excitement.

Not all of the animals knew what was happening, but for those that did, the hero of the hour was now marching down the length of the cage-room, now stacking crates, now grabbing the scalpel firmly once more in his teeth and climbing the crate moun-tain. Slowly and carefully he twisted each of the four screws that were holding the ventilation grille in place, before disappearing inside the large hole in the wall.

Suddenly there was silence. All of the animals held their breath as they waited to see what would happen next.

The room vibrated with noise and excitement once again as soon as they heard footsteps coming from inside the ventilation shaft. Along the back-wall, the little doggie ran. Turning right, the footsteps then proceeded down the full length of the cage-room, straight through to the other room.

Inside the shaft, Ooyay was growing warmer. He came to a grille that looked out onto the reception-area, but he kept going. Finally he reached a left-turn. Within a few feet, however, there was a sudden drop down into darkness. The small dog hovered on the edge of this hole, wondering what to do next, as a wave of hot air wafted over his face.

Should he risk this leap into darkness? Did he have a choice? Where was this hot air coming from anyway? His mind was still muddled from the chloroform and he was unsure what this heat meant. ...Still, he could take this leap or he could go back the way he came -Back to his cell to await the same fate that had befallen ole golfeyeball.

Just then he had another idea. Retracing his footsteps to the last grille, he looked down now into the reception-area below. Yes! This just might work!

Excited animals howled and cried out all the more to see the escapee return from the hole in the wall and once more march through to the outer room. Whatever was going on here, it was worth forsaking a night's sleep for the excitement alone.

"You have rung the wrong number. Don't bother leaving a message. ....BEEEEEP!"

Ooyay found it strange, but not unpleasant to hear a familiar, friendly voice. In fact, the voice was that of the answer machine message that he himself had left. He was hoping that Crasty would have answered, but decided to risk it nonetheless.

"...Crasty?" he whispered into the mouthpiece of the phone as he looked around the office. "...Are you there Crast? ...If you're there pick up!"

A few seconds passed by with no sound from the other end of the line.

"I'm in... I don't know... I think it's an animal shelter of some kind... wherever the local dog warden takes dogs possibly -probably..."

Realising the ridiculousness of the situation, Ooyay suddenly burst out with laughter. *How* had it been possible that the dog warden might have caught him? If true, that would be one funny state of affairs. After all he had been through -after all he had *invented*- to find himself possibly prisoner to the local dog-warden was a joke beyond belief.

"Beep!" went the phone on the other end of the line as the answer machine reached the end of the message time allowed.

The sound of the phone-line's busy signal acted like a scissors, cutting the last contact the small dog had to the outside world. He allowed himself flop from the counter and remained curled-up, whimpering behind the desk for some time. Where was Crasty? Was he asleep? *Didn't he care?*

Laughter had turned to sadness. Sadness lead to inaction as he considered how and why he had gotten into this situation. Anger then followed as Ooyay decided that *he* would fight this on his own -in his own way -on *his* terms. He would get out of here - and when he did, he would have a thing or two to say to *Professor* Marcus Crastinator. ...Things were going to change around here! He would make sure of that himself! There was no point in waiting for that loafer to decide if he should climb out of his bed!

Ooyay would have to get out of this in his own way. How could he expect Crasty to rescue him? After all, on his own, Crasty *was* quite useless at just about everything.

Returning to the cage-room to a hero's cheer, Ooyay now set about freeing each of the animals one by one. How else could his own single cage-escape be explained? It wouldn't have been possible to climb back into his cage without leaving some evidence behind. Anyway, with a mass of animals all over this place, when Seamus Shafford came back in the morning he would almost certainly not miss a certain little doggie slipping out the door in all the hubbub.

This plan... just might... actually... work!

ADULTHOOD

PENNY'S TURN

Although Matthew was a brilliant student, his tolerance for any one subject was always short-lived. He spent *years* in college hopping from one course to another, excelling in all of them (to his teachers' delight), but never completing a single one.

Mr. Kratinsky had a word with him on more than one occasion, pointing out how hard his sister worked to pay for his education. By this time, the downstairs garage was being rented-out and used as a private car park, which also helped pay for Matthew's costly upbringing.

No matter how determined he was to "stick with it this time", however, within a few months Matthew became bored and his grades slipped. Soon he could no longer keep up with the class.

He assured Mr. Kratinsky that he wasn't doing it deliberately, but no matter how hard he appeared to try, once Matthew lost interest in the subject, he could not hold any of it in his mind.

Penny secretly blamed the Flock-in Occulorum films that he constantly watched now. They distracted him too much while he should be studying. However, she never told him to stop watching and she never reprimanded him in any way for dropping out of any particular class. Matthew was her last remaining link to the family she once had. She had spent all her life looking after one family member or another. She really didn't know how to do anything other than to 'be there' for her family and to do whatever was needed on their behalf. She didn't see it as a sacrifice that needed to be done. For Penny, that *was* her life and her reason for being. If Matthew finished college and got a job, and maybe got a life of his own... what would Penny do then? What would she be? *Who* would she be?

So she was happy for Matthew to stay studying and for her to stay mothering him forever more. He needed her help and she was happy to provide it. Penny was Penny and Matthew was Matthew.

But one day, that world came to an end...

It was on Matthew's birthday that it happened. Penny went out, as she often did at lunchtime, with the sandwich-board around her neck to advertise the Flock-In Occulorum. She had arranged with Matthew that they would meet and go for a meal just after she had let the three o'clock audience into the cinema.

A film called *Things in my Pockets* was playing that day, which obviously wasn't very popular, which was why Penny had to go around town advertising the cinema. The following week, *Women with Hoola Hoops* was to be the main show. There would have been no need for Penny to advertise the cinema at that time.

Matthew finished his studies early that day, so he arrived at the Flock-In Occulorum some time before three to find that his sister wasn't back yet. He stood in by the front door, away from the wind and the rain as he waited. After a few minutes Mr. Kratinsky came out the front door and was annoyed to find Matthew standing there with his hands in his pockets.

"What are you doing there?" he cried. "Go! Why don't you go find your sister -out there in this miserable weather! Here!" he added, handing him an umbrella. "Bring her this -The poor girl out there getting soaked to the skin!"

Carrying the sandwich board had been Penny's own idea. In truth, the sight of her wearing two large wood panels with pictures of himself (and the building) embarrassed Mr. Kratinsky more than anything else. He had told her not to do it, but the ever-practical Penny would only smile and shrug and say it was good for business.

It wasn't that Matthew was a nasty person. It was just that he never really considered anyone else. Despite the great losses in his life, he was spoilt. His head was all the time stuck in books or on the screen and he was too busy with everything *inside* to even think about having a good look *outside* at the world and at the people around him.

After trudging crankily up the main street, he came to an intersection with pedestrian crossing. Leaning against the building on the other side of the road was Penny. She had stood-in during a particularly bad shower, but as soon as she spotted her brother, she stepped forward and waved joyously.

"HAPPY BIRTHDAY!" she shouted across the busy road at the now red-faced Matthew.

Just then a car sped by and soaked his sister's face, hair and the front board that covered her body. Since she had just embarrassed him so much, Matthew couldn't help but break out in laughter.

Penny turned away from the road so as to shake her sopping hair, but as she did, a massive gust of wind whooshed up the street. Like it would with the sail on a boat, the wind was trapped now by the body-length panel attached to Penny, and so sent her flying into the oncoming traffic on the main road. At the same time, the driver of a large truck had increased his speed slightly so as to dodge the light that was just about to turn red. Instead of catching the green light, however, the truck caught a flying sandwich-board girl.

Matthew witnessed the whole thing. In fact he had *participated* in it by simply being there. The world swirled. A crowd gathered around his sister at the other side of the road. He needed to be there for her now, but he felt as if that crowd and that whole accident-scene was slipping away from him. It was as though he was looking at that scene through a long tunnel -and the tunnel was growing longer. Nothing was really working in Matthew's head by then, but his legs stepped forward onto the road. His body carried him down the long tunnel toward a man who was holding his sister's wrist. Matthew's arm stretched outward as though he was handing the umbrella to the raised hand of his sister. Just then, the man looked up into Matthew's eyes.

"She's dead," he cried.

It happened the first time a family member of his had died, but it hadn't happened since. Now it happened again: Matthew collapsed on the spot.

PAUSE BEFORE LIFT OFF

At six hundred and ninety one miles west, two hundred and nine miles south of their current position there lay a small island with a Bullet hole, but no name. That is to say, no name appeared over the map on the computer console once the Professor keyed in the coordinates. At least this time it was obvious that there was indeed an island at those coordinates.

"That's it!" cried Lucy. "It *has* to be! How else could it have no name!? Everywhere has a name!"

The Professor could think of nothing to add or take from Lucy's point. He had no better idea on what to do next or where to go, so he merely shrugged and slid along the rounded seating, away from the console.

When two people first meet, they need words to fill in the silent gaps and to explain what they are thinking and how they feel and what their outlook on life is. Once they come to know and trust each other and have a common purpose and common goals, or once they have an understanding on what type of person each one is, there is less need for words all of the time. A nod or a shrug or a half-closed eye or a particular type of breath can say everything needed to be said between people who belong together at any one moment.

Without thinking, Lucy knew why the Professor had slid away. He hadn't told her or looked at her, but she knew at once what to do. At the same moment, both of them reached out, took safety goggles from the space below the central table and put them on. The young girl then slid in front of the main console, gave a brief look to the old man, and pressed the red launch button.

Lucy only ever had one grandfather and one grandmother. Her mother's parents used to take her for walks when she was younger. The three of them went on the train together to the country or to the beach. She used to stay in their house sometimes if her own parents had to go away for some reason. It was like a second home to her.

Nowadays they didn't go anywhere together. Thankfully they were both still alive and well, but Lucy felt sad that she didn't seem to see them as much.

'Why don't I see them as much now?' she wondered sorrowfully to herself, before resolving to visit them as soon as she returned home and to give them both a big hug.

She never knew her dad's parents. They were both dead since before she was born. To be honest, she had never given them much thought, but now she felt sad and missed them a lot.

Over the past few days, Professor Crastinator had become like the grandfather she never knew. He was cranky and silly and useless, but he never pretended to be anything else with her. Most people are too busy trying to be nice or helpful or busy trying to get you to do something. This man never asked anything of Lucy, which made her determined to help him all the more. He was never anything but *himself* since they had set out. He no longer had his dog to hide behind so his guard was down.

The ATV sank into the ground.

"I'm getting that sinking feeling, Blurt," said the computer. "Get ready for the three beeps. On the third beep, the only way is *up!* ...This time we're off to..."

When a computer seems so unsure of itself that it fails to finish a sentence, it would usually lead to uncertainty, doubt and possibly even panic. In this case, however, Lucy and Professor Crastinator just looked at each other and sniggered. They both knew that wherever it was and whatever it was called didn't really matter any longer. They had a serious reason to go there, but this search had taken on a life of its own. Despite the trauma they were going through, they were equally curious about what would happen next. Neither of them had experienced or ever considered anything like they had been through recently. Finding out what was about to happen was no longer something they feared.

'Bring it on!' their sniggers said, although neither of them needed to actually use those words.

Lucy paused and checked the old man. He seemed sad, despite his laughter. He looked *alone.*

"...Can I call you Crasty?" she asked. Somehow it no longer seemed right to call him Professor.

The Professor looked at her softly as the first beep sounded from the computer. She gazed into the tinted eyes behind the goggles. Lucy wasn't certain, but she felt there were quiet tears in there now for some reason.

He smiled and shook her hand. He had never had children of his own and so he never considered having a grandchild -or a great-grandchild for that matter. Seeing and being with this child now, he realised that if he had, he could never have asked for a better one than Lucy. She was a good kid.

He didn't feel the need to answer yes or no. Such words weren't necessary. The second beep sounded.

"...That's what Ooyay calls me," he simply said, throwing his head back into the headrest.

Lucy smiled and did the same, as the third beep rang out and the Bullet launched up and out of the tube.

BEAUTY AND THE BEAST

Days passed as Matthew slept in his hospital bed. Tests and scans showed that his brain and senses were still functioning, but nothing could be done that would wake him. He didn't require medical attention, but clearly he was no longer capable of surviving day to day without assistance. Nobody knew when or if he would ever awaken.

As the days turned to weeks, Matthew was transferred from ward to ward by medical staff who were too busy to deal with a patient who wasn't exactly sick. Mr. Kratinsky would often spend the first hour of each visit wandering the wards and corridors of the old City General Hospital, in search of the travelling sleeper.

Finally, after months had passed without any change in Matthew's condition or his treatment, Pierce Kratinsky demanded that Matthew be put on a Procliner.

The Procliner was a quite recent medical invention that was actually a self-cleaning bed. It was hooked to a Central Process Store (CPS), located elsewhere in the building and could administer food and medication, via tubes, to a patient in need of life-support assistance. As well as feeding and disposing of a patient's waste, it also had an inbuilt massager that ensured the patient's muscles retained some strength for the day when he or she might require it.

The only problem was that Matthew was not, technically, in need of life-support assistance. His brain was still functioning and he didn't require any *medical* attention.

Nonetheless, the owner of the Flock-In Occulorum spent months pleading with anyone in the hospital that would listen. Matthew was being ignored and maltreated, he told them. The staff were too busy and they were forgetting him all of the time. On one occasion, Mr. Kratinsky spent the day looking for Matthew, only to eventually find him in his bed, hidden away in the janitor's closet with the buckets and mops.

After that, he threatened to go public with news of the shabby treatment. A middle-aged surgeon by the name of Dr. Miles Folkard-Nockwell also spoke on behalf of the patient, saying that he was a friend of the family and that a Procliner should be assigned to Matthew because he was the last member of a large family that did not deserve to be forgotten.

Eventually, having been asleep for two years and showing no sign of waking up, Matthew was the first non-critically-ill patient in the hospital to be awarded a Procliner. He was also placed permanently in the building's west-wing, on the fourth floor, in a public ward, so that if and when he did awaken, it would be noticed and dealt-with at once.

Matthew slept. As he slept, he dreamt.

Time ticked by. Life and sickness and sometimes death occurred within feet of Matthew's sleeping form, but no drugs or loud noises or tickles could wake him.

In his dreams, Matthew was back in the countryside with his younger brother, Martin, and his sister Penny. They walked hand in hand, whistling and singing and picking flowers. Martin was always sick and weak, but he never died. Oh no, of course he didn't die. In these dreams there is no such thing as death. They called him Mucus and they all laughed and had fun as they skipped through the fields chasing butter-flies.

Matthew had grown to be quite a dashing man by then and some of the nurses jokingly referred to him as "Sleeping Beauty." They began saying that he was awaiting the kiss of his one true love -"*Only then would he awaken,*" they giggled.

As soon as a new female staff member joined the hospital, it wasn't long before she was led to the last ward on the fourth floor in the west-wing of the main building to find out if she was 'The One'.

Penny was always feeding him in his dreams.
"Eat up," she would tell him, and he would -eat up. He ate soup. And when he looked at the soup, it was now a strawberry cake. Mucus loved strawberries, but for some reason, Jenny would never let him eat them.
"You'll die if you eat those strawberries!" she told Mucus.
"What do you mean Jenny?" asked Matthew. "You're mad, you are - everybody knows there is no such thing as death in this dream!"
Jenny laughed as she realised it was all a dream and said "Of course! That's true! It's all a dream!"

So they had a party and they all ate strawberries -Mucus too. And of course he didn't die at all, because nobody dies in this dream.

Over time, other patients in the ward noticed what was happening. Staff were drawing the curtains around a sleeping patient and queuing to kiss him! Some people complained and several staff members were disciplined. The Ceremony of the Kissing ceased at once.

Matthew slept. As he slept, he dreamt.
He stole apples from an orchard and threw them to Penny and Mucus below. He built a tree-house and the three of them lived there forever. Then his sister Joan knocked on the tree-house door and asked if she could come in.
"Come in my sister Joan," cried Matthew. "I never even knew you really."

After a number of years elapsed, Matthew now became a kind of horror-legend among the staff. They told each other confused and half-true stories of how one day he had been the cause of several nurses being fired. Somehow *he* had caused confusion and turmoil in the haunted ward and workers had fought with patients and patients had fought with doctors and in the end, a number of staff members had to be fired. And it was all *his* fault.

Someone then misheard this story (either by mistake or on purpose) and it turned into a tale whereby the sleeping patient had caused a hospital worker to *catch* fire.

People feared to go near the living corpse. ...It wasn't natural for a person to stay alive for so long, but yet, clearly not be living like a normal person.

Matthew slept. As he slept, he dreamt.
Laughing women were on the beach -His mother and Joan and Jenny and Penny. They were all playing with hoola hoops and the men (himself, Mucus, Mike and his dad) were all whistling and cheering and jeering and clapping.

After a while, the legend grew and Matthew (who had never done anything in the hospital besides sleep) became known as "The Zombie". Rumour had it that he was regularly found wandering the corridors, drinking pints of blood in the early hours of the darkest nights.

Nobody wanted to work on that floor, and the poor misfortunate patients who were assigned to the same room often became ill from the tension and apprehension surrounding them at all times. Of course, Matthew was then blamed for the number of nearby patients whose sickness grew worse. '*Somehow, he must have caused that,*' people thought quietly and uneasily to themselves.

Matthew slept. As he slept, he dreamt.
He was looking at an empty room. His father walked in backwards, holding a book. The book was the book of his life and his father read it backwards.
As he came to a particular part of the story, Matthew himself walked in and stood next to his father.
His dad then dropped the book and Matthew hugged him tightly. Both of them cried.

Frightening tales of mysterious happenings at last reached the hospital Board of Management. Clearly the stories were rubbish, but they *were* affecting staff and patient morale. The Board couldn't banish an innocent patient just because of silly superstition. Could they? ...Of course not!

Matthew's mother sat on a chair in a room. She rocked back and forth, reading a book to herself. He knew that she was reading backwards because her rocking was also backwards. She went forth and back instead of back and forth. The old family dog walked in backwards and sat down by the fire. Matthew had forgotten all about him. As his mother read, Penny walked in and stood beside her. She turned and smiled at Matthew as his mother read.

As his mother read, Mike walked in holding his head. He looked to be in pain, but once he stood next to Penny he laughed and held out his hand, waving to Matthew.

Joan and Jenny and his dad and Mucus all joined the moving family-portrait as his mother continued reading the story backwards.

Government Health Cuts finally gave them the excuse required to close the ward entirely. It was "no longer feasible" to maintain the old ward on the fourth floor on the west wing in the main building. Patients and staff were to be relocated to other areas.

At the end of their meeting, someone asked the question that everyone else was deliberately trying to avoid...

"What about the zombie?"

Since nobody had a better idea, it was decided that Matthew would remain where he was. That was "easiest all round," they figured. He didn't require any assistance, but just in case something happened, someone was to be sent up there once a day to check on him.

Matthew slept. As he slept, he dreamt.
"I know!" cried Matthew and all of his family suddenly looked at him, curious about what he would say next. They always liked his suggestions and he was always able to make them stop being so busy and to play with him, just by making some great suggestion.
He turned now to Penny, who was sitting in the chair. "Why don't you read that story backwards, Penny, and when we are all in the room, continue reading it backwards until we're all babies at the same age. Then we can start it all again -only in new ways this time. We can all play together every day and never die!"
"That's a great idea!" they all cheered Matthew's suggestion and Penny began to read. Backwards.

As you can imagine, a deserted old hospital ward that was rumoured to be haunted was not a nice place to have to enter every day. So once-a-day became once-a-week, which lead to "now and again." Soon nobody could recall whose task it was to go up there. The janitor conveniently decided it was an orderly's role. Orderlies were certain some nurse did it. The nurses knew that only a trained doctor would know how to handle the situation if the zombie was found to have woken up.

More time passed and eventually people forgot about "The Upstairs Zombie" altogether. The elevator now only ever travelled to the third floor on the west-wing and the stairs were boarded up.

Matthew was forgotten.

Matthew slept. As he slept, he dreamt.

OOAY

Due to the direction in which the planet turns, six hundred and ninety miles was too far a jump for a direct westerly journey. This meant that they had to travel once around the planet in order to reach the island with no name. Even using the various tools at their disposal to speed-up the journey, it had taken them almost eighteen hours in total. Thankfully they had stocked up on food reserves at Harrumph! and it had been a lot of fun chasing after their grub in zero gravity. Also, they both needed a rest after all the floating and travelling and eating and excitement, so sleeping in space actually proved to be possible -although Crasty's snoring kept Lucy awake for a long time.

Now they had landed on the unnamed island and were sitting in Blurt's ATV, waiting for their energy to return, before climbing out of the Bullet.

Lucy looked to her friend.

"Crasty?" she asked, testing the name out.

"Yeah-s?" answered the old man slowly, sensing some difficult question was coming.

The young girl waited a few seconds before continuing.

"...What type of dog *is* Ooyay?" she asked. "I mean, where did he come from? How come he can *talk?*"

Crasty scrunched up his mouth and puffed out his cheeks and knotted his eyebrows. He then sucked in his cheeks and puckered his lips. Clearly he was considering his answer and it was now clear that he at least *had* an answer to consider.

"...Ask me again later," he told her finally, stretching to stand and to prepare for what they might find outside.

Lucy wasn't happy, but she was satisfied now at least that he *would* tell her soon.

It was a jungle out there. Massive green leaves, bamboo chutes, multi-coloured giant plants grew everywhere. The air was so thick there was a kind of swirling, damp haze floating in front of their faces, but as they reached to grasp the haze, they found nothing in their hands.

There wasn't any immediate sign of human life here,

although their craft and the Bullet Hole itself was in the centre of a small clearing, which would certainly require maintenance to stop it from becoming overgrown. Four paths lead into the jungle, apparently in each compass direction. There was nothing to distinguish one path from another. They all looked like 'a standard jungle path' -whatever that looked like.

It sounded as though millions of insects were creaking continuously in a high-pitched, low-volume refrain. Some of them creaked quickly, some more slowly. Together they formed an almost-deafening, hypnotic continuous jungle rhythm.

Above that sound, from high in the trees, out of sight came bird or monkey clicks and whoops and screams.

"Kuh kuh kuh kuh kuh kuh"

"Crrrrlllllllkkkkk Crrrrlllllllkkkkk"

"Neeeeeeeeeeeeeeee Neeeeeeeeeeeeeeeee   Neeeeeeeeeeeeeeeeee"

"Ooo ooo ooo ooo ooo ooo AH AH AH AH AH OOOWAAA OOOWAAA OOOWAAA!!! Ooo ooo ooo ooo ooo ooo AH AH AH AH AH"

Into this mix, Crasty decided he would throw his own voice.

"HHHELLLLLLLO!" he yelled into the jungle.

Suddenly silence crashed on top of them. It was like someone had turned off the television in the middle of a really loud explosion. Only at that point did they both realise that the jungle noises had in fact been very, very loud. Now though, they both felt like their hearing had left them completely.

"Bah!" shouted Lucy gently, just to make certain she hadn't gone deaf.

She was pleased to note that she hadn't, so she said it again.

"Bah!"

She turned to Crasty, who was busy checking each of the pathways. Clearly he couldn't think of a reason to choose one over any other so he turned to Lucy and shrugged. Lucy gave each path a cursory glance of her own, before shrugging back to the Professor. Now Crasty half-smiled, shrugged again, pointed toward one of the paths and began walking in that direction.

As they walked, they slowly became aware that the various animal and insect noises had each started up once more. Neither of them noticed any one particular noise starting for the first time, but at one stage or another, both of them noticed each sound and noted that it too had once more joined in the tropical tune.

Although the path appeared to be going in a straight line, after travelling just a few feet into the jungle, it was no longer possible to see the ATV behind them. They could see the path a few feet in front and a few feet behind, but there was nothing visible except for heavy vegetation beyond that in either direction.

Suddenly Lucy gasped from fright as she saw a man silently standing within reach, to her right hand side. But as she moved her head to see him properly, it turned out to be nothing but a large leaf.

"What is it?" whispered Crasty, quickly spinning around.

Lucy smiled and waved him on.

"Nothing," she puffed, laughing now, examining the veins in the leaf more closely. "I just thought I saw something."

Crasty continued. Soon Lucy saw something else out of the corner of her eye and snapped to see it, but it was gone.

"What was that?" she wondered to herself.

Only then did she realise that she had thought she had seen a horse. Again she laughed, knowing how ridiculous that would be, and continued following the old man.

Once more it happened. She quickly turned to look, but whatever it was had vanished. ...No, that wasn't right... What she had seen this time was a tree -she could still see the tree standing there now, but before she had taken a proper look, she had believed it was a dog -possibly even Ooyay. She didn't tell any of this to her friend, because none of these visions were actually real in any way. She knew that.

Soon they reached the end of the path and Crasty made way for Lucy to walk up and see past where he stood. Beyond the end of the path lay jagged rocks. Turbulent waves smashed across the rocks, almost touching the two travellers. There was no way to continue and they could see nothing but rocks and water. With a shrug, they headed back along the same path in order to try another direction.

Professor Crastinator too had seen things that weren't there, but he had said nothing. He knew that jungles played such tricks on the eyes. Still, each time he snapped left or right he had been convinced that *this* time there definitely was something there, but each time it turned out to be a tree or a plant or a flower or a mixture of all of the above.

He had already begun trying *not* to turn around in order to see whatever-it-*wasn't*-that-he-might-think-that-it-was for longer, but each time his head would snap to the left or to the right before his brain could tell it not to.

It seemed to him that it was going to be impossible to see something out of the corner of his eyes and *not* turn to look directly at it.

Then, just as they reached the clearing, he did it. The corner of his left eye registered something and he managed to stop his head from checking it out. He continued walking slowly and his brain seemed to complete the image of what wasn't there:

A small, sickly young boy stood there, looking toward the ATV. Crasty could *see* him as clearly as though he was looking straight at him.

Suddenly he swung to his left as he jumped backwards. He landed with his back to the Bullet they had arrived on. As he did, he saw a blue flower and some greenery behind. None of it looked anything like the child he had seen.

"Did you see him!?" cried Crasty, pointing at the blue flower.

Lucy smiled and almost laughed.

"No," she simply answered.

But Crasty was certain she didn't understand. This wasn't one of the standard apparitions that they both had been seeing. He had carefully controlled himself this time and he was absolutely *convinced* that the boy had actually been standing there before he turned.

"But how could that be?" he asked himself silently, knowing it was impossible.

It *was* clearly just a blue flower and some leaves and things. Nothing more.

Resting against the ATV now, he occasionally glanced back to where he had seen the boy -just to make sure he was still not there.

"So we try another path?" Lucy half-suggested/ half-asked.

Crasty nodded toward a second track and groaned.

"Uh" he said.

This path turned out to be a little wider than the first one. Neither Lucy nor Crasty experienced any apparitions (or premonitions or mirages or whatever they were) for quite some time. Finally, when they reached around the halfway point, Crasty sensed something to his right and managed to contain his curiosity. He didn't turn, but kept walking slowly.

"What is it?" he wondered quietly to himself, then at once he realised that it was a piano.

Looking straight ahead, but concentrating on something in the corner of his eye caused the eye to water-up. There was something else next to the piano -some other shape, but the moisture in his eye now blocked any further examination. At last he stopped and rubbed his eyes and looked quickly to where he had spotted the piano. Now though of course there was only jungle. Nothing even vaguely piano-shaped was to be seen.

"This is too much," he cried in a half-whisper.

"I know," said Lucy from behind. "I see them too."

"You do!?" he gasped. "Did you see that piano?"

The girl shook her head.

"I thought it looked more like an old man," she admitted.

"Was he there? Right there?" he asked, frantically pointing at where he was sure he had seen a piano.

"No," said Lucy. "He was over there!" indicating the opposite side of the path.

The track ended with the same view as the last one: Rocks and water. There was nowhere else to go and nothing else to see. So they turned back.

Shortly after doing so, the Professor saw the piano again. It wasn't in the same place as before though. This time he didn't slow down. The image seemed to be changing slightly as he walked, but still it was the same -as if it was coming into focus in the corner of his eye. Standing next to the piano was a man... *and something else... it's a woman... no wait... the woman is sitting on a rocking chair and the man is bent into the piano.*

The Professor now threw his hands up to his face. He knew that was an impossible image. They were hundreds of miles from anywhere out here and nobody was tuning pianos in this jungle. Deliberately, he blocked his peripheral vision with his hands for the rest of the journey back to the Bullet. Since they weren't there anyway, there was no need to look at these silly images.

After reaching the clearing once again, Lucy noted how the Professor was breathing heavily. These 'visions' were just tricks being played by the movement of the leaves and the trees. Even *she* knew that. He was being silly, but she didn't laugh at him because he was clearly upset that they still hadn't found his dog. She doubted now that they would find Ooyay here in this jungle, but they should at least check the last two pathways.

"Let's go," she said at last, starting now toward the third path. Crasty hesitated, then thought of Ooyay out there in the jungle, and stepped ahead of the young girl once more.

Here now he found the same pale-faced young boy as before. Crasty didn't look, but walked a little faster. The young boy seemed to move alongside the Professor, but soon slipped back behind Crasty's vision as though he couldn't keep up. Then a little further on, something else appeared at the corner of the same eye... a young girl was walking alongside him now, pulling the smaller boy behind. Quickly the Professor turned to see the boy and the girl, but they were not there.

As before, the path came to an abrupt end with rocks and water.

"What's the point in these paths if there is nothing there!" complained Crasty, visibly annoyed now at these paths and this island and the visions he was seeing.

On the way back, he passed another, older boy and two more females. Each of them seemed to be just sitting there, looking.

"Do you see those people?" Crasty asked Lucy when they reached the ATV again.

"Yes" she laughed. "Well, I think I see *some* people, but when I look they're not there. I thought I saw my friend Milo a while ago, then I saw a pony and cars and one time I thought I saw an elephant!"

"Hmm" said the Professor. He clearly wasn't finding this as funny as Lucy was.

Were these *really* imaginary visions? Was there something else going on here? Where *were* they anyway? What did any of this *mean*?

"Well just one path to go!" laughed Lucy, walking away now.

"No!" cried Crasty, shaking his head. He had obviously had enough. His dog wasn't here. "I can't go on. What's the point? There is nothing there. There is never anything there. It's all lies."

The young girl stepped toward him carefully now. She took his hand and patted his wrinkled knuckles.

"It's ok Crasty," she said. "I'm here with you. ...Let's have a look. ...We'll find Ooyay and we'll bring him home. You'll see!"

This jungle made her nervous too, but Lucy no longer feared what she couldn't see. In a strange way, she was now kind of enjoying the feeling that just about anything could pop into the side of her field of vision.

All the way along the last path, Crasty couldn't stop himself looking at the visions as soon as they appeared. In fact, he deliberately didn't try to stop himself looking. Now he looked to make sure they weren't there. And as he guessed -*they weren't.*

The end of the fourth path was something unexpected: It was the same as the other three. Both Lucy and Crasty had felt certain that they'd find *something* substantial here, but it appeared not.

On the way back, Crasty figured that if he was not going to find something substantial, then he might as well check out those insubstantial images once again as best he could.

Concentrating on not turning once more, it wasn't long before something floated into view (or into 'non-view' to be more accurate). This time he saw a bed. A young man was sleeping in the bed. As Crasty walked, the image stayed with him. The bed was in a large, empty room. Crasty continued to walk and the bed and the room remained in sight in the corner of his eye. Now others were standing around the bed. Crasty knew at once who they were. They were the young man's mother and his father and his brothers and his sisters. His family was standing around him, tucking him in and patting his head while he slept.

At once, Crasty threw his hands to his head and ran the rest of the way back to the Bullet. These images were now haunting him like nothing had before. He had to escape the imaginary scenes as quickly as possible. It was surely madness for him to think about what these ghost images could mean.

MEMORIES OF DUST

You, reader, are a tiny little dust particle floating in a very large, dusty old hospital ward. Shafts of sunlight stream through broken window shutters, sometimes highlighting your faint movement across the room.

Only if someone looked very closely and for long enough would they notice that you are headed along a particular path. You seem to drift slightly in one direction before gliding a shorter distance backwards.

Time means nothing to a dust particle, but inevitably it becomes clear that you are floating ever so slowly toward a man lying in the only bed in the large room.

You are closer now to this man and almost on top of his head. He breathes in and you float a little faster now toward his left nostril. He breathes out and you are pushed back almost as far as you had come.

Just as you are about to be pulled into his nose, he whispers something that would be barely audible if you had ears to hear.

"Mucus," he sighs, which throws you far away.

However, after doing so, he takes a deep breath and you whoosh straight up his left nostril.

Take something small... *a football?*
No, smaller... *a tennis ball?*
No, smaller... *an acorn!*
No, smaller than an acorn. Something <u>tiny</u>. Take the <u>tiniest</u> thing...
a speck of dust!

Ok. Now add another of the same... *two specks?*
Then another, then another. Slowly and methodically, build using this smallest item.

In time you have something new... *a handful of dust?*
Add a small drop of water and what do you have?... *a mud pat?*
Put that to the side and start again from scratch.

In time you have... *another mud pat?*
Put that aside and do the same, until you have hundreds of the same. Now bring them all together. What do you have?... *a mud castle?*

Start from the top. Make many mud castles. Bring them all together and squeeze. Squeeze tighter than is possible to squeeze. Then squeeze harder. It now fits in your hand. Open your hand. What is it? *...a stone?*

Put that aside. Start from the top. Make many stones.
People will laugh! -Ignore them, they don't know anything different. Yet.

Bring all your stones together. Squeeze tight and make a rock.

From the top once more...

Speck, mud, stone, rock.
Speck, mud, stone, rock.
Speck, mud, stone, rock.

Bring them all together. *...Make a wall?*
Yes, make a wall, but not a wall like you've seen before. Make a new type of wall -make it in a way never thought of. Make many walls. Bring them together. *...You have a building.*
Now you have a building. A unique building. ...Now a village. Now it's a city. Now a country. Now the world! *...Your world!*

Made by you. For you. Live the world. Live <u>your</u> world. Nothing else exists except your world. *...Nothing else exists except the world <u>we</u> make. <u>We</u> will change the world. <u>We</u> will do it together.*

Matthew opened his eyes.

He had been dreaming, but he had also been awake. What had happened? Was he talking to someone else just now? Was somebody else in the room with him?

"Heh... Hello?" he said aloud. He didn't have the strength to move his head and he was even unsure if he was actually speaking out loud or if it was still just inside his head.

"Hello? Is someone there?" he asked again.

There was silence for a long time. As he began to shut his eyes once more, a voice spoke up from someplace -out of sight.

"Yes" came the reply and for a minute Matthew could think of nothing to say.

"Who are you?" he asked the other voice at last since he could see nobody around and he could not move his head.

"Who are you?" asked the voice.

Matthew considered the question. It had been a long time since he considered that question -Years in fact. There was only one name he remembered now.

"Mm... Mucus?" he replied, unsure, but knew that wasn't it. "Mu?... Ma?... Mar?... Mar-cus!"

"Hello Marcus."

"Who are you? What is your name?" he asked the voice.

"I am Ooyay. I'm here to be your friend. I will look after you now."

Marcus cried for the rest of that day. It had been a long time since he had anyone to talk to, let alone a friend.

Lucy climbed quietly into the ATV. Her friend, the Professor was sitting inside, gazing blankly at the revolving computer-generated globe. Tears streamed down his face.

Lucy bit her lip, wondering if now was a good time to ask. Then she asked...

"Where did Ooyay come from Crasty?" she asked her friend softly. "What type of dog is he?"

Marcus Crastinator paused only briefly as he turned his head upward a notch and looked to the ceiling.

"...He's a figment of my imagination," he told the girl.

Lucy immediately had a hundred questions, but bit her lip again instead of piercing the moment with the sound of her voice. A friend knows how long to wait for the silent invitation to speak.

"Oh he's real enough," he looked her straight in the face now, with his glassy, old eyes. He knew that would answer the first question she hadn't asked.

"I don't understand it myself to be honest... I was sick for a very long time. I lost everyone.

"...My imagination grew as I lay there in the hospital bed. One day everything could no longer fit in my head and things began to crumble for me. Then Ooyay was there. He spoke to me and wanted to help. He took the burden of my imagination. At first I could only hear his voice, but time passed and one day I opened my eyes and he was there before me -the same as you've seen him yourself.

"...We spent years in that bed together, doing nothing... thinking, talking and doing nothing. First *I* was telling *him* everything. Then we were deconstructing, examining, building *together* for a long time (*all inside our heads, you understand*). Then Ooyay began to take the bigger load and I began to rest and my strength began to grow. I had collapsed on my 30th birthday. I found out later that it was on my 60th birthday that Ooyay lead me from that building. Thirty years I lay there in all... The last ten (or more) with Ooyay."

Lucy was blind from tears. Her eyes were wide open and she was directly facing the Professor, but the wall of tears that shimmered and held in her eye sockets caused her to be incapable of seeing what was before her. Finally the wall broke and Lucy collapsed into her friend's chest with a bursting cry. She gave him the biggest hug that was in her power to give. He squeezed his nose into her hair, trying to stop himself from bursting out in a loud cry in case it upset her further.

They sat there in the Bullet like that for some time before the Professor reached over and pressed a button to mark their next destination. He knew the location without even thinking. Whether it was going to help or not, there was something now that he felt had to be done.

AN EXTRAORDINARY BREAK

Ooyay awoke and immediately hopped in the air. He was amazed to find that he was back in his cage. How did that happen? The last thing he remembered, he was crouched down by the front door, waiting for Seamus Shafford or that other guy to come along so he could escape. Had he fallen asleep? How utterly unlike him! How could he have allowed himself fall asleep at such a crucial time?

Looking around now, it seemed that all the animals were back in their cages. Again, how did that happen? He had freed almost all of the animals –all the ones in the lower cages at least. How come he slept through their discovery and recapture? There must have been pandemonium going on here while he snored his brains out. Could it be that he was more tired from the effects of the chloroform than he had realised? All that running around must have taken more out of him than he had thought. It now looked like any normal day here in this... wherever he was. Nothing had changed.

Just then he noticed that Seamus Shafford was working his way through the cages, bringing a dish of food and a dish of water to each dog on Ooyay's line.

Opening the cage next to Ooyay now, Seamus placed the two bowls in front of the collie that had the red lipstick-line drawn across her bare side. Only now did Ooyay notice that this shaved area had already been bandaged up and that the collie was able to raise her head enough to eat from the bowl.

"There, there girl," whispered Seamus as he slipped something into her food. To Ooyay it looked like a blue tablet.

"It won't be long now," Seamus added softly, rubbing her head as she ate from the bowl.

He came next to Ooyay's cage, gave an incredulous stare, then laughed.

"Ah you're back to us!" he cried. "I named you well I did, Sleepy! You'd sleep through an explosion in a fireworks factory!"

Placing two bowls into the cage, he gave a short tap on Ooyay's head before moving on. The little dog examined the food bowl, but since it didn't appear to contain any tablets and since he *was* starving, he decided to eat. He ate it all in no time and licked the bowl clean afterwards. Just as he looked up from taking a drink of water, he noticed a young, blonde-haired boy stretching to look into his cage.

"How about this one, dad?" asked the boy sweetly, pointing at Ooyay as he looked to the man who was now walking toward the cage.

"Why not take a look further up first?" suggested the father, walking past Ooyay to examine the rest of the animals. But if the young boy was unsure at first, now he was certain.

"No!" he stated firmly, "I want this one!"

The father stopped a few feet away and pointed at some other dog on the lower shelf.

"How about this one, Timmy? Here -have a look at this little fella," smiled the father excitedly, trying to distract his son.

Now the son was getting angry. He had said which dog he wanted and his dad kept annoying him to look at others. Why don't fathers ever listen to their sons?

"I - WANT - THIS ONE!!" he shouted, pointing directly at Ooyay.

The little dog didn't know what to do. Crasty would likely be coming for him any minute. He couldn't leave now!

"All right!" said the father, giving up at last, walking back to his boy.

Ooyay was in a panic. Who knew where these people were going to take him!? He didn't want to leave this safe place with *them*. The boy wasn't exactly nice to his father. Surely such a boy would mistreat a dog too.

"We'll have this one," the father called to Seamus Shafford, pointing at the captive canine inventor.

Ooyay turned toward the back of his cage, eager to escape from whatever this sudden change might bring. As he did so, a little gas escaped his posterior and a deep pong quickly filled the air all around.

Seamus approached and was about to open Ooyay's cage, when the boy changed his mind, even as he pretended not to notice the stench.

"No," he stated with his nose in the air. "How about that one instead? I'll have him!"

"Are you sure Timmy?" asked the father. "You seemed pretty certain about the other guy."

Timmy shot a stabbing stare at his dad.

"Just bring the dog, dad," he commanded as he turned and walked from the room.

Seamus opened the cage and lifted the newly-arrived golden labrador to the floor, before following along with the father where the boy had lead.

Ooyay couldn't help but laugh. His flatulence had been a lucky break indeed. However, as he glanced past the open cell next to his, he now noticed the grille on the air duct had been replaced. More than that, it looked unchanged from before he had unscrewed it. He was sure he had at least damaged the paintwork around some of those screws while he fiddled with the scalpel, but the grille now looked to be as untouched as ever. And those boxes looked to be stacked much the same as they ever were. Why would a cleanup operation have been done so thoroughly? And what did Seamus mean when he laughed at Ooyay's sleep? Maybe he meant that he had been asleep for *so long*? Maybe he never woke after being on that table and that everything else had been a dream!? Now he was uncertain of everything. Had he set the other animals free? Had he left a message on the phone?

"Oh no," he whispered quietly to himself as he curled up in a little ball in the back of the cage once more. He had just missed possibly his best opportunity of escape since he had arrived. ...If proof was needed, there was no better evidence than this: Farting had its price.

THE WORLD IS TURNING

By this time I, Stanley Rumm, had slept with the Empathy Stone under my pillow. Not that I totally believed what that famous author had said to me about it, but -well, *why not?* -The Professor, Lucy and Blurt had all rubbed the stone while they were in the shop and I had nothing to lose by trying it out.

Amazingly, it worked! As I slept, I saw Matthew Cratchett and his family and at once I knew the whole story of the amazing life of Marcus Crastinator and his dog. For Lucy and Blurt I could also see everything from their perspective, but I have to admit to being most curious about the Professor. His story had amazed me. At last I could see how a single man (or the dog that was a kind of extension of himself) could have invented so many marvellous things. His imagination had roamed free on four legs.

However, at that time I only knew his story up until the moment when he rubbed the stone, so I was now desperate to discover if he had succeeded in retrieving his beloved Ooyay. I would have given anything just to know if they were ever to be reunited.

Imagine then my surprise to find this same old man and his young friend, Lucy, walk into the clearing in the centre of the Grot Shop! I leapt at once from my stool and ran to shake his hand.

Despite the freezing cold outside, I noted that he was now carrying the gorilla costume under his right arm, so I was unable to shake his hand as vigorously as I would have liked. Nevertheless I lost no time in explaining all about how the Empathy Stone had told me everything and that I was there to help in any way I could. I even pulled the stone from my pocket as I walked slowly backward to my stool and I almost cried for joy when he took it from my hand to examine it more closely. I knew at once I would later be able to sleep soundly and to discover what had transpired since last they had visited. He then handed it to Lucy, who checked it briefly before passing it back to my now sweating hands. There really wasn't too much to see in the Empathy Stone. It looked like a very ordinary piece of hacked rock. Neither of them believed what I was saying, or even gave it much thought if truth was known.

I pulled up a chair for the old man to sit on, but he simply held out the gorilla suit for me to take.

"I want the dog back," he declared. "Susan. I give you this in return."

I was surprised he had come back for her to be honest, but I figured that he had been upset when Blurt handed her over and that he now meant to reunite her with her owner. Possibly he felt that would give him at least a small bit of hope too.

"She should never have been used as an exchange in that way," he added sorrowfully.

Just then, Susan herself ran into the clearing, quickly followed by my assistant, Onoshi Han. He was laughing loudly and wildly and flailing his arms all over the place. Susan was leaping and turning and barking and wagging her tail furiously.

When he saw who was standing next to me, Onoshi silently rolled forward on the floor, scooping Susan quickly into his arms, continuing his forward roll, then came to his feet directly in front of us. Susan was delighted to once again see the young girl and the old man.

"Yap!" she said to them as she stood on Onoshi's outstretched open hands and wagged her tail. Clearly she was happy to see them.

Lucy laughed aloud.

"Hello girl!" she waved, before turning to Onoshi.
"I do that roll too all the time," she smiled, pointing at where he had just performed his acrobatics.

Instead of snapping at her this time, my assistant returned the smile.

"It's good fun isn't it?" he giggled. "I like it when the world is upside down. It only lasts a second, but that second is one you remember for a long time after."

I had to smile and blink as he spoke. A transformation had come over Onoshi Han since meeting Susan. For one thing, he let her do all the barking. Not once did he snap or have a bad word to say to anybody over the previous few days. On the contrary, he kept coming out with these bizarre statements as though he had suddenly turned into a fortune cookie or something. He was a changed man and it was all because he had found this dog.

Indeed they seemed to have found each other. Susan too seemed happier now than I remembered seeing her in my dreams. She wasn't unhappy before, but now she seemed to be over the moon.

The thought of having to separate these two was not something I wanted to consider, but yet I would have been unable to refuse Professor Crastinator anything. If he wanted to bring Susan back to Blurt then I was not going to stop him.

Actually, concerning Blurt... I did like the man. He was impossible not to like. But still I suspected he had another motive at the time that he handed Susan over. I didn't 'see' this motive while I slept with the Empathy Stone under my pillow, but I think he even fooled himself most often. I'm really not that certain that giving up his dog was as big a sacrifice as he thought it was... I think he was secretly happy that now he had an excuse to abandon his four-legged helper.

Blurt would never have admitted (even to himself) that she was not an ideal companion for a man like him. Some part of him *must* have known that. He had spent a long time nursing bruises and broken bones as a direct result of her inability to be a proper guide-dog. But if he was to admit that she had been no good at her job, he would then have had to admit that *he* had been wrong to choose her in the first place. The man had simply too much self-belief to *ever* do that.

Still, I think he could easily have fooled himself into believing that he was handing over his helper and favourite companion for a kind of greater good.

I was about to say something on Onoshi's behalf when I turned to the Professor. He was looking and smiling at Susan and her newfound friend. He then reached out and rubbed the top of her head gently. Obviously he had already seen how well the two of them got along together. I knew at once that he wasn't going to separate them. By now, Onoshi and Susan were inseparable. In time they would become even more so.

With a soft smile and a nod from Professor Crastinator, Onoshi laughed and danced out of the clearing, rocking Susan in his arms and swooping her through the air as they went.

I had to laugh, but when I turned back and saw the Professor leaning heavily on the desk with his two hands, I quickly grabbed the nearest chair to help him sit down.

"I'm all right!" he insisted. "I don't want to sit."

Flapping both arms until Lucy and I stopped holding him, he looked again at the gorilla suit he had tossed on the desk. A few seconds of silence passed while myself and Lucy stared at each other, wondering what we should do.

"I... " said Crasty at last. "I want to make a wish."

What could I say? I wasn't sure the suit would work as a wish-giver, but *I* wasn't going to be the one to tell him that.

"Certainly Professor," I told him. "No problem," I said, bowing to this great man, hoping with all my heart that the wish table would grant this one wish above all others.

I cleared my throat, then softly stated the lines I had always said at such times.

"Place your item on The Wish Table and tell me your wish. Remember: it must be something of immense value -and worthless."

Then something happened that I was not at all expecting. Removing his hand slowly from the pocket of his pyjamas, he reached over to the Wish Table and gently placed something there with a soft tap. Taking a deep breath, he withdrew his hand and at last the object could be seen. First of all I thought it was a piece of an old wine-cork, but looking more closely, I discovered it to be... an old-looking... acorn.

GO GET THAT DOG!

They were back inside the ATV now. Lucy was quietly settling into her seat whilst keeping an eye on the Professor. Completely gone now was the aged, uncertain, incapable Crastinator. In his place was a man who seemed to know exactly what he wanted and even how to get it. He had borne a look of grim determination the whole way down the mountain and Lucy had been afraid to open her mouth in case it caused his concentration to snap. This Crasty had a goal and a plan and a new confident strength. By now Lucy knew enough to sit back and to let her friend take care of whatever needed to be done. She was certain he'd be able to cope with anything that was to come.

Following a few taps on the keyboard in front of him, the computer-generated globe above the console began to spin rapidly. Crasty stood up. Now he sat down. Now he stood again. Now he sat. Once he was moving up and down as quickly as his age and health allowed, he shut his eyes, then thrust his index finger into the swirling sphere. Immediately the globe stopped spinning and was automatically replaced by the map of a small island. The Professor opened his eyes as the computer announced their new destination.

"You have selected... DR. FLOCKY NOCKY'S ISLAND," said the female voice, before adding in her calm, dispassionate tone, "...I like the cut of your jib."

Lucy was shocked. There it was: "Dr. Flocky Nocky's Island." There could certainly be no doubt now. It was as simple as that the whole time and they could not see it.

"Crasty's not going to like this one bit," she cringed, thinking to herself.

The old man flopped into his seat.

"There it was the whole time!" he pointed and laughed.

Lucy laughed too, even though she didn't really find it funny. She laughed from relief in seeing the Professor laugh. She had been afraid he would never laugh again, but now he laughed long and hard and she gladly joined in the laughter with him.

Finally the laughter subsided and Crasty gave a giggling sigh as he slid away from the console. Lucy shifted into place and was about to press the launch button when she remembered something.

"What about Blurt?" she asked. "Shouldn't we go visit and make sure he's alright?"

Again Crasty smiled (this Crasty seemed more smiley than the older, crustier one) and waved Lucy on.

"If there's one thing I know about Mr. Blurt Johannsen," he said, "it's that he's gonna be alright no matter what happens. There'll be time enough to visit him after we get my dog back. Let's drive on now Lucy... the world is turning."

THE LOOK OF FEAR

Seamus Shafford entered the room and gave a brief look into the cage beside Ooyay before turning his back and folding his arms.

"She's ready," he softly declared.

Seamus's assistant now opened the collie's cage. Quickly and quietly, he carried the apparently-sleeping dog from the room.

Once they had left, Seamus wiped his nose, bowed his head, then placed his hands on his hips. Ooyay couldn't see his face since his back was still turned.

Finally Seamus spun around toward the door, but as he did, his eyes were caught in Ooyay's gaze. Both felt something as they looked in each other's eyes. To Seamus, it seemed as though the small dog had seen and understood everything. To Ooyay, it was clear that Seamus was upset with having to 'dispose' of unwanted animals.

"He probably does this job because he loves animals," Ooyay could see at once, *"but he can't forgive himself for taking part in their destruction."*

Both man and dog held that silent bond as if one was a fisherman and the other was a hooked fish at the end of his line. They were locked together and now drawn together. Neither one could be certain which was the man and which the fish.

Seamus's red eyes seemed to be pleading with the little dog now for forgiveness. Ooyay didn't forgive the actions, but he did somehow feel sorry for the man who might yet end up killing him.

The dog inhaled as he opened his mouth.

"You're a lost soul Seamus Shafford," he was about to inform his captor, but before the words came out there was a shout from the basement.

"COME ON WILL YOU SEAMUS!" called his assistant. "YOU NEED TO OPEN THE DOOR!"

The line was now snapped and the moment lost forever. Seamus turned and ran from the room without another glance to his judge.

A MOMENT OF REFLECTION

"Well done again Blurt" said the computer once more. "Your bravery knows no bounds. We have now landed in... Dr. Flocky Nocky's Island."

You could write a book about the silent stares in this book, but for a number of reasons, Lucy and Crasty's silent stare to each other and around the inside of the ATV at this point beat all others. For one thing, they were trapped there, unable to move until their bodies adjusted to the Earth's gravitational pull. It's hard to lift your own body when it has been weightless for so long.

For another thing, neither of them much wanted to speak at that time. There was no point in talking because they both had mostly the same thoughts and the same fears and the same questions to ask themselves: Will we find Ooyay here? Will Flocky Nocky hand him over willingly? Are we in danger? What if Ooyay isn't here at all? Maybe Flocky Nocky is holding him elsewhere? How are we going to make the doctor tell the truth?

As well as these, each of the passengers in the blind man's Bullet had his or her own considerations that also did not warrant mentioning out loud:

"Do my parents know I didn't go on the school trip yet?"

"What if Flocky Nocky had nothing at all to do with my dog's disappearance?"

"How am I ever going to be able to explain what has happened -or why it happened -or how?"

"How did I get here? It seems like only yesterday that I was walking the meadows with my brother and my sister. I refuse to lose Ooyay like I've lost everyone else!"

Although the Doctor was the younger man, he had usually spoken to the Professor like a teacher would speak to a student. One time, Flocky Nocky had spent almost an hour on videoconference "proving" to Crasty that they *should* join forces and work as a team. At the end of his speech he then began to ask questions about what he had been saying to Crasty.

"Do you recall my fourth point concerning the liberalisation of the post-Enlightenment-era perspective analyses vis-à-vis freedom in selection through 'The Relevant Process'?"

Crasty never had a clue what the man was talking about, but would instead just sit there, waiting for an opportunity to say goodbye. Most of the time, he would roll his eyes or scratch his elbow or sometimes grunt during a pause from the Doctor.

Yet at the end of each of their conversations, the Doctor had always insisted they had "made headway" or "cleared some thought-debris" or that it had been nice to "enfranchise some progression."

Sitting here now in the Bullet, outside Flocky Nocky's house, Crasty began to actually consider for the first time what he already knew of the person who had spoken with him for so long over so many evenings.

The man he had met and gotten to know, actually had no interest at all in the Professor or his life or his dog, he now realised.

This scientist had never questioned Crasty about what he had been working on or why or on how he approached his work. This scientist was merely eager to share points of view in any way he could. He liked to talk about "the experimentation process" more than anything else.

Crasty suddenly was *certain* that the doctor had never heard of Ooyay, much less had him kidnapped. He didn't have to meet the man in person to know that. A moment's reflection with a clear mind was all he had required.

Professor Crastinator now *knew* beyond doubt that Dr. Flocky Nocky did not have his dog. Ooyay was somewhere else ...but where?

DOUBT

That night, Ooyay felt too tired to move. What was the point in trying to escape? Nothing was going to work. Not now. Even if his earlier escape *had* been a dream, any escape would clearly end that way anyway. How could it happen any differently? Obviously, the front door was locked at night and that air duct would never open out to the outside.

...And the phones were likely switched off at night time anyway. And if they weren't, Crasty would never answer the telephone -he probably wouldn't know how to -poor guy. Ooyay loved his master, but without those mental exercises that he set for him all of the time, Crasty would just lie there and eventually forget how to do anything for himself, including how to eat. He would fall back into his deep sleep and this time there would be nobody to bring him back.

His one regret in all of this was that the old man was never going to be able to survive without Ooyay to look after him. In fact it was very likely they would both fade away at the same time.

"Crasty is probably there now, lying in bed, waiting for the inevitable, just like me," thought Ooyay. *"Why fight it?"*

CONFESSION

Dr. Flocky Nocky's Island was quite small. Apart from a little beach and a large, well-kept field, it consisted of only two distinguishing landmarks: The first being a single tall palm tree. The second was a standard-looking two-storey house that would not look out of place in the middle of a city-centre council estate. It had redbrick walls and double-glazed windows. Because it was such an ordinary building, it stuck out like a bold girl's tongue, here in such an extraordinary location.

The front door was made of a dark, strong-looking wood. It had three fogged-glass panels, not vastly different to those in any other type of front door. Protruding from the frame of the door was an ordinary-looking doorbell.

"DING DONG" went the doorbell as soon as Crasty pushed it.

It was a pleasant day -not too hot, not too cold, not too windy, not too still. It looked like it might rain a little later on, but other than that ominous possibility... it was pleasant.

"Looks like there's nobody home," sighed Crasty, who wasn't really too upset since he had already decided that Flocky Nocky was not the man they were looking for.

"Look!" cried Lucy in a whisper. "Someone's moving inside!"

Sure enough, beyond the clouded panels on the door, they could make out the unmistakeable shape of a human being approaching.

Tension mounted as the shape stuck its face up to the glass in an effort to see outside without opening the door. Only then did the visitors see that it was a man (of some sort). One of his eyes bulged larger than possible. The other was smaller, but badly out of shape. His mouth seemed to be where his cheek belonged and his tiny nose sat next to his mouth instead of above it. He was hideous and Lucy almost screamed at the sight of him.

Suddenly the face snapped back. There was a click and a brief rattling of chains before the door swung open to show the man in all his disfigured glory: His head was almost bald except for a large clump of grey hair jutting out from above the forehead. His eyes were large and reddened, but quite normal looking -both were the same size. His nose did not warrant any special attention other than to say that in fact it did lie below his eyes. And below that again sat his perfectly ordinary-looking mouth. It was clear now that the glass had artificially distorted the man's features.

A pair of spectacles hung around his neck. His clothes were comfortable, casual and non-descript. To Lucy's youthful gaze, this man was as old as Professor Crastinator, but in fact he was only sixty-two years of age.

He stood now before them, unsure of who or what he was seeing. He looked at Crasty, then to Lucy, before turning again to the old man.

"Pro... Professor?" he blinked, pulling on his spectacles for a closer examination.

"Professor!" he declared with excited surprise and unhidden joy. "It *is* you! My good man, how do you do!"

Without giving Crasty time to reply, he took the old man's hand and shook it vigorously before quickly adding: "I thought it was a delivery. They usually just leave it at the door.... Come in! Come in!"

The inside of the house was the same as the outside had suggested: It was a standard, two-up/ two-down, terrace type home with old wood and plaster walls. Facing them, on their right as they entered the hallway, was an uninteresting, narrow, carpeted stairway leading to the upstairs.

To their left, was a room with little ornaments and statuettes adorning a glass cabinet. In the corner was a dusty 25" television set. A large single-seat couch was situated next to the TV, pointing into the room. Lucy and the Professor couldn't see behind the door in this room, but it was not unreasonable to assume that there were matching single and three-seat couches inside, probably situated around a magazine-topped coffee table. Before the man pulled the door shut, Lucy noticed the non-vacuumed, dark blue carpet within.

"He has the same carpet as my grandparents!" she noted at once, but didn't feel it was worth mentioning.

"You'll have to forgive the mess," muttered the owner of the house with some embarrassment. "...I'm not used to visitors. Come down to the kitchen -I was just having a bite to eat. Please join me!"

The kitchen was a small room at the end of the short hall. Apart from the sink, cooker, fridge and washing machine, taking up almost all the space inside this room was a single table, which was pushed against the wall, leaving room for three seats. On the table was a coffee pot, a milk jug, a cup, a loaf of bread, some butter, cutlery and a plastic container full of what looked to be tuna pasta.

"Here, help yourselves," said the man, grabbing two plates, cups and some cutlery. "There's plenty for everyone. Don't be shy!"

He then sat down and urged his guests to do likewise. The Professor silently prepared, then tucked in to some tuna pasta sandwiches and coffee. Lucy placed some pasta on her plate and half-filled a cup with milk. She didn't like fish and she knew the rest of the dish was now contaminated with that fish-taste, but she didn't think the time was right to ask for a burger.

As she picked at the pasta, Lucy suddenly noticed that nobody was talking. Crasty seemed to be enjoying his food, unconcerned with anything else. The house owner looked shy and embarrassed, but not surprised or curious as to why they had come so far to visit.

"Excuse me," she asked the man at last, "but are you Dr. Flocky Nocky?"

The man smiled and looked to Crasty (who didn't respond), before turning again to the young girl and answering with a simple "yes."

"Do you have the Professor's dog?" she wasted no time in asking.

Again the man looked to Crasty, now appearing genuinely confused.

"Dog?" he asked. "No. I have no dog here... I never knew you had a dog?" he said to Professor Crastinator.

The Professor now took a proper look at Dr. Flocky Nocky for the first time since arriving. As he looked, he ate his sandwich. He did nothing else, except look the Doctor straight in the eyes whilst eating that sandwich. Flocky Nocky became flustered under the silent gaze.

"I -I don't go out much nowadays..." he stuttered. "I'm -I guess you could say I'm retired."

Still the Professor ate his sandwich and stared at the Doctor.

"I'm glad you called, Marcus, I really am," continued Flavius, "but... well I... I never expected you would come *here*," he said waving around, obviously speaking of the house.

"It used to belong to my parents, this house," he said, clearly preferring to talk rather than endure the silence. "I grew up here! - Well not on this island, but in this house. I had it shipped out here brick by brick a few years back. This place is my *home*. I've never felt at home anywhere else. I guess this is where time stops for me. When everything gets too much and the world is changing too quickly, there is one place you want to keep..."

The doctor didn't finish his sentence. Or perhaps he did. He sat now and gazed silently at some unseen point. He was deep in thought. Or possibly his mind was a blank.

"Do you have a good home, young lady?" he cheerily enquired as he suddenly snapped out of his trance.

"I do," answered Lucy with a quiet smile. "I live with my parents at home," she continued, seizing the opportunity to throw some life into this dull conversation. "It's nice there I guess. ...But I pretended to them that I was going on a school trip and I pretended to the Professor that my parents let me go looking for his dog with him..." she added, turning to the Professor, who didn't seem to be paying any attention.
"...And my name is Lucy Lucey," she said, offering her hand to Dr. Flocky Nocky, who shook it with a polite smile.

"How do you do, Lucy?" he said. "...Y'know, you should be nicer to your parents. You'll never be as happy and as safe as you are in your own parent's home. Isn't that right, Professor?"

The Professor seemed to be caught in the same daydream that had affected the doctor just now. He sat with a far-off look in his eyes.

"Yes," he said simply.

An awkward few seconds passed before Dr. Flocky Nocky again punctured the silence.

"I have to tell you something..." he stated, shaking his head, keeping both eyes closed. "I am not the man you think I am -not really."

The Professor sat up as though waking from a deep sleep, but he kept silent, waiting for the Doctor to continue.

"You -You humble me with your presence..." stammered the Doctor. "...I know I've talked to you in the past as though I am your equal, but... well... I'm... well I'm *a fake*."

Still, Crasty didn't say a word. Dr. Flocky Nocky was saying plenty by himself.

"...I'm just -I *was* just a lab scientist -research and development - that kind of thing. ...Well, a little over twenty years ago I discovered the non-stick magnet *-the magnet that doesn't stick to iron, but still reacts with other magnets as normal*. ...Well I didn't know what to do! What could I have done with such a discovery? I had no idea what use it would be. ...So I sold it. ...I sold my discovery to a nameless, faceless venture capital company. ...And that's about all I've *ever* done.

"A few years later, they came up with a use for it -uncrashable cars. Great idea! ...but they needed a *name* and they needed some kind of 'angle.' ...Everybody knew Professor Marcus Crastinator - well they wanted their own Professor Crastinator.

"So they came back to me. ...and I was only too happy to oblige! '*Use me*' I said, '*use my name*,' ...at last I was famous!

"Then they invented the ATV and the Bullet holes and they too had my name and my hand all over them... but I never had anything to do with any of them really. ...I only ever made one fluke discovery and I've been living with that lie to my name ever since. ...I'm a fake, Professor... forgive me!"

Crasty took some time to consider what he had just heard. Flocky Nocky's admission had been heartfelt -that much was plain- and it was absolutely clear to him now that the Doctor knew nothing of Ooyay's abduction.

"So how come you spent so long talking to me about 'the process' of inventing and why we should work together?" he asked at last out of curiosity.

Again the Doctor looked embarrassed and began to tap the spoon by his cup.

"I..." he began. Clearly he didn't want to continue, but knew the question required an answer. "Well... it gets a bit lonely out here all alone sometimes. ...Working with you was something of a dream for me. ...I like to talk at times, but you weren't saying much so I... well I kind of *filled in the blanks* somewhat.

"It became obvious to me that you were not going to work with me (I don't know what I'd have done if you agreed to in the first place), so I pretended to be an even bigger man than I had before.

"...In the presence of the greatest man I know, I pretended to be an equal." Dr. Flocky Nocky sobbed now as he looked into Crasty's eyes. "You, Professor, are my hero. You always were. I am *honoured* to have met you."

He stretched his arm across the table to shake the hand of the man he had looked up to admiringly for the past thirty years.

But Crasty refused to take it. Instead he leapt from his seat and turned at once to look out the window at the well-kept back garden and private beach beyond.

"You're no fake," he informed Dr. Flocky Nocky. "I don't deserve to have a friend like you. I'm the fake here. I'm a fake in every way. ...I've never done *anything*..."

EAT UP

The next day began like any other since Ooyay had arrived. Nothing changed in this place. The only difference today was that Seamus didn't enter the room with the cages. Ooyay could hear him outside in the other room throughout the morning, but he didn't once leave the front desk. The little dog tried stretching to see around the bars in his cage, but he couldn't make out much.

"Didn't I have something here to help me?" he wondered, searching the floor of his cage now, unsure what he was looking for.

Just then he yelped as he stood on a sharp object, hurting his paw. The cage door opened and Seamus's assistant placed two bowls inside.

"What's this?" enquired the assistant, picking up the piece of mirror that Ooyay had stowed away. "How did this get in here?" he asked himself aloud.

He then examined Ooyay's bleeding paw and rubbed it until the wound dried.

"It's only a scratch," he told the dog, patting him quickly on the head before closing the cage door again.

"Eat up now," he commanded. "...Soon you won't feel a thing."

Ooyay knew what to expect when he heard those words, and sure enough, once he checked his dinner, he saw that buried in the meat and the granules was a small blue tablet.

Still it came as a shock to see it there. Was this the end? What should he do now?

"Eat it," said the assistant as though reading the dog's mind.

Ooyay hadn't been aware that he was still there watching, but now he slowly began to eat on command. The food tasted good and his pace quickened as he ate more.

When finally he had finished, he threw his head back and smiled into the face of the assistant, who had remained standing in front of the cage the whole time. The only thing left in the bowl now was the blue tablet.

"Go on!" urged the assistant. "You'll only make it worse on your-self if you refuse it!"

Looking into his eyes, Ooyay could see that this man was telling the truth. He might not have *wanted* to force the dog to swallow the tablet, but with one glance, Ooyay could tell that he *would* have done so.

So what choice did he have? None really. He bent and licked the last morsel from the bowl, before turning and curling up at the back of his enclosure.

"Good doggie," said the man softly, moving on to the next cage.

OUTSIDE

"Wow!" gasped Dr. Flocky Nocky after the Professor finished telling his story.

They had moved outside to the patio area by the back door and the Professor had spent the last number of hours going over his life story and describing the events that had occurred before they reached this place.

"...So you see, my dear Doctor," said the Professor in conclusion, "if there is any fake here it is clearly *me*."

For a long time Dr. Flocky Nocky said nothing more. This tale had been far too bizarre to comment on right away. The top of the overhead parasol turned and squeaked in the gentle breeze. Then the wind stopped and a deathly silence filled the air. The two men gazed out at the garden and the beach as they sat without saying another word. Both minds were preoccupied with memories and dreams and half-baked notions on what to do next.

Lucy had volunteered to fetch some refreshments and as she now returned to the garden, she had to laugh at the sight of the two old men. For the first time, she noticed how Crasty's large bald patch was in the same place as where all of Flocky Nocky's hair grew. She imagined taking the tuft of hair from Flocky Nocky and placing it over Crasty's upper-forehead -or surrounding Flocky Nocky's tuft with the flowing locks from Crasty's head.

"What do you find so amusing young lady?" asked Crasty with a curious smile as she placed the tray with jug of iced tea and three glasses on the table.

"Nothing," replied Lucy. Some thoughts are not meant to be shared.

Flocky Nocky still sat in silence, but Lucy's levity had given Crasty a newfound pep. Taking the handle of the jug, he reached for the first glass.

"Shall I pour?" he asked grandly, then immediately flopped back in his chair, deflated like a broken whoopee-cushion.

"What now?" enquired Lucy, unable to keep up with all these sudden swings from happiness to sadness with nothing in-between. What had happened to cause this latest swing?

"It's nothing," muttered Crasty. "It's just something I always said to Ooyay. ...*Shall I pour?* ...It seems so long ago now. ...Now it seems like a memory rather than something that is real right now..."

He allowed his voice and his thoughts to drift away in the breeze that had picked up again once more. Lucy and the Doctor both looked to him sadly, unsure what to do or say. He was clearly thinking hard about Ooyay and the times they had together.

"...And there is something else..." said Crasty now, "...something I've been thinking of for a while..."

"What is it?" Dr. Flocky Nocky asked, suddenly realising he no longer knew what to call this man -Marcus? Matthew? Professor Crastinator? Cratchett?

From his sunken position, Crasty looked to his two friends.

"Today is my birthday," he said at last with tears in his eyes.

Under normal circumstances, the young girl and the Doctor would no doubt have automatically yelled Happy Birthday to such a statement. But looking at Crasty, they both immediately sensed it wasn't what he wanted to hear. It was also clear that Crasty had something more to add.

"That's right," he informed them. He knew they were paying close attention. "Today I am ninety years old ...My life has run in thirty-year cycles... I spent the first thirty years with my family - losing each of them one by one... Then, beginning on my thirtieth birthday, I spent the following thirty years asleep (-or in a hospital bed at least).

"...Ooyay has lived my life with me and *for me* during the last thirty years..."

He didn't finish his thoughts out loud, but it was clear to everyone present where they were going... *Today is the start of a new era for Matthew Cratchett. ...What course would that era take and where was it going to bring him?*

"...Plus ça change, plus c'est la même chose," muttered Flocky Nocky.

"Indeed," agreed Crasty sadly. "I've felt it myself. I've changed - but what does that mean for Ooyay?"

"Yes," said Flocky Nocky slowly now. "But what if..." he paused and looked to Crasty before continuing, "...what if Ooyay isn't real?"

INSIDE

"Not real!?" cried Lucy. "How do you mean not real? Of course he's real! ...Tell him Ooyay's real, Crasty!"

        Dr. Flocky Nocky waved his hands and tried calming his guests.

"Please," he begged, "just hear me out...

"Is there anyone else that can verify the existence of this dog? Who else has he spoken with besides you two?"

        The Professor didn't like the approach Flocky Nocky seemed to be taking, but he decided to go along with it for now.

"Nobody. Up until recently, Ooyay only ever spoke to me," he informed the Doctor.

"So (please don't take this the wrong way)... if, as you say, Ooyay is a figment of your imagination, is it not possible that you have always imagined that he was there? ...You had been traumatised by the loss of your family... you wanted someone to look after you... you dreamt of a happy life... and when you woke up, your imaginary friend took care of you for the next thirty years! ...but *actually* your own split personality was taking care of things for you!? ...Would that not be more realistic?"

"It would," conceded Crasty, "except for two things... First of all, Ooyay is a real dog. I know he is. I've lived with him for thirty years -and secondly, there is the small matter of Lucy here..."

"Ah yes -Lucy," Flocky Nocky smiled and sat back in his chair. "...Uh... Let me say this and I will leave it at that... In all my years I have never heard of a talking dog. I do not deny what you believe and I do not think either of you are foolish... but I *have* heard of mass-hysteria, where a group of people are convinced they have seen and interacted with the same impossible events...

"In short, I find it *slightly* easier to believe that Lucy has imagined the same thing you have imagined, rather than believe a story of a talking dog. I'm sorry Professor. I feel I need to say these things because it is the only sensible explanation I can see."

        Lucy was confused and not at all certain she had understood everything the Doctor was saying... "*Ooyay doesn't exist and*

I only dreamt him or something? How could that be? Who had driven the Hamsterball if Ooyay didn't exist?"

Crasty nodded softly, then sighed deeply as he patted his knees and stood up.

"What you say makes sense, Doctor," he agreed, "but I'll need time to consider it all. -Right now I'd better get this little runaway back to her parents. Come along Lucy -I'm taking you home!"

They walked slowly, but directly to the ATV. All the while Dr. Flocky Nocky apologised for speaking his mind so forthrightly. Before the visitors climbed inside, Flocky Nocky gently pulled Crasty back by the shoulder.

"I know you didn't want to hear that, Marcus, but how about this..." he said. "...If Ooyay *is* your four-legged imagination ...you said yourself you feel different now... you've been dreaming in your sleep and you imagined you saw your dead family back on that jungle island...

"...If he *is* your imagination -and your imagination *is* back inside your head... then where is Ooyay?"

Crasty was too stunned to reply, but still Flocky Nocky had more.

"... Ooyay has come from your imagination," he said. "...If you were angry at him, might you not want to *suppress* that imagination in some way? -To *lock him up?* ...Perhaps Lucy here witnessed the physical manifestation of that suppression?

"...Maybe..." said Flocky Nocky, "Ooyay is trapped -up here," tapping the centre of the Professor's forehead.

Still Crasty was gob smacked. Could it be true? Had he himself been responsible for Ooyay's disappearance? Was it possible he had trapped his precious doggie inside his own mind?

As Lucy lead him into the ATV, Dr. Flocky Nocky again grabbed and shook the Professor's hand.

"Goodbye my friend," he told the old man. "...You are my all time hero and I hope you find your Ooyay."

Within minutes, the two were back in space, on their way home. This time, their minds felt as topsy-turvy as their bodies. Neither knew now what to think or what to say or what to do next. Everything was a muddle.

COMING HOME

It took only a couple of hours before landing at their local airport. In all their time together, Lucy had never seen the Professor so confused. When they had set out, at least he could walk and talk and he made *some* sense. He was able to pretend he was in control long enough to fool others at least.

But now! -Now he was holding his head and not responding to anything Lucy said. His eyes were closed and he walked through the airport as if his head would fall off if he didn't keep it in place.

Thankfully, Lucy recalled the presence of a homing switch on the Hamsterball. Once she had seated Crasty in the chair, she crouched over the white beach ball steering device, shut the doors and hit the Home button.

Without delay, the Hamsterball set off, avoiding traffic and pedestrians and obeying signal lights of its own accord.

"We're nearly home now Crasty," said Lucy softly, but looking back, she saw that he wasn't aware of anything in the world around him.

He still clutched his head and his eyes were shut tight in deep concentration.

When at last the Hamsterball rolled in to the grounds of Professor Crastinator's house, control reverted once more to the white beach ball. Lucy managed to manoeuvre the vehicle to the front door before switching off the engine.

If Crasty was listening, he didn't respond, but thankfully he was able to move his own legs in the manner and direction Lucy instructed.

"Do you have a key?" she asked as they reached the front entrance.

"It's me," he simply said from behind his hands and at once the door opened.

Lucy guided him past the mountain of newspapers and mail, down the corridor toward the office where she had first seen Crasty and Ooyay speak.

On a small table in the hallway, outside this office, sat a telephone and answering machine. At first Lucy didn't even notice the table, but as she lowered her gaze to the door-handle, her attention was caught by something in the corner of her eye. Turning at once (for it is impossible not to turn at such times), she noticed a red number 1 flashing on the box.

"Wait here," she instructed the old man as she stopped and stretched and hit the large play button.

At once the noise of amplified silence echoed through the hall. Nobody spoke at the other end, but it was clear that someone had left a message. Then a low throaty growl was heard, followed by a slight whining sound like a dog's cry. Now the sound changed to something like a whispering bark. Suddenly the barking was replaced by a familiar voice.

"I'm in... I don't know... I think it's an animal shelter of some kind... wherever the local dog warden takes dogs possibly -probably..." said Ooyay through the machine.

Crasty couldn't believe his ears. It was Ooyay! Beyond a doubt, that voice was his beloved, lovely, blue dog! He was real and he was there and he had left a message! For the past number of hours, Crasty had been trying hard to pull Ooyay from his head, but all this time Ooyay was real and now here was the proof.

Throwing his arms in the air he screamed for joy and ran for the front door.

"WAHOOOO!" he cried. "It's Ooyay! It's my doggie!"

Lucy too jumped in the air and danced out the door and into the Hamsterball after him.

RESOLUTION

Seamus Shafford looked into Ooyay's cage and saw the small, lifeless dog lying there. His assistant made to move past him, but Seamus pulled at once on his shoulder.

"No," he said with bowed head. "*I'll* do it."

Taking a deep sigh, he opened the cage door and scooped the drooping animal into his arms.

Crasty and Lucy burst in the front door of the animal shelter as the assistant strolled back to the reception desk.

"Can I help you Granddad?" he calmly asked the old man with a smile.

"Quick!" cried Crasty. "You have a blue dog! He's mine! I'm here to take him home!"

The man behind the desk shook his head.

"No, you're mistaken," he said. "We have no blue dog here."

Inside the cage-room, Ooyay decided the time had come to make his move. Unfurling his tongue, he spat the blue tablet from his mouth before telling Seamus Shafford exactly what he thought of this place.

"YOU HAVE NO RIGHT TO KEEP ME HERE LIKE THIS, Y'KNOW!" he *would* have cried, but for some reason all that came out was "WOOF WOOF WOOF WOOF WOOF!"

Ooyay stopped barking and wiggled wildly in Seamus's arms. But Seamus knew how to hold a dog and Ooyay did not escape.

"*How could that be?*" Ooyay wondered to himself. He was certain he used to be able to talk. "*I thought I could talk?*" he considered now to himself. "*...Wasn't I able to talk at one time?*"

Then he caught sight of Seamus in a mirror on the wall, but *that* Seamus was carrying a different dog. The dog in *that* Seamus's arms was white.

"Hey who's that white dog in your arms?" Ooyay *meant* to ask, but instead he said "Woof woof woof woof woof!"

Seamus had already been walking in the direction of the basement when the dog had begun barking. He was unable to think of anything to do now except continue in that direction and to get it over with as quickly as possible.

As he passed the front desk however, an old man called out to him.

"Please!" said the man. "I'm looking for my dog... He's blue... I think you have him here!"

Seamus stopped and looked at the face of the imploring, familiar-looking old man.

"Blue?" repeated Seamus, holding the white dog who had stopped struggling. "There's no such thing as a blue dog."

Ooyay didn't recognise the newcomers or pay them any heed. Noticing now that Seamus seemed distracted, again he began to wiggle and cry.

"WHAT DO YOU MEAN YOU HAVE NO BLUE DOGS?" he *wanted* to shout, "WHAT DO YOU THINK *I* AM!?" but instead, only barks escaped his mouth once again.

Just then, Lucy caught sight of something -some twinkle in this white dog's jet black eyes.

"Wait a minute!" she cried as Seamus began turning away.

Ooyay stopped barking now and looked directly at the young girl. She seemed familiar in some way...

"Ooyay?" called Crasty, unsure of what he was seeing.

Once he approached and took a more careful look at the beautiful sparkling black diamond eyeballs there was no longer any doubt. Those deepest twin echoing caverns were unmistakeable no matter what colour the animal was. With a single stare into this dog's eyes, Crasty knew that the old companion who had taken such care of him for thirty years would now need to be cared for himself. And if he barked now instead of talked, then no matter -there was no denying him. ...This dog was his very own Ooyay and he was delighted to have him back.

"*Crasty?*" called Ooyay inside his mind, but outside he merely whined and licked the old man's crinkled face.

Crasty cried and laughed and the white dog licked the tears from his eyes.

"Ooyay!" cried Crasty. "It is you! What has happened, boy? What have I done? I'm sorry Ooyay! I'll never shout at you again! Come on boy -let's go home. I'll take you home Ooyay and from now on it's *my* turn to look after *you.* ...I'll never let you down again."

Hugging and kissing his little white dog, Professor Crastinator turned and walked from the animal shelter with a tearful Lucy in tow.

MATURITY

PLUS ÇA CHANGE, PLUS C'EST LA MEME CHOSE!

I called to see him a number of years later -naturally- I had a story to finish. In fact, I had taken a long time to come down off my mountain and ten years had elapsed by then. Thankfully, the Professor was still going strong at the grand old age of one hundred.

At that stage he had already invented window wipers for spectacles, the Radar Necklace for blind people, and many more items.

[The Radar Necklace is made up of a number of sensored-rings and is worn by people with little or no sight. Depending on the size, speed, height, distance and location of nearby objects, the necklace gives its wearer little jabs of varying pressure and height and position throughout the neck, which informs him or her of nearby obstacles.]

I wasn't sure he'd remember me. After all, we had only met twice and he had been under some pressure at the time, but as soon as he opened the door my fears proved unfounded.

"Ah my dear Stanley!" he laughed. His voice had a little more warble than before, but there was still a certain excited air about him. "...I was wondering when you'd show!"

Quickly he turned and bid me follow him down the hallway, which I did.

"Who was that at the door, Crasty?" called a familiar male voice from inside the first door on the right.

Crasty opened the door and looked in.

"You remember Stanley Rumm," he said. "I told you he'd call to check up on us one day!"

Standing aside, the Professor gestured for me to come and see. As always, what greeted me was a surprise: Blurt Johannsen stood in the centre of the room, apparently trying on a new type of hat. It was like a full leather helmet covering his head, but on the top was what looked to be a satellite dish.

"You remember Blurt Johannsen, my Marketing Director, don't you Mr. Rumm?" said Crasty. "I have him testing a little idea I had for an update to the Radar Necklace..."

"How are you Blurt?" I asked. "I thought you found your happiness in Harrumph!?"

"I did," he told me, "but once I finally shared my money with my newfound family they all left the village and the island. I guess they needed to find themselves -Or something," he laughed.

Blurt seemed less frantic than before. More relaxed. More at peace with himself and the world. Despite the satellite dish on his head, it was immediately clear that he was less showy than he used to be. This Blurt had no need nor wish to impress anyone.

"Hey! How about that guide dog of mine?" asked the blind man. "Y'know I never replaced her. I hope you've been looking after my dear old Susan?"

I hung my head and spoke softly.

"I have bad news I'm afraid," I informed the two men. "My assistant Onoshi Han had an accident one day while he played with Susan on the mountain. The two of them fell from a great height."

"Oh no!" cried Crasty.

"They both lived, thankfully," I quickly added to ease their minds, "but Susan got lodged in the hump of Onoshi's back. The doctors said it could be life or death for either or both of them if they were separated. ...So they stayed that way. ...You should see them!" I laughed. "They're as happy as ever together and she's like a parrot, nesting on his shoulders. Now they truly are inseparable!"

We laughed and talked of some other shared memories before I finally asked Crasty about Ooyay. Had he found his dog? (I still hadn't known anything about it at that time.)

"Come with me," he told me at once, shuffling from the room.

I bid farewell to Blurt and followed behind the old man. We walked further down the hall and turned left, through what looked like an ordinary entrance to another room, but in fact this door brought us outside. It was sunny and warm out there, (which was strange because when I called it had been snowing).

"Where are we going?" I asked the Professor, who was leaning on my arm as we slowly made our way up a grass-lined mountain path.

"You'll see," he said with a casual wave.

As we walked I asked about the girl.

"Do you still see Lucy Lucey now?" I enquired.

"I do," he informed me, "but she's off at college would you believe? ...How time flies! She calls by all the time, but she's busy of course -Aren't we all!"

I guessed at once what she would be doing at college.

"I bet she's studying science to be a great inventor like yourself!" I told him.

"Ha!" he said, "You lose... she's studying History and English Literature, but I guess you can't have everything..."

We turned now from the path before reaching the top of the mountain, but as we did, we wound our way around the hill and came to an old oak tree. I knew this place at once -though it seemed a little smaller now than in my dreams. I didn't look, but I was positive that I would find a little stream further on if I went to check (although I didn't have to in order to know that it was there.)

At the foot of this tree, a little white dog was resting peacefully.

"There you are fella!" cried Crasty, rubbing now on the animal's tummy. "Snoozing again are you!?" he laughed as he tickled him gently.

The dog didn't seem to want to wake, but he soon began wagging his tail and purring like a contented cat. Crasty gestured for me to pat the dog's head, which I did at once.

"So this is the mighty Ooyay," I said, happy to have finally met him, still unsure what I had missed in order to find him this colour.

"Hello boy!" I patted and smiled and played with the friendly, though old, hound for quite some time.

Before showing Crasty the work I had already started on this book, and asking for his blessing, I informed him that I had something that I wanted to hand over.

As I reached inside my coat pocket however, he quickly caught my hand to stop me from removing it.

"Don't!" he warned, then smiled softly.

"...I have this place ...and I have my dog and life is good," he said.

"I've had luck and I've had a long life... you keep it," he told me, "...whatever it is."